D0276203

Presented with the compliments of the author.

Willis,
May, 1982.

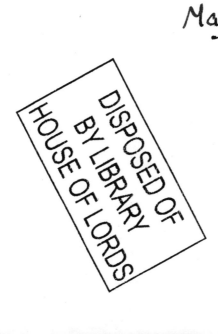

DISPOSED OF
BY LIBRARY
HOUSE OF LORDS

The Most Beautiful Girl in the World

It began when Kitty Higgins won a beauty contest and the title Miss Greater London. After that she was due to be 'packaged and processed for success' in international contests, and she didn't want that. Then she was kidnapped. After a massive police search, it was assumed that she was dead. Only her boyfriend, Steve Ugley, clung to the belief that somewhere, somehow, she was still alive.

Ugley was lucky to make contact with a soldier of fortune named Barr (the hero of Ted Willis's earlier and hugely successful thriller *The Churchill Commando*). They acquired two additional – and very engaging – recruits to the team of four that was to begin the quest for Kitty Higgins.

The four, who adopt for themselves the title of the Baker Street Runners, discover names and details of other girls who have vanished: all young, all exceptionally beautiful. And these disappearances have happened across the world, in France, Guyana, India, Sweden and elsewhere. Barr discovers a link – and the link leads him and the Baker Street Runners to a Caribbean island called Jerusalem.

This island is in the grip of a powerful religious sect with worldwide connections. And it is in and around Jerusalem Island that many mysteries are hidden and much violent action takes place.

This is a most unusual thriller that moves at a cracking pace from page one and holds the reader through all its strange twists and turns to the final show-down. Ted Willis' most exciting thriller to date – the work of a master story-teller.

by the same author

Death May Surprise Us
The Left-Handed Sleeper
Man-Eater
The Churchill Commando
The Buckingham Palace Connection
The Lions of Judah
The Naked Sun
Woman in a Dressing Gown and Other Plays
Whatever Happened to Tom Mix? (autobiography)

THE MOST BEAUTIFUL GIRL IN THE WORLD

Ted Willis

Macmillan

ISBN 0 333 32764 0

First published 1982 by
MACMILLAN LONDON LIMITED
London and Basingstoke
Associated companies in Auckland, Dallas, Delhi,
Dublin, Hong Kong, Johannesburg, Lagos, Manzini,
Melbourne, Nairobi, New York, Singapore, Tokyo,
Washington and Zaria

Printed and bound in Great Britain
at The Pitman Press, Bath

To Jack Wayland

Chapter One

The man sighed with pleasure and closed his eyes as the girl's thumbs circled the bunched muscles at the back of his neck. Beneath the sensuous perfume of the oil, the firm yet soothing motion of her hands and of her body on his, all the jagged tension seemed to be slipping away.

The tension had begun to worry him. In the past, up until a few months before, he had never known a moment of concern before an assignment, even the most difficult ones. But on this occasion, as with the time before, his whole body had somehow tightened up. He had hardly slept for two nights, and he had felt as though his nerves were at breaking point.

He still did not know the actual target, and he had found some consolation in this, wondering if the uncertainty was the cause of his stress; but in his heart he knew that this was simply an excuse, that the truth had deeper roots. He was like a fighter-pilot who had flown too many missions: he felt as though he had used up his luck, that on this mission or the next, fortune would desert him.

All these fears seemed to be absurd now. He could feel his strength and confidence returning and wondered why he had ever allowed himself to become a victim of such doubts. It had been a simple matter of tiredness, nothing more. Tomorrow, after a few hours sleep, he would be his old self again, ready for anything. Only he must not, dare not, sleep yet. He had to be ready for the call when it came.

'Over,' said the girl, giving his shoulder a little pat as though in farewell. 'Turn over.'

'Not yet,' murmured the man. 'Do that again.'

'You like it, do you?'

'I like it.'

'It will be extra,' she said, 'the extra time, you see.'

'You'll be paid.'

He felt himself slipping down into sleep and forced his reluctant eyes to open. The girl slid from his body and he heard her move round the bed. He turned his head and checked his watch. It was 8.40. He had fifteen minutes.

The girl came into his line of vision. He could see her from the waist downwards, the spiky blond triangle of hair between her legs, the light film of sweat on the fair skin. A faint line encircled each leg like a tidemark: below it the skin was slightly coarser and carried the light brown of a faded sun-tan, but above the line the flesh was as smooth and white as milk.

7

The sandalwood fragrance of the oil drifted down to him from her body. He put out a hand and touched her thigh, sliding his fingers upwards. She laughed lightly and snapped her legs together, imprisoning his fingers.

'Is that what you want, darling?'

'It will be extra,' he said, mocking her tone.

'Of course. But I'll make it interesting. It will be worth it, you'll see.'

'Later, perhaps.'

She released him and moved away. A moment later the bed creaked as she knelt over him once more, her breasts brushing his shoulders. She flexed her fingers, poured a little of the oil on to his brown skin and pressed down with her hands, gently kneading the strong, well-muscled body.

'You've got a lovely tan, darling,' she said. 'I bet you didn't get that here, not with the summer we've had.'

'No. I didn't get it here.'

He thought about the island, and the beaches, and the soft warm sea, and his eyes half closed again. Sleep, sleep – if only he could sleep!

'What do you do, darling?' asked the girl. 'I mean, what do you do for a dollar?'

'I'm a bishop,' he said, smiling at his own joke.

'You wouldn't be the first bishop I've had between my legs,' she said.

He smiled again, and then a great wave of drowsiness swept over him, he could feel it bearing him away into sleep. He fought against it frantically, struggling round until he was lying on his back, looking up at the girl.

'What's the matter?' she asked.

'You're too good,' he said. 'I nearly dropped off.'

'I'd better do something to wake you up then,' she said. She eased herself downwards and began to massage his thighs, making little circular motions with her fingers. From time to time she drew her nails lightly across his skin. He began to stiffen beneath her, and his breathing became more urgent. She adjusted her position again, and guided him into her.

'It's beautiful,' she whispered as she rocked gently above him, 'it's beautiful.' She was professional enough to make it sound as if she meant it.

Ten minutes later he was asleep, lying back on the pillow and snoring gently in a way that reminded her of a cat purring. She got down from the bed and looked at him for a moment. Her face was expressionless except for a hint of mockery in the eyes.

His jacket was hanging across a chair by the window, and for a moment she was tempted to explore the pockets. But she resisted

8

the impulse, remembering the time when she had been severely beaten up by a client who had caught her going through his clothes. She moved to the fitment which served both as a writing-desk and dressing table. The key to the room was there, together with a little card which bore the room number, the name of the hotel and the man's name.

H. van Norden.

A Dutchman, she thought. But, on the other hand, she had detected no accent. Anyway, what did it matter?

A good quality but clearly much-travelled suitcase lay on the fitment near the door. She noticed that the locks were undone, and this time the temptation overcame her. She took a swift look at the sleeping man, and lifted the lid.

Her face widened into a smile at what she saw. On top of the unpacked clothes, there was a pile of about a dozen glossy photographs. The top one showed an attractive smiling girl posing in a bathing-suit; there was something familiar about the face but she could not place it. She shuffled through the others to find that they were all of different girls in similar poses. There was nothing remotely pornographic about any of them and she found that rather puzzling.

She was used to porn: indeed, she had done a little posing of that sort herself. Men like the one asleep on the bed often carried pornographic pictures around with them. But these were different, they were the sort of thing you might find reproduced in any respectable women's magazine. Was he something to do with a model agency? Or in the rag trade perhaps?

She soon altered this assessment of her client. There was a bulge under one of the folded shirts and, once more, curiosity proved too much for her. She turned back the shirt and then stepped back as though she had suddenly been struck in the face.

A gun lay there, a flat black automatic, its outline sharp against the whiteness of the clothes on which it was lying.

Her heart fluttering, she closed the case, picked up her clothes and headed for the bathroom. At the door the man's voice checked her and she stood there, rigid with fear. Had he seen her going through his things?

'What are you doing?' he murmured.

She closed her eyes, feeling the blessed relief flow through her body. 'I was just going to get dressed,' she said breathlessly.

'What time is it?' Then, without waiting for her answer, he checked his watch himself. 'Ten minutes past nine! Holy Christ! You bloody cow – why didn't you wake me!'

'How was I to know —' she began, but he cut her short.

'Switch on the television!' he shouted. 'Switch on the bloody

9

television!'

'No need to shout,' she said, pouting. 'What channel do you want?'

She hurried to the set and switched it on with fumbling fingers. Pictures of a beauty contest began to fill the screen, the bland voices of a man and a woman describing the parading girls. One of them, she felt sure, was the girl in the photograph.

'There,' she said. 'What's so important about that?'

The man was already out of bed, pulling on underpants and a pair of slacks. He went to his jacket, pulled out a wad of notes and gave her £40. His eyes scarcely left the television screen. She had intended to ask for £50, but the sight of the gun and the man's manner had frightened her; all she wanted to do was to get dressed and leave.

Luckily the man had the same idea, for as he gave her the money he said, 'Take that and get out.'

While she was dressing in the bathroom, the telephone rang. It was a brief call, for within seconds he had replaced the receiver.

'Number nine. Right.' That was all she heard him say.

When she left, he ignored her. He was sitting on the edge of the bed, engrossed in the beauty contest on the television. The pile of photographs now lay beside him.

Maybe that was the sort of thing that turned him on, she thought, though on reflection she felt that to be unlikely. But it wasn't important, and by the time she reached the street she had dismissed the subject from her mind.

But it came back to her the next morning when she opened a copy of the *Daily Mirror* and saw, on page three, a picture of a girl in a bathing suit. It was the girl in the photograph, the one whose face she had found familiar. She realised now that she had seen a similar picture in the newspapers a few days before.

The accompanying news item identified her as a certain Miss Kitty Higgins. She had won the previous night's contest and been duly crowned as Miss Greater London. Later in the year, said the story, she would be competing for the titles of Miss England and Miss United Kingdom.

On her wrist she wore a disc which plainly revealed the figure 9.

Three days later Miss Greater London, better known as Kitty Higgins, left the offices of Paragon Promotions in Curzon Street, Mayfair, climbed into her canary-coloured Mini and headed northwards through the heavy, Friday evening traffic towards home. Home was a flat in Parkhill Road, Hampstead, which she shared with her friend, Lucy Syms.

She paid no attention to the big black Volvo estate car which pulled in behind her as she moved off and which stayed on her tail

10

throughout the slow tortuous drive.

Her thoughts were elsewhere. She was thinking, with a mixture of amusement and irritation, of the lecture she had just received from Mr Digby, the managing director of Paragon Promotions.

It was not the first time he had lectured her but she was determined that it would be the last. Mr Digby, who was quite famous as a promoter and organiser of beauty contests, had once again taken Kitty to task for her irreverent disregard for her own success and for the important, not to say momentous, business of being a Beauty Queen.

Everything, he declared, everything was in her favour; in his opinion, based on years of experience, she could go right to the top, she could win the very highest international crown.

And he meant it. When he had first seen her, in a small local contest, he had known, with a thrill of excitement, that he had found a potential star.

Her hair, dancing on her shoulders, had the colour and sheen of burnished bronze and it framed a face of extraordinary radiance. There was a golden flicker in the wide green eyes, a delicious tilt to the nose, and an inviting though not over-emphatic sensuality in the strong full mouth. Her lightly tanned skin glowed with health, her firm, high-riding breasts and her long smooth legs were exact and right in their proportions, and she moved with an easy-flowing grace that made men and women alike turn their heads in wonder.

But all these magnificent qualities would be useless, he told her, unless she applied herself. A Beauty Queen held a special position in society: she was constantly in the public eye and she had to behave with a dignity appropriate to her situation. He had known dozens of beautiful girls who had failed to reach the top because they lacked self-discipline and character. He hoped that Kitty would now pull herself together.

And so on and so on, in much the same vein.

Kitty sighed as she took a left turn and drove up Haverstock Hill. Mr Digby was such a *sincere* man. Sincerity clung like syrup to his voice, it gleamed in his pale eyes and on his pink earnest face. She would have liked to please him, for she understood that the Beauty Queen business was his whole life: for him it was a vocation, a sort of religion. And because she was more intelligent than he realised, she understood also that for Mr Digby there could be no other way. He had to believe in what he was doing: if he allowed his belief to waver for a single moment, the total absurdity of the thing would become obvious and his whole tinsel world would collapse.

The fact remained that to her it *was* absurd, at best a game, at worst a fraud. She had been persuaded to enter her first contest by teasing friends and had done so as a sort of challenge. After winning that, it had been easy enough to go after yet another crown and then

11

another. But now she had become tired of the joke, she felt soiled by it all. The Miss Greater London title was as far as she could go on a local scale: to continue would mean entering national and even international contests and that would mean giving up more and more of herself. She would be packaged and processed for success and the thought repelled her.

Tomorrow, she decided, she would do what she ought to have done an hour earlier. She would write to Mr Digby and tell him that she wished to go no further.

She parked the car and ran up the path to the front door. Searching her handbag, she realised that she had left her keys in the flat that morning and, hoping that Lucy would be home, she rang the bell. She was lucky. A towel round her wet hair, a smiling Lucy opened the door.

'Thanks,' said Kitty.

'You'll forget your head one day.'

The door closed behind them, and the three men in the black Volvo settled down to another wait.

Kitty went directly to the bedroom and took off the suit she was wearing. After a shower, she put on a pair of jeans, cowboy boots, a red polo-necked sweater and a shirt. She packed an overnight case with pyjamas, fresh underwear, and a toilet bag, then checked her purse to see that she had enough money for the weekend. There was almost £30 in notes and silver, more than enough to see her through.

The doorbell rang and a few moments later she heard the deep voice of Dick Owen, Lucy's boyfriend. An uncharacteristic pang of jealousy gripped her for a moment. Dick was staying for the weekend: his visit was the main reason why Kitty had decided to spend a couple of days with her parents. Lucy and he were in the middle of a passionate affair and although Lucy had assured her that there was no reason to leave, she felt that her presence would be an intrusion.

This apart, she knew that having a man around the place would remind her of another Richard, the man with whom she had shared her life for eighteen months. For almost all that time he had hovered weakly between her and his wife, and only under pressure from Kitty had he decided finally to return home – or rather, since he had never actually left it, to break off their relationship.

He still rang her from time to time, in the hope that she might agree to see him, but she had steadfastly refused all advances. She knew that he had simply used her, that he was not worth another moment of her time; all the same, she had been in love with him, and a little of the feeling still lingered. He had left a gap in her life which she found difficult to fill.

There were men, of course, more than enough men who kept crowding her for dates. She thought of Steve Ugley, a young minicab driver whom she had met almost by accident and whom she quite liked. She smiled to herself. Ugley. It was an odd name but somehow it suited him. He wasn't really ugly – craggy or homely would serve better as a description – and he was a light-hearted amusing companion who at least treated her as a person and not a beauty package. But she wasn't really ready to embark on any relationship which threatened to become serious or permanent.

Dick had opened a bottle of wine and when she went to the kitchen to say goodbye he pressed a glass upon her. He was a big, simple, hearty young man and as he raised his own glass he said, 'Well, here's to Miss Greater London.'

'Get lost,' said Kitty amiably.

'When's the next contest?'

'I doubt if there'll be one,' she answered. She felt vaguely depressed and didn't want to prolong the discussion.

'Shit!' said Dick. 'I told everybody at work that I know the future Miss Universe. Did a lot for my prestige.'

'I can imagine,' she said drily. There was a touch of male condescension in his tone which added to her irritation. She drained her glass and turned to Lucy. 'I've left my blue suit on the bed. If you're passing the cleaners —'

'I'll drop it in tomorrow morning.'

'Thanks. I'll be on my way then.' Relenting a little, Kitty added, 'Have a good time you two. And don't do anything to frighten the horses.'

The telephone rang as she turned to go and Lucy said, 'It might be for you. That boy Steve – Steve Ugley – rang about an hour ago, said he'd ring back.'

Kitty wavered for a moment. She could always go to her parents later, or even the next morning. An evening with Steve would be pleasant and undemanding. She suppressed the thought.

'If it is him, say I've left already. Tell him I'll be back Monday evening.'

'You're sure?' Lucy studied Kitty's face, sensing her mood.

'Sure.'

It was Steve, and as Kitty picked up her case, she heard Lucy making sympathetic noises into the phone. She took a light raincoat from the rack in the hall and went out to the car. It was dusk now and as she drove away she switched on the sidelights.

She pulled in at a garage on Haverstock Hill and put five gallons of three-star in the tank. Further on, near the Underground Station, she stopped again and bought a spray of flowers for her mother. It was now 7.20pm and the night seemed to have closed in suddenly.

She headed northwards across the Heath, through Golders Green and Elstree towards the A5, settling herself for the forty mile drive to

13

her parents' bungalow. From time to time she noticed the black Volvo in her rear-view mirror, but it did not occur to her that she was being followed.

Normally she enjoyed driving but tonight she found it difficult to relax: the feeling of depression, overlaid by irritation, seemed to be taking a firmer hold. The irritation arose partly because she was essentially a cheerful person, not much given to moods, and partly because she could not find a reason for her state of mind. She was only conscious of a vague dissatisfaction with life in general and with her own life in particular.

It was, perhaps, because of her mood that the incident occurred. Just before reaching the A5, she pulled over to the outside lane, indicating her intention to turn right, and was met with a concerted and angry blast of the horn from a large Rover. Looking in her mirror, she realised that she must have cut across the other car too abruptly, and raised a hand in apology.

At the road junction, the other driver drew in alongside her, his face distorted with anger. Winding down his window, he shouted, 'Where the hell do you think you're driving – in the bloody Sahara?'

'Sorry.' She mouthed the word. And because he seemed not to have heard she released her seat-belt and, reaching over with difficulty, opened the passenger window. 'Sorry,' she said again.

'Bloody women drivers!'

She got out of the car, ignoring the impatient cars behind her, and went round to him.

'What did you say?' She smiled down at him with a deceptive sweetness.

He was a thin middle-aged man with a small moustache and there was a regimental badge on his blue blazer. Her appearance – perhaps her extraordinary beauty – seemed to startle him and he began to climb down.

'You ought to be more careful, you know,' he muttered.

'You said something about women drivers.'

'Well —' he said and stopped, quelled by the look in those green eyes.

Then, to his astonishment, she reached inside the car and took the keys from the ignition. He was too stunned to respond as, with the same enchanting smile on her face, she said, in a voice that was no more than a husky whisper, 'You know something, you want to know something? I think you're full of shit, totally full of shit.'

Then she hurled the keys over the car into the darkness of the grass verge at the side of the road.

A driver, sitting high above them in the cabin of his huge truck, honked his approval, and in the dim light Kitty saw him raise his thumb to her and grin. Before the man in the Rover could recover his wits, she regained the Mini, engaged gear, and drove off. She gave a final derisive toot of her horn as she moved away.

She smiled, feeling a sense of liberation as a result of this odd encounter. And she was humming gently to herself, fully relaxed and at ease, when she turned off the A5 just before Fenny Stratford and took the road which led to her parents' home at Bragenham. It was then that she became aware of the black Volvo behind her and remembered seeing it before. She was not concerned: she wondered for a moment if it was on the way to Bragenham also, and then put it from her mind.

As the road narrowed, curving through woodland, the driver of the Volvo flashed his headlights, as if indicating that he wished to pass. She drew over to give him room. He came alongside, she saw the dim outline of two other men inside, and then, to her astonishment and growing fear, the Volvo passed her and cut directly across her path.

The Mini slewed to a halt, narrowly avoiding a crash, and as she fumbled with her seat-belt, the door opened. A man's face looked down at her, and a voice said, 'Good evening, darling.'

At 9.30pm Kitty's father, Pat Higgins, rang the flat in Parkhill Road. He was concerned that Kitty had not yet arrived and wanted to find out if anything had happened to detain her.

He tried to get through three times, but the line seemed to be permanently engaged. In fact, Lucy and her boyfriend were in bed and they had taken the phone off the hook so that their pleasures would not be interrupted. It was not until 10.30 that Lucy replaced the receiver and he was able to speak to her. By this time his concern had turned to real anxiety and it was not alleviated by the news that Kitty had left Hampstead over three hours before. Even allowing for exceptional traffic, she should have reached her destination by 9pm at the latest.

Lucy promised to ring round some of their friends to find out if Kitty had called in to see any of them. It was unlikely, she felt, for Kitty was a thoughtful girl and she would almost certainly have rung her parents to alert them to any delay. Lucy was not surprised when she drew a negative response from each call.

By midnight, with a rising feeling of panic, she called various hospitals which were more or less on Kitty's route, to see if she had been involved in an accident. Again the response was negative.

At 12.30am Lucy rang the Hampstead police to report that Kitty was missing. Pat Higgins made a similar report to the police station at Leighton Buzzard. A description of Kitty and of the yellow Mini was put out immediately, but it was not until 2.30pm on the following day that there was a positive development.

15

A police constable discovered Kitty's car in King's Wood, a few miles from her parents' home. It had been driven a short distance into the wood and was partly screened by the autumn foliage.

Nearer the road, not far from the abandoned car, the police found signs of a struggle. Grass and bushes had been beaten down: there were tracks in the soft earth which suggested that Kitty had tried to make a run for it, and had been pursued by two men. And they discovered some recent tyre tracks on the verge which indicated that another, larger vehicle had been at the scene.

Her handbag was found under a clump of bushes nearby. Its contents, including Kitty's Access credit card and money, were intact, but the bag itself was damaged, as if it had been used as a weapon. The detectives found other evidence, including threads from her red sweater, which indicated that a fierce struggle had taken place. The spray of flowers was still on the back seat of the car, but the case containing her clothes had gone. Forensic analysis revealed no trace of blood.

By Monday morning, the story was headline news. Photographs of Kitty, in her role as Miss Greater London, decorated the front pages, together with potted versions of her brief career. A certain call-girl, seeing the photographs and remembering the man with the gun and his strange obsession with the beauty contest, toyed with the idea of going to the police with her information. In the end, she decided not to get involved and more or less dismissed the matter from her mind.

Nevertheless, within two days the police were able to put together a clear picture of Kitty's movements from the time she left the flat. They traced the flowers back to the shop where she had bought them, and the garage on Haverstock Hill where she had filled up the car with petrol. The man whose keys she had so abruptly thrown away and the driver of the heavy truck both came forward, after seeing her picture on television, to confirm that they had seen her on the evening in question and that she had taken a right turn on to the A5.

Convinced now that they were almost certainly dealing with a case of rape and probably of murder, the police organised a ground and helicopter search of the countryside within a radius of fifty miles of the abandoned Mini. They were looking, in particular, for tyre tracks which might match those they had found near Kitty's car and for signs of a shallow grave. The search was thorough, but it yielded nothing. Hundreds of men with past convictions for sexual offences against women were interviewed and several were held for further questioning, but in the end all were released for lack of evidence. Within ten days the case dropped out of the newspapers.

Lucy Syms and her boyfriend Dick Owen took two weeks' leave from work and spent the time in a private search of the area around

King's Wood. Helped by Steve Ugley and Kitty's father, they checked and rechecked every remote building, every stretch of woodland and wild common on the local map.

They had no success either. Lucy and Dick were forced to give up and return to work, but Steve and Pat Higgins stubbornly continued their forlorn search. After another week, they also gave up.

Pat and the others, along with the police, resigned themselves to the near certainty that Kitty was dead and that time would reveal her body and the truth.

Only Steve Ugley, without reason, and in the face of all the facts, clung to the belief that somewhere, somehow, Kitty Higgins was alive.

Chapter Two

Barr woke that morning at about eleven o'clock with an evil taste in his mouth and a throat that felt as if it had been lined with old fur. There was also a steady painful hammering in his temples which rose to a crescendo of protest when he tried to move his head.

Slowly, very slowly, his mind began to focus. He had spent the previous evening at the Queen's Head in Camden Town, in the company of Mike Noonan. It had started as a celebration of Noonan's birthday, but had gone on beyond that. Noonan was the publican and after closing time they had continued the party in the back parlour, just the two of them, drinking whisky and yarning about the old times in Biafra, Rhodesia, the Congo and a half-dozen other places.

How many bottles of Scotch had they knocked back between them? Barr hadn't drunk so heavily since those days in Africa but yesterday, he recalled, had been a bad, bad day. To start with, he had fallen out with Vicky, a circumstance which was becoming too common for comfort of late. It arose, as he well knew, from his own deep sense of frustration. He was on the run-up to his fortieth year, his money was giving out, and he still did not know what to do with his life.

Ten or fifteen years ago he would simply have found a nice local war and sold his military skills to whichever side would pay the highest rate. Noonan and he had fought together in most of Africa's wars, pausing at intervals to spend what money they had earned on women and on drinking bouts which were almost as savage and dangerous as the battles.

It began to change, for Barr at least, when they went to Nigeria to serve the Biafran leader, Colonel Ojukwu.

Up until this time he had been a straightforward soldier-of-fortune, a gun for hire, with a cynical eye for all causes, but in Biafra he had found himself involved as never before, involved both morally and emotionally, and the experience changed him. He found it impossible ever again to play the role of pure mercenary and this had rather cut the ground from under him. Increasingly he found that the sort of people who wished to hire mercenaries were not the sort of people he wished to serve.

So, apart from his brief association with General Wilcox about six months before, he had not followed the profession of war for almost a year. He knew now, in his heart, that he would never do so again. During the spring he had spent some time on his father's farm in the West Country in the hope that this contact with his roots would

18

provide him with some answer to the problem of his future, but the experiment was a failure. After a couple of weeks of utter peace and contentment, the old restlessness, the old familiar urge for action and excitement had begun to stir in his blood.

And so he had returned to London in a mood of desperation to make contact with an old friend, Harry Benedict, Deputy Director of Operations at MI6. He had served the department in a freelance capacity on several occasions in the past and he hoped that Benedict would be able to offer him some sort of permanent position in the field. Yet here again, he was faced with disappointment. MI6, like every other government department, was being asked to make economies: the establishment had been cut back and there was no vacancy for Barr to fill. Benedict had promised, for old times' sake, to try and use him whenever possible but in six months no call had come. The truth – which Benedict took care to keep from his friend – was that the departmental chiefs objected to Barr on two grounds. He was thought to be too unorthodox in his methods and too independent of mind to suit their purposes, and at thirty-nine years of age he was considered to be too old for active service in the field.

So here he was in the tiny flat in Hampstead facing another day, a day in which he knew he would somehow have to come to terms with himself. Yesterday, apart from the violence of his row with Vicky, there had been the incident at the bank when, on presenting a cheque for cash, the cashier had smiled politely and asked him to wait. A few minutes later the manager, with an equal measure of politeness, had drawn Barr's attention to the paucity of his resources and informed him that he had reached the limit of his credit.

The pounding in his head had stopped now and with careful steps he picked his way to the bathroom. As he cleaned his teeth and tried to rinse the taste of fur from his throat, he became aware that something had changed. The glass shelf above the sink looked strangely uninhabited: he opened the whitewood cabinet and found that, apart from his spare razor and comb, it was empty.

He went back into the bedroom to check the wardrobe. All Vicky's clothes, except a blouse, had gone. The blouse was lying in a crumpled heap on one of the wooden shelves and Barr picked it up. He ran the thin material through his hands and imagined for a moment that he could smell the faint womanly scent of her body. The momentary regret was soon overcome by a feeling of relief that their brief affair had come to so painless an ending.

In the last few weeks the passion which had fuelled the relationship at the beginning had begun to fade and without that the affair had become empty and meaningless. He realised now that they had been drawn together by a mutual loneliness and that they had found their

19

greatest happiness in bed; when the joy had gone from that, they had faced each other as virtual strangers, with little in common.

In the untidy sitting-room he found a brief sensible note.

> Tommy, dear, I'm sorry. But it isn't working and it isn't going to get any better, is it?
> Thanks for everything. At least we can say it was good while it lasted. I still think you're a smashing bloke and I hope you'll find what you're looking for – as they say in the movies. I wish I knew what it was, so that I could help you. Good luck. Be happy. Love, Vicky.

He moulded the note into a ball and threw it into the wastebin. That, then, was that. It had ended at the right moment and in a simpler and better way than he had expected or deserved.

The hammering in his head began again, sharper and more distinct now; it took Barr a moment or two to realise that this time the sound was coming from outside, that someone was knocking at the door. He slipped on his worn robe and went to answer it.

'Mr Barr?'

A young man stood in the doorway, smiling at Barr with a certain diffidence.

'Yes?'

'My name is Ugley, Stephen Ugley.' The young man's eyes hardened slightly, as though he expected some response to this, but Barr simply leaned against the door-jamb and repeated himself:

'Yes?'

'You don't know me. But we have a mutual friend who suggested that I ought to come and see you. I have a proposition that —'

'Who's the mutual friend?'

'Mr Boyd.'

'Boyd?'

'Mr Alexander Boyd, of Murray, Boyd and Owen. He's a solicitor.'

'Alex Boyd.' Barr nodded.

'I've had this fantastic piece of luck, you see,' said the young man. The brown eyes gleamed with an enthusiasm which had a touch of appealing innocence about it. 'And Mr Boyd thought – with your experience —'

'Look,' said Barr, 'I can't talk now.' For some reason, his thoughts were elsewhere: he was wondering about Vicky and where she had gone. 'What did you say your name was?'

'Steve Ugley.' Again the defensive look appeared in the clear brown eyes, but Barr gave no indication that he had seen it.

'Can you meet me in, say, an hour?' asked Barr wearily.

'Yes. Of course. Back here?'

'No. At the Queen's Head in Camden Town. Saloon bar.'

20

'Great.' The young man glanced at his watch. 'Queen's Head at twenty past twelve.'

'Give or take ten minutes,' said Barr and closed the door.

He waited for a moment, listening to the sound of the young man's footsteps retreating down the stairs, then went into the sitting-room. After checking the directory, he dialled a number on the telephone.

'Murray, Boyd, Owen and Partners,' said the impersonal female voice at the other end of the line. 'Can I help you?'

'I'd like to speak to Mr Boyd, please.'

'Mr Alexander Boyd or Mr Stanley Boyd, sir?'

Christ, thought Barr, old Alex has taken his son into the partnership. He remembered Stanley Boyd as a precocious and almost unbearable twelve-year-old. It made him feel the weight of his thirty-nine years.

Aloud, he said, 'Mr Alexander Boyd, please.'

'May I ask who is calling?'

'Tell him Tom Barr.'

'I'll see if Mr Boyd is available.'

Mr Boyd was available and to prove it he came on the line immediately. He spoke with genuine warmth.

'Tom! Tom Barr! How are you?'

'Couldn't be better,' said Barr. The lie, honed to perfection by months of regular use, tripped lightly off his tongue. 'Listen. Who is this fellow you sent to see me?'

'Ugley?'

'That's the one.'

'A nice young fellow. How did you get on?'

'We haven't talked yet. We're meeting later.'

'Excellent. I hope you'll be able to advise him.'

'About what?'

'I rather think I ought to leave him to tell you that.'

'He said he'd had a fantastic piece of luck.'

'Yes,' said Mr Boyd carefully, 'yes, indeed, you might call it that. Tom, listen. I don't want to influence you one way or another. The – er – the proposal that Ugley wants to discuss with you – well, in some ways, it has a certain appeal.' Boyd chuckled. 'If I were a younger man I might be tempted to become involved myself. On the other hand, looked at from a rational viewpoint, I am afraid that it might be – shall we say – just a little far-fetched and impractical.'

'You want me to talk him out of it?'

'Not exactly. I mean, not necessarily. Just – just give him your candid opinion.'

'I'll do that,' said Barr.

'Excellent,' said Boyd. 'And thank you, Tom. The lad means well, and he can be trusted, I'm certain of that.'

'You sent him round to my place. How did you get my address?'

'From your father, naturally. I had dinner with your parents about ten days ago when I went to my Devon cottage for a break. They asked me to look you up. They're concerned about you, Tom.'

'No need to be.'

'I'm sure of that. But if you could drop them a line – or telephone.'

'How were they?'

'Fine. Not getting any younger of course, but who is? Listen, Tom, how about taking a spot of lunch with me one day soon?'

'I'll give you a call sometime and we'll fix something up.'

Once again the lie came easily enough, but he felt a twinge of guilt about it just the same. Alex Boyd was a good friend of the family and he had once given notable help when Barr had run into certain difficulties with the authorities as a consequence of his service in Biafra. But at this time he could not face the thought of a lunch, and all the questions and conversation that would go with it. Boyd was nobody's fool and he would quickly penetrate Barr's defences and get at the truth of his situation. And then it would somehow find a way back to his parents – the last thing Barr wanted.

They exchanged farewells and Barr hung up. On the way through to the kitchen to make some coffee he retrieved Vicky's note, smoothed it out, and read it again.

Alex Boyd, for his part, took a toffee from the tin in the bottom drawer of his desk and unwrapped it carefully. It was an indulgence he had allowed himself since giving up smoking. He popped the sweet into his mouth and sat back with a satisfied smile.

He was thinking of yesterday and of the moment almost exactly twenty-four hours before when young Steve Ugley had sat in the chair opposite and of the look of amazement blended with bewilderment with which the young man had heard the astonishing news.

Boyd sucked happily at the toffee, unconcerned about the smacking sounds that came from his lips. It had been, he thought, a supreme moment. Never, in all his twenty-seven years as a solicitor, had he known anything like it.

It was the kind of letter that you might expect to find in a story or a play but not in real life. Steve Ugley had to read it four or five times before he was able to take in the sense of it.

It was brief but courteous, neatly typed on paper of the finest quality, with an embossed heading which exuded respectability. MURRAY, BOYD, OWEN & PARTNERS. An address in Bedford Square, in the Holborn area of London. A list of partners headed by Alexander Boyd, LL.B., and followed by a half-dozen other names.

22

Dear Sir,

Re: Estate of Stephen James Ugley, deceased.

We act for the executors under the will of the above named deceased, late of Tradewinds, Antigua, West Indies, who died on October 1st last year.

A grant of probate has now been obtained and we are in the process of administering the estate under the said will. We now write to you in connection therewith.

We should be grateful if you could attend this office at 11am on Wednesday, March 21st, when you may learn something to your advantage.

Should this date or time be inconvenient kindly telephone this office in order to arrange a mutually convenient alternative appointment.

There followed an indecipherable signature.

Steve read the letter yet again, the thoughts tumbling and racing in his mind. He ought, he supposed, to feel some grief at the passing of someone who had meant a great deal to him in childhood, and whom he remembered as a warm, rumbustious character with an outrageous sense of fun. But what he felt was regret, rather than grief. And though he tried to put the thought aside, his mind kept coming back to the letter.

'Learn something to your advantage.' What did that mean, in practical terms? Would there be enough for the new car he so badly needed?

He telephoned the office of the minicab company for whom he worked as an owner driver, told the manager that he would not be available and then regretted the decision, for he spent the rest of the day mooning around, wondering about his stroke of fortune, warning himself not to build his hopes too high.

The following morning, after a disturbed and virtually sleepless night, clad in his one and only suit and wearing a borrowed tie, he found himself sitting in Mr Boyd's office, facing the gentleman himself. The secretary, who stared at Steve with undisguised interest, served them coffee and then retreated.

Boyd, the senior partner of the firm, was a plump man with kindly eyes and a voice that cracked and crackled like morning cornflakes, but in spite of his friendly manner – or perhaps because of it – he seemed quite unable to get to the point. Each time he appeared to be reaching the nub of the matter he veered away again, as if he were determined to extract the maximum drama from the situation.

'How well did you know your uncle, Mr Ugley?' he asked.

'Not well at all really. I saw quite a bit of him when I was a boy, but

23

he went abroad when I was ten. I heard from him occasionally after that, but it wasn't much more than a card at Christmas. Oh, yes, and when I was eighteen – on my eighteenth birthday – he sent me £100 as a present.'

'Where was he at the time?'

'In the Argentine, I think.'

'Did you write to him?'

'I wrote and thanked him for the money, of course. And I sent him a letter every year telling him what I was up to – that sort of thing. I never knew whether he received the letters – he never acknowledged them, not even when he sent a card.'

'How did the family look upon him?'

'Well —' Steve hesitated. 'There was a sort of rumour that he went abroad because he was in some kind of trouble with the law – and that he couldn't come home for the same reason. I'm only guessing really. My parents never mentioned it to me. In fact, they hardly mentioned Uncle Steve at all. But if his name came up, there was a sort of atmosphere, if you understand me. My parents would look at each other and change the subject. They thought I didn't notice, but I did.'

'Children do,' said Mr Boyd.

'I liked him,' said Steve. 'I always used to look forward to his visits when I was a kid. He had a great personality – used to tell the most fantastic stories. He'd just drop in and whisk me off for the day – we'd go fishing or to the cinema or the zoo. Once he even took me on an aeroplane to Glasgow and back, all because I'd never been in a plane before.'

'A man of some character.' Mr Boyd nodded approvingly. 'He lived a full and exciting life by all accounts. And one could say, I suppose, that even his death had a touch of the adventurous about it.'

'How do you mean?' Steve straightened up in his chair.

'Oh, I'm sorry. I am sorry,' said Mr Boyd. 'Of course, you don't know. Your uncle was drowned, I'm afraid. He owned a house called Tradewinds on the West Indian island of Antigua. According to evidence given at the coroner's inquest, he took a boat and went out fishing. He was alone. He did not return that evening as planned. The next day some fishermen found the capsized boat about two miles out to sea. Your uncle's body was washed ashore at a place called Pineapple Bay.'

'That's terrible,' said Steve. He had a sudden mental picture of his uncle as he had once known him, a roaring unquenchable man who seemed to take life and its obstacles like a hurdler. He shook his head, angry with himself because he could find no other, more adequate words to express his sorrow.

There was a silence broken only by the clink of china as Mr Boyd

24

stirred his coffee. He felt increasingly drawn to the quietly modest and sensible young man who sat opposite. He found himself comparing him to his son Stanley – to the latter's detriment – and immediately checked this unfatherly line of thought.

It was Steve who spoke next. 'How did you find me?'

'Ah.' Mr Boyd's eyes twinkled. 'It wasn't easy at first. Your uncle left no information as to your whereabouts. We thrashed about a bit, making enquiries here and there, and then, quite suddenly, I had a brainwave. I looked in the London telephone directory! And lo and behold, there was only one Ugley listed. Yourself!' He leaned back, his face beaming with triumph.

'That was a bit of luck,' said Steve. The first time, he thought wryly, that the name has done anything for him.

Ugley. From that early moment in infant school when the teacher's calling out of his name had produced a fit of giggling from the rest of the class, he had been conscious that he was burdened with a label that was an invitation to instant mockery, like the red nose of a clown.

It would have been a simple matter to change it, of course, and there had been times in his youth when he had seriously considered such a step. These moods did not last long. Pride, obstinacy, and a certain wry humour, partly inherited from his father and partly developed in the many battles fought with mocking detractors during the growing-up years, made him determined to stick with what he'd got.

It was said in the family that the name went back to Saxon times and was derived from a Cumberland village where, for centuries, the Ugleys had run the local blacksmith's forge. Steve, who was born and brought up in that part of Kent which touches the outskirts of London, had never bothered to check the family tale. It was sufficient that the name was now in his keeping, and his own honesty had long since persuaded him that the fates had shown a certain shrewd judgment when they arranged for him to become an Ugley. Only the wide brown eyes redeemed a face which a privileged friend had once described as being 'like a loaf of homemade bread'.

All the same, by the time he was fourteen, there were very few people who dared to joke about the name. One look at the challenge in those brown eyes, and another at those broad blacksmith shoulders, persuaded most of them to pursue the path of discretion.

Mr Boyd's voice crackled in his ears, bringing him back from his thoughts.

'It is rather an unusual name.'

'Suits me, I suppose,' Steve said, with a smile.

'Oh, I wouldn't say that.' Mr Boyd smiled in return, and then, because they both understood that he was being polite, their smiles grew larger.

'Your parents are dead, I understand,' said Mr Boyd, returning the conversation to more serious matters.

'Yes. My father died three years ago. A heart attack. My mother went a few months later. I don't think she ever really got over Dad's death.'

Mr Boyd made a clucking sound to indicate sympathy, allowed a moment or two of respectful silence to pass and then said, with a sigh, 'Well, shall we press on?'

'Please,' said Steve. He tried not to sound too anxious.

'First, I have to tell you that you are your uncle's principal legatee.' Mr Boyd shuffled the papers in front of him. 'Apart from some small bequests to – er – certain ladies, the bulk of the estate comes to you.'

'Ladies?'

'Your uncle was married three times – didn't you know that?'

'No.'

'And there were other associations. Several in fact. As I said before, he was quite a character.'

Steve had a sudden recollection of the day, years before, when his uncle had taken him to the London Zoo. On the way back they stopped at a toy shop in St John's Wood High Street and Uncle Steve bought him a kit with which to make a model of a VC-10 airliner. They then went to an apartment overlooking Regent's Park where young Steve was given Coca-Cola and cakes and ice-cream and generally fussed over by the very pretty and sweetly-scented lady who lived there.

After tea, Steve had been left in the sitting-room to assemble his model airplane while his uncle and the lady went into another room to 'discuss some boring old business matters', as Uncle Steve had put it. Young Steve had almost finished when they came to him again but he had been so absorbed in the model that he thought nothing of the incident. It had never even occurred to him to wonder why the lady had changed out of her clothes into a frilly blue dressing-gown.

Now he smiled inwardly at his own innocence, and felt a glow of affection for this larger-than-life man, mingled with regret that circumstances had separated them for so long. It had been good of the old man to remember him at the end. Principal legatee! Would there be enough, he wondered again, to buy that new car? Or even a good second-hand one? The old Ford that he drove as a minicab had over 100,000 miles on the clock and was pretty well clapped out.

As if he had read Steve's thoughts, Mr Boyd said, 'Have you any idea of the value of your uncle's estate?' There was a chuckle in the dry voice.

'Not really.'

'Then I have a pleasant surprise for you, Mr Ugley. Your uncle was a wealthy man – a very wealthy man.'

26

For the first time in the interview Steve looked startled. The coffee cup and saucer rattled in his hand and he put it down on the desk quickly.

'We have no idea how he made his money and, in any case, it is not our concern,' Mr Boyd continued. 'The assets are largely in the form of cash and jewellery, deposited with banks in Zurich and New York. In terms of property there is Tradewinds, the estate on Antigua, in the West Indies. Do you know the island, Mr Ugley?'

Steve shook his head, too shaken to speak.

'Ah. I had the good fortune to spend a holiday there two or three years ago. A most attractive place. I stayed at a hotel called Callaloo, not very far away from Tradewinds. I didn't see inside your uncle's place, of course, but from the outside it seemed to be a most impressive property.'

'Have you any idea —' Steve heard his own voice, faint and crackling like an old gramophone record, and stopped. Mr Boyd came to his rescue.

'How much your share of the total estate is worth? Is that what you were going to ask?'

'Yes.'

'A reasonable question.' Mr Boyd peered through his half-moon spectacles at a sheet of paper. Then he looked up again and smiled. 'Fasten your seat-belt then – and here we go. Tradewinds, the property on Antigua – which comes to you – has been valued, with its contents, at a figure of £350,000. In addition, after the smaller bequests have been settled, you will inherit cash, jewellery and invest-ments to an approximate value of eleven million pounds sterling.'

And, as if he were afraid that Steve might have missed the figure, or perhaps out of a sense of the dramatic, Mr Boyd repeated it. 'Eleven million pounds sterling.'

Not surprisingly, this statement was followed by a silence. Then Steve, who felt it necessary to make some comment but found the right words difficult to come by, cleared his throat and said diffi-dently, 'Thank you.'

'Not at all,' said Mr Boyd politely.

There was another pause. Steve still could not think of anything suitable to say and Mr Boyd, as he was to reflect afterwards, was savouring the most exciting moment in his long career. Later, after the young man had adjusted himself, in some measure at least, to the sensational change in his circumstances, they talked quietly about his future plans.

It was as a result of this conversation that Mr Boyd suggested that Steve should go to see Tom Barr. And this was how the two men – the former soldier-of-fortune and the newly-created millionaire – came to be sitting together in the saloon bar of the Queen's Head shortly after noon the following day.

The Queen's Head was a Victorian pub which had managed success-fully to survive a half-dozen misguided attempts at modernisation. It looked what it was – old and comfortable and full of character. The original beer pumps were still in operation and one of them actually dispensed real ale. The only apparent concession to change was the presence of a television set. When Mike Noonan took over as land-lord, one of his first acts was to consign two juke-boxes to the rubbish dump.

Tom Barr and Steve Ugley sat near the door with the window behind them. Outside, the rain, which had begun earlier as a drizzle, had quickened to a downpour and was running in swift streams down the opaque glass. A few regulars were in their usual places, confront-ing their usual drinks, and some casual customers, driven in by the weather, were standing at the long curving bar behind which Noonan himself was serving.

'You said you'd got a proposition,' said Barr.

'Sort of,' said Steve.

He fiddled with his glass of ale, wondering where to start, how to explain his idea without appearing to be foolish or childish or both. He looked at Barr, but found no help there. The other man's face was expressionless; there was no hint either of sympathy or curiosity in his eyes. Resisting an impulse to drink up and get out, Steve blundered on. 'What I have in mind,' he said, 'what I'd like to do, is set up a kind of special detective agency. Know what I mean?'

'No,' said Barr, still giving nothing.

'It's something I've always wanted to do. I don't know why, but ever since I was a kid I've had this thing about being a private detective. Well, not exactly a detective, if you know what I mean, something a bit more. It's hard to explain. I mean, I'm not interested in following unfaithful wives, that sort of thing. Bigger stuff than that, more interesting, more – well, more exciting, more meaningful!' Steve stopped and his rugged face coloured slightly. 'I expect you think I'm crazy or maybe just stupid.'

'It is a pretty stupid idea,' Barr said.

'In that case —' Steve half rose from his seat, inwardly relieved that he had the opportunity to escape further embarrassment.

'Sit down,' said Barr, 'and tell me more.' His face eased into what might have passed for a smile. In truth, he was beginning to feel sorry for this naïve young man. Steve saw the little smile and mistook it for condescension or ridicule. His eyes hardened and he made to leave again. Barr took his arm quickly.

'No. Don't get uptight. I'm interested. Tell me why you've always had this urge to be a kind of super private eye.'

28

'I can't explain it.' Steve relaxed and sat down. 'Maybe I watched too much television when I was young. It just seems to me that there is a lot of trouble in the world – a lot of people in trouble. Some of them are up against big organisations, governments even. They haven't got the muscle or the power to defend themselves, so they get screwed, know what I mean?'

'I know what you mean,' Barr said.

'Well, maybe it sounds stupid —'

'It does, but keep going.'

'I'd like to start an organisation which could handle those sorts of cases.'

'What sorts of cases?'

'We'd take on a lot of straightforward jobs, of course – the bread and butter work, but every now and then I hope there would be something with more scope.'

'Like what? Give me an example.'

'Like some years ago an English kid of fourteen was sent to prison in Turkey. His mother tried to fix an escape. They were captured at the border because he tried to get through with a botched passport. I'd like to think that my organisation would cater for those sort of people – and that we wouldn't botch the job.'

Barr nodded. 'Anything else?'

'Well,' Steve hesitated. 'There'd be, like, the sort of case that never gets in the papers because nobody knows anything about it. Or if it does get mentioned, nothing happens. You know what I mean,' he finished lamely.

'No, I don't. Tell me.'

'Well, like when I was up in Manchester a couple of years back I heard about this old fellow with a shop. A tobacconist's shop. It was slap in the middle of some big property development but he refused to move. Then one night the place went up in flames while he was out visiting his daughter. Inconvenient for him – very convenient for the developers. Nobody was ever caught.'

'What would you have done?'

'I don't know. I did try, in an amateur sort of way, to find out more about it, but I hadn't got the time to do the job thoroughly. I had to earn a living.'

'And now?'

'Like I told you this morning, I've had this fantastic piece of luck. Money's no problem now.'

'Won the football pools, have you?'

'Better than that, much better.'

'Good for you.'

'What do you think?'

'Think?' Barr drank the last of his whisky. 'I like it.'

29

'You do?' Steve's eyes brightened and his face broadened into a smile of relief.

'Yes. To tell you the truth, I was beginning to wonder about your generation. Wonder where all the spark and drive had gone. I thought you'd all been ruined by television and pop. I was wrong. There is something there. A hell of a lot. I apologise.'

'Then you'll help me? Mr Boyd said —'

'Hang about,' said Barr, 'hang about. What I like is the idea. The idea. But that's as far as I go. It won't work – what's your name again?'

'Steve.'

'It won't work, Steve.'

'Why not?'

'You see yourself as a cross between a private eye, a secret agent and a boy scout. A sort of white knight on a charger, riding to the rescue of whoever happens to be in distress. That's a noble thought. But it's strictly for storybooks, Steve. Real life is something else.'

'I don't see —'

'Wait. Let me finish. Take your little man in Manchester who had his shop burned out. I'd lay odds that if you'd followed that one through, you would have ended up with a couple of broken arms. Or worse. As for that kid in Turkey – if the Turks had caught you trying to help him, they would have picked your bones clean.'

'You're trying to tell me that it is risky?'

'Not risky, not risky. Dangerous. Very, very dangerous.'

'And that frightens you?'

There was a silence. Barr stared at the young man coldly. An ambulance went by in the street outside, its siren screaming.

'Yes, it frightens me,' Barr said quietly. 'Danger scares me. I'd be an idiot if it didn't.'

'But Mr Boyd told me that you —'

'Never mind what Mr Boyd told you about me. Let's just say that maybe, because of what I was, I know a bit more about danger than you do. And it won't go away if you wave a cheque-book at it, Steve.'

'OK.' Steve sighed. 'So it will be dangerous. What else?'

'All sorts of things. How are you going to start, how are you going to operate? Open an office, stick up a nameplate, wait for a queue to form at the door? Advertise in the papers?'

'We'll need an office, of course. But I thought of keeping the organisation small – three or four key people, no more. When we needed extra help, we'd hire it. And all the other things, technology and so forth, we'd buy that as and when it was wanted.'

'Do you intend to charge for your services?'

'We'll charge what people can afford.'

Barr smiled. 'You'll go bust in a month on that basis.'

Steve returned the smile. 'I don't think so,' he said. 'I told you, money is not the problem.'

'Then why don't you just go ahead?'

'Because I need someone like you as a partner. Your experience, your contacts, your know-how – I need all that. I will go it alone if you won't come in with me. My mind's made up on that. But I'd be a damned sight happier if it was the two of us.'

'It's crazy,' said Barr.

'Let me get you another Scotch,' said Steve.

'It's my round.'

'But I told you —'

'Listen,' said Barr, 'there's one thing you'll have to learn. You may have money coming out of your ears, but when it's my shout, it's my shout. OK?'

'OK,' said Steve happily.

Barr picked up the empty glasses and went to the bar for a refill.

'You're doing a lot of talking over there,' said Noonan.

'Yes,' said Barr.

He watched thoughtfully as Charlie 'Kid' Brown, a genial but ring-scarred former light-heavyweight boxer who doubled as barman and chucker-out, squeezed past Noonan and went through to the public bar. He was a product of the post-war immigration from the West Indies – a black cockney. Barr lowered his voice and leaned forward. 'Listen, Mike,' he said, 'I want you to ask the Kid to do me a favour.'

Noonan knew Barr too well to be surprised at any request he might make and he listened, a faint smile on his face, as Barr outlined what he wanted. Then, as Barr took the drinks back to the table, he went through to the other bar to find and brief the Kid.

'Do you realise,' Barr said as he sat down, 'do you realise that you hardly know me?'

'I know enough,' Steve said. 'Mr Boyd told me quite a lot about your – your career.' He smiled. 'Do you know what he said?'

'How could I?'

'He said you were the only man he knew who was a free spirit.'

'Crap!'

'I think he envies you.'

'Then he's a mug. Or a romantic – or both.'

'I believe he understands more than you realise.'

'Let's forget me. Let's talk about you. I don't know anything about you, do I?'

'There isn't all that much to know.'

Barr sipped his whisky. Two tables away, three elderly ladies were discussing the shocking price of funerals, and from the public bar he could hear the sound of men's voices raised in argument over a game of darts. The outer door swung open and Kid Brown entered, as if he had just come in from the street. He was wearing a jacket now and

31

looked like an ordinary customer as he stood in the doorway brushing the rain from his shoulders. He glanced at Barr, gave him an almost imperceptible grin and moved to the bar.

Steve had his back to the door and saw nothing of this. In any case his mind was on the conversation with Barr, and he pressed him for a response.

'Well, what do you think?'

'It needs a lot of consideration,' said Barr.

'If it's money —' began Steve.

'It isn't money.'

Kid Brown moved away from the bar, a large foaming glass of ale in his hand. As he came up behind Steve he staggered and fell against the young man: the glass shook in his hand, spilling half the contents over his clothes and then it fell, shattering to pieces on the floor.

The table rocked, and Steve's own glass tilted and turned over. He jumped up as the beer began to flow over the edge of the table towards him. As he did so, a huge black hand clamped down on his shoulder.

'What the hell do you think you're doing, man!' growled the Kid. It was an accusation, not a question.

'I didn't do anything!' protested Steve mildly.

'What's that then?' The Kid pointed to his broken glass. 'Who did that?'

'I didn't,' said Steve. He shook himself free of the other man's grip.

'Don't get smart with me, man!' said the Kid with greater belligerence.

'Look,' said Steve, 'I don't know what happened. But I'll buy you another pint if it will make you happy.'

'Oh, yeh.' The Kid's tone was heavily sarcastic. 'You'll buy me another pint, will you?' And what about my bleeding clothes then – what about them?'

The hand went out once more and gripped Steve's shoulder.

'Don't do that,' said Steve quietly and without emphasis.

'I'll bloody do more than that!' said the Kid, tightening his grip. 'I'll flatten you, man, I'll really flatten you!'

Steve looked at Barr, whose face showed no reaction, and lifted his shoulders slightly in a shrug of resignation.

'All right,' he said. 'Try it.'

The words were hardly out when the Kid pulled him round, released his shoulder, and sent a straight right towards his chin.

Steve swayed inside the punch just in time, and retaliated with a one-two: the left clipped the Kid's jaw and the right thudded into his stomach.

Most other men would have gone down under the blows, but the Kid merely gasped, recoiled a little, and stood looking at Steve with a

32

puzzled expression on his craggy face. He turned and glanced towards the bar, towards Noonan, as if mutely asking for further instructions. It was Barr who intervened.

'All right, all right,' he said. 'That'll do.'

'I can take him,' said the Kid.

'Leave it,' said Barr.

Noonan came out from behind the bar and led the bewildered fighter away.

'Give him another pint, landlord,' called Steve. 'And the same again here.' He looked down at Barr. 'What was all that about?'

'How should I know?' said Barr.

'You set it up, didn't you? What for? To get rid of me or to test me out?'

'You did all right,' said Barr. 'Only one thing. You should have put him down when he turned his head. He was wide open then. Rule Number One. If you get into a fight, finish it.'

'I didn't want to hurt him,' said Steve.

The two men eyed each other and then Barr broke the tension with a wry smile. Steve relaxed and sat down as Noonan brought a fresh round of drinks and swabbed down the table. Steve studied the golden froth on top of his beer and drew a faint line across it with his fingertip. Then he looked at Barr.

'I've got a feeling I'm wasting my time,' he said.

'Who said?'

'You're not interested in my proposition.'

'Who said so? Did I say so? As a matter of fact, I think I might give it a go.'

'Great!' Steve's face brightened into a broad smile. 'Great! When could you start?'

'Well,' Barr said. 'I don't happen to have my diary with me. But how about today? Like now?'

'Great!' said Steve again, and shook his head as if he could hardly believe it.

'Well,' said Barr, 'don't just sit there. Tell me what we do next.'

A shadow loomed over Steve's shoulder and, half-turning in his seat, he looked up into the smiling pug-face of Kid Brown. 'Oh, no. Not again!' he said.

'No hard feelings,' said the Kid.

'No hard feelings,' said Steve warily.

'That was a good punch,' said the Kid. 'The one you gave me in the guts. A hell of a good punch, man.'

'Any time,' said Steve.

'Would you like to try it again?'

'Try what?'

'Try the same punch.'

33

'No, Kid,' said Barr abruptly. 'No!'

'Aw, come on,' said the Kid, 'what's the harm?' He spread himself so that his muscled stomach presented an open target. 'Come on, son, hang one in there again.'

'What for?' asked Steve.

'Just want to see if you can hurt me,' said the Kid.

Steve shrugged and got to his feet. 'Do you really mean it?'

'I wouldn't ask if I didn't mean it, would I?' said the Kid. 'Come on, put it in there – put it in there, man!'

'Don't do it!' said Barr.

'He wants it. He's begging for it!' said Steve, bunching his fist.

The buzz of conversation in the bar died away. The small circle of men at the bar turned to watch. The three old ladies, funerals temporarily forgotten, scuffled their chairs round to get a better view.

'If you hurt me, I'll buy the drinks,' said the Kid.

'How will I know?' asked Steve.

'You'll know,' said the Kid.

Steve seemed hardly to move, but his arm shot out, straight as a piston, and his fist thudded into the other man's stomach. The Kid smiled broadly and then as Steve stood there, his arms hanging loose, he suddenly hit back. Steve folded up like a nutcracker as the ex-fighter's fist rammed into his solar plexus, and he fell to the floor, fighting desperately for air.

'That's the way to do it, man,' said the Kid amiably.

'What the hell did you do that for!' said Barr.

'He hurt me!' said the Kid, in a pained voice. He pulled Steve to his feet and sat him in his chair. 'I'll get the drinks.'

'Christ,' said Barr, 'you asked for that. You were standing there like a clown asking to be hit!'

'I didn't expect it,' said Steve. His face was the colour of pumice-stone and the words came out in short painful bursts.

'You've got a lot to learn,' said Barr.

'He's got a stomach like cast iron,' Steve said ruefully, looking at his bruised knuckles. 'But I'll get him next time.' The colour was just beginning to return to his cheeks.

'Next time,' said Barr, 'he'll slaughter you.'

'I'll tell you something,' said Steve. 'We could use him.' He looked towards the bar, where the Kid was setting up yet another round of drinks. 'What's his name? You called him Kid.'

'Kid Brown. Former light-heavyweight champion of Britain and Europe.'

'Oh, my God!' Steve's eyes widened. 'And you just sat there and let me take him!'

'You want me as a partner or a babysitter?'

'A partner.' Steve looked towards the bar again. 'Listen. We could use him too, don't you think?'

'The Kid? What for? We haven't even started yet. We haven't even got a case.'

'Oh, yes, we have,' Steve said.

'Would it be asking too much for you to let me in on it?' asked Barr.

'We have to find a girl,' said Steve. 'A girl named Kitty Higgins. And I reckon it might be quite difficult.'

Chapter Three

It was the scream of fear that woke Kitty from her long, troubled sleep and moments passed before she realised that the scream had come from her own lips. When she opened her eyes the light was so bright and painful that she closed them again quickly. She could feel the fear pricking her skin like so many needle-points, and the sheet beneath her naked body was damp with sweat.

She shuddered as she remembered fragments of the dream. The thin grey mist swirling around her as she ran, the black mud sucking at her feet, the dark, howling wolf-like creature snapping at her legs, drawing blood with its fangs. And then it was upon her; even now she could see the one red malevolent eye and smell the awful foulness of its breath, as the creature dragged her down . . .

Gradually the echoes of the nightmare faded away and, once again, the terrible tiredness that seemed to hang like a weight on her limbs urged her back to sleep. She fought against it with all her strength, knowing vaguely that she had slept too long and too much, that somehow she must force herself back into the waking world. There were questions in her mind to which she could give no shape or coherence, but they were there nevertheless: questions which she glimpsed as through a mist, darting elusive questions which appeared and then vanished again before she could grasp them.

She opened her eyes slowly, adjusting them to the white glare of the room. Her ears picked up a low humming noise, but she was unable to place it. High on the wall before her something glinted in the sunlight, something which looked red and malevolent, like the eye of the creature in her dream. Shivering, she looked away, around the room. It was small and, apart from the bed, contained only a round white-topped table and a tubular steel chair. A vase of flowers stood on the table, unfamiliar exotic flowers to which she could not put a name.

A hospital? Was she in a hospital, or a nursing home perhaps?

A diagonal pattern of black lines on the wall behind the table puzzled her. Then she saw the pattern flicker momentarily and realised that it was a shadow. A shadow of what? She turned her aching head towards the window and the sunshine and saw the criss-cross of bars behind the gleaming glass.

She sat up in sudden fright, so quickly that her body flooded with nausea, and it took her a good half-minute to steady herself. Bars! A barred window! Was she going mad? Was she mad?

Her hand dropped to her breast and, for the first time, with a renewed sense of shock, she saw that she was naked. She turned back the top sheet and looked down at her body with dull, uncomprehend-ing eyes as though it belonged to another person. It was all beyond her understanding, her mind was too tired to focus, to wring sense out of the situation.

Lying back on the pillow, she tried again to concentrate. Simple things, the simple things first. What was her name? Kitty Ann Higgins. Where did she live? Parkhill Road, Hampstead. What was the number of the house? With an effort she dragged the answer out of her reluctant memory. Number 50. 50, Parkhill Road, Hampstead, London. And she lived there with her friend, Lucy Syms. Somehow all that seemed a long way away and a long time ago, but remember-ing helped her; she was no longer in limbo, she was a person with a name, an identity.

She heard a faint click and then became aware that the low humming noise had suddenly stopped. Her mind was a little clearer now and when she saw the box-like grille on the outer wall she realised that the noise had come from an air-conditioning system. Such a thing was still a rarity in Britain. What kind of a place would have bars on the windows and air-conditioning in the rooms?

The silence, the absence even of this small sound, increased her sense of isolation. And then she remembered something else. Movement. And the faces. She remembered brief intervals when she had woken as though from a coma, to find strange, unknown faces looming above her. Doctors? Nurses? There had been a suggestion of white overalls but she could not be certain; she recalled only the faces and even those were not clearly established in her mind.

And in those short waking intervals she had felt some sort of movement, a rocking motion, which puzzled her, but which she found vaguely soothing. It had reminded her of some previous experience but she had been too listless and tired to work out what it was.

Now the answer came to her and with it the fear came surging back. Two years before, she and Lucy had gone on a fourteen-day cruise around the Mediterranean. The movement she had felt was that of a ship!

But there was no motion now, she was on land. Had she been on a ship? And where, in heaven's name, was she now?

Gathering all her resources, she swung her legs out of the bed and touched the coolness of the tiled floor with her feet. Another wave of nausea swept over her and she sat there, head down, hand over her mouth, trying to bring her body under control. The nausea passed and gripping the headboard, she pulled herself up. Her legs quivered violently, uncontrollably: they seemed to be dissociated from the rest of her and to lack the strength to respond to her needs.

She pushed herself off and took two or three tentative, stumbling steps towards the window. A short stretch of lush green lawn came

37

into view and beyond that a high wall, its whiteness broken by a thick, hanging mass of red and purple flowers. Just outside, to the left of the window, a banana stalk threw a long shadow on the gravel path which ran between the lawn and the building: she would not have recognised it but for the hands of small green fruit that hung from its branches.

And, to her increasing bewilderment, in the middle distance there was a stand of coconut palms, their fronded heads rising above the wall.

She closed her eyes, trying to keep a grip on her senses, and when she opened them again she saw a man crossing the lawn. His face was shadowed by a wide-brimmed straw hat, but when he turned momentarily to look up at the sky, she saw that he was young and black. He paused by the wall to pick up a hoe, shouldered it, and then continued on his way.

Her control snapped suddenly and seizing the bars which separated her from the window, she screamed at the man, shaking the bars and calling out for help. If he heard, he made no sign, and a moment later, he was gone.

In despair, Kitty turned away. She took a step towards the door, but the effort was too much for her. Her strength exhausted, she collapsed on the floor, sobbing not out of self-pity but for her own utter helplessness.

'A most interesting specimen, Doctor,' said the Comptroller in his usual high-pitched, precise tone. 'When will she be ready for auditing?'

'In two, perhaps three, weeks,' answered the Doctor.

'So long?'

'I am afraid so, yes.' Dr Christa Bauer picked up her clipboard and ran a heavy finger down the neat line of figures on the chart. 'Yes. The subject is exceptionally strong-willed and high-spirited, you see.'

'She hardly looks that way at present,' said the Comptroller. He turned back to the television monitor on which Kitty could be seen lying where she had fallen.

'Perhaps,' replied the Doctor. 'But it meant that she resisted the drugs for quite a time. We had to increase the dosage – to quite a formidable degree. And now we have gradually to reduce the daily intake until the subject is restored to normality. So it will take time.'

'If her temperament is all that you say it is, the emotional-training and auditing period may well be extended beyond what is normal.'

'That is not my department,' said Dr Bauer rather stiffly.

'Of course, Doctor,' said the Comptroller. He assumed the bland official smile for which he was noted.

38

'I sometimes feel that they go too far with the auditing of subjects,' continued the Doctor. 'Beauty lies not only in the body, but in the personality also. To remove that personality, or even part of it, is to reduce the total attraction.' And she added hastily, lest it be thought that she was being disloyal, 'Of course, that is only my humble opinion.'

'But if the subjects become too troublesome? They do occupy a rather special position in the Community, you know.'

'There are ways of dealing with troublesome girls,' said the Doctor. There was a strange huskiness in her voice which the Comptroller was quick to notice.

'Of course. I'm sure you would know how to discipline them, Doctor,' he said. 'Would you like me to arrange an audience with Mr Dunlop, so that you might express your view?'

'No,' she answered quickly, too quickly. 'I mean – I wouldn't dream of – he has so many other things – and he knows what is best.'

'Yes,' he said, 'indeed. His judgment – takes my breath away sometimes. So lucid, clear. And right, always so right.'

'Always,' she echoed fervently.

'I am sure he will be delighted with this new subject,' said the Comptroller. 'She really looks quite perfect. There are no defects, I assume?'

'A tiny scar on the scalp. Probably caused by a fall when she was a child.'

'Not visible, I trust?'

'No, no. It is above the hair-line, quite hidden.'

'Excellent. How old?'

'The documents indicate that she is just over twenty-one.'

'Intact?'

'I am afraid not. At that age —' The Doctor spread her hands in a gesture of resignation.

'Exactly. Fortunately, Mr Dunlop does not insist on virginity,' said the Comptroller. 'Well, Doctor, I will leave you to your work.'

He turned to take another look at the television monitor. 'Ah, yes. A remarkable specimen. Quite beautiful.'

'I'm most grateful to you, Comptroller, for your advice and help. Most grateful. You are always so kind,' she said.

'You are a very valued member of the Executive, Doctor,' he said, and patted her arm.

She watched him waddle away, an immensely fat man, the huge stomach thrusting forward, the fleshy neck bulging over the collar of his loose white silk tunic. The way he stiffened his back to take the strain of the weight in front reminded her of a heavily pregnant woman, and her eyes darkened with contempt. He was neither the one thing nor the other: he was an in-between, a sexless nothing, a eunuch! She hated him for what he was and for his position of power in the Community. Above all, she hated having to screen her real feelings, she hated herself for fawning upon him. But there was no other way; a word from him and her privileged place, perhaps her life, could be in jeopardy.

Why was it, she wondered, that Mr Dunlop held him in such esteem?

And even as she asked the question, she shuddered at her own temerity. To doubt Mr Dunlop's wisdom, even in the smallest instance, was the worst of crimes. He was all-knowing, without fault, infallible. And good, he was good. Had he not brought her – and everyone in the Community – out of darkness into the light? She was wearing his ring, the ring with his seal, which signified that she was a Founder, someone who had been chosen by him for special duties.

She held the hand which carried the ring flat against her heart in the ritual gesture of submission and silently prayed for release from her feelings of hatred and envy, for forgiveness for her doubts.

She saw on the television monitor that the girl called Kitty Higgins was still lying on the floor of her room and appeared to have gone to sleep. What on earth were the Custodians doing, to leave her like that!

Refreshed by her anger, Dr Bauer strode down the corridor. She inserted her plastic master-key into the lock of the steel grille which barred the entrance to the Special Rooms and waited impatiently for it to rise. When she had passed through, the grille closed automatically behind her.

As she reached Room 7, she met the Deputy Chief Custodian coming from the other direction. He stood stiffly to attention as she upbraided him for neglecting his charge, and then dismissed him. Again, she used the plastic key to open the door to the room.

Kitty lay on her back, her head to one side, breathing heavily. Dr Bauer knelt and checked her pulse. It was slow, but that was consistent with the drugs, and it did not worry her unduly. She held a hand to the girl's forehead for a moment: it felt cool, perhaps cooler than it should be, but that again could be attributed to the drugs.

'Come on, my lovely,' she said, 'let's get you back into bed.'

She slid her arms under Kitty's shoulders and, without undue effort, pulled her up into a sitting position. The girl's eyes fluttered open momentarily and she murmured incoherently as the Doctor drew her to her feet. She staggered and would have fallen, but the other woman fielded her deftly and carried her in her arms, like a child, to the bed. With a sigh of relief, Kitty turned on her side and went back to sleep.

Breathing more deeply now, though not from exertion, the big woman stood looking down at the girl. Her dull eyes brightened as

40

they probed every curve of the firm flesh, her lips gleamed with moisture. She wondered, with a spasm of disgust, what man had taken this lovely creature's virginity, what other men her body had entertained.

And, forgetting herself for a moment, she slid her hand gently over the smooth buttocks, along the line of the thighs, over the rounded stomach and up to the breasts. She leaned forward, impelled by a desire to kneel and touch the breasts with her lips, to lay her face against them, to worship the whole body with her mouth, her hands, her fingers . . .

Then, with a surge of guilt and fear, she remembered. The Custodians would be watching on the closed-circuit television monitors in the Control Room; they would have registered every movement. Perhaps she had already gone too far.

With an effort, she brought herself under control and assumed her best professional face. Forcing herself not to hurry, she drew the sheet over Kitty, and then, with studied care, made an entry on the clipboard which hung near the bed.

Only then did she leave the room, locking it behind her.

Slowly, over the next few days, Kitty felt her strength and health returning. She no longer slept so heavily or for so long, and she began again to take an interest in food. She had always been a healthy eater and she had no complaint now about the meals, which were wholesome and tastefully cooked. There was always a wide selection of fresh fruit, some varieties of which were strange to her, but she tried them all and, as the days passed, the lustre came back into her eyes and her skin took on its former characteristic glow.

And memory returned also, at least, in part. Painfully, step by step, she built a mental picture of her last interview with Mr Digby, of the flat in Parkhill Road, of driving out to see her parents, and of those frenzied moments when the black Volvo had hemmed her in. She recalled her fierce struggle with the two men as they dragged her from the Mini; strange little details came back to her so that she could almost feel again the coarse, unshaven skin of one of them as her fingers and nails raked his face in the darkness. And then the brief, fearful interlude of escape as she broke loose and fled into the woods. She remembered one man calling out and strained to recall the words. What had he shouted? The odd phrase echoed in her mind with a sudden rush: 'Don't mark her! Don't mark her!'

After that she could remember nothing except the dull ache of waking, the faces bending over her, the strange movement which she now felt certain was that of a ship.

That she had been kidnapped was beyond question, but her own

41

calmness in the face of this awesome fact astonished her. Who had carried out the abduction, and why, and where she was, were questions which still had to be answered and she found herself examining them steadily, without panic, trying to fit together what snippets of information she already had, in the hope that this might yield a solution to the problem.

Oddly enough, she felt only occasional spasms of fear. The comfort of her surroundings, the solicitude and even respect with which the attendants treated her, was puzzling, but it all served to allay any feelings of immediate danger.

She was visited at regular intervals by a woman doctor whom she got to know as Dr Bauer, and by two people, one man and one woman, who seemed to be nurses, though she suspected that their responsibilities went beyond this and that they were her guards also.

They were kind, almost unbearably so, treating her more as an honoured guest than as a prisoner. The smiles and the courtesy seemed genuine enough, but there was something strange about them all, something which she could not place. It was as if they were not quite whole, as if some part of their personalities was elsewhere.

They refused, with grave politeness, to answer any question which referred to her present position, turning it aside with the vague promise that all would soon be revealed to her. Here again, she was surprised at her own patience. It was as if she instinctively understood that she could do nothing until her health and strength had completely returned.

Her custodians seemed to be delighted with her steady recovery and desperately anxious to do everything to please her. When she requested clothes to cover her nakedness, they brought in her own familiar weekend case, containing the spare underclothes she had packed on that critical Friday evening, together with her toilet-bag: and with these things they brought half a dozen dresses, two swim-suits, and a beachrobe.

The new clothes surprised her. They were exquisitely made in various colourful patterns of sea-island cotton. They fitted perfectly as if made to measure and she had to admit that they were exactly the sort of things she would have chosen herself. Someone in this strange place either shared her taste or had gone to great lengths to match it.

But when she asked the female nurse for the return of her jeans, or for a pair of slacks, she received an odd reply. The nurse, a kindly, motherly Irish woman named Maura, smiled and shook her head.

'No, my dear. Your jeans were destroyed. Women are not allowed to wear such things here.'

'Here?' asked Kitty. 'Where is here?'

'Here,' said Maura, with a little laugh. 'Here is here.'

On another occasion, Kitty asked Gunnar, the young Swede who

42

shared duties with Maura, the name of the red and purple blossom that flowed in such profusion over the white wall outside.

'Why, that's bougainvillaea,' he answered. 'Don't you recognise it?'

'I do now,' she said. 'I saw some in Greece and Italy when I went there on a cruise.'

'It is beautiful, is it not? Look, do you see the way it is growing – in one direction? That is because bougainvillaea loves to grow with the prevailing wind. Later, when you go outside, you will see many other wonderful plants and flowers. Hibiscus, water hyacinth, oleander, orchid, jacaranda, frangipani. They say that when God made the world, he touched this spot with his little finger to give it a little extra beauty.'

But Kitty was thinking, with a surge of hope, of what he had said about going out.

'When will I be able to go outside?' she asked.

'Soon, I think,' said Gunnar. 'It is not for me to say. But I will speak to the doctor.'

The next day, a smiling Dr Bauer came to the room. 'We are pleased with you, Kitty,' she said. 'You have made excellent progress. This afternoon you are to be allowed to go to the Compound.' She put a hand on Kitty's arm and squeezed it gently. 'You will enjoy that, I think. You can try out one of your swimsuits.'

Kitty drew away, avoiding the Doctor's touch and the odd, intense look in her eyes. 'The Compound? What is that?'

'A very special place, for very special persons, believe me. You will be able to swim, sunbathe, relax.'

She spoke in a placatory way, as though telling a child of some treat in store, and at last Kitty's anger broke through the thin unnatural seal of patience which had been keeping it in check.

'What is this place, Doctor?' she asked, in a low tense voice. 'Don't try and put me off. I want to know!'

'I've told you —'

'No, no. Not what you call the Compound. This place.' She waved an arm at the room. 'This whole place. And don't give me any of your usual bullshit! I want to know!'

'You will be told in due course. When you are ready,' said the Doctor anxiously.

'You keep saying that! I want to know now, now!'

'You mustn't upset yourself, dear, really. You've made such progress. Don't spoil it!'

'Spoil it!' Kitty opened up now. 'Spoil it! Bloody hell!'

'Sh, sh,' said Dr Bauer, her eyes wide with alarm. 'That sort of language is forbidden here. I must tell you —'

'Tell me nothing!' shouted Kitty. 'Bloody hell! Bloody hell! All the claptrap you keep giving me! I'm not a child or an idiot! I've been

43

kidnapped, I'm being held here against my will! Don't you know that that's a criminal offence? Don't you know that the police will be looking for me? And they'll find me, never fear – and you and all the others will be for the chop!'

Dr Bauer stepped back and clicked on her pocket intercom. 'Come in here – Room 7. Quickly.'

Within seconds the door opened and Gunnar came in with Maura. Kitty looked round desperately, picked up the vase of flowers, and emptied the contents on to the floor. She held the vase up in a threatening gesture.

'Don't you come near me! Don't touch me!' she hissed.

'The subject has had a relapse,' said Dr Bauer. 'She must be sedated.'

'No, you don't!' shouted Kitty.

And as Gunnar moved towards her, she hurled the vase at his head. He dodged the missile easily, with a smile, and it smashed in pieces against the door. He pinioned the struggling Kitty, his partner moved in to help, and together they carried her to the bed.

'Hold her there! Don't mark her!' said Dr Bauer. She moved in closer, a syringe in hand, and looked down at the helpless Kitty.

'You are a very foolish girl,' she said with what sounded like genuine disappointment in her tone. 'You will have to be punished for your outburst. There will be no visit to the Compound for you today – or tomorrow, if your behaviour doesn't improve. I'm here to help you get better. I don't want to sedate you – you've had enough drugs, more than enough, but really, you leave me no choice.'

Kitty looked up into the heavy face, and shook her head. 'No, please,' she murmured, 'no, no.'

Dr Bauer hesitated. 'I told you, I don't want to use this. You were doing so well. If I leave it this time, will you promise to behave?'

Kitty nodded, relief flooding through her.

'Very well. But I want to tell you something, something rather important. You spoke about being kidnapped. That is not the way to look at it. I can tell you now that you are a very privileged person. You are a Chosen One. That is a rare honour. Many are called, but few are chosen. Now, will you promise to be good?'

Kitty nodded again and they released her. After they had gone, she lay back on the bed trying to collect her thoughts. What had the Doctor meant about her being privileged? A Chosen One? What on earth did that mean? Had she landed up among a group of madmen?

One word surfaced in her mind. Escape. But she would have to be cunning and careful. These people, whoever they were, madmen or not, were clearly well organised and powerful, and escape would not be easy. She was a girl alone, one person against many. She had no friends here, no weapons, and she didn't even know where she was being held.

The only thing to do was to play their game, convince them that she had submitted, lull them into a false sense of security and await her opportunity. In the meantime she would have to control her unruly temper, school herself to be patient, build up her strength.

The broken vase had not yet been cleared away and, on an impulse, she retrieved one of the jagged pieces and put it under the mattress. It wasn't much, but it was better than nothing, and the time might come when she would need some sort of weapon.

Chapter Four

Steve Ugley's flat on the first floor of a house in the Highbury district of London was bigger than Barr's own place but because of the clutter of books, magazines and files, it seemed smaller. To Barr, it looked like the dusty store-room of some mad second-hand book-seller.

The books were everywhere, stacked up in seemingly haphazard fashion in the living room, the bedroom, the tiny entrance hall and even the bathroom. Most of them dealt with crime, from novels by eminent and not so eminent crime writers to factual accounts of notorious crimes or famous real-life trials.

There was a huge stack of books describing the organisation and methods of the world's leading police forces, and another, even bigger, which dealt with the history and activities of the principal secret service and intelligence agencies. There were books and magazines about guns, about spies and their exploits, about confidence tricksters, about security systems and modern methods of surveillance.

Nothing, as far as Barr could see, had been overlooked. If he needed proof of the seriousness of Steve's obsession, it was here in abundance. He must, Barr thought, have spent every spare penny and hundreds of man-hours on this extraordinary collection.

He found the only departure from the theme of crime in the bedroom where there was a selection of poetry, mostly in the form of paperbacks, ranging from Milton to Ted Hughes. There was also a sophisticated Marantz hi-fi system and a collection of records and tapes which appeared to be dominated by Mahler, Mozart and Beethoven on the one hand and by Ella Fitzgerald and Frank Sinatra on the other.

They had come back to the flat after their talk at Noonan's pub and while Barr wandered in astonishment from room to room, Steve stayed in the kitchen, rummaging through the cupboard section of a Welsh dresser. As far as Barr could see, the dresser contained more books and files than food or crockery.

Steve must have noticed his amused look for he said apologetically, 'I don't eat here very much.'

'I'm not surprised,' said Barr. 'You wouldn't have room to swing a fork, would you?'

'Coffee. I could make some coffee,' Steve said, as though he had suddenly realised that, as host, he had certain responsibilities.

'Coffee? Why not? Always assuming you can find some,' said Barr.

Steve took a manilla folder from the dresser and put it on the table. It was fat with notes and newspaper clippings. 'That's the case notes, so far.'

'Case notes?' asked Barr.

'For our first case.'

'Ah. The Kitty Higgins affair.' Barr sat down at the table and pulled the file towards him.

'No,' said Steve and, as Barr looked up sharply, he added, 'I mean, not yet. I want to fill you in on the background first.'

'OK. You're the boss.'

Steve filled the kettle and plugged it in to an electric point. Then, to Barr's surprise and approval, he produced some coffee beans and an earthenware jug from behind a pile of books.

'Do you mind your coffee made this way?' Steve asked.

'I prefer instant,' said Barr, with a straight face.

'Oh,' said Steve, 'I haven't got —'

'Get on with it,' said Barr. 'And tell me about this Kitty Higgins. Was she the one who was in all the papers a few weeks back, the model who got herself murdered?'

'She wasn't a model,' said Steve.

'Something like that,' said Barr. 'Don't let's split hairs.'

'And she wasn't murdered.'

'Oh?'

'Her body was never found. Apart from the police search, I spent almost three weeks going over the ground with her father. We found nothing.'

'Was she your girl?'

'Not exactly. I met her when I was driving the minicab. Took her out a couple of times, but there was nothing special between us. As a matter of fact, I rang her flat on the evening she disappeared. I had some free time and wanted to spend it with her. But she had already left. She was going to stay the weekend with her parents.'

He switched on the coffee-grinding machine and for a time the kitchen was filled with its high-pitched whine. The clean enticing aroma of freshly ground beans floated on the air. Steve stopped the machine and said wistfully, 'She was a beautiful girl, you know. Beautiful.'

'Even you speak as if she is dead,' said Barr softly.

'I don't mean to. I think she's still alive, I'm sure she was kidnapped.'

'Why? Does she have money? Are her parents rich?'

'Far from it.'

'Then what would anyone hope to gain by hijacking her?'

Steve warmed the jug with some of the boiling water, swilling it round thoughtfully. 'She was – I mean, she is – a beautiful girl.'

47

'You're beginning to repeat yourself,' said Barr, watching as Steve finished making the coffee. Leaving a pan of milk to heat up, he came to the table and sat down opposite the older man.

'Listen,' said Steve. 'I naturally asked myself the same question, the obvious question. Why would anyone want to kidnap Kitty? She had no money to speak of, no rich relations, no influential friends. And, in any case, there has been no demand for money or for anything else from the kidnappers. So what do we deduce from this?'

'Jesus. You sound like one of your books!'

'Sorry.'

'It doesn't matter. It's obvious that the kidnappers weren't after money, or that kind of loot. Is that what you're saying?'

'Correct! So why else would they go to such elaborate lengths to take her? What else did she have that they wanted? Only one thing. Her looks. Her looks. Believe me, she is fantastic, a real stunner.'

'I believe you,' said Barr. He shook his head. 'But no. It's too far-fetched.'

'Maybe. But if you eliminate every other possible explanation, whatever you have left must be the answer, no matter how improbable it may seem.'

The phrase sounded familiar to Barr, but he did not press the point. Instead, he said, 'OK. Let's assume that someone took a fancy to your beautiful Kitty, and decided to take her for himself. It isn't so easy to kidnap someone and keep them hidden, you know.'

'I know,' said Steve. 'Not easy, but not impossible either if you have the resources.'

The milk began to hiss in the pan and he jumped up just in time to stop it from boiling over. As he prepared coffee in two enamel mugs, he went on, 'I got on to the next line of development almost by accident. One day, shortly after Kitty went missing, I spoke to a Chief Superintendent, one of the senior detectives on the case, and asked him whether he thought it was possible that she had been kidnapped just for her looks. He was a bit sharp with me – he obviously thought I was intruding on police territory and should mind my own business. He said that it was far more likely that her good looks had attracted a maniac, and that she had been raped and murdered. He said that there was no case on record of a woman being kidnapped simply for her beauty, and with no other motive.'

'You should have told him about Helen of Troy,' said Barr.

Steve smiled. 'The stupid sod would have told me that Troy didn't come under his jurisdiction!'

He brought the coffee to the table, set out a packet of sugar, and sat down. Barr waited for him to continue.

'A day or so later, I met a detective sergeant who had been with the Chief Superintendent at the time I spoke to him. He was much more friendly. He told me that he'd been thinking over what I'd said. He was pretty vague about it, but he said that there had been another case, about a year previously, where an attractive girl had disappeared in suspicious circumstances and apparently without reason. The only other thing he could tell me was that this girl was called Gabrielle something or other and that she was a French actress.'

He sipped his coffee and looked anxiously at Barr. 'Is it all right?'

'Whatever else,' said Barr approvingly, 'you know how to make coffee.'

'Anyway,' Steve continued, 'I decided to go into it. There wasn't much more than an odd paragraph or so in the British papers, so I went to Paris and did some checking there. I discovered that the girl's name was Gabrielle Joyeux, and that she was twenty years old. She disappeared one night shortly after leaving her flat in Paris, without leaving a note or any message. She was on her way to dine with her agent and an American film producer. She never turned up and she was never found.'

'Were there signs of a struggle?' asked Barr.

'None. Her car, a Renault, was in the street, untouched.'

'Then that's quite different. She could have had a lover and just decided to shoot off with him.'

'She was having an affair with a young actor at the time. He was on stage in a small theatre in Montmartre that evening and was supposed to join her after the show.'

'A pretty girl can have more than one lover,' said Barr. 'It has been known. She could have gone off with someone else.'

'Without packing? Leaving her passport, her car, her clothes, everything? And just as she was about to sign a contract which would have taken her to Hollywood and probably made her an international star?'

'OK,' Barr said. 'It isn't likely. But kidnapping isn't any more likely. And I don't see the connection between this case and Kitty's.'

'Gabrielle Joyeux was beautiful also.' Steve opened the file and drew out some glossy photographs. 'See for yourself.'

Barr studied the pictures, which showed Gabrielle Joyeux in various poses, nodding as he did so. They had obviously been taken for the purpose of publicity but even so, there could be no argument about this girl's beauty.

Her dark hair had been cut short in a soft, carefully untidy style that emphasised the impudent, urchin quality of the face. The small nose, the clean, strong sweep of the chin, the disarming dimples that softened her cheeks, all added to the impression of delightful roguishness; the bright, glowing eyes held a hint of mockery, and the mouth, with its full lower lip, was both an invitation and a promise.

Other photographs confirmed the impression of beauty and sensuality. She was of medium height, but perfectly proportioned; narrow waisted, with fine legs, firm breasts and a voluptuously

49

rounded bottom.

Barr turned again to the photograph which showed only the girl's face. The physical features were well-nigh perfect but it was the personality, the cheerful mockery in those lovely eyes, which informed the whole and added that mysterious plus which distinguishes the truly beautiful from the plastic imitation. There was a quality in Gabrielle that could not be applied from a make-up kit, or explained solely by her physical attributes.

'She's a winner all right,' Barr said. 'I wouldn't mind kidnapping her myself.' He sipped his coffee. 'So. In the space of eighteen months, two girls disappear in rather strange circumstances. The only link between the two, as far as I can see, is that neither of them was seen again, dead or alive, and that they were both rather special in the looks department.'

'More than that,' said Steve, correcting him. 'They were more than just good-looking, they were stunningly beautiful.'

'Granted,' said Barr.

'And they both had their pictures in the papers. Gabrielle more so than Kitty. It means that they could have been seen and noted by the kidnappers.'

'All the same —' Barr began, but Steve interrupted him.

'Suppose I were to tell you that there have been others?' he asked.

'Other disappearances? Like this one?'

'Yes. After I learned about Gabrielle, I decided to do some more checking.' He put his hand on the file. 'The results are in there. In the last three years, eight girls have disappeared. Vanished. In similar circumstances.'

'You're kidding!' said Barr.

'No way. From Guyana, a local beauty queen. From India, a young fashion model. From Gothenburg in Sweden, a girl who won a national award as the best hospital nurse of the year. From Hong Kong, a film actress. From Spain, a singer, an entrant in the European Song Contest. From the Philippines, a beauty queen, Miss Manila of 1979. Plus Gabrielle Joyeux and Kitty. Eight in all. The cuttings and notes are in the file.'

'Hang about,' Barr said, 'hang about! If that's true, why haven't the police put it all together? Why aren't they working on the same angle?'

'They may be, for all I know,' said Steve. 'Only so far, they don't seem to have come up with any answers.'

'And you have?'

'Not yet. But I will. Or rather we will.' He smiled and picked up the coffee jug. 'Want a top up?'

'Thanks.' Barr watched as Steve refilled the mugs. 'OK. Let's assume that there is something in your theory. Not a lot, but something. You admit yourself that you've run into a dead-end with Kitty. So where do we start? Where the hell do we start?'

'We check every one of these other cases.'

'Gothenburg, Hong Kong, the Philippines and what-have-you! Are you crazy?'

'No.'

'It'll cost a fortune!'

'I've got a fortune.'

'And it'll take weeks, maybe months.'

'Maybe. We must be prepared for that. Patience and persistence are more important to an investigation than a gun or a black belt in judo,' said Steve solemnly.

'Which book did that come from?' asked Barr acidly.

'Sorry.' Steve blushed. 'Actually, it was an American criminologist who said that.'

'Bully for him,' said Barr.

'Seriously,' said Steve. 'What we have to do is collect a lot more information than we have now. And that can only be done on the spot, don't you see?'

'OK. But what are we looking for?'

'Some common factor.'

'Apart from the fact that all the girls were good-lookers?'

'Yes. Something else that is common to all the disappearances. Apart from Kitty, the most recent case was this girl in the Philippines. Miss Manila. I think we should start there.'

'It might save time if we split our forces,' said Barr. 'Do you know the Philippines?'

'No.'

'I do. Suppose I go there and do some checking. You take somewhere else. Hong Kong, say. That way we'll be only a few flying hours away from each other.'

'Great,' said Steve, 'great!'

'There is just the little matter of money,' said Barr.

'There's a travel agency in Islington High Street,' said Steve. 'Let's go and get fixed up now.'

'Money,' said Barr.

'I told you. I've —'

'I know, you've come into a fortune. But how much is a fortune? I don't want to find myself stranded in Manila with empty pockets.'

Steve blushed again. 'Actually, I've come into quite a lot. From an uncle. Mr Boyd told me yesterday.'

'What do you call quite a lot?'

'Eleven million pounds,' said Steve apologetically.

Barr looked at him in astonishment. 'Eleven million!' He mouthed the words.

'That's right. It's crazy, isn't it?'

'Crazy? It's incredible! And what's more incredible is that all you

51

can think to do with – with all that loot – is to set up as a bloody private eye!'

'Well, like I said, it's something I've always wanted to do. And, of course, I shall do other things with the money when I get round to it.'

'I'm relieved to hear it. Like what, for instance?'

'Well, there's a few odd relatives. I shall have to see that they're all right. And I guess I might get myself a new car, maybe some clothes – you know.'

'Don't go too mad, will you,' said Barr drily.

'Of course, I can't pretend that the money won't change my life,' said Steve earnestly. 'After all, it's giving me the opportunity to do something I've always wanted to do. But I've thought about it very seriously, and I'm determined not to let it change me as a person. I mean – I hope that doesn't sound bigheaded.'

Barr had to work hard to keep a straight face, but like Mr Boyd before him he found himself warming to this young man, who was such a strange mixture of determination and artlessness. At least, he thought, at least he has his priorities right.

'No,' he said solemnly, 'you're not bigheaded. And what's more, I don't think you'll change. If I see any sign of that, my friend, you can rely upon me to kick your arse!'

Steve smiled and put out a hand. Barr was not given to such gestures, but he took the hand and shook it awkwardly. For the first time, he felt that what he had committed himself to was more than a temporary diversion which would fill an empty space in his life.

It was a serious enterprise because Steve thought it so, and there was no way now that Barr could back out or let him down.

Barr had never believed in what he called random luck. In his view, you could only get lucky if you worked to create the right circumstances. You had to be there, you had to arrange your life so that you were in the right place at the right time. It was rather like a lottery. A man had to be in it before he could win it.

Maybe the fact that he was in the Philippines went some way towards proving his theory. At any rate, his bit of luck arrived only a few hours after his arrival at the Manila Hotel on Rizal Park, when he discovered that the man in charge of Metropolitan Manila's Criminal Investigation Bureau was an old friend, Captain Placido Mascardo.

They had worked together about five years before when Barr had gone to the Philippines on a one-off job for British Intelligence. At that time Mascardo had been third-in-command of the State Security Office of the Philippine Government, with special responsibility for counter-espionage. It had been in Mascardo's interest to help Barr, and together they had organised the exposure of a much-wanted Soviet agent who had used his job as a consultant engineer with a prominent British firm as a cover for his activities.

Mascardo insisted on sending a police car to collect his friend, which greatly improved Barr's standing with the hotel, and greeted him personally at the entrance to the imposing modern police building. He was a short, stocky, handsome man with dark mischievous eyes and a smile to match.

'My friend!' he said, clasping Barr's hand. 'It is good to have you back.'

'It's good to be back,' said Barr with real warmth. It was more than the conventional polite response. Barr felt a genuine affection for the Philippines and its friendly smiling people.

They spent a preliminary half-hour over a drink in the police club, discussing Mascardo's promotion and generally catching up on the years between this meeting and the last.

'How many children now?' asked Barr.

'Seven,' said Mascardo, with a touch of pride.

'You always wanted a son,' said Barr. 'Did you get one?'

'No, alas,' said Mascardo sadly. 'They are all girls. Very beautiful, that goes without saying. I am fond of them all. But to live in a house where one hears only the chirrup of female voices —' He broke off, and shook his head.

'You've given up now, have you?' asked Barr.

'Given up? Never! We shall keep trying, my wife and I. It is not much to ask, after all — just one son. Perhaps God will relent. And you, my friend, not married yet?'

'How can you tell?'

'You have the look.' Mascardo cocked his head to one side and smiled at Barr with a certain sympathy. 'You should try it, my old friend — marriage is not as bad as I make it appear.'

'I've left it a bit late,' said Barr.

'Forgive me,' said Mascardo gently, 'forgive me for asking. But what happened to the girl — the Australian girl, Iris?'

'Oh, just one of those things.' Barr looked down at his drink, twisting the glass in his hands.

He had met Iris Hughes on his last visit to Manila and their relationship had lasted for almost three years. There had not been too many women in Barr's life: apart from Vicky, with whom he had lived for seven months, no association had survived for more than a month or so, and that made Iris something special.

He had left her, quite suddenly, in Port Moresby in Papua New Guinea, and he had never quite got over the feeling of guilt. He had fled, paradoxically, not because he no longer cared, but because he found himself caring too much: he was afraid that his emotions were taking too strong a hold and that they would destroy his indepen-

53

dence. It had been a near thing, for she had pierced all his defences, thrusting herself deep inside him like a knife, and the pain was still with him.

Barr had a sudden vision of Iris lying beside him in the big bed in their rented bungalow in Port Moresby, her eyes closed in sleep, her incredibly fine fair hair floating across the pillow. Iris, he thought, oh Christ, Iris, Iris, Iris!

'I am sorry.' Mascardo's voice gently interrupted his reverie. 'I did not wish to intrude.'

Barr looked up, forcing a smile. 'Just one of those things,' he said, repeating himself.

Later, in Mascardo's office, Barr explained why he had come to Manila.

'Of course,' said Mascardo, 'I remember the case well. The file is still open. The girl's name was Mila, Mila de Jesus. Even in a country that is noted for the beauty of its women, Mila was exceptional, a jewel. The case created great indignation, you understand, for she was most popular. The President himself intervened, and took a special interest in the case.'

'Do you think she was murdered, Placido?' asked Barr.

'I think it is possible, yes.'

'Why?'

'What else? If Mila had been kidnapped, we would surely have heard from those responsible. But there was no ransom demand, nothing. Only silence.'

'But you haven't found a body?'

'No. That is true, that is true.'

'Perhaps there could have been another motive for kidnapping her?'

'What? In my experience, kidnappers work for money, and only money.'

'I was thinking of what used to be called the white slave traffic.'

'No, no.' Mascardo laughed shortly. 'In Asia, at least, they can buy all the girls they need for their brothels at very low prices. There is no point in kidnapping – it is too complicated and too expensive.'

'What about boyfriends? A jealous boyfriend?'

'No. We investigated all that, believe me. Mila was engaged to be married to a young attorney. They were very much in love, very happy, and faithful to each other. There were no complications, at least that we could find. Of course, we considered the possibility that the crime had been committed by some sort of sex maniac, but that proved to be a dead-end. In any case, sex maniacs of that sort are usually solitary creatures, they operate alone, in the shadows. And we know that at least three men were involved in the kidnapping.'

Barr looked up with quickening interest. 'How do you know that?'

'They were seen. Mila lived in an apartment in Quezon City. She was getting ready to go to a dinner at the Cultural Centre on Manila Bay – a special function which she was attending in her capacity as Miss Manila. A message came through on the housephone to say that an official car was waiting for her downstairs. Her maid took the message. Mila was surprised because she had expected to drive to the Centre in her own car. But she was also pleased by this attention. The maid saw Mila leave, and watching from the window, saw her move out into the street. The car was there, a black limousine. A man, dressed like a chauffeur, saluted Mila and opened the rear door of the car. The maid saw Mila hesitate and draw back, but then the chauffeur pushed her into the car and another man pulled her from inside. It was all over in a second or two. The limousine drove off. The maid caught a glimpse of Mila sitting between two men on the rear seat. And that was the last time she was seen.'

'Didn't the maid raise the alarm?'

'Not for some time. She is not a bright person. She waited for a while, wondering what to do, and then when her boyfriend turned up to take her home, she told him. Luckily, he had the good sense to contact us.'

'Did she take the number of the car?'

'No. But we found it the next day in a car park in Batangas City, a few miles south of here. We found Mila's fingerprints – matched them up with samples taken from her apartment. And our forensic department also found certain threads which came from her evening wrap. The car turned out to be stolen.'

'And the men?'

'The maid was fairly certain that the one in chauffeur's uniform was white, a European. As for the others, she did not see their faces.'

Barr got up and walked to the window. In the street below a small traffic jam had built up around two jeepneys which were facing each other almost head-on. Neither driver appeared to be willing to give way: each was gesticulating and swearing at the other.

Other jeepneys – old American jeeps which had been adapted as miniature buses, and decorated with all the Filipino flair for colour – were honking their horns impatiently. Looking down on them, Barr was reminded of Derby Day at Epsom, with its parade of Romany caravans. A flash of white caught his eye and raising his head he saw, beyond the line of coconut palms that fringed the waterfront, a yacht sliding gracefully across the smooth, deep blue waters of the bay.

He turned back to Mascardo. 'Did you check the shipping?'

'We searched every ship in the harbour. And put a check on all airports.'

'It's not easy to search a ship. Too many nooks and crannies —'

'I know, I know. But we did our best.'

Barr followed the white yacht with his eyes for a moment and then returned to his seat. He sat back, pressing his hands on the bamboo arms, shaking his head thoughtfully.

'It doesn't make sense, Placido,' he said, 'it doesn't make sense.'

'No,' said his friend, 'I agree, I agree. There is no motive either for murder or for kidnapping.'

'No obvious motive,' said Barr.

'You have something else on your mind, my friend?'

'No. At least, nothing definite.' Barr hesitated, thinking aloud. 'Could you get me a list of all the ships which were berthed in the harbour around the time the girl was kidnapped?'

'Nothing would be simpler. May I perhaps ask why you would want such a thing?'

'I'm not sure. Except – except that Mila de Jesus could have been taken out of the country. And the most likely way to do that is by ship.'

'Well, you shall have your list,' said Mascardo. 'And I wish you well. I tell you this, Tom, my friend. If you find Mila de Jesus, you will be a national hero here. We will strike a medal in your honour!'

Barr stayed in Manila for two more days, making what enquiries he could. He spoke to the maid who worked for Mila de Jesus, and to her fiancé; he studied and re-studied the police report of the case; he wandered around the harbour area asking questions. At the end of all this he knew little more than he had learned in that first hour with Mascardo, and he decided to go on to Hong Kong. He telephoned Steve to tell him that he was on his way.

Steve met him off the midday flight of Philippine Airlines the next day and drove him to the Miramar Hotel on Kowloon side. He chattered breezily enough to Barr on the journey from the airport, but to the older man there seemed to be a note of desperation in his cheerfulness.

It turned out that he had learned about as much as Barr, which, in the event, was very little and did almost nothing to advance their investigation.

The film actress, a Chinese girl named Hua Yen-ping, had disappeared eighteen months before. She was working on a film at the Run Run Shaw Studios at the time, and left the set at six o'clock one evening to drive out to see a friend in the New Territories. She did not arrive. Her car was found abandoned the next morning and, as with Kitty Higgins, the police discovered signs of a struggle.

The pattern was much the same as with the other disappearances. No demand came in from the kidnappers, no body was found, no real motive could be established. The Royal Hong Kong Police were

56

helpful, but it soon became obvious to Steve that as far as they were concerned the case of Miss Hua Yen-ping was virtually closed. He could not find it in his heart to blame them. They ran a territory which teemed with people and problems, and they were woefully short of man-power. There was a limit to the time and energy they could spend on an individual case.

As he pushed through the crowded streets under the grey, rain-heavy skies, Steve could only wonder not that the police did so little, but that they achieved so much. A Welsh journalist whom he met in the Captain's Bar of the Mandarin Hotel told him that Hong Kong was laced with corruption. It depressed but did not surprise him. In such a city, where there was no space and the only way to build was upwards, where everybody seemed to be hustling and hurrying, where illegal immigrants from the mainland arrived in their thousands every month, where drugs were an everyday currency – in such a city, how was it possible for a man to avoid the pollution which affected almost everything around him?

That evening, strolling along the noisy pavements of Kowloon in the strange half-light cast by hundreds of competing neon lights, past window displays of amber and jade and hi-fi equipment and clothes, past shop doors so plastered with credit-card labels that scarcely an inch of glass was left visible, Steve and Barr discussed their next move. It seemed that there was little more that they could do in Hong Kong and that the only thing to do was to move on.

It was then, more as a matter of routine than with any sense of hope, that Barr, remembering that he had the shipping list for Manila in his case at the hotel, suggested that they should get a similar list from the Hong Kong harbour authorities for around the period when Hua Yen-ping had disappeared.

By ten o'clock the next morning an obliging Scotsman in the offices of the harbour authority had provided them with the information they needed and over a cold beer in a nearby bar they checked one list against the other.

One ship, and one ship only, appeared on both lists. She had sailed from Manila the day after Mila de Jesus had been kidnapped, and from Hong Kong two days after the disappearance of Hua Yen-ping.

The ship was the *SS Leandro*, registered in Panama, owned by Burnham and Company of London, a firm trading in bananas and other tropical fruits. She had berthed in Hong Kong for two days only, seemingly with no other purpose than to take on supplies. On the other hand, in Manila, she had picked up a small cargo of bananas and avocados.

Barr and Steve sat in silence. Both men were pondering the next, the obvious, question.

Had the *Leandro* also picked up Mila de Jesus and Hua Yen-ping?

57

Chapter Five

Two days after the outburst in which she smashed the vase, Kitty Higgins was taken to the place they called the Compound.

It was to be a strange, bewildering and frightening day. An air of unreality was established from the beginning, when Dr Bauer, with a simpering, schoolmistress-like smile and the air of one bestowing a great favour, told her, 'We're going to have a lovely picnic, my dear. On the beach! Now – what do you say to that?'

'Goody, goody,' said Kitty coldly.

The Doctor gave her a quick, sharp look. 'You are going to enjoy yourself,' she said, and made it sound like an instruction. Then she smiled again. 'You look beautiful in that dress, my dear. It suits you, it really does. Do you know something? You have wonderful skin, so cool, so smooth. It's the truth.'

She ran a finger down Kitty's arm and a faint flush of redness glowed momentarily on her normally sallow cheeks. Then, as though remembering herself, she withdrew the hand and said briskly, 'Have you remembered your swimsuit?'

'Yes.'

'Good.' Dr Bauer clapped her hands as if she were bringing a class to order. 'Let us go then.'

She led Kitty out into a wide, tiled corridor, on either side of which there were four doors. Two of them stood open and the rooms beyond, which looked to be much the same as the one she had just left, seemed to be unoccupied.

Since her arrival Kitty had not seen anyone other than the Doctor, the two attendants, Maura and Gunnar, and that brief glimpse of the young West Indian in the garden, and she wondered if there were others, like herself, locked away in this strange prison.

That word prison trembled in her mind again when at the end of the corridor they came to a gleaming steel grille which blocked the way forward. It was a strange and formidable obstacle: the cold metal, winking in the light, the intricate pattern of the bars, made it seem like some baleful animal standing menacingly at bay.

She watched curiously, her heart-beat quickening, as Dr Bauer pulled at a chain around her neck and drew up an oblong of plastic which, to Kitty, looked rather like a credit card. It was, in fact, a coded key: the Doctor inserted it in the lock, waited a second, and then withdrew it. There was a faint whirring of machinery and the grille lifted itself into some upper recess. When they had passed through, Kitty turned and saw that it was coming down again, back into place.

Beyond this there was a door, which Dr Bauer opened with the

58

same plastic key, and they moved on into a large and comfortably-furnished room. The bamboo armchairs were spread with brightly patterned cushions which matched the drawn curtains, and a scatter-ring of rugs broke up the impersonal coldness of the tiled floor. On a low, marble-topped table Kitty saw a large bible, the inlaid gilt cross on its black cover glinting in the pure, bright light which streamed in through two panoramic windows.

The white walls were bare of ornament or decoration except for a large head-and-shoulders portrait of a middle-aged man. He seemed to be wearing some sort of loose-fitting robe and he was holding his right hand, on which there was a single, heavy signet-ring, across his heart in a kind of salute. His head was tilted upwards in a way that emphasised the determined firmness of the chin; the face itself was full and fleshy, the lips slack and sensual.

But it was the man's eyes that dominated the portrait, over-shadowing all else. Of a piercing violet colour they glittered, like crystal, with a fierce, almost hypnotic quality. Moving closer, Kitty saw that the portrait was, in fact, an enlarged photograph: even so, it was impossible not to feel the personality and power of this man, who seemed to be half priest, half pirate.

Dr Bauer noticed Kitty's interest and came to stand beside her.

'Do you know who that is?' she asked.

Her voice trembled slightly as she spoke and she seemed eager to have the girl respond. But Kitty was not prepared to give her even that small satisfaction and so, with a studied air of indifference, she shook her head.

'That is Mr Dunlop,' said Dr Bauer, in a low reverential tone. She looked at Kitty expectantly.

'Oh,' said Kitty mischievously, 'I knew a Mr Dunlop once.'

'Not this Mr Dunlop,' said Dr Bauer carefully.

'No. The one I knew was a schoolmaster, at the comprehensive school I went to. Dirty old sod. Hands like a commercial traveller – you know, always on the move. Always trying to touch you up.'

Dr Bauer looked shocked and she said sternly, 'You will wait here.'

She went out, locking the door behind her, and Kitty moved to one of the windows. It gave a view of well tended, emerald-green lawns lined with flowering shrubs and confined by a wall which seemed to be an extension of the one Kitty had seen from her room. Beyond this again she saw more palm trees and, in the far distance, she caught a glimpse of low purple hills, patterned with light and shade. And once again, the inevitable questions came pounding back.

Where was she? What place was this? Why had she had been kidnapped and why was she being treated in this strange fashion?

The one obvious thing was that these people – whoever they were – had brought her to some tropical or sub-tropical land. It could be

59

any one of a dozen places. A chill touched her heart at the thought that she could be hundreds or, more probably, thousands of miles from home.

Home! What were the people at home doing about it, she thought bitterly, what were the police doing? Her disappearance must have been reported, enquiries must have been made. She could not put an exact measure to it, but at a guess she must have been in captivity for some weeks – a month, perhaps, or even more. Surely in that time, the British police, for whose skill and persistence she had great respect, would have come up with some clue to her whereabouts? Perhaps – and with the thought there came a tiny surge of hope – perhaps they were even now on her trail, closing in on the kidnappers, preparing to pounce?

The door opened, cutting across these thoughts, and to her surprise, two girls entered, followed closely by Dr Bauer. They seemed to glide rather than walk across the room, and to do it, moreover, in perfect unison as though joined together. And when they paused and turned, it was with the same graceful co-ordinated motion.

They were identical twins, so clearly look-alike that each was a mirror image of the other. Small and delicate and beautiful, with honey-coloured skin, glistening black hair, and dark eyes that were wide and wondering, they stood together shyly like two frightened fawns.

'Now, look who we have here!' said Dr Bauer, beaming at Kitty. 'Two companions for you, two friends. This is Susheela and this is Jasmine.'

Each girl put her hands together in turn and made a slight inclination of the head towards Kitty.

'And this is Kitty,' said Dr Bauer.

'Hello!' Kitty said, with a smile. And, with a quick glance at the Doctor, she added maliciously, 'Are they letting you out for the day too?'

'Kitty!' said the Doctor sharply.

'Sorry,' said Kitty. 'I only wanted to know if they were here of their own free will or if you'd kidnapped them too.'

'That is enough!' snapped Dr Bauer. 'We have been very patient with you, my dear, very patient. But if you persist, you will learn that we can also make things rather uncomfortable for you. Painfully uncomfortable. Do you understand me?'

'You know something, Doctor?' said Kitty with a brightness she did not feel. 'You're a fantastic person, you really are. I think you should be stuffed.'

'Let us go,' said Dr Bauer coldly.

*

60

They went outside into a heat which was almost oven-like in its intensity after the coolness of the building they had left. Then, with Gunnar at the wheel and the Doctor beside him, they were driven in a Range Rover along smooth tarmac roads across a flat plain that even to Kitty's inexperienced eye seemed to be immaculately culti-vated. Neat stands of coconut palms, fields of sea-island cotton, sugar-cane, banana and pineapple lay on either side.

Small groups of people were at work in some of the plantations and Kitty fancied, though she could not be sure, that she could hear them singing. There were men, women and some older children, and they looked to be a mixture of races. They were all dressed alike, in a sort of bush-type uniform of a khaki-green colour, with skirts for the women and slacks for the men. The Range Rover slowed down at one point and she caught a glimpse of thin, worn, exhausted faces. Even so they smiled at the occupants of the car and, one by one, offered the same sort of salute as the man in the photograph.

A little further on they were held up by a work-gang which was repairing the surface of the narrow road. As Gunnar braked to a halt, waiting for the men to manhandle their heavy roller off the track, Kitty, on a sudden impulse, put her head out of the window and called out to them:

'Here – you – listen, listen! Get the registration number of this car – or whatever you call it – and give it to the police! My name is Kitty Higgins. Higgins. I was kidnapped. These people kidnapped me. The British police will know. Help – please! Please!'

Even as the words came tumbling out, she realised that they sounded hopelessly ridiculous and melodramatic.

The men paused in their work and looked towards her. Most of them seemed surprised by her outburst and she fancied that she saw a flicker of fear on one or two of the tired faces but no-one responded.

'For God's sake!' Kitty's voice rose in desperation. 'Listen, for God's sake! Don't just stand there! Tell the police – anyone – please!'

Most of them smiled at her now, as though she had made some kind of joke or was mad and needed to be humoured, and put their hands across their hearts in the now familiar salute. She noticed then that some of them were wearing rings similar to that worn by Dr Bauer.

She sat back in her seat, fighting down tears of anger and frus-tration, and within moments the Range Rover moved forward again. Neither Gunnar nor Dr Bauer had made any move to restrain Kitty and the only comment came when the Doctor said, quite mildly, 'You are a very silly girl, you know!'

'Get lost!' said Kitty through her teeth.

The two Asian girls, Susheela and Jasmine, had remained

seemingly unmoved by this small confrontation. They sat stiff and silent beside Kitty, their shoulders touching, as though they were afraid to lose contact with each other. Only their dark eyes moved, restless and eloquent with fear.

'Haven't you got anything to say?' said Kitty angrily. They trembled slightly like twin leaves, but made no response, and she went on, more gently now, 'Where are you from?'

Without moving their heads, the girls gave her a slow sideways look but again there was no reply. Dr Bauer screwed round in her seat and intervened, 'Susheela and Jasmine are rather shy.'

'Or scared,' said Kitty softly.

'They are not like you. They have accepted the situation.'

'What situation?'

'They understand that they are privileged. In time, you will come to see that also.'

The Doctor turned to the front as the Range Rover took a left turn along another narrow road. In the distance, not much more than half a mile ahead, the sunlight glittered on an enormous golden cross that seemed to be suspended in the sky high above the tops of the palm trees. Beyond this it was just possible to see a curve of golden sand and a stretch of gleaming turquoise-coloured sea.

All this was lost to view as the road went into a steep decline, and they came to a wooden bridge which spanned a wide and curving channel of water. On the opposite side the water was bordered by a rampart of sandy earth, some ten or twelve metres high, which in turn was almost completely covered by hundreds of large, savage-looking cacti.

The approach to the bridge was barred by a painted iron gate, rather like a frontier post and, just before this, there stood a small brick-built building which was obviously some kind of guardhouse. Two men wearing olive-green combat uniforms and armed with sub-machine guns came forward to check the Range Rover. Gunnar showed them a pass which they studied carefully, passing it from one to the other. They stared at Kitty and the two Asian girls with undisguised curiosity and then signalled to the guardhouse. There was a faint whirr of machinery, the gate swung back, and Gunnar, engaging gear, drove the Range Rover over the bridge and on to the road beyond.

'Welcome to the Compound!' said Dr Bauer softly.

Nothing she had so far experienced, however extraordinary, had prepared Kitty for what she was to see in the next few minutes.

Within a few yards of the bridge, the road opened up on to a wide avenue lined on either side by trees that blazed in a riot of colour.

Neat white houses stood beyond the trees, each one uniformly edged with an oblong of neatly clipped lawn and low flowering shrubs. Here and there a sprinkler played on the grass, the drops of water sparkling like diamonds in the sunlight.

A little further on they passed what appeared to be a school. About fifty or so children of varying ages were cavorting around a large recreation ground in front of a long, low building, playing, as far as Kitty could see, the same sort of games that children played back home.

And, as if to reinforce the impression of suburban normality, just beyond the school there was a large supermarket, half covered and half in the open, where men and women were shopping, pushing trolleys laden with goods, as they might have done in Tunbridge Wells or Kentish Town.

Except, she thought, that this looked much more like a market in an army camp than a superstore in an English town. Men and women alike were clad in the same neat bush-style uniforms she had seen before. Those who went hatless revealed short hair, cut in the old crew-cut style for the men and briefly bobbed for the women. Despite the military style of the dress, no-one appeared to be armed.

There was another difference, something missing, which puzzled Kitty and it took her a minute or so to work out what it was. Then she realised that there was no traffic on the avenue, no automobiles parked alongside the market or, indeed, outside the houses they had just passed. Theirs was the only vehicle in view, and it was not surprising, therefore, that it drew the attention of the people on the street. Here again, she noted that most of them smiled and that some performed the ritual salute.

Quite suddenly the avenue divided and became two roads running on either side of a grassed arena which was as smooth and large as a football field. Royal palms, tall and majestic, stood around this area like grey sentinels and below them there was a wide paved walk, beautifully patterned in a mosaic of coloured tiles; wooden benches, painted, like almost everything else, in gleaming white paint, stood at intervals along this walk and here and there were occupied by people sheltering from the hot sun.

'We call this the Square of Peace and Love,' said the Doctor.

Kitty lifted her shoulders in a gesture of indifference and the Doctor glared at her.

'Stop!' she ordered.

Gunnar brought the Range Rover to a halt and Dr Bauer pointed to the far end of the arena.

'Look!' she said, in a tone that was a mixture of pride and reverence. 'The Tabernacle!'

Despite her determination to remain unimpressed, Kitty felt a

63

sense of awe as she looked towards the tall building which dominated the whole arena, the same sense of wonder that she had once felt in Athens on her first sight of an ancient Doric temple. Indeed, there was something Grecian in style about this building, from the great columned porch with its terracotta figures to the wide flight of stone steps, running the whole width of the arena, which led upwards to the entrance. A wing had been built on either side of the main structure, each one sloping slightly backwards, so that the general shape was rather like that of an arrowhead aimed at the field and at the buildings beyond.

And on the highest point of the roof the great gleaming golden cross they had seen in the distance lifted itself to the blue skies, towering above the palms and casting a solemn swathe of shadow over the ground below.

'Well?' asked Dr Bauer.

'Well what?' said Kitty.

'What do you think? Is it not beautiful?'

Once again Kitty detected a note of anxiety in the other woman's tone and decided obstinately not to indulge it.

'I've seen better,' she said. 'It's a bit on the flashy side for my taste.'

'Kitty,' said Dr Bauer, and she spoke almost sadly, 'I've seen girls like you before. Full of spirit, unable – at first – to conform. At first, I say. For I tell you this – you will learn humility, you will learn to accept, you will learn to obey. And in that acceptance you will find true and perfect happiness.'

'Garbage,' said Kitty viciously. 'Absolute garbage! I shan't be here long enough to accept anything. And when I do get out of here, I'll have the police down on you so hard you'll wonder what's hit you.'

Dr Bauer sighed and looked first at her watch and then at Gunnar. 'We should go to the Lagoon, I think.' And she added, with a sharper edge to her voice, 'I would not wish Kitty to miss a moment of the ceremony.'

'We call it the Lagoon,' said Gunnar, 'because that's what it once was. A kind of lake, made by the sea. We made it deeper and wider and reinforced the sides. And made other changes, as you will see.' He spoke in a flat conversational tone, as one would to a visitor, but when he looked at her she saw concern in his eyes. The look puzzled Kitty. It was like a signal, which she could not understand.

He shifted away from her stare, glancing nervously at Dr Bauer, and Kitty turned her attention to the scene around her. The Lagoon itself did not impress her unduly, except that she would have loved to have plunged into its limpid green water. For the rest, it seemed to her to be rather like a luxurious outsize pool, with tiers of seats for spectators rising on either side, and high diving boards at one end.

The only difference that she could see was that, instead of the usual ladder, a flight of steps led up to the very highest board.

She was sitting with Susheela and Jasmine in the front seats of what appeared to be a private box, with Gunnar and Dr Bauer on either side. It was comfortable enough; a smiling West Indian woman in the now familiar greenish-khaki uniform supplied them with ice-cold lime drinks and there was a dish of fruit on a table to one side, but Kitty noted that two armed guards were posted at the door of the box. To keep us in or other people out, she wondered.

Dr Bauer turned aside to speak with some people who had entered the adjoining box and suddenly, as though he had been waiting for this moment, Gunnar touched Kitty with his elbow, gently pressing it against her side. Without moving his head and through half-closed lips he murmured, 'Listen. Don't look round. I wish you to know that I am your friend. Do not be afraid. I wish to —'

He broke off abruptly as Dr Bauer straightened up in her seat and turned towards them, a little frown puckering her heavy face. Kitty covered her eyes with a hand for a second, lest they should show any sign of the hope that had begun to surge inside her. What Gunnar had said was little enough, but it had, at a stroke, destroyed the terrible sense of isolation which had weighed like a millstone on her spirits. It was as though she had once again made contact with the human race.

'Are you all right?' asked Dr Bauer.

'Yes, yes. I'm fine,' Kitty said quickly.

'Look, look. This is something you must see.'

On the opposite side of the pool, a group of about thirty men and women was being brought in under armed escort and conducted to two rows of reserved seats. They were dressed like all the other people she had seen, except that the letter W was displayed prominently on their tunics.

'Who are they?' asked Kitty.

'Ah. This is very interesting,' said the Doctor. 'Those poor people are Waverers. The Community takes special care of them. In time, with love and understanding, we shall bring them back.'

'From what?'

'From their wavering, of course. Restore them once again to spiritual health. You know, Gunnar was a Waverer at one time. Isn't that true, Gunnar?'

'For a short time,' Gunnar said uncomfortably. 'But I was saved.'

Kitty turned, looking at the young Swede, and said teasingly, 'You don't look saved to me! Tell me, what would have happened if you had carried on wavering?'

'That is unthinkable!' said Dr Bauer. 'All Waverers return in the end.'

'You're kidding yourself,' said Kitty. 'You don't really believe it.'

65

'That is enough!' said the Doctor.

'Suppose you wanted to leave this place. You or Gunnar. Could you? Could you leave?'

'That is enough, I say!' There was a shrill edge to the Doctor's voice, and a hint of real fear in her eyes. Reaching forward, she grabbed Kitty's arm in both hands and twisted the flesh just below the elbow in opposite directions. Her grip was masculine in its strength, and though she tried to pull free, Kitty could do nothing against it. As the fingers dug in harder, stretching the skin, she let out a small scream of pain.

'Christ! That hurts!'

'It was meant to,' said Dr Bauer spitefully, releasing her.

A flurry of activity drew Kitty's attention away from her aching arm. Other spectators, a few families among them, had filled the rest of the seats and now, as if at a signal, everyone rose and stood with their hands across their hearts.

'Stand up!' hissed Dr Bauer. 'Stand up!'

As she spoke, she rose to her feet and joined in the salute. Gunnar followed suit, and the three girls, bewildered by all this, got up and stood beside them.

There followed a few moments of tingling silence, and then the Comptroller, followed by a half-dozen guards and attendants, entered the box almost immediately opposite. He waited, looking round and returning the salute, before taking his seat. As he did so, the spectators relaxed and sat down also.

Four uniformed guards came in at the far end of the Lagoon, drawing behind them on a rope a young man whose hands were bound together. Naked except for a loin-cloth, his thin white body contrasted strangely with the healthy sun-burned faces of the burly guards. He stood as if in a daze, screwing up his eyes against the fierce sunlight.

'Who is he?' whispered Kitty. She felt possessed by a terrible unknown fear.

'Quiet!' whispered the Doctor in an urgent voice. She was leaning forward in her seat, her eyes staring, her tongue thrusting through her lips like a small pink snake.

The crowd was silent, gripped by a tension which was almost unbearable, as though the air itself were crackling with electricity. And, as if it did not choose to be outdone, nature took a hand also, adding a new measure of drama to the scene. The blue brilliance of the sky began to fade to a sombre grey and a column of black clouds moved in from the west, veiling the sun. In the gloom that followed a fresh wind began to stir the fronds of the palm trees and to flick at the water of the Lagoon, churning it into small angry waves that surged hungrily against the concrete sides.

66

One of the guards stepped forward, armed with a knife, and looked up at the Comptroller, who nodded almost imperceptibly. Two more guards seized the prisoner and held him tight: he struggled a little, his head rolling from side to side, but he was no match for them.

Kitty saw the raised knife and shuddered, closing her eyes. She heard the man's high-pitched agonising scream and felt sure that he had been killed, but when she looked again she saw that he was still wrestling feebly with his guards. After a few moments his strength abandoned him and, giving up the futile struggle, he hung between the two men, sobbing and moaning.

And she realised now what the knife had done. The prisoner had been slashed across the body and the arms, his skin scored just deep enough to draw the blood which was dribbling down his body in a dozen streams.

Kitty half-rose to her feet but Dr Bauer had anticipated her reaction. The two men at the back of the box had moved in behind, and they seized the girl, pinioning her arms and forcing her down. She tried to scream, but nothing came out except a low dry rattle. Susheela and Jasmine sat motionless beside her, their faces touching, their eyes wide and staring.

A low murmur of anticipation now came from the crowd. One woman, overcome by the tension, fell forward in a faint, but no-one moved to help her. The murmuring became more uniform, turning into a kind of deep keening sound and the watchers began to sway from side to side in a strange hypnotic rhythm.

They were looking away from the prisoner towards the other end of the Lagoon, where the sides turned in sharply to a narrow entrance, rather like the neck of a bottle. There was a movement below, and the water began to chop more viciously, as two iron shutters slid open, inching slowly into their underground recesses.

The swaying and the keening stopped abruptly as the crowd turned back to the prisoner. They had cut his hands free and he was now climbing the flight of steps towards the high board. Clinging desperately to the rails, he hauled himself up one step at a time, and when he hesitated the guards jabbed at him with their guns, forcing him upwards.

The blood was still streaming from his wounds, staining the steps and leaving crimson marks at intervals on the handrail. When he reached the top platform he was forced, in the same manner, to move along the board, inch by painful inch, until he had reached the very end.

He stood there for a long, terrible minute, swaying with the motion of the board, the criss-cross of red lines standing out against the whiteness of his body. The swaying increased and he tried desperately to restore his balance: then, with a half-strangled scream that

67

brought a murmur of exultation from the crowd, he fell forward and plummeted into the Lagoon.

Surfacing almost immediately, he beat at the surface with his hands, thrashing his legs in panic and as he went down again, the blood from his wounds began to darken the water.

And now there came a dark flash of movement from the narrow end of the Lagoon. At first it looked like a small dark object sliding smoothly and with great speed through the water, but then, below this dorsal fin, the outline of the shark appeared.

Dark and malevolent, the great head extending on either side of the skull like a hammer, the long vicious teeth gleaming in the crescent mouth, it swept down on its prey. It turned under the helpless man, the water thrashing in waves against the sides of the Lagoon. Kitty saw the white face once more and then it was finished. The Hammerhead slid back to its lair and the iron shutters began to close behind it.

Dr Bauer motioned to the guards, indicating that they should release Kitty, and they stepped back. The girl began to shiver uncontrollably, and a wave of nausea swept through her body.

'It's all right, it's all right,' whispered the Doctor soothingly.

Kitty looked at her without comprehension, her eyes still dark with the horror she had just witnessed.

'That man was a Judas,' continued the Doctor. 'He came to the island pretending to be a friend, asking to join the Community. But he was a spy, he wanted only to discover our secrets and to sell them.'

Kitty tried to speak, but it took a moment or two for the words to come. In a cracked, wavering voice she said, 'It was horrible, horrible. It was murder, you murdered that man.'

'No, my dear,' said Dr Bauer. 'It was justice, retribution. He was tried and convicted by the High Court of our Community. I wanted you to see so that you would understand.'

'Understand?'

'That we mean what we say. That our purpose is firm. That there is no escape for you, no way back. Do you think we did not know of the piece of china hidden in your room, and what you hoped to do with it? Put away such foolish thoughts, my dear. You are one of us now, a special, privileged member of the Community. If you submit, we shall cherish you, offer you nothing but love and kindness. But if you refuse to take our hand, if you continue to dream of your old life, if you nourish thoughts of escape —'

She paused, shaking her head, and took Kitty's cold and trembling hand in her own. Then she went on, 'The choice is yours. There is no way back, believe me. You can decide either way. A wonderful new life of service with us or – well, I do not think that I need remind you of the alternative.'

68

The sky above had darkened still further and the Doctor's earnest face showed white in the gathering gloom. The palms were bowing their heads before the strengthening wind and from out over the ocean there came a rolling cannonade of thunder. Rain began to fall heavily, dancing on the dark restless water of the Lagoon.

'Come, my dear,' said Dr Bauer.

Chapter Six

Barr was in a dark mood when he returned to London with Steve Ugley. His mind nagged on the fact that the trip to the Far East had been so barren of results: in ten days all they had discovered was the existence of a ship called the *SS Leandro* which might, or more probably might not, have some connection with their case. It was, he thought bitterly, a small return for a long and expensive journey.

But it was not only this. The truth was that Britain depressed his spirit, bringing to the surface a streak of cynicism that had been growing within him in recent years. Flying homewards, looking down on the patterned fields of Kent and Sussex, he had felt, as always, a momentary lift, a return of the old feeling that this small green island was, after all, the best place in the world.

The feeling did not last long. Heathrow, like most international airports, sickened him. Huge and impersonal and grubby, it was like a great glasshouse in which people were confined, numbered, controlled by echoing, disembodied voices, and through whose weary corridors they trudged like hostages, longing for the moment of release. And when he came up from the Underground into Piccadilly, it seemed that London had caught the same infection. With her littered streets and tawdry buildings, she was like a tired old lady with shabby skirts and smelly underwear.

Steve, bright as ever despite the long flight, said cheerfully, 'Glad to be home?'

'Not particularly,' said Barr.

'Why?'

'Can't you smell it?'

'Smell what?'

'Decay. The smell of decay. I get a whiff of it every time I come back to this country. Lately, it's been getting stronger.'

'Ah, come on!' said Steve uncomfortably.

'I mean it. These are bad days.'

Barr paused as two young men and a girl shoved their way unceremoniously between them, dropping empty plastic cups on the pavement as they did so. One of the young men looked at Barr with arrogance, almost as though offering a challenge, and then went on his way with a triumphant chuckle.

'Do you know the feeling I get when I look around this country?' Barr continued. 'It's the feeling of weightlessness. The ordinary natural laws don't apply any more. People are floating. There's no weight, no direction. They can't make sense of things, the problems are too big, so they've given up. They don't even bother to hope. They

70

just float along, using as little energy as possible, living on old, dead dreams.'

'Christ!' said Steve, shifting his suitcase from one hand to the other. 'Are you always like this after a long flight?'

'Nearly always,' Barr smiled ruefully.

'And do you include yourself in this scenario? Come to that, do you include me?'

'I'm no better, no worse, than the others. I see the problems, I think. Some of them anyway. I mean the real problems; not the ones that grab the headlines. Like there are over five million new people being born on this planet every month, sixty million more bellies to fill every year. Pretty soon there won't be enough cornflakes to go round. Up to now we've found consolation in the idea that no matter how bad it is for us, our children will have it better. Doesn't apply any more. Now that's a terrible thing, a frightening thing.'

'So what will happen?'

'The big bang – that's what will happen.'

'The bomb?'

'What else? When a man gets to the end of his tether, when he feels choked, when he can no longer see a way out, he does one of two things. He blows out either his own brains or someone else's.'

'And me? You didn't say where I fit in.'

'You? I don't know, I'm not sure. I hope you'll be a survivor. You're young and you're full of foolish optimism. You'll need a lot of that when you come to start up the world again.'

An hour later, after a shave and a shower and a change of clothing, Barr's spirits began to improve. But with Vicky gone and no word from her, there was an emptiness about the flat which was almost like a presence in itself, and he decided to go down to the Queen's Head and Noonan in search of drink and company.

As he was leaving the telephone rang. It was Steve, and there was a note of excitement in his voice.

'I've got some news!' he said.

'Why else would you ring?' said Barr.

'Where shall we meet?'

'Can't you tell me now?'

'On the phone?' Steve sounded shocked.

'Listen,' said Barr wearily, 'don't let this private eye business go to your head, son. Nobody's tapping this phone. I'm not important enough.'

'You don't know,' said Steve. 'And when you don't know, it is safer to assume the worst.'

'You've been at those books again,' said Barr and sighed. 'All right. Meet me in the Queen's Head in twenty minutes.'

*

Steve was waiting at a table by the window when Barr arrived at the pub. He had already ordered a round of drinks and Barr's large Scotch was winking a welcome in front of an empty seat. The third place at the table was occupied by a very large woman.

'This,' said Steve, with a touch of pride, 'is Mrs Lavinia Harcourt. Vinnie – this is my partner, Tom Barr.'

The large lady lowered her glass of Guinness, favoured Barr with a confident smile and held out a hand that looked as big as a brick. 'Pleased to meet you.' She had a deep throaty voice, seasoned with a cockney accent, and the handshake she exchanged with Barr would have made a lesser man wince.

'Glad to know you, Mrs Harcourt,' said Barr warily.

'Vinnie,' she said bluntly. 'Call me Vinnie, love.'

'Vinnie,' he murmured obediently, and sat down. He gave Steve a slightly puzzled look, waiting for him to explain.

'Vinnie is an old friend of mine,' Steve began.

'Ah.' Barr nodded, as though this explained everything to his satisfaction, and wondered for a brief crazy moment at the nature of the association between the young man and this huge, genial chunk of middle-aged womanhood.

'She used to be manageress of the minicab company I worked for,' Steve continued, adding with a smile, 'and a holy terror she was too. Eighty-two drivers and she had us all running scared.'

'I never had any trouble with my boys,' said Vinnie affectionately.

'We were too bloody frightened!' said Steve.

'You're not working for the company now?' asked Barr.

She glanced at Steve, who said quickly, and with a certain awkwardness, 'No. She left. Actually, Tom, I've asked Vinnie to work for us.'

'I've had the minicab business – up to here,' said Vinnie. 'I did a lot of the calling, you see, running the radio link. That's why I talk as if I've got a rusty throat – well, you can hear it, can't you? I liked working with the boys but the bleeding customers got me down. People have got worse, you know – the last three or four years, they've got worse. No patience any more and no bleeding manners.'

'You could be right,' said Barr carefully.

'We need an office,' said Steve, 'and someone to run it properly. Vinnie can do that standing on her head. I asked her just before we left London. I would have told you before but I wasn't sure whether she would agree. Then, when I phoned her from Hong Kong —'

Vinnie cut in, turning her keen brown eyes on Barr, 'I told him, I told him that it would be down to you. After all, you're his partner. So I told him – if your mate doesn't want me, if he doesn't like the look of my face – and I wouldn't blame him for that – then it's all off.'

There was a moment or two of silence as they both looked at Barr, waiting for him to react. To their relief, the coldness left his eyes and, with a little smile, he lifted his shoulders in a shrug of acceptance.

'If Steve says you're OK, I'll go along with him.'

'Great!' said Steve enthusiastically.

'I won't let you down,' said Vinnie.

'You'd better not,' said Barr. 'Now, you said you'd got some news. Was that it? Or is there some more?'

'Plenty more!' said Steve. 'Tell him, Vinnie.'

'When Steve phoned from Hong Kong, he told me about this boat, the *Leandro* —'

'Ship,' said Barr.

'All right. This ship. He asked me to dig into it a bit. The first thing I found out was that she sailed from Barry Docks, in South Wales, the day after Kitty Higgins disappeared.'

'Where was she bound?'

'The West Indies.' Vinnie reached down, pulled up a huge, worn handbag and, from the jumble within, produced a new black notebook. Flipping this open, she continued, 'Yes. The Windward Islands. Dominica, St Vincent, St Lucia, Antigua. She carries fruit, mainly bananas.' She looked up. 'I've got more details here, if you want them.'

'Go on,' said Barr, impressed in spite of himself.

'The *Leandro* was built in 1971/72 in Greenock. Gross register of six thousand tons. Three lower holds and eight tweendecks – whatever the hell that means. She's got suites for passengers, four double and four single.'

'Did she have any passengers when she left Barry?'

'No. No passengers were listed, any road.'

'The owners. What was their name again, Steve?'

'Burnham and Company,' said Steve.

'Did you check on them?'

'Of course I did,' said Vinnie briskly. 'I went up to see them, didn't I? This afternoon as a matter of fact.' She turned a page of her notebook, and frowned at it for a moment. 'Can't read my own bleeding writing. Ah, yes. Burnham and Company, Leadenhall Street. Saw a man with a double-barrelled name. Whitney-Hythe. Mr Whitney-Hythe. A right toffee-nosed twerp he was and all. And little with it, if you know what I mean – he was like two pennorth of scrag-end to look at. Well, they're all the same, you know, the little ones are all the same. He tried to dodge me at first, told his secretary to make an appointment, but I wasn't having any of his old madam, was I? I barged into his office and sat down and said I wasn't moving until we'd had a little chat.'

Barr had a mental picture of the scene and smiled. He felt a tiny surge of sympathy for little Mr Whitney-Hythe: to face Vinnie

Harcourt when she was in full cry would be a frightening experience for any man. Aloud, he said, 'You didn't tell him why you wanted to know about the *Leandro*? I mean, the real reason?'

'What do you take me for?' she answered scornfully. 'Do I look as if I just came out of the egg? No, I told him I was interested in buying the bloody boat – I mean, ship.'

'Yes, I see,' said Barr, feeling that there was no answer to that one.

'I told him I'd seen the *Leandro* when she was at Barry Dock a few weeks back and that I liked the look of her. I said my idea was to spend a bit of money and have her converted into a private yacht. I sort of gave him the impression that I'd got more money than sense – made the odd million or so in the scrap-metal business. You should have seen him – his greedy little eyes were standing out like chapel hat-pegs by the time I'd finished.'

I bet they were, thought Barr. He was still enjoying his mental replay of this extraordinary confrontation.

'He was all over me after that,' she continued. 'Butter wouldn't have melted in his mouth. Anyway, the upshot of it all was that he said I couldn't buy the *Leandro* because it had been leased out to another firm. They'd had it on lease for over two years, with an option to buy at the end of three.'

'The name of the company?'

'Hold on. I've got it here. Yes. J. D. Winston, Redcliffe Street, St John's, Antigua.'

'My uncle left me a house in Antigua,' said Steve, with some surprise.

'It might come in handy,' said Barr. 'What else do you know about these people, Vinnie?'

'They're in fruit – bananas and suchlike. Mr Whitney-whatsisname said they were very good customers. Very reliable. He thought that they would almost certainly buy the ship when the lease came up. But he did offer to find me another one just like the *Leandro*. I told him I'd think about it.'

'The *Leandro* must figure in this business somehow,' said Steve. 'She seems to have been around almost every time a girl has disappeared.'

'Could be coincidence,' Barr said.

'Maybe. But it's the only lead we've got.'

The conversation was halted by the arrival of Charlie "Kid" Brown, who came over from the bar with a fresh round of drinks. Barr noticed that there were four glasses but before he could comment, the ex-boxer pulled in another chair and joined them.

'Don't tell me, let me guess,' said Barr wearily.

'Mr Brown has agreed to come in with us,' said Steve quickly.

'Has he really?' said Barr. 'Welcome aboard, Charlie.'

'Hi,' said Charlie.

74

'Is there anyone else I ought to know about?' asked Barr.

'No,' said Steve. 'We'll need a sort of secretary in the office, but that can wait.'

'Have we got an office?' asked Barr, with only a trace of sarcasm.

'As a matter of fact, yes,' said Steve. 'I asked Vinnie when —'

'When you were on the phone from Hong Kong. That call must have cost a fortune. Where is it – this office?'

'You'll never guess,' said Steve, with a small apologetic grin.

'Christ!' said Barr. 'Are we going to play games now? Where the hell is it?'

'Baker Street.'

Barr sighed. 'Ask a silly question,' he murmured.

'On the first floor, over a store,' said Vinnie. 'Three nice rooms, a reception area and a small kitchen. All in very good nick. Carpets, double-glazing, the lot.'

'What do we call ourselves?' said Barr. 'Son of Sherlock Holmes Limited? The Baker Street Runners?'

'I thought the Baker Street Investigation Agency,' said Steve tentatively. 'But if you've got a better idea . . .'

'No,' said Barr. 'I'm relieved. I was afraid you'd come up with something really fancy.'

He smiled, suddenly struck by the absurdity of it all. Big Vinnie, Kid Brown, Steve with all his naïve enthusiasm, and himself, the ex-mercenary: we must, he thought, be four of the unlikeliest private investigators in the world. On an impulse, he lifted his glass.

'Well,' he said. 'To the Baker Street Bureau. Cheers.'

'I like the Baker Street Runners. Got a nice ring to it,' said Vinnie. And, her big pleasant face opening in a grin, she added, 'Anyway, cheers and bon voyage, whatever it is they say.'

'What's the bon voyage for?' asked Barr.

'Well, someone will have to go to the West Indies to check up on this bloody banana boat, won't they? And knowing the way you men fiddle things between you, I'll lay all Chelsea Barracks to a sentry-box that it won't be me.'

'No,' said Steve, after a pause, 'I think we should all go. And especially you, Vinnie.'

'I was only kidding,' she said.

'I mean it. Mr Whatsisname – the fellow with the double-barrelled name —'

'Mr Whitney-Hythe,' said Vinnie.

'Well, he may have made contact with the people in Antigua, told them of your interest. If you call in – say that you're taking a holiday out there – it'll look as if you are just following up your London call. But if one of us goes to see them, they'll start wondering why so many people have suddenly become interested in the *Leandro*.'

'Makes sense,' said Barr. 'But surely all it needs is you and Vinnie. You won't want Charlie and me as well.'

'Maybe not. But on the other hand, we might. The people behind this thing must be well organised. We may need all the hands available.'

'I've never been further than the Costa Brava,' said Vinnie, her eyes shining. She leaned across and gave the startled Steve a big, smacking kiss. 'You're a lovely lad,' she said, 'a lovely lad.'

It was raining when the British Airways 747 landed at Coolidge International Airport, Antigua, raining with such an intense tropical fury that it seemed as if nature had abandoned all her other tasks to concentrate on this one particular downpour. Yet, oddly enough, it brought no relief to the atmosphere: after the cool elegance of the aeroplane, the air seemed to scour the skin with a furnace-like ferocity.

The plane had been full and by the time Barr and the others reached the tiny terminal building it was packed with passengers jostling for a place in the queue which led to the Immigration Control desk. This was manned by a solitary officer who seemed quite unconcerned by the rain thundering on the roof or the clamour of the steaming crowd; he worked with a kind of methodical languor, examining each passport with enormous care, and wearing on his face that unconcerned expression which is common to such officials the world over. It was as if he knew that all these wet and weary people were in his power and was determined that they should wait upon his authority.

'Bloody hell!' said Steve, eyeing the crowd. 'It will take them all the afternoon to clear this lot!'

'I feel like I've just been put through a washing-machine,' said Charlie. 'This heat! The rain!'

'I thought you'd be used to it,' said Vinnie.

'Don't talk through your skull, lady!' said Charlie amiably. 'I ain't never been to these parts before. My Mum and Dad come out from Montserrat but me, I was born in Kilburn.'

'Mr Ugley? Mr Ugley? Mr Steve Ugley?'

It was hard to tell where the voice was coming from, but when Steve signalled his presence a slight, middle-aged man pushed his way through the crowd towards them. Wearing a shining white shirt with a tie, khaki shorts with knee-length socks to match, and immaculately polished shoes, he looked crisp and fresh and totally unaffected by the stifling heat. He put his head to one side in a curious sparrow-like gesture, smiled and said, 'Mr Ugley?'

'Yes.'

76

'Good show! My name is Pullar. Gordon Pullar. There are four of you – correct?' He spoke with a marked English public-school accent, and the words came out in little bursts, as though he were throwing handfuls of pebbles at his listeners.

'That's right. Four,' said Steve.

'Good show! Well, the first thing is to get you out of this blasted inferno, eh, what? Give me your passports and baggage claims and follow me. This way, this way.'

The crowd, some members of which greeted him by name, parted before his brisk onslaught and Barr's party followed him with eager relief. Within minutes the remarkable Mr Pullar had cleared them through all the formalities, organised a porter to take their luggage to a waiting station-wagon and ushered them into a small private room where a large electric fan gave at least some illusion of coolness. Rum punches, clinking with ice, were brought to them by a cheerful Antiguan girl and as they relaxed, their smiling host explained his timely intervention.

'Mr Boyd cabled me you were coming, Mr Ugley. I'm a solicitor, by the way. Used to look after your uncle's interests on the island. Well, strictly speaking, I'm still looking after them – but on your behalf now, of course.'

'Thanks for meeting us,' said Steve.

'Oh, it's my pleasure entirely.'

'We could have perished in there,' said Vinnie.

'I doubt it, Mrs Harcourt. Anyhow, getting you through was no great trick. I know the people here – do them the odd favour from time to time and they like to repay me when they can. And in any case, the fact that Mr Ugley is his uncle's nephew is a great help. Your uncle was well-liked on the island, Mr Ugley, very popular, so you start with a pretty good credit rating, if you see what I mean.'

'How far are we from the house, from Tradewinds?' asked Steve.

'Nowhere is far on Antigua, Mr Ugley. It's a small island, only just over one hundred square miles in all. The roads aren't good, but on the other hand they're not all that bad. It will take us thirty minutes to get to your estate. A beautiful place, I promise you, one of the love-liest on the island, and that is to say a great deal. You'll enjoy your break, no question of that.'

'Well, it's not exactly —' Steve said, and hesitated before going on. 'I mean, we're not exactly here for a holiday.'

'Of course not,' said Mr Pullar. 'You'll want to run the rule over the estate and so forth. Quite understood. It's all ship-shape and Bristol fashion, I assure you.'

'Tell me,' said Barr, turning the glass in his hands. 'Do we go through St John's on the way to Steve's place?'

'We could do, of course,' said Mr Pullar.

77

'Good. I'd like you to drop Mrs Harcourt and me off there for half an hour or so. We've a little bit of urgent business to attend to.'

'Certainly.' If Mr Pullar was surprised by this request, he did not show it. 'We can send the car back to pick you up when you're ready.' He gave Steve a small apologetic smile. 'Actually, it's your car. A big Ford station-wagon. Goes with the estate. Since there were four of you, I took the liberty of telling Joe Bradshaw – he's a sort of general factotum around the place – to bring it out here to meet you.'

'I'm glad you did,' said Steve. He was still finding it hard to adjust to the idea that he was a man of property.

'Where do you want us to drop you in St John's, Mr Barr?' asked Mr Pullar, lifting his glass.

Barr consulted the back of an envelope. 'We want to pay a call on a firm called J. D. Winston. They're on Redcliffe Street, or so I'm told.'

Mr Pullar stopped with his drink almost touching his lips: for the first time, the crisp confidence left his face and a faint shadow darkened the pale blue eyes. It was only for a moment, but Barr knew the man had been shaken.

'Do you know them?' he asked. 'Do you know the firm?'

'I know of them, of course,' said Mr Pullar, somewhat recovering his poise. 'But I can't say I actually know them, if you follow me.'

He got to his feet and, as though anxious to change the subject, he added, 'Well, shall we make a start then? The rain has stopped, but then, it seldom lasts long in Antigua.'

The West Indian midday break, which is longer than the average European lunch interval but not long enough to rate as a siesta, was just about over when they arrived in St John's and the narrow streets of the island's capital were filling with people once again: with the locals, moving at their own sensible, languid pace under the blazing sun, and with the tourists, mostly white, marching grimly from point to point as if they had been programmed to a fixed time-scale by computer.

The roads and sidewalks were sadly in need of repair, and the few modern shops and offices stood out in sharp contrast to the mass of old, sun-baked wooden buildings which surrounded them.

Barr had seen many such places in his time, shabby, colourful towns where decades of colonial neglect had combined with latter-day mismanagement, laziness and poverty to create a picturesque and ever-present seediness. He wondered, not for the first time, what emotions were aroused in the local people, with their small ramshackle huts, by the sight of the luxury hotels and homes which dotted the island.

'It's a busy little town,' said Mr Pullar, 'but there isn't a lot to see

78

here. The cathedral, perhaps, that is interesting. And the market on Saturday mornings is well worth a visit. Otherwise, the main places to see are in other parts of the island. English Harbour, and Nelson's Dockyard, of course. Nelson was Commander of the British Navy out here for some years and he certainly left his mark on the islands.' He paused as the car slowed down. 'Ah, there is the place you want, Mr Barr.'

He pointed across the street to an office over which there hung a sign: J. D. WINSTON & CO LTD – IMPORT AND EXPORT. Brightly painted, with tubs of flowering shrubs lining the verandah, the building seemed to stand disdainfully aloof from the unkempt, raggle-taggle properties on either side. A brown-skinned youth, in an olive-green bush jacket and slacks, leaned over the rail of the verandah, staring down at the car.

As Vinnie and Barr got out, Mr Pullar who seemed to be suffering from a return of his former uneasiness, said, 'You'll be a half-hour, you say?'

'Don't really know,' Barr replied. 'It may only take a few minutes.'

'In that case, I think we might wait for you at the Spanish Main. It's an excellent bar and restaurant on East Street, not far from here. Much patronised by the local business community. It'll give me an opportunity to call in at my office. This is rather a busy time for me. Yes, I'll drop Mr Ugley and Mr Brown at the Spanish Main and send the car back to wait for you. Does that sound agreeable?'

'Whatever you say,' said Barr.

'Good show.' And as Vinnie and Barr got out of the car, Mr Pullar said with a smile and a touch of his former waggishness, 'See you in church.'

'Sure,' said Barr, with a straight face, 'I'll be taking the collection.'

The car drove off and Barr steered Vinnie across the road. The youth on the verandah followed them with his eyes as they climbed the wooden steps towards him, and greeted them with a careful smile.

'Hello there.'

'Hello,' said Vinnie, returning the smile and mopping her forehead and neck. 'It's a bit cooler up here than it is down there.'

'Yes,' said the youth politely. 'If there's a breeze, I guess we get the benefit.' He was a large, athletic-looking young man with well-trimmed hair and a Zapata-style moustache; his speech had strong overtones of New York but there was a slight Spanish accent in there somewhere and Barr, who was no expert in such matters, guessed that he was probably a Puerto Rican.

But if this was a guess, Barr was certain of one thing. The man was a thug. He had seen the type often enough to be able instantly to recognise it. And the military-looking olive-green uniform suggested

79

that he was employed as a security guard of some kind, an impression which was reinforced by the appearance, through a door further along the verandah, of a tall, thin, white-skinned man in similar dress, who glanced at them without too much interest and then withdrew.

As Vinnie tried to move forward, the young man moved across her path, blocking the way with a casual, polite, but menacing ease.

'Can I help you?' he asked.

'I'm looking for Mr Winston,' said Vinnie.

'Mr Winston?' Teeth sparkled as the young man smiled and repeated, 'Mr Winston? I'm afraid you won't find him here, ma'am.'

'Isn't this Mr Winston's office?'

'Ah, you mean the sign, ma'am? Yeh, I guess that could be a little confusing. Truth is, this used to be Mr Winston's office, used to be his business, but that isn't so now, not any longer.'

'What happened?' asked Barr.

'Well, Mr Winston kinda sold out, you might say, sir.'

'Who to?'

'The present owners.'

'And who are they?'

'Might I ask the reason for this enquiry, sir?'

'Might I ask who you are?'

A shadow passed across the young man's eyes, obscuring their brightness for a fleeting moment, and there was a threatening cold-ness in his tone as he replied, 'I am employed here, sir.'

'Good,' said Barr. 'Then perhaps you will tell the new owner or the manager or whatever that we should like a few minutes of his time.'

'Might I ask the nature of your business, sir?'

'Look, sonny boy,' said Vinnie, who was growing tired of this polite fencing, 'it's hot, I've had a long flight and I'm tired. I came here to speak to the engine-driver, not the oil-rag. So just tell your boss that I'm here to talk about a boat – ship – called the *Leandro*. OK? And while you're doing that, I'll take the weight off my feet if you don't mind.'

The young man stiffened angrily under this onslaught but, before he could react further, Vinnie had shoved him aside and planted herself on an upholstered bench which stood between two potted shrubs. In the next moment, two things happened: the young man's hand went to his waist and Barr, moving in swiftly, clasped his wrist. The bush shirt fell back into place, but not before Barr had glimpsed the gun protruding from the man's belt. It looked, though he could not be sure, like a Colt .45 Automatic.

'Now, now,' said Barr. 'Why don't you be a good lad and do what the lady wants?'

'Eddie!'

The young man pulled himself free and swung round to face the

80

tall man who had appeared previously. He now came towards them, a frown on his long, lean face.

'What seems to be the trouble?'

Vinnie rose from the bench and placed herself massively before him. 'No trouble, no trouble. Just a little hiccup, you might say. Now, tell me, are you the boss here?'

'I don't understand.' The frown deepened. 'If you're from RRA —'

'I'm from London,' she interrupted brusquely. 'I've never heard of RRA, whatever the hell that is. I came here to see Mr Winston.'

'Mr Winston is not here now,' he said warily.

'I told her that,' growled the young man.

'Look, don't let's go over that again!' said Vinnie. 'Mr Winston sold out and took off. All right, all right! Let's try again, eh? Are you the boss here?'

'I'm in charge,' said the tall man.

'Good. Now we're getting somewhere. What's your name?'

'Lavender. Simon Lavender.'

'Right, Mr Lavender. Now, which is your office?'

'The end door.' He responded automatically as though bemused by this large lady who stood so commandingly before him, the sweat pouring down her determined face.

'Great! Let's go in there and have a chinwag, shall we? It won't take long. Excuse me.'

She edged the beweildered man aside and walked down the verandah, the wooden boards creaking under her tread. At the last door she stopped and turned, as if surprised that the others hadn't followed.

'Well,' she said, 'are you coming or not?'

She disappeared into the office and Lavender, recovering his wits, hurried after her. Barr paused and tapped the gun at the young man's waist.

'I didn't know you were allowed to carry guns in Antigua.'

'It's licensed,' said the young man. His dark eyes were hard and angry, and there was a twitch in his right cheek which had not been there before.

'Import and Export. That is still your line of business, isn't it?' asked Barr.

'So?'

'So what are you afraid of?'

Before the young man could answer, Barr turned and, walking with considered ease, went along to join Vinnie.

Bobby Branker and his wife Janice were New Yorkers and, in a modest way, they were also miracle-workers. They had taken a beauti-

81

ful but decaying colonial house on the outskirts of St John's and transformed it into a small hotel: in doing so, they had succeeded in preserving its former charm and grace to an extraordinary extent, so that the old house seemed to have slipped naturally and even proudly into this new role, as though grateful for its deliverance.

It was here, in the bar and restaurant of the Spanish Main, while they waited for Gordon Pullar to return, that Barr and Vinnie told the others of their brief and unsatisfactory visit to the offices of J. D. Winston & Co.

'Weird,' said Vinnie, 'that's the only word for it. Weird. Gave me a strange feeling in my funny-bone.'

'But what did you learn about the *Leandro*?' asked Steve.

'Nothing. Not a damn thing we didn't know already. But there isn't a J. D. Winston anymore – leastways, he's not around. These new people are running the firm. Couldn't make head nor tail of who they are, except that this Lavender bloke is the manager. They're in the same line as before – bananas, fruit and suchlike. Or so he says.'

'Did you find out where the *Leandro* is now?' asked Steve impatiently.

'Lavender did the stonewall bit. Said it was none of our business.'

'Then it was all a waste of bloody time!'

'I'm not sure,' said Barr thoughtfully. 'Like Vinnie said, it was a weird set-up. There were maybe half a dozen people there – I caught a glimpse of four at least in the rooms next to Lavender's office – and they were all in the same sort of gear, like a uniform. The goon who stopped us at the top of the stairs was carrying a gun. And Mr Lavender was obviously very edgy about our visit.'

'Jumpy. As if someone had put a shovelful of earwigs down the back of his shirt,' said Vinnie.

'What's more,' said Barr, 'when Vinnie introduced herself as Mrs Harcourt, it registered. You could see it in his eyes. I'll lay odds that he'd heard the name before.'

'The agent in London could have tipped him off,' said Steve. 'But why?'

'He probably did it quite innocently,' said Barr. 'All in the line of business. Probably telephoned the people out here to say that he'd got a prospective buyer for the *Leandro* and would they surrender the lease for a consideration.'

'OK,' said Steve, 'we'll give him the benefit of the doubt.' He paused, and then continued gravely, in his best investigative manner, 'Now, let's check what we've got. We know that the *Leandro* was involved somehow in the disappearance of Kitty and some of the other girls.'

'We think we know,' corrected Barr. 'It could be coincidence.'

'Do you think it is?' asked Steve. 'Do you think it is just a coincidence?'

82

'No.'

'Right. The next point. We now know that the name J. D. Winston is just a front for a peculiar outfit which puts its staff in uniform and has a man with a gun to keep guard. What's all that for? Who exactly are they? It will be interesting to find out. But most important of all, they almost certainly know where the *Leandro* is now.'

'So must a lot of other people,' said Barr. 'A ship is a ship is a ship. Not easy to hide. If she's in these parts, we ought to be able to get a line on her from someone.'

Charlie Brown, that man of few words, spoke for the first time. 'What was the name of the guy you saw?'

'Lavender,' said Vinnie, snorting at the incongruity of the name.

'I could maybe sort him out,' said Charlie diffidently, knuckling a large black fist into the palm of the other hand. 'Persuade him like, persuade him to sing a little bit.' And he added, as though anxious to reassure them, 'I mean, I wouldn't hurt him. Well, not much. Just enough.'

'It might come to that,' said Barr, 'but not yet.' He was looking over Charlie's shoulder, towards the door. Gordon Pullar had just entered and was moving briskly towards them, his face beaming with good fellowship.

'Hello, there,' he said. 'You're back, I see. Good show. Righteo, then, shall we saddle the horses and get out to Tradewinds? You must all be ready to drop!'

'Give it a few minutes,' said Barr. 'I need another drink. This heat takes it out of you. Sit down, Mr Pullar, let me get you something.'

'We could have a drink back at the house,' said Mr Pullar.

'I like it here,' said Barr. 'In fact, I like it very much. A very nice bar. Now, what will it be?'

'A lime-juice, if you insist.'

Mr Pullar pulled up a chair and smiled round at them. Barr signalled to the pretty waitress who was serving at the tables, and when she came over he ordered a fresh round of drinks. As she moved to the bar, he turned to Pullar.

'We want some information, Mr Pullar.'

'Information? Well, if I can help, I will, of course.'

'How long have you lived on the island?'

'All my life, old chap. Except when I went to England to school, and to get my qualifications. Oh, yes, and I spent the last two years of the war in the RAF.' He put his head on one side and shrugged modestly. 'Squadron Leader Pullar. Bombers. Seems a long century ago, it really does.'

But you've never been able to forget it, thought Barr, never grown out of it. Frozen in time, all the old slang carefully preserved. And then, reproving himself, he remembered that he also was a man who

83

drew nourishment from the past. The old days in Biafra, when he had truly felt himself to be part of a decent cause, were never far away from his thoughts. Men like Mr Pullar, unheroic little men, had once defeated the Nazis and, in so doing, had been touched by a brief heroism. For some, it had been the only adventure of their lives. Small wonder, then, that it should have set a stamp on them.

'I remember,' Mr Pullar was saying, 'I remember after the war, I met a German tourist on the beach. Here, in Antigua. He asked me if I'd ever been to Germany. Do you know what I told him?' He chuckled at the recollection. 'I told him – oh, yes, I've been to Germany many times. But I never stayed.' He laughed again, anxious that they should catch the joke. 'I was in bombers, you see. Over there night after night – but I never stayed!'

'What did he say?' asked Vinnie bluntly.

'Oh,' Mr Pullar hesitated. 'As a matter of fact, he took it in good part. I mean, we all did it, didn't we? Both sides. London – Berlin, Coventry – Dresden. I wonder about it now, I mean, if the bombing —' He broke off and shook his head briskly. 'No use speculating. Water under the bridge, eh? Now, you said you wanted some information, old man.'

'J. D. Winston,' said Barr. 'We want to know who runs the firm now. Why do they wear uniforms, why do they employ armed guards? And we want to locate a ship called the *Leandro* which they have on lease from an agent in London.'

'I don't think I can help you,' said Mr Pullar and his voice was so quiet that it was scarcely audible.

'I think you're lying,' said Barr.

Mr Pullar flushed and seemed about to protest, but he was interrupted by the arrival of the waitress with the drinks. He waited until she had set them down, collected the used glasses, and moved away. Then he said, his voice still low, 'Is that why you are here – to find out about these people?'

'We think so,' said Steve. 'It's a kind of chicken and egg situation. We shan't know if they're the people we're looking for until we know who they are, if you see what I mean.' And he added tactfully, 'That's why we were hoping that you might be able to help us, Mr Pullar.'

Mr Pullar studied his face for a while, as though trying to assess his sincerity. Then, one by one, he applied the same scrutiny to the others.

'I must ask you one thing,' he said at last. 'And you must answer me truthfully. Are you from RRA?'

'Never heard of it,' said Steve promptly.

'The goon up at the office asked me the same question,' said Barr. 'What the hell is RRA?'

'It is something they don't like, Mr Barr.'

84

'They?'

Mr Pullar made one last effort to pull back. 'Take my advice. Don't pursue this. Forget your questions. Come out to Tradewinds and enjoy the sea and the sunshine.'

'Don't stop, Mr Pullar,' said Barr. 'Carry on with what you were saying before. Who are they?'

Mr Pullar sighed, gave a little nervous glance around and then fell to the contemplation of his finger nails.

'These are dangerous waters,' he murmured.

'It is important that we know,' said Steve. 'Please.'

'Very well. I will tell you what I can. But I still beg you, for your own sakes, to leave well alone. Perhaps you will see why when I have finished.' He paused and gulped down some lime-juice before continuing. 'Have you heard of a semi-religious sect which calls itself the Community of New Jerusalem?'

'No.' said Barr.

'Vaguely,' said Steve. 'Wait! Yes. A year or so back a couple of people came to my door and tried to put the bite on me for money. They seemed nice kids, sincere. Spoke a lot about cleaning up the earth, getting away from materialism and back to basics, to nature. They said it was an idea whose time had come.'

'That would be right,' said Mr Pullar. 'The Community does – or rather did – have some quite admirable aims. It has supporters worldwide and is reputed to be extremely wealthy. It has settlements in Bolivia and Guyana but by far the most important of its projects is Jerusalem Island. That's the jewel in the crown, so to speak. The island is two or three miles off the coast of Antigua and is entirely owned by the Community. The name attracted them, I suppose. Jerusalem Island. That was how Columbus christened it in 1493 and the name stuck. Until 1964 it was owned by an English family but for one reason or another they neglected the place, let it get so run down that only a handful of people lived there. In 1966, the Community bought it, moved in a large number of its members and set up headquarters there. And, in a remarkably short space of time, they transformed the place. Built a settlement and what they call a Tabernacle, reconstructed the harbour, reclaimed the land – and so forth. And a couple of years ago they leased the *Leandro*, so that they could independently export produce and develop trade.'

'The *Leandro*!' said Steve quickly. 'You know about her?'

'Oh, yes. She puts in from time to time, to take on produce for shipment to Europe. That is why the Community maintains an office here in St John's, and on some of the other islands. It is a legitimate trade that brings us some benefits.'

'What happened to Mr J. D. Winston?' asked Vinnie. 'Did he fall or was he pushed?'

85

'I suppose you might say that he fell.' Mr Pullar smiled wryly. 'He was one of our more successful local businessmen, in the import-export business. Built up a thriving concern. Then, quite suddenly it seemed, he announced that he had become a convert of the Community of New Jerusalem and intended to hand over all his property to them. Within a week, he had done just that. He moved his entire family to Jerusalem Island and the Community took over his business, his house, his car, everything.'

'Nice going,' said Barr. 'That's the quickest way to make a million these days – start up a new religion.'

'Do you know where the *Leandro* is now?' asked Steve.

'She's docked at Jerusalem Island,' said Mr Pullar.

'How soon can we get over there?'

'You can't, Mr Ugley.'

'Why not?'

'I thought I'd explained. The entire island is privately owned. And the Community actively discourages visitors.'

'Why?' said Barr. 'Don't they want people to see all their good works?'

'There have been incidents,' said Mr Pullar. 'You asked about RRA. Those initials stand for Relatives Rescue Association. It is an organisation of people who are related to members of the Community of New Jerusalem and similar extreme sects. It believes, to put it crudely, that most Community members have been brainwashed, and its aim is to get them out and de-programme them.'

'You said there had been incidents,' said Barr.

'A couple of groups from the RRA tried to visit the island. They were turned away. In one instance there was some quite considerable violence.'

'Well, we're not from this RRA,' said Barr. 'So what is to prevent us going over and having a look-see?'

'I shouldn't try it, Mr Barr.'

'Why not?'

Mr Pullar shifted uncomfortably. 'The Community has considerable influence and power – well, considerable is an understatement. It is very powerful. And, in many ways, it is quite ruthless in the pursuit of what it deems to be its best interests.'

'They can't set themselves up above the law, surely?' said Steve.

'Sounds as if they can and they do,' said Barr.

'Please – be advised,' said Mr Pullar earnestly. 'Don't meddle with the Community. Stay away from them. This is a beautiful island. Three hundred and sixty-five beaches, one for every day of the year. Why not relax and enjoy yourselves?'

86

Chapter Seven

'I am not sure that she is ready, Comptroller,' said Dr Bauer.

'The Terminal Experience?' asked the Comptroller testily. 'She witnessed the Terminal Experience at the Lagoon, did she not?'

'Yes, Comptroller.'

'Well, did that have no effect?'

'She was shocked, naturally. But she is a person of considerable willpower and mental resilience. The experience seemed to increase her resistance rather than diminish it.'

'I cannot understand this delay, Doctor!' The Comptroller fixed the nervous woman with his chill, fish-like eyes. 'Is there, perhaps, some other reason for holding her back?'

'No, no,' said Dr Bauer hastily. 'None at all, I do assure you.'

'How long have you been in charge at the Reception Centre?' He waved a plump hand. 'I have the records, of course, but just remind me.'

'Almost three years, Comptroller.'

'Hm. You have done excellent work, there can be no argument about that.'

'Thank you, Comptroller.'

'On the other hand,' he said softly, 'on the other hand —' She waited, trembling, for him to continue. 'We all know how much importance Mr Dunlop places upon the Regeneration Experience. A spell in the fields, performing the primal tasks of the Community, renewing one's ancient partnership with the earthforce. We have all been a witness to its blessings, have we not?'

'Yes, indeed, Comptroller.'

'It is, after all, a basic concept of the Community. One might even say that it is *the* basic concept.' He gave her a sad look. 'The trouble is, the real trouble is, that we seldom understand our own needs. We become so immersed in our work, in our daily duties, that we fail to perceive the necessity for renewal.'

'I did volunteer, Comptroller,' she said quickly, perhaps a shade too quickly. 'Earlier this year, when you announced the new Clearance Project at Morgans Bay.'

'Did you indeed! Excellent. Excellent. I should have checked the records before you came. How long were you with the project?'

'Three days, Comptroller.'

'Ah.' He sounded disappointed.

'It was all I could manage. We had a new intake at Reception, I had to get back. I was reluctant, but I had no choice. Even so, those three days helped me enormously.'

'Of course.' He shifted his great bulk and the chair squeaked a response. 'Well, let us get back to Sister Higgins. Can I assume that you will hand her over to Sister Eleanor for the auditing process?'

'Immediately, Comptroller.'

'Excellent. I shall look forward to receiving a progress report, Doctor.' And then, in the same soft, silky voice, he added another threat which disturbed her as much as the first: 'If the girl doesn't respond in reasonable time we shall have to cut our losses. She can always be sent to the Beach of Pleasure. A great waste of precious beauty, but there it is.'

In what was both a salute and a dismissal, he laid a hand on his heart. She responded in kind, murmured her thanks, and hurried from the room.

Outside the building, the Doctor sat down on a bench in the shade of a geranium tree to compose herself. It had been cool in the Comptroller's office but despite this she could feel the sweat still bubbling on her skin, soaking her clothes. She shuddered as she recalled the interview and the Comptroller's implied threat.

The very thought of the Regeneration Experience terrified her. It lasted for a minimum period of three months, depending on the assessment made by the Comptroller's office: some people had been attached to the Work Units for over a year, with no sign of release. There was no respite for the members of these units: they were expected to labour in the plantations from sunrise to sunset every day of the week except on the Sabbath, when they were graciously allowed to break at noon. The diet was basic. Rice and beans, rice and gravy and, occasionally, if you were lucky, fruit which, for one reason or another, was not fit for export.

In some ways even the Waverers received better treatment. True, their diet was much the same and they were assigned to the most back-breaking tasks in the Community, but at least they had frequent breaks when one of the Teachers from the Tabernacle gave them spiritual instruction.

And then there was the Comptroller's threat to send Kitty to the Beach of Pleasure. Why did the idea concern her so deeply? Was she becoming soft, so attached to the girl that her sense of priorities, of values, was being affected? Or was it the thought of Kitty with those men?

Once again, she felt hatred for the Comptroller seething inside her. His flabby bulk, his cold eye, his hypocrisy, repelled her. What would happen to him if he were ordered to take the Regeneration Experience, she thought angrily. It would kill him in two days! She smiled with grim satisfaction at the mental picture of that gross body bent in labour in the sun-scorched fields, of those soft moist lips sucking in a ration of rice and gravy! She had been fortunate enough

88

to dine at the Comptroller's table on a number of occasions and seen the sort of food he ate; only the best, exquisitely cooked by a member of the Community who, in his previous life, had been a master-chef at the Connaught Hotel in London.

And that same tantalising, dangerous question which lurked like an unwelcome predator in the shadows of her mind, surfaced yet again. Why did Mr Dunlop tolerate the Comptroller and his effete life style? It flew in the face of all his teaching, of all the basic tenets of the Community. After all, Mr Dunlop lived simply enough or so it seemed. It was true that he had splendid, not to say, luxurious accommodation in the Tabernacle, but that was understandable. He was the Founder and Leader of the Community: one could not expect such a man to live in a hut like a peasant. People, important people, came from all over the world to see him and it was necessary that he should receive them in some style, with a dignity befitting his high standing.

Even so, Mr Dunlop had not allowed himself to be corrupted by his surroundings or his authority. He always wore simple clothes: a neat Chinese-style tunic or the colourful, though not flamboyant, smock which the local people called a dashiki. And his taste in food was plain and more or less vegetarian; in the early days she had lunched or dined with him on several memorable occasions and he had eaten only a simple meal – a salad, or an omelette.

In the early days . . .

A drift of bright orange blossom floated down from the tree and settled on the Doctor's sleeve. She looked at the shining petals for a long moment, then brushed them away with a small unhappy sigh.

Yes, in the early days it had been wonderful to be part of the Community. There had been an energy, a drive, an excitement, the like of which she had never known. Borne along on a great tide of love and faith, the people had achieved miracles – coaxing new crops from the barren and neglected earth, building a network of roads, a hospital, a school and, most splendid achievement of all, the Tabernacle of Grace. It had been hard, gruelling work but nobody had complained. Inspired by Mr Dunlop they had marched to the fields singing.

She sighed again, remembering with regret the joy that had possessed her at that time. It was as if she had been born again, her whole being transformed by the shining power of the love which had lifted her up and wrapped her in its beauty.

Before then, before the Community, her life had been meaningless, without purpose. She had been forced to leave her work in a hospital at St Veit in southern Austria following the exposure of her relationship with a young student nurse called Erna. She had gone off to Vienna with Erna, holding her head high in defiance, and for a while, life had been good. But her money had soon run out and she

89

had found it difficult to get work in her profession. Then, when things were at their lowest, Erna had abandoned her, simply gone away, leaving a brusque note in which she announced that she had met a young man and intended to marry him. There was no word of love or of thanks in the letter.

How petty and stupid it had all been, thought the Doctor. Yet, at the time, she was so weighted down with grief and bitterness that she had come close to the point of suicide. And then, miraculously, she had met the two young people from the Community of New Jerusalem. They had shown her genuine, unselfish affection, offered her hope, made her understand how narrow and self-centred her life had been. Later, when she was accepted into the Community, she had served her twelve month apprenticeship as an Apostle, collecting funds for the Community on the streets and drawing new converts into its orbit. Then came the great moment when she learned that she had been chosen as a Pioneer, to go to Jerusalem Island and help build a society which would be an example to the whole world . . .

What had gone wrong with the dream? At first, it had been wonderful, better than she could ever have imagined. But now – and even to think the thought frightened her – something seemed to be going awry. In her mind, she associated the decline with the emergence of the Comptroller, but honesty compelled her to admit that he was probably an effect, not a cause.

No. It went deeper than one man. There were several disturbing indicators. The fact that Mr Dunlop was seen so seldom, for a start. It was two years since she had met him on a personal basis as she had done at the beginning. And instead of appearing regularly at the weekly service in the Square of Peace and Love, it was months since he had shown himself. Nowadays, he seemed to make all his pronouncements through the Comptroller.

Then there was the violence. In the early days, violence had been regarded as a sin: now they were told it was necessary to defend the Community from the enemy without and the backslider within. Hence the Lagoon and the so-called Terminal Experience, and the other practices which had crept into Community life. The punishment of children for lack of achievement or lack of discipline was now officially approved. Only a week or so before she'd had to treat a ten-year-old boy who had been so badly beaten that his skin was in ribbons: when she asked about his crime she learned that he had stolen a coconut from a Community truck. It was now common, she knew, to put a microphone to the mouth of a child during punishment so that its screams would be amplified and serve as a warning to others.

There were the guards, the élite Guards of the Tabernacle, with their clubs, guns and military-style transport. They had become a law

90

unto themselves, a police force with arbitrary powers, which was steadily turning the island into a prison. Merely to express the wish to leave the Community was now rated as a serious crime: the last family to do so, father, mother and two daughters, had been stripped naked in public and scourged before being sent to the Waverers.

The worst thing of all was that such public expressions of violence seemed to have caught the imagination of the Community. The members enjoyed the Terminal Experience at the Lagoon and other similar manifestations and were clamouring for more. There was even talk of reviving the ancient practice of stoning sinners and Waverers!

It was as if the sanction of violence had released some sleeping demon in the heart of the people. The Doctor recognised the disease in herself. At first, the Terminal Experience had horrified her: but later, she had been drawn back to it, feeling a strange mounting excitement from the spectacle, and drawing from the bloody climax a tingling pleasure which was almost sexual in its intensity.

She stood up suddenly, terrified by this flood of faithless thoughts, and shook her head as if to free her mind of such pollution. There was Mr Dunlop, she told herself vigorously, there was always Mr Dunlop. If things went too far, he would see and understand and guide the Community back to the proper path.

But as she began to walk back to the point where she had parked her little open-sided Rustler run-about, she knew that she had not expelled the treason from her mind, merely driven it into some dark recess where it would wait to emerge and torment her once again.

The man called Van Norden was relaxing in a cabin at the Beach of Pleasure, on the western side of the island, when the Comptroller's messenger came for him.

He cursed the interruption silently. The Sisters in attendance at the Beach were dedicated to the gratification of its patrons and their skills in the pursuit of that objective was unmatched, even in his consider-able experience. For the last hour he had been lying with two of his favourites, Diana and Karin, and their sensual revel, with all its delicious permutations, was fast approaching the summit of excite-ment.

Nevertheless, a summons from the Comptroller was not to be disobeyed. For one thing, the setting aside of this small secluded bay as a playground for the privileged had been the Comptroller's idea and access to its facilities was within his gift. The approach to the Beach was guarded and few ordinary members of the Community knew of its existence: only the élite guards and some others like Van Norden were allowed to sample its range of pleasures. He had no intention of depriving himself of the many diversions and entertainments that the Beach could provide: without them, as he well knew, life on the island could be a grinding bore.

And there was another, deeper reason for obeying the summons without delay, a reason which Van Norden would have admitted to no-one and which he scarcely admitted to himself. He was an insensitive man, not given to fear, but he was afraid of the Comptroller. And because he feared him, he hated him also.

He knew, by instinct and experience, that the man could turn from beneficent patron to implacable enemy in seconds, and he knew, above all, that he had the means and the power with which to satisfy this hostility. There was scarcely a country in the world which did not boast a Chapter of the Community: its Apostles were everywhere, an army of zealots who, on instructions from the Comptroller (always issued in the name of Mr Dunlop), would hunt down any enemy, whether real or imagined, to destruction. He had seen it happen: indeed, on many occasions he himself had been the instrument of the Community's wrath.

Ten minutes after the arrival of the messenger he presented himself to the Comptroller, who waved him to a chair.

'I'm afraid we shall have to interrupt your little holiday,' said the Comptroller, smiling at him from behind a long rosewood table: looking down, Van Norden could dimly see his reflection on the surface of the gleaming, mellow wood. The Comptroller lifted a bottle of wine from an ice bucket, wrapped it in a napkin, and held it poised over two glasses.

'Wine?' he asked.

'Thanks.' Van Norden was wondering, with a touch of apprehension, what mission the Comptroller had in store for him. He prayed silently: please God he doesn't want me to snatch another model or beauty queen! So far his luck had held, he'd got safely away with his captives, but deep inside he had this tremulous feeling that the next time would be the last, that the odds were stacking up against him. He was relieved, therefore, when he heard the Comptroller say, 'We have a small problem. Mr Dunlop wishes you to look into it.' He raised his glass. 'Bless you, brother.'

'Bless you,' said Van Norden automatically. He sipped the wine, a first-rate Moselle, and reflected that the Comptroller knew how to look after his personal well-being. Had he been asked to describe the furniture in the room, he would have dismissed it as a bunch of antiques, junk out of a museum. But secretly he had to admit that the place had something. The word that came into his mind was class. And he guessed that it must have cost a fortune to furnish this room alone.

'You're looking well,' said the Comptroller. It was years since he had left his hometown of Kingstree in South Carolina, but he had retained the soft, slow, Southern accent: some might have thought that he had even cultivated it deliberately. His voice was a quiet benevolent purr, as he continued, 'Very well indeed. Much more relaxed than when I saw you last.'

'I was a bit tired,' said Van Norden. 'But I'm fine now.'

'Enjoying the Beach?'

'It's great.'

'We have Mr Dunlop to thank for that particular inspiration,' said the Comptroller smoothly. 'As, indeed, we have to thank him for all our blessings.'

'I thought the Beach of Pleasure was your idea, Comptroller,' said Van Norden tactfully.

'Heavens, no. No, no, no. Definitely not. No. No. I am – how shall we put it? – I am merely an instrument of execution.' His fleshy face widened in a smile at the thought. 'Yes. That would be it. He is the architect, and I serve him in the humble capacity of builder. Take the Beach of Pleasure as an example. In a sense, the very concept of such a place might be said to run contrary to the principles of the Community. I argued as much. But Mr Dunlop, in his great wisdom, saw beyond that.'

He paused to sip some wine and to dab at his moist lips with a fresh, neatly folded handkerchief. Van Norden watched him, wondering when he would get to the point, yet knowing that he would not be hurried.

A thought came to him, followed by an image and he smiled inwardly. Yesterday, at the harbour, he had seen a huge Jewfish which had been brought in by one of the fishing boats. Six feet in length and weighing around five hundred pounds, the giant sea bass, with its wide flabby mouth, cold eyes and plump body, had reminded him irresistibly of the Comptroller.

One of the fishermen had told him a remarkable fact about Jewfish. Like all groupers, he said, they start life as females and produce eggs: then, later on, they change sex and become fully functional males. It amused Van Norden to imagine that the Comptroller was going through a similar process, though perhaps in reverse!

And then his mind drifted to the stiletto that was locked away in his cabin. Only slightly thicker and longer than a bodkin, it was his favourite weapon, just as one of his favourite dreams was to imagine what it would be like to plunge it deep into the Comptroller's flesh, to pierce him again and again and again . . .

He dragged himself back from this fantasy as he heard the Comptroller continue, forcing himself to concentrate.

'Yes, Mr Dunlop saw clearly that for those members of the Community who render special service and who are therefore placed under a special strain, there is need for special consideration. A few extra privileges, concessions and so forth. Like, for example, the – er – the private financial arrangement we made with you, Mr Van Norden.'

For every assignment Van Norden undertook outside the island he received the sum of twenty-five thousand US dollars, paid into an account in the Bahamas. A bonus of five thousand US dollars was paid on completion of each successful mission. So far he had registered no failures and his private bank account, including interest, stood at over a quarter of a million dollars.

He knew that the Comptroller had only mentioned the matter as a veiled reminder that he was the paymaster. It was unlikely that he would bring the arrangement to an end since Van Norden had proved himself to be a reliable and efficient agent, but it was in his power to do so. Van Norden loved money – the thought of it, the feel of it, the sense of security that came with it – and for this reason he said quickly, deferentially, 'I am grateful to you, Comptroller.'

'Grateful to Mr Dunlop, you mean.'

The Comptroller's eyes went to the big portrait of Mr Dunlop which hung above a blue and white Adam fireplace at the end of the room and Van Norden swivelled round to add his gesture of homage.

The vivid, violet-coloured eyes seemed almost real as they looked down at him. Van Norden was only a nominal member of the Community: he went through the bare motions of belief more as a cover than for any other reason, knowing that he had been recruited by the Comptroller for one purpose and one purpose only. Yet each time he saw the portrait of Mr Dunlop and looked at those eyes, he was affected by it. A strange force seemed to flow out of the man, an hypnotic power which had a weird intensity . . .

'Mr Dunlop wants you to go to Antigua,' said the Comptroller, and when he saw the relief in Van Norden's eyes he added, 'Quite. Not a long voyage this time. Someone has been making enquiries about the *Leandro* and we wish you to find out what is behind it.'

'Who is this person?'

'A woman calling herself Mrs Lavinia Harcourt. She enquired in London and at our offices in St John's about purchasing the *Leandro*. From the reports, she appears to be a most unlikely ship-owner. She's English, but our Chapter in Britain can find no information on her – who she is, where she comes from and whether she has that kind of money.'

'You think she is from the RRA – the Relatives Rescue Association?'

'That's for you to find out. She went to our office in St John's with a man named Barr. And she was seen with two other men. According

94

to our contact at the airport, Mrs Harcourt and Barr arrived from England with a black man named Charlie Brown, probably of West Indian origin, and a white man named —' The Comptroller paused as though for effect, and then added, 'An Englishman named Stephen Ugley.'

'Ugley?' Van Norden sat up in the chair, a startled look on his face. 'Can't be. Ugley – well, you know about him, Comptroller . . .'

'I know nothing!' snapped the Comptroller. 'I know nothing except that Mr Ugley died in an accident at sea. The official verdict was accidental death by drowning, I believe.'

'Of course, of course,' said Van Norden hurriedly.

'The young man who arrived yesterday is the nephew. Also called Stephen Ugley. He was met by Mr Pullar who was the late uncle's legal representative. The word is that the young man has inherited the bulk of the estate, including Tradewinds.'

'What do you wish to know, Comptroller?'

'Mr Dunlop wants to know,' said the Comptroller firmly. 'He wants to know why this woman is interested in the *Leandro*. Who exactly is she, and who are her companions? The late Mr Ugley was antagonistic to the Community and gave practical help to our enemies. Do they share that antagonism? And so forth and so on.'

'If they have come out to try and harm the Community, do you want that I should . . .' Van Norden spread his hands and tilted his face to one side.

'No,' said the Comptroller after a moment's thought. 'We have a delegation from New York and London arriving the day after tomorrow to look at the work of the Community. Mr Dunlop would not wish anything to disturb that visit. Simply go to Antigua, find out what you can, and report back to me.'

'Very well, Comptroller.'

'On the other hand,' the Comptroller said softly, 'on the other hand, there is no reason why you should not – shall we say – make them and their friends just a teeny-weeny bit uncomfortable. You understand?'

'It will be a pleasure,' said Van Norden with a smile.

'I don't think you will frighten these people away, but one never knows. And at least we can make it clear to the locals that they are to be avoided, and not helped.'

'You mean, like we did with —'

The Comptroller cut him off icily. 'I do not wish to discuss the details. You are employed – and well paid – to take care of those.'

He leaned forward and topped up the wine glasses. A half-dozen rings glittered on his fingers and a bracelet jangled as he poured.

'Do you like the goblet?' he asked, with a smile.

It took Van Norden a moment to realise that he was referring to the wine glass. His mind had been on other things and he had scarcely noticed the long-stemmed, decorated glass with its gilt rim. Now he lifted it and made a pretence of admiring the workmanship.

'Beautiful,' he murmured, 'very beautiful.'

The Comptroller seemed to be gratified by this response. 'Beautiful, yes. They are over two hundred years old, did you know that?'

'Really?' said Van Norden in what he hoped was the proper mixture of awe and surprise.

'Made in Bohemia and engraved by Silesian craftsmen,' said the Comptroller. He picked up the goblet and held it to the light. 'Do you believe in beauty?'

'I like it,' said Van Norden, thinking not of the glass but of Diana and Karin and wondering if he would have time to go back to them before leaving for Antigua. And then he thought of all the girls he had brought to the island and wondered if he had been wrong about the Comptroller. He had not set eyes on any of the girls since handing them over. Did the Comptroller keep them for his personal pleasure? Or for Mr Dunlop's pleasure perhaps?

The Comptroller touched Van Norden's glass gently with his own. His voice trembled slightly as he said, 'To beauty. I'll give you Mr Dunlop's own toast. To the beauty of the past, to the living beauty of the present, and to the beauty which is yet to come . . .'

The Comptroller's face, reflected in the polished table, reminded Van Norden once again of the Jewfish. And from that his thoughts returned to the stiletto. Aloud, he said, 'To the beauty of the past, to the living beauty of the present, and to the beauty which is yet to come.'

'I want you to meet Sister Eleanor,' said Dr Bauer.

The woman who came towards them smiling was straight and tall and very handsome. She wore the familiar olive-green costume of the Community but it had clearly been cut and tailored to suit her and seemed to enhance her femininity rather than disguise it. The wide dark generous eyes, the smooth erect carriage, the cinnamon skin suggested the Far East but when she spoke it was with a quiet New England American accent. Kitty judged her to be about forty.

'Hi, there!' she said and stretched out both hands in greeting.

'Hi,' said Kitty and, in spite of her resolution, she found herself taking the woman's hands.

'I've been longing to meet you,' said Sister Eleanor. She moved back until she was holding Kitty at arm's length and looked at the girl with open admiration. 'My, but you're beautiful, Sister. You *are* beautiful!'

96

'My name is Kitty!' said the girl, pulling herself free. 'I'm not your Sister, I'm not anyone's Sister.'

'We're all sisters really, don't you agree? All sisters under the skin.' The woman seemed quite unperturbed as she turned to Dr Bauer. 'You can leave her safely in our hands now.'

'You will let me know when I may make the final assessment, Sister?'

'Of course.'

The Doctor turned to Kitty. 'I'll say goodbye then, for the time being.'

'Where are you going?' Kitty could not keep a note of alarm from her voice. She had no particular love of Dr Bauer but at least she knew her: now she was being thrust into the unknown once more and the prospect sharpened her fear.

'I have to get back to my work, dear,' said the Doctor, as to a child. 'You'll be all right here with Sister Eleanor and the others. Just try to accept what they say. Co-operate. I told you – that is the only way.' She patted Kitty's arm. 'The only sensible way. You are privileged, you know, especially privileged.'

As she moved to the door, Kitty stopped her with a cry. 'Doctor!'

'Yes?'

'Susheela and Jasmine. Aren't they coming?'

'No, my dear. They were not —' She paused as though seeking the right words and then, abandoning the search, she added briskly: 'At any rate, they will not be joining you.'

'Where are they?' A mental picture of the two shy, gentle, sad-eyed girls, clutching hands as if in fear of being separated, wrenched at Kitty's mind.

'They will be well looked after,' said the Doctor, not with complete conviction. 'No need to concern yourself.'

She went out quickly. The door closed behind her with a note of finality and Kitty braced herself, as best she could, for what was to come.

In the past day or so, and especially since the Experience at the Lagoon, she had felt a growing sense of hopelessness. She now realised that she was on an island and that in itself added a new and difficult dimension to the possibility of escape. She had taken some heart from the words of comfort that Gunnar had whispered to her at the Lagoon, but since then she had scarcely seen him and there had certainly been no opportunity to follow up his remark.

The Doctor had brought her to the Compound again, past the guards and the roadblocks, to what seemed to be a wing of the great Tabernacle, so that she was once more on strange, unfamiliar ground.

So, more than ever now, she felt herself to be alone, disorientated

97

and drifting, in this extraordinary community which smiled and talked of love even as it kidnapped and murdered people. England and her friends seemed far, far away, shadows that diminished with each day. She had tried to maintain her resolution, to put on an air of defiance but it was becoming harder to do so. For the first time she had begun to think that perhaps it would be easier not to struggle, to accept, to go along with what these people wanted.

Or, at least, to go along until she found out what exactly they did want of her. The Doctor had said it again, a few moments before: *You are privileged, my dear, especially privileged.*

Now, perhaps, she was about to find out what that meant. She would go that far, she decided and, by so doing, she might win their confidence, make them feel that they had succeeded in breaking her spirit, and so relax their guard that she might, somehow, be able to organise her escape.

The woman called Eleanor put her hands on Kitty's shoulders and smiled into her face. 'You're not afraid, are you?'

'No,' murmured Kitty, shaking her head.

'Good.' Eleanor leaned forward and kissed the girl on the cheek. 'We're going to be friends, I can see that.' She took Kitty's arm and led her to a high-backed chair which had been placed in the centre of the room. 'Sit there, my dear.'

Kitty sat without protest and watched as the woman crossed to the windows. They were on an upper floor in a room, long and almost oval in shape, which overlooked part of the great arena. It was bare of furniture except for a low curved couch which stood against one of the walls and another chair similar to the one on which Kitty was seated. On the wall facing her was a large portrait of Mr Dunlop, seated at a table and looking benevolently out on to the world.

Eleanor pressed some buttons on a wall-panel and the heavy curtains swished together. At the same time, an overhead lamp came on, enclosing Kitty in an island of rose-coloured light and she heard, in the background, a faint, regular sound, a ticking beat like that of a metronome.

Crossing to the couch, Eleanor picked up a high-necked cotton robe and slipped it on. It fell to her ankles, covering her uniform and, as she came towards the circle of light, the white cloth seemed to emit a gentle luminous glow, as of phosphorescence.

'What are you doing?' Kitty's voice was a whisper.

'Sh.' Eleanor smiled and put a finger to her lips. Above the whiteness of the robe the raven-dark eyes gleamed like polished ebony. She brought the other chair and sat facing Kitty, drawing herself so close that their knees were touching. Kitty tried to move back, but Eleanor stopped her with a warning gesture of the hand.

They sat in an eerie silence for a long time, the woman smiling, the

98

girl unable to look away from the dark glowing eyes. The regular beat seemed to grow louder and Kitty began to feel that the monotonous rhythm had taken possession of her mind. She tried to force herself to think of other things: of her yellow Mini, of her flat, of Lucy, of Steve Ugley, even of Mr Digby and his beauty contests. But the thoughts were as elusive as birds and, inexorably, she was driven back to the metronome's beat and to the woman who sat motionless before her.

At last, just as she was about to explode into a scream, Eleanor spoke: 'Kitty.'

'Yes?' she said eagerly.

Eleanor leaned forward and lightly brushed Kitty's forehead with a fingertip. 'Hello in there. Hello, Kitty. The real Kitty. Shall we begin?'

'Begin?'

'I want to hear about you. Tell me about your life. Everything about your life, from the beginning.'

'Why?'

'Just tell me. Later, you will understand and be grateful. Later.'

'First, tell me why I am here.'

Once again, the fingertip drew an invisible line across Kitty's forehead, and the soft, hypnotic voice replied, 'Don't you know? You are here because you are beautiful. You are here because you are the most beautiful girl in the world.'

Behind Eleanor, glittering in the shadows, the eyes in the portrait seemed to have taken on a greenish tinge. Glittering like emeralds, they stared at Kitty as though possessed of life and sight. And the metronomic sound rose in volume again, beating in her ears like muffled thunder.

It took her a moment or two to realise that she was listening to the wild beating of her own heart.

At two o'clock the following morning, Dr Bauer was aroused from a troubled sleep by Gunnar. With him, she hurried to the hospital wing in which the Special Rooms were situated. Gunnar paused at the entrance to the room occupied by Susheela and Jasmine and allowed the Doctor to move past him through the open door.

The two girls were hanging from the upper crossbar of the iron grille which blocked the window. The nooses around their necks, and the ropes, had been fashioned from strips torn from bed-sheets and from their clothing.

Susheela's right hand was clasped so tightly in Jasmine's left that they had to cut them down together and even then it took the combined strength of the Doctor and Gunnar to prise them apart.

'We checked at midnight,' whispered Gunnar. 'They were asleep then.'

99

'They were to be sent to the Beach of Pleasure tomorrow,' said the Doctor.

'I know. Poor devils.'

'Did you tell them? You didn't tell them?'

'No. Only that they were to be moved from here.'

'Perhaps they guessed. From the way you said it.'

'It is possible. In any case, I think they had made up their minds to die.'

'Cover them,' said the Doctor. 'We shall have to report this in the morning.' She looked at the two girls and then at Gunnar and shook her head.

'What is happening?' she whispered. 'Suddenly, everything seems to be —' She checked abruptly, as if she felt that she had already said too much. He touched her arm – the first time he had ever done so – and for a brief moment she gripped his hand.

'I understand how you feel. Tomorrow, perhaps we can talk tomorrow,' he murmured.

The Doctor nodded. As she released his hand she felt herself tremble with the apprehension of one who has taken the first step on a dark and dangerous journey.

Gunnar brought a sheet but before he covered the bodies, the Doctor laid the cold, dead hands of Susheela and Jasmine together again, the one touching the other.

Chapter Eight

Daniel Ackland-Pryce, known to his friends and associates as Acky, half-owner of Sugar Bay Water Sports Ltd, was a man so fat as to merit the use of the word gross.

His ample flesh, stained to a dark mahogany by the sun, hung in blubbery folds over the edges of the air-mattress. A thin scrap of covering – little more than a jock-strap – drooped from that part of his body which, in earlier days, had been a waist. He wore nothing else apart from a pair of sunglasses with large round lenses and a whistle which was attached to a piece of cord around his neck. Colouring apart, he looked to Barr and Steve like a beached porpoise.

'Mr Ackland-Pryce?' asked Steve.

The big man did not open his eyes, although it was hard to tell this through the dark sunglasses. Neither did he move or speak. Inwardly he hoped that this immobility would persuade the intruders, whoever they were, to go away.

Steve stirred the great bulk with the toe of his canvas shoe, and repeated the name, louder this time. Acky sighed and opened one eye, squinting at the two white faces that stared down at him. Bloody tourists, he thought. He made a living, an excellent living, by ripping off tourists but, like most expatriates, he held the geese that laid his golden eggs in deep contempt.

'See Lindy,' he said, waving a hand in the general direction of the beach. He dropped his arm as if the effort of moving had exhausted him and closed the eye.

Barr and Steve looked down to the beach where a nubile lady in a very brief bikini was initiating a man and a small boy into the mysteries of a pedalo. She had firm, full breasts, a smoothly-rounded bottom and looked about eighteen. Barr was the first to look away.

'We'd like to talk to you,' he said. 'Joe Bradshaw from Tradewinds said you could help us.'

Acky opened both eyes now and, easing himself up on one elbow, scrutinised the two men. Selecting Steve, he said, 'Good Lord! You must be the chap who has taken over at Tradewinds!'

'That's right.'

'You're the spitting image of old man Ugley. Right out of the same mould.'

'Thanks,' said Steve, who wasn't sure how to take this.

'I heard you were on the island. Look, help me up, would you mind?'

Steve and Barr exerted their combined strength and pulled the

101

mass of flesh into a standing position. Upright, the man stood at over six feet and the blubber appeared to be fairly evenly distributed: even so, he looked enormous. For such a huge person he had an oddly thin and reedy voice: he sounded, to Barr, rather like an adolescent English public school boy.

'Sorry,' he said apologetically. 'I turn the scale at twenty-three stones give or take a bit. Three hundred and twenty pounds.' Slapping his stomach to emphasise the point, he added wistfully, 'It's glands, you know. Doctors can't do a thing. Glands.' He lifted the sunglasses so that they rested above his forehead, and stared at Steve.

'Well, well. The likeness is uncanny. Younger version of the same face. Well, well.' He held out a hand. 'Daniel Ackland-Pryce. Nobody uses it. Call me Acky.'

'Pleased to meet you,' Steve responded. 'I'm Steve. This is my friend and associate, Tom Barr.'

Acky nodded and turned his small, smoky-green eyes on to Barr. He took the other man's hand in a firm grip and then, suddenly, he put the whistle to his lips and blew three shrill notes.

The girl called Lindy and a West Indian girl who looked equally glamorous came scampering across the sand towards him. They stopped and looked at the big man with adoring eyes, like a pair of young puppies.

'A jug of pina colada, my darlings. Pronto!' He slapped the nearest one on the bottom and she ran off with a delighted squeal. He followed her with his eyes, and said happily, 'They love their work.'

He did not expand on this and neither of the two men pressed him.

'We came to hire a boat,' Barr said.

'Joe Bradshaw said you'd be able to fix us up,' said Steve.

'We want it as soon as possible,' added Barr. 'Like now, this minute.'

'Of course, of course,' said Acky, in a pained voice. He looked from one to the other, and shook his head. 'How long have you been here, gentlemen?'

'A couple of days,' answered Steve.

'Exactly. You're still on the old European tempo.' He snapped his fingers. 'Everything must be done – snap! – like that. Take my advice and ease up. You're in the West Indies now – different climate, different people, different rhythm of life. Don't fight it, gentlemen. Enjoy it. Adjust. That way you'll live longer.'

'Everybody keeps singing the same song,' said Barr. 'Relax, take it easy.'

'Why not?' said Acky. 'That's why you're here, isn't it?'

There was a brief silence as their eyes met. Then Barr shrugged and smiled, 'Sure,' he said. 'We're here to relax. But they say there are three hundred and sixty-five beaches to relax on. It's going to take time to sort out the right one. I figure the sooner we get started the better.'

Acky led the way into a small hut which was furnished with four canvas chairs, a table and a humming refrigerator. A strong smell of fish hung in the air. Through a half-open curtain at the rear, Barr caught a glimpse of a king-size bed covered by a crumpled sheet.

The girls had already set a large jug, three glasses and a bowl of ice on the table. Acky waved them away, stacked the glasses with ice-cubes and filled each one from the jug.

'Ever tried this?' he asked.

Steve sipped the light brown liquid tentatively at first and then with greater enthusiasm.

'It's good! What's in it?'

'Rum, coconut, pineapple juice and a touch of bitters. Always keep a jug ready-made in the old ice-box. Daytime drink, mind you. In the evening, I hit the Scotch. But before sundown this is the best tipple. Have a seat. Drink up. Plenty more where that came from.' But as Steve was about to lower himself into one of the chairs he added quickly, 'Not that one!'

'Sorry,' said Steve.

'No problem,' said Acky with a smile. 'But this one is reserved for me. Specially reinforced, you see.' He lowered himself carefully into the chair, which creaked a little but otherwise stood firm. He looked long and hard at Steve.

'So. The old man left you all the loot, eh?'

'Not quite all,' Steve said carefully.

'Tradewinds?'

'Yes.'

'That's enough. That would suit me nicely.'

'The boat,' said Barr brusquely.

'Tell me,' said Acky, turning his head towards Barr with a kind of slow deliberation, 'were you born impatient or did you have to take lessons?'

'What can you offer us?'

'Anything, within reason. What do you want? Look out of the window. There's all sorts out there. A speedboat? Sailing dinghy? Or something bigger?'

Barr rose, went to the tiny window and pulled aside the ragged curtain. Beyond the row of beached pedalos, speedboats and other pleasure-craft, he saw a cabin-cruiser tugging gently at her moorings on the end of the wooden jetty. She needed a fresh coat of paint but looked sturdy enough. Barr could just about make out the name: *Carib Beauty.*

'How about the cruiser?' he asked.

'Your choice, old friend,' Acky replied. 'She's not much to look at, but she's reliable. One hundred per cent reliable.'

'How much?'

Acky scratched his stomach reflectively, making a faint white line on the dark skin. 'To you sixty US dollars per hour.'

'Including boatman?'

'Including everything except food and grog. There's a stock of drink on board but you pay extra for it. And one of the girls will fix a packed lunch.'

'We'll take it,' said Barr.

'For how long?'

'Three, maybe four hours. Maybe the rest of the day.'

'Where do you plan on going?'

'Just for a cruise around. A look-see,' said Steve carefully.

'And maybe a little fishing,' added Barr.

Acky nodded and once more applied himself to the whistle, blowing two long blasts. This time the West Indian girl arrived alone.

'These gentlemen want to hire *Carib Beauty*, Mandy.'

'She's all ready, Acky,' said the girl. She flashed a smile of pleasure in Steve's direction. Her straight dark hair, threaded with hundreds of tiny different-coloured beads, framed her gleaming, impudent face like an open curtain. She had an air of greater maturity than Lindy, and Steve guessed that she could give the other girl three or four years.

'This one is Mandy,' said Acky. 'She'll take you out.' And as Barr's forehead wrinkled in doubt, he added, 'Not to worry, old friend. She can handle that boat better than most men.'

'A whole lot better,' said Mandy. 'It's the truth. Did the gentlemen bring food?'

'No,' said Steve.

Without realising what he was doing, he watched a glistening pearl of sweat roll down from the girl's neck and disappear into the valley between her breasts. She smiled again and he looked away in embarrassment.

'I better fix the food,' said Mandy. 'Do you want the ten, twenty or thirty dollar packed lunch?'

'This is Mr Ugley, Mandy,' said Acky, with a faint note of rebuke in his voice. 'He's the new owner of Tradewinds.'

'Is that so?' Her dark eyes twinkled. 'In that case, nothing but the best. I'll bring the fifty dollar special.'

As the girl hurried away, Acky refreshed the glasses. 'Relax. She has to get the hamper from the Arawak Bay Hotel, just up the beach. Going to take a little time.' He looked at Steve. 'You planning to stay on the island?'

'I haven't really made any plans. Not longterm, anyway,' said Steve. He sipped his drink, looking at the fat man over the rim of the glass.

104

'How well did you know my uncle?'

'Pretty well. He was a good scout. Awkward cuss, mind you. But I liked him. And I miss him.'

'I read the Coroner's report,' said Steve. 'Not very illuminating. Nobody seemed to be able to work out how it happened.'

The man's reaction was almost imperceptible but Barr, watching keenly, noticed that he stiffened slightly and that his stubby fingers tightened around the glass. Then, with a rueful shake of the head, he said, 'The sea never changes and its works, for all the talk of men, are wrapped in mystery.' And he added, with a little smile, 'That's not me. That's Conrad.'

'According to the evidence, there was no storm and hardly any wind. And according to Joe Bradshaw my uncle was an experienced sailor and a strong swimmer. He'd been out in that same boat hundreds of times.'

'The sea has no respect for experience or skill.'

'All the same,' said Steve obstinately, 'you were his friend. Didn't you find it odd?'

'My old friend, there is nothing odd about it. The greatest mystery is the sea and no sailor or scientist has ever come up with an answer to it.' He added amiably, 'Have you read much of Conrad?'

'*Lord Jim. The Heart of Darkness*,' said Steve. 'Not much else.'

'I read him all the time,' said Acky. 'Over and over. He's the greatest in my view, the greatest.'

'What do you make of this strange mob on Jerusalem Island?' asked Barr abruptly.

Acky's eyebrows went up. 'Heavens, you are a direct person.'

'What do you make of them?'

'Live and let live. They don't interfere with me, and I return the compliment.'

'But they are a very strange lot.'

'My old friend, who isn't? I've no doubt that many people think I'm strange, but I don't allow that to disturb my sleep. The world is full of weird sects and religions – and there are going to be more of them, mark my words. Our civilisation, if I may so abuse the word, has reached the end of the road. From now on it's reverse gear all the way. That breeds panic and uncertainty and in such a situation people will take hold of anything that removes the need for thought. In the next few years we'll see more prophets than you'll find in any bible, believe me.'

'Prophets who take people for suckers?' asked Barr. 'Who rob people blind? Who line their own pockets?'

'That sort most of all,' said Acky. 'Most of all. And as fast as you cut one down, another will rise up in his place.'

'Did my uncle have any connection with the Community of New

Jerusalem?' asked Steve.

'Connection is the wrong word. He was hostile to it and said as much on various occasions. Rather unwisely, in my humble view.'

'Why?'

Acky shrugged, as though he found the conversation uncomfortable. 'They're powerful. Wield a lot of influence. But like I said, live and let live. If you leave them alone, they won't interfere with you.'

'Why was he hostile?'

'I suppose he didn't like their style. No, it was more than that. He had a good friend on the island. Jonah Winston. Had a fair old business in import-export. A good family man. Then, quite suddenly, his wife left him, taking their two sons, and joined the Community on Jerusalem Island. Jonah Winston almost went out of his mind. He went over to find them and never came back. He simply issued a statement saying that he, too, had been converted to the Community. And he handed over all his possessions to them.'

'We went to his office,' said Barr. 'The Community had a couple of thugs in charge.'

Acky's face showed surprise and curiosity. 'Why did you go there?'

'On business,' said Barr. 'You were telling us about Jonah Winston.'

'Well, that was it, really. Mr Ugley's uncle got uptight about the whole thing. Demanded to see Jonah to check out whether he had acted under duress. The chief administrator of the Community, a man they call the Comptroller, was quite bland about the whole thing. Said he would gladly arrange such a meeting. Mr Ugley went over to see Jonah, who told him that he didn't want to know. He was quite happy with life on Jerusalem Island – never been happier in his life. Mr Ugley still wasn't satisfied. He threatened to bring in lawyers to challenge the Community in the courts, and even went to the police. Generally made a nuisance of himself, you might say.'

'And then, one sunny, peaceful day, he was drowned at sea,' said Barr.

'Yes,' said Acky.

'Quite a coincidence.'

'It was an accident. There was nothing to prove otherwise. A tragic accident.'

'And a convenient one. For the Community.'

Mandy suddenly appeared in the doorway, casting a sharp-edged shadow across the table. 'All ready!' she called cheerfully. 'All aboard!'

Acky pulled himself to his feet with evident relief. 'Enjoy your trip, gentlemen!' he said, rather breathlessly. 'It's been good to talk to you.'

The *Leandro* lay in deep water with her bow anchor out, just beyond the Blue Water Reef. A ship's boat was negotiating a narrow passage through the reef, heading for the stone jetty and the cluster of tin-roofed buildings which made up the tiny port of St Marks on Jerusalem Island.

Barr studied the ship through the glasses he had borrowed from Gordon Pullar but they told him nothing. A seaman moved across the deck, gulls hovered on spread wings above the bridge house, the sun drew a flashing gleam from glass or polished metal – that was all.

He turned to follow the passage of the boat. It had reached the jetty and three men were going ashore. White men. One officer in tropical gear and two seamen went into one of the long, low buildings. Nearby, three men and a woman, all wearing the olive-green uniform of the Community, were unloading a truck stacked with hands of green bananas. Beyond them, the land was as flat as a pancake, save for a line of low, blue-tinted hills in the middle-distance and, to the east, the high sharp dominating outline of Dreadnought Hill. It was here, in 1781, that Admiral Lord Nelson had built one of his famous forts to defend the approaches to Antigua: Barr could vaguely make out the tier upon tier of breastworks which rose to the sturdy grey blockhouse at the summit of the hill.

'We'd better move on now.'

Barr looked down into the smiling face of Mandy, and saw behind the smile, a touch of nervousness. He tossed the glasses to Steve and scrambled down from the roof of the cabin.

'See anything?' asked Steve.

'Not much. I'd like to get in closer,' answered Barr.

'No. That would not be wise!' said the girl quickly. 'Look – they are watching us.'

She pointed to the deck of the *Leandro*. Two men were standing at the rail and one of them was staring down at them through a pair of binoculars.

'What is there about this island that puts the fear of God into everybody?' asked Steve.

'Let's take a trip around it,' said Barr. Mandy threw him a quick puzzled glance, as if she were trying to read his intentions, and he gave her bare shoulder a reassuring pat. 'Look, girlie, we're paying sixty dollars an hour for this tub. That's a rip-off in any language. So let's have our money's worth, OK? Take us right round the island. And my friend Steve – he's the rich one – will give you twenty extra, on the side, as a personal bonus.'

She grinned at this and turned back to the controls. The engine quickened, and she sent the *Carib Beauty* around in a half-turn, moving away from the *Leandro* and taking a course parallel to the shore-line. Steve lifted the glasses and took a last look at the two men on the deck of the banana-boat.

'They're still very interested in us,' he said.

'Look at the coral,' begged Mandy. 'It's very beautiful.'

Steve and Barr looked down obediently. Beneath the boat the water was dark blue, but a yard or so away, where the reef lay just below the surface, it turned to a vivid green. Angelfish, groupers and rainbow parrot fish glided through the honeycomb maze of pink coral, accompanied by swarming schools of tiny multi-coloured cardinal fish. Here and there the tips of ivory bush coral thrust through the water like the branches of a small tree and, a little further on, the prevailing pink was broken by rough outcrops of green star coral and glistening mauve sea fans. A blue-spotted cornetfish appeared suddenly and took swift evasive action, the strange whip-like growth on its tail flailing as the long tubular body slid through the water.

'Have you seen a coral reef before?' asked Mandy.

'I haven't,' said Steve. 'It's great! Really fantastic!'

Barr didn't answer. His eye had picked up a movement on the shore and, taking the glasses, he focused on a small sandy bay. He studied the scene for quite a long time, and the smile on his face prompted Steve to ask, 'What is it?'

'Some people,' said Barr gravely as he handed over the binoculars, 'some people might say that it was more interesting than coral.'

At first sight, Steve was puzzled by Barr's interest. Four sun-tanned and beefy young men wearing identical, dark blue swimming trunks were tossing a beach ball from one to the other, while two girls darted between them, jumping up and down in frantic efforts to intercept the passing. It took him a moment to take in the fact that the two girls were naked.

Further up the beach, their bodies partly shaded by a large striped umbrella, a man and two girls were lying together in a strange contortion of writhing limbs. Nearby, the black body of a young girl lay straining beneath the whiteness of a bearded middle-aged man.

A tall girl, wearing only a short apron, came out from a low red-roofed building with a tray of drinks and picked her way delicately across the sand. She paused at the threesome for a moment and the man suddenly reached up and pulled her down into the tangled group, scattering the glasses.

'Jesus!' Steve whispered. He glanced towards Mandy but she was occupied at the wheel and did not seem aware of their new interest. He returned quickly to the view. Higher up, standing in a half-circle around the red-roofed building he counted eight small cabins and further back still, where the ground sloped upwards in a slow gradient, he fancied he could make out a high wire-mesh fence.

As he panned back to the group, he saw that one of the girls had managed to catch the beach ball. Laughing, she ran with it into the sea with one of the young men racing after her. Suddenly, he checked

108

and stared out towards the *Carib Beauty*. He waved to his companions and seemed to be shouting something. He turned and ran towards the buildings, pursued by the girl: the others, as though governed by the same impulse, followed suit.

In a few moments the beach, fast receding from view, was empty. Only the beach ball, bobbing in the fringe of surf, and the striped umbrellas confirmed that the scene had been no illusion. Lowering the glasses, Steve rubbed his eyes as if to wake himself.

'Jesus!' he said again.

'It's all right, you know,' said Barr. 'So long as it's between consenting adults, it's all right.'

'But it's supposed to be a strict religious community.'

'No wonder they're winning so many converts,' said Barr.

They rounded a small headland, putting the beach out of sight, and came to another, smaller bay which appeared to be deserted.

'Mandy,' said Barr, 'I'm hungry. Let's eat.'

'OK,' she said, 'I'll switch off and drop anchor.'

'No,' he said. 'Not here. We'll picnic on that beach.'

Once again, he saw a hint of fear in her eyes. 'We can't take the boat in,' she said. 'The reef.'

'There's a channel. Look.' He indicated a break in the reef where a bridge of bright blue water pointed towards the shore. Still she shook her head.

'Why not?' he asked.

'It is forbidden.'

'Who forbids it?'

'The island is private property. They are very strict about trespassers.'

'Darling, we're not going to invade their bloody island. Only take a picnic. You needn't come ashore, you can stay in the boat if you're scared.'

'If there's any trouble —' she began.

'I'll take the blame,' he said.

She hesitated a moment longer and then, with a shrug, slowed the engines and headed the boat towards the break in the reef. But as they reached it and turned for the shore there was a sudden, sharp, echoing explosion and a bullet seared through the air above the cruiser.

Mandy cut the engine at once and turned to the others, the fear and shock now openly showing on her face. Barr seized the glasses and studied the low ridge above the little bay, and as he did so he caught the flash of rifle fire as another warning shot arched over them.

'I don't like that,' said Barr, 'I don't like that at all. I'm going in to have a word with those bastards.'

'Not without me, you're not,' said Steve.

'Let's go,' pleaded the girl.

'They're only firing to scare us off,' said Barr. 'Stay here and wait, you'll be OK. Or move further out if you like and come back to get us when I give the signal.'

'I'll wait,' she said, shivering a little.

'Good girl.'

The two men plunged overboard and struck out towards the shore. Three more shots cut into the water but they ignored them and swam on. As they drew near the beach, two men in combat uniforms rose from behind the ridge and moved across the sand towards the water's edge. Barr and Steve touched bottom and began to wade forward.

'That's far enough!' The taller of the two guards, a tall, narrow man with a thin angular face, lifted his gun. Barr saw that it was a Uzi, an Israeli weapon. He had used one himself in Biafra, and knew that like most Israeli hardware it was more efficient than it looked. The other man was also carrying a Uzi: both weapons looked new and Barr guessed that someone had been doing a little shopping in the Lebanon, where such arms could be picked up with relative ease.

'What do we do?' asked Steve, pausing for a moment.

'Keep moving!' said Barr. 'They're bluffing.'

'I hope you're right,' grunted Steve, wading after him.

In a lower voice, Barr said, 'We may have to take them. Watch the smaller one. Keep on your toes. And if I say go, then go for him with all you've got.'

'Jesus!' said Steve, and made it sound like a prayer.

'This is private property!' shouted the first guard. 'Get back to your boat!' He shook the Uzi threateningly, but he was clearly puzzled by their refusal to be scared off. And as Barr and Steve stepped from the water, he and his companion fell back a couple of paces.

Barr shook the water from his hair and favoured the tall guard with a long slow stare. 'For two pins,' he said at last, 'for two pins or even one, I'd wrap that bloody gun round your bloody neck.'

'It was a warning. And I'm still warning you. You're trespassing,' said the guard.

'Shit!' said Barr. 'You're full of shit. I don't like being fired on, sonny boy. Especially by a couple of toy soldiers.'

'Get off this beach, mister!' said the guard in a low angry voice. He took a step forward.

'That's a Uzi, isn't it?' said Barr, nodding towards the man's gun. 'New model. Haven't seen that one before. Good weapon. Light, easy to handle. I see you've got it on safety.'

The man, startled by Barr's sudden change of direction, looked down at the gun. In that second, Barr leaped at him, shouting to Steve at the same time, 'Go, Steve, go!'

Barr grabbed the gun and jerked it upwards. In his surprise the tall guard let go and the Uzi caught him under the chin. The impact was enough to force his head back and, as this happened, Barr brought a knee up sharply into the man's crutch.

With a shout of pain, the guard doubled up and Barr hit him behind the ear with the gun. He fell slowly to the sand, his eyes bulging, and a trickle of spittle came from his gaping mouth. Barr flicked the Uzi control to automatic and stirred the fallen man with his bare foot. He wasn't exactly unconscious, but he was in no shape to give any further trouble.

Steve was having a little more difficulty with the other guard, a swarthy little man with a barrel-like chest and muscles to match. They were rolling in the sand trying desperately to get at the other Uzi which had fallen by a small outcrop of rocks. Barr strolled across and picked it up. It was on single fire. He switched it to safety and sat down on the rocks to watch the progress of the contest.

A momentary glimpse of Barr sitting calmly with the two guns seemed to knock some of the spirit out of the second guard. Even so, he struggled on for another minute or so, and contrived to land one cracking blow to the side of his opponent's jaw. Eventually Steve managed to turn him over, plant a knee in the small of his back and twist his arm into a savage lock. The man lay there grunting and spitting sand while Steve sucked in great lungfuls of air.

'You're out of condition,' said Barr.

'You picked the easy one.'

'They were both easy,' said Barr. 'Bloody amateurs. Let him go.'

Steve released his hold and stood up. As the guard rolled over, Barr moved across and pressed the barrel of a Uzi into his cheek. The man's eyes swam in fear as Barr switched the control from safety to single fire.

'Where you from, comrade?' Barr asked.

The man hesitated and Barr jabbed the gun in harder. He winced and stammered, 'From Mexico. From Mexico City.'

'How long have you been here?'

'Maybe three months, I think.'

'You're not a regular member of the Community?'

'Please – I do not understand this.'

'You were hired as a guard – right?'

'Si, senor. As Guardian.'

'Guardian. How many Guardians are there?'

'How many? Forty, I think. Maybe fifty.'

'All armed like you?'

'Si, senor.'

'And your job is to keep out intruders?'

'Si. We patrol the beaches.'

111

'To keep out intruders and to keep in the others?'

'I do not —'

'To stop people from leaving the island?'

'Si. This is why we fire at you. We think maybe you come with boat to take away somebody. We do not shoot to kill, only to warn not to come.'

'A lot of people want to leave, do they?'

'Some peoples, yes. But is not permitted.'

'Where did you get these guns?'

'I do not know, senor. Are issue to us. I think maybe they are bring in by big boat.'

'The ship that's lying off the island now. *The Leandro*?'

'Si, senor, I think so.'

'It brings in arms and supplies?'

'Si, senor.'

'Does it bring in girls too?'

'I do not understand, senor.'

The man had a small gold ring in his left ear and Barr tapped it lightly with the gun. 'If I blow your ear-ring off – will that help you to understand?'

The man's sallow face grew visibly paler. 'Sometimes people come in the ship. New peoples for the Community.'

'Girls?' Barr touched the tip of the man's ear with the gun.

'Sometimes, yes, I think so.'

'And where do they keep these girls?'

'I do not know, senor.' Barr tapped his head with the gun, less gently this time, and the man winced with pain. 'Please, senor. Some special girls live in Tabernacle, I think so. But I am only Guardian, not permitted to see. Is truth, senor, I tell truth.'

Barr nodded and stepped back. The guard rested his head in the sand, his eyes moist with relief. Nearby, his companion had climbed to his feet and was making desperate efforts to stand erect. He staggered towards them and Barr cracked the gun sharply across his left shin. He howled with pain and sat down abruptly, nursing the injured leg.

'I think I'll take a look around,' said Steve.

'No,' said Barr.

'Why not?'

'For a start, because you'd stand out like a whore at a wedding. You heard what the man said. There are forty or fifty armed guards on the island – they'd pick you off like that.' He snapped his fingers.

'What then?'

'We go back. Sort out what we've got. Think it through. Find a way to get back and take a proper look.'

'How?'

112

'Hell, I don't know. Not yet. But we'll work out something.' He saw the doubt on Steve's face and shook his head. 'Steve, I know what you're thinking. But I told you once before – riding to the rescue like a white knight on a charger is strictly for the storybooks. You'll be no good to Kitty Higgins or anyone else if you get yourself wasted now. This one wants thinking about. And the first thing we do is to see about organising ourselves a little help. Reduce the odds. Come on.'

He picked up the other gun and waded into the sea. When it reached waist-high, he swung each Uzi in turn and hurled it into deep water. The sky was beginning to darken and, as Steve came out to stand beside him, a light wind with a fresh cool edge to it began to stir the surface of the water. Barr held his face up to it.

'Feel it?' he said. 'In these parts they call that the Undertaker's Wind.'

Chapter Nine

Gordon Pullar had taken lunch with a client at the Admiral's Inn at Nelson's Dockyard and was feeling in a mellow, relaxed mood. The grilled lobster and the Chablis had been excellent as always, the business discussion satisfactory, and the only slight shadow over his sense of well-being was cast by the thought that he had, perhaps, over-indulged himself.

Still, he thought, as he drove back across the island to his office on Thames Street in St John's, there was nothing wrong that a short nap wouldn't put right.

Mr Pullar was a great devotee of the after-lunch nap. He had read some years before that his idol, Winston Churchill, had taken a regular daily rest throughout his tenure of office as war-time Prime Minister, regardless of whether the news from the battlefronts was favourable or disastrous: from then on, Mr Pullar had embraced the ritual, reasoning that what was good enough for Churchill must be good for him.

Indeed, he had at one time taken up cigars and brandy in further imitation of his hero, but Mrs Pullar had stamped down firmly on such indulgences. He was secretly relieved by her decree, for he had found that cigars did not agree with him and that he had no taste for brandy.

He parked the car and headed up the flight of wooden stairs towards the couch which stood waiting in his private office. It was now just after three o'clock and his next appointment was not until four: Mrs Colson, his secretary, had been with him for fifteen years and she knew that it was almost more than her job was worth to allow any caller, by telephone or in person, to come between Mr Pullar and his siesta.

'I'm back, Mary,' he called as he passed the open door of her office on the way to his own. 'Just going to have my usual tickle-and-slap.' Tickle-and-slap, meaning nap, was a survival from the half-forgotten days of Cockney rhyming slang: it was an old joke between them, a kind of codeword.

'Mr Pullar!' She stopped him on the threshold of his office and he turned with a touch of annoyance. She hurried towards him and he noticed that there was an unusual flush of colour in her thin, yellowish, sun-dried cheeks.

'What is it?' he asked.

'This man. He's been waiting. He would not go. Insists on seeing you,' she whispered. Her voice, even after twenty-five years on the

114

island, was still strongly flavoured with the accent of her native Scotland.

'You know I can't see anyone at this time!' He raised his tone in the hope that the intruder might hear. 'I have those papers to prepare. Make an appointment.'

'I want five minutes of your time.' The man, wearing a well cut, chocolate-coloured shirt-jacket with short sleeves, and matching slacks, had come to the doorway of Mrs Colson's office. He was thickly built, his face was lean and hard, and there was about him an air of confidence, as if he were used to getting his own way.

'If you will make an appointment with —'

'Now!' said the man, interrupting him. His eyes flickered with a look that was almost contemptuous and a vague unspoken threat seemed to hang in the air between them.

Mr Pullar mentally retreated a step or two. He was no match for the man himself and, short of calling the police, there was nothing he could do to get rid of him.

'What is the nature of your business?' he asked, attempting, rather feebly, to put the visitor in his place by cold formality.

'It's private,' said the man, glancing at Mrs Colson.

'Oh, very well,' said Mr Pullar, with a show of irritation. 'You'd better come through to my office. But I warn you, I can give you no more than five minutes.'

He led the way into his private room, switched on the fan, and sat back behind his desk. A picture of his wife stood beside the blotter and he shifted it an inch or two, making the movement deliberate so as to disguise any nervousness on his part. With the same sort of deliberation he took his old Parker fountain-pen from his pocket, unscrewed it, and examined the nib.

His pleasure at this performance was somewhat dispelled when he looked up. Without waiting to be asked the man had drawn up a chair and was now seated across the desk from him. Once again, Mr Pullar had the odd sensation of being under threat.

'Perhaps you'd begin by giving me your name,' he said, holding the pen poised above the yellow legal pad on the desk.

'My name is Van Norden,' said the man.

'Address?'

'You can always reach me at J. D. Winston's office on Redcliffe Street.'

Mr Pullar's fingers tightened around the pen as it skidded nervously across the paper. He looked up into the man's mocking eyes. 'J. D. Winston?'

'That's what I said.'

'Then I can take it that you come from the Community of New Jerusalem?'

'You can take what you like.' Van Norden could sense the fear rising in the other man and his voice was keen with contempt. 'Now, let me ask the questions. First, you went to Coolidge Airport earlier this week to meet four Brits. Three men and a woman.'

'That is correct.'

'What is your connection with them?'

'Really, Mr Van Norden —' Mr Pullar gave a little frown of protest.

Van Norden reached across the desk and struck the photograph of Mrs Pullar with the back of his right hand. The blow had sufficient force to send the heavy frame crashing into a metal filing cabinet some yards away, where it fell with a crunch of breaking glass. Mr Pullar looked down at the wreckage with wide, fearful eyes, and then turned to his visitor.

Van Norden smiled and spread his hands in a gesture of mocking apology. 'Sorry,' he said, 'sorry. That sort of thing is always happening with me. I'm accident prone. Can't help breaking things – all kinds of things. Photographs, glasses, arms, legs – you name it, I've broken it.'

Some cars in the street below hooted noisily at each other but to Mr Pullar the sound might have been coming from another world, thousands of light years away. He felt an extraordinary sense of unreality, as though, caught up in this strange confrontation, he was suspended in time and space.

He had his dreams of heroism and, over the years, both in his own mind and to his friends, he had modestly played up his role in World War Two. His performance had not been without merit, but time and Mr Pullar had given it a gloss: what he remembered now, and exaggerated, were the moments of triumph, while the tedium, the failures and the fear of other times were forgotten.

Yet in his heart, in those rare periods when a man truly looks at himself, he knew that he was not really a brave man. Violence and the threat of violence frightened him: he would always go the long way round to avoid it, or choose the path of compromise. But now, rising through the fear, he felt a sense of outrage surging in his blood, and anger lent him a boldness which he found astonishing and exhilarating.

'Mr Van Norden,' he began. His voice was pitched on too high a note and he stopped, clearing his throat. The sneering smile on the other man's face lent him fresh spirit and he went on, in a firmer more resolute tone, 'Mr Van Norden. I don't know who you are, or what you want. But I have absolutely no intention of discussing my clients or their affairs or my relationship to them with you or anyone else. Now, I have work to do, and I must ask you to leave. At once.'

He felt his hand tremble as he slid open the centre drawer of the desk and gripped the round ebony ruler that lay there. Van Norden continued to smile but made no effort to move.

'They're your clients are they?' he asked.

'They are my clients. That is all I will tell you. Now, will you leave or must I call the police?'

'The police!' Van Norden spat the words out contemptuously. He got to his feet very slowly and Mr Pullar shrank back a little. Van Norden looked round the office and nodded.

'You have a good business here. Very good, I'd say. But in your line it is all a question of goodwill, wouldn't you say? I mean, one day you've got a list of clients as long as a man's arm, and the next – whoosh – it's gone. Vanished. Suddenly they've gone off you, maybe they've been frightened off, know what I mean? I should have thought a man like you, with your experience, would realise that it is important to keep in with the right people – and keep out of the way of the wrong ones. We could put a lot of business your way, you know. On the other hand —'

He stopped, smiled and shook his head. Moving to the door he paused by a wooden cupboard, the top half of which was stacked with law books. He glanced at Mr Pullar, shook his head again, and smashed his foot into the door at the base of the cupboard. The wood splintered and broke, revealing the small stock of hospitality liquor within. Reaching inside, Van Norden grasped a bottle of white rum, uncorked it, and holding the bottle high, poured the contents on to the floor. When the last drop had gurgled out he tossed the empty bottle in to the air, caught it deftly, and hurled it at Mr Pullar's head.

Mr Pullar ducked and the bottle crashed on the wall behind him, narrowly missing a group of photographs of the British Royal Family and Winston Churchill.

When he looked up again, Van Norden had gone. With shaking hands, Mr Pullar reached for the telephone and called Steve at Trade-winds.

It took Barr a long time to get through to Noonan in London and when he did so, he was disconnected three times. However, at the fourth attempt the gremlins departed and he heard Noonan coming through loud and clear from the back parlour of the Queen's Head.

During their service together in Biafra and in some of the other troubled countries in Africa, Noonan had proved himself to be an awesomely efficient Sergeant-Major and, to Barr's relief, his touch had not deserted him. Despite the fact that Barr had got him out of bed in the middle of the night he showed no irritation and no surprise at the nature of the request. He asked only the most practical and essential questions, and concluded with a brisk promise that the merchandise would be delivered on schedule. Checking his watch, Barr noted with a smile that the entire conversation had taken only eight minutes.

The main homestead at Tradewinds stood on a slight rise and, from the panoramic windows of the wide lounge, Barr could see Steve and Charlie Brown relaxing on the sea-front terrace beside the neat open-sided bar. Vinnie was swimming nearby, shaking up the placid blue water with a powerful, if clumsy, overarm stroke. The sea looked inviting and Barr decided to join her.

Joe Bradshaw's wife, Rose, had tidied his room and made the bed: fresh towels had been set out in the bathroom and Barr noted, with approval, that the soiled clothes he had left off only the evening before were lying on the bed in a neat, freshly ironed pile.

It was part instinct, part experience, that made Barr check as he opened a drawer to get at his swimming trunks. It was his habit, part of his training, to put his things away in a certain regular order and he saw at once that this drawer had been disturbed. The handker-chiefs which he had placed to the left on the top of some leisure shirts were now on the right. A box of aspirin was missing.

He found the aspirin in another drawer and, again, there was evidence that someone had been riffling through his things. And he found the final proof when he pulled out the old leather case in which he kept his papers, passport and other travel documents. Someone had forced the lock and the case was open. As far as he could see, the contents were intact, nothing had been taken.

But clearly someone had turned over the room in search of something. Not money, for his traveller's cheques and about £15 in English currency were still in the case. Rose? Barr had met her and liked her, and he could think of no possible reason why she should do such a thing. No. Had she wanted to go through the wardrobe, she could have used his clean linen as an excuse to go to the drawers, but she had left it for him to check and put away.

Barr got on the housephone to Steve and Charlie and summoned them to the house. A quick check of Charlie's room revealed that it had also been searched but that nothing was missing. Steve's room appeared to have been given a more thorough going-over than the others and the intruder had taken less care to replace the various articles. It was as if he (or she) had begun to panic, to throw caution aside as time passed.

Steve's briefcase, newer and slimmer than Barr's, was lying on the bed with the locks open. He searched anxiously through the contents: his passport, cheques and air-ticket were all untouched. But then Steve remembered and his hand slapped his forehead in a gesture of anger and frustration.

'Oh, bloody hell!'

'What is it? asked Barr.

'The file. They've taken the file!'

'What file, for God's sake?'

118

'*The* file! The one with all my case notes about Kitty and the other girls – and the press clippings – and the photographs.'

'You're sure the file was in the case?'

'Sure I'm sure. And the case was locked in the top drawer of that bureau.'

'What's wrong?' Vinnie, wrapped in a voluminous robe that made her look like a bedouin tent, put a red face round the door.

'We think we've been done over,' said Barr.

'Think! We bloody well have!' said Steve miserably.

'Check your room, Vinnie,' said Barr. 'Especially check any papers you might have which refer to Kitty or to the *Leandro*.'

When Vinnie joined them in the lounge five minutes later, they were discussing the affair with Joe Bradshaw and Rose. Steve broke off the questioning and looked at her.

'Well?' he asked.

'Only one thing missing that I can see,' Vinnie said. 'My black notebook.'

'What was in it?'

'All the stuff I found out about that boat – I mean ship – the *Leandro*.'

'That's all?'

'It's enough,' she said gloomily. 'I hate the thought of some villain going through my things with his greasy hands. Ugh! If I catch the bastard I'll pulverise him. Invasion of privacy, that's what it's called, you know. Besides, that bloody notebook cost me the best part of a pound!'

'It looks as if they broke in this morning,' said Steve. 'Rose was out at the market, and Joe was decorating one of the guest cabins, well away from the house. It must have happened then.'

'I'm sorry,' said Joe. He was huge and black, and towered over his small, pretty, light brown wife. Both of them looked unhappy and crestfallen.

'Not your fault, Joe. Mr Pullar had an unpleasant visitor yesterday afternoon – enquiring about us. He warned me. I should have anticipated that they'd try something, and taken precautions,' said Steve.

'They? Who are you talking about?' asked Vinnie.

'The Community. Couldn't be anyone else. Obviously, they were anxious to find out why we are here.'

'And now they know,' said Barr.

'Now they know.'

Joe led Rose from the room, his strong, muscled arm resting on her slender shoulders. At the doorway he paused and turned back to the others.

'They are a bad lot,' he said. 'They gave your uncle a bad time.'

'I think they gave him more than a bad time,' said Steve. 'Which adds one more item to the account.' He paused reflectively, rubbing the side of his nose with a finger in a characteristic gesture. 'One thing. This break-in confirms what, up to now, we've only suspected.'

'How?' asked Vinnie.

'The only things they took were the photographs of Kitty and the other girls. And your stuff on the *Leandro*. Why? Because they don't want evidence like that kicking around. So we can be pretty sure that we were right. Kitty was kidnapped and taken to Jerusalem Island on the *Leandro*. And she's there now. It's a logical deduction.'

'While you're on your great detective bit, you could come up with another deduction,' said Barr. 'They know now that we've come here after Kitty. They won't leave it at that. Somehow or other, they have to stop us pushing our enquiries. And judging from their track record, they won't be too gentle about it.'

'Well, there's no point in just sitting here on our backsides waiting for them to barge in!' said Vinnie aggressively. 'What do we do?'

Steve turned to Barr. 'When will your reinforcements get here?'

'In two days, maybe three.'

'We can't wait that long. The only real proof we'll have that they are holding Kitty is if we find Kitty herself. They might decide to destroy that proof. I wouldn't put it past them.'

'Kill her?' asked Vinnie, her eyes wide. 'You mean, they'd kill her?'

'Kill. Waste. Extinguish. Terminate,' said Barr. 'Whatever the word, the result will be the same. Finis.' He drew a finger across his throat. 'I'd like to get on that island and take a good look around. And I have an idea how to do it.'

'It should be me,' Steve said thoughtfully.

'Why?'

'Well,' said Steve uncertainly. 'In the first place, I brought you here. I got you into this.'

'We aren't in anything yet. In the second place?'

'Kitty is my girl, sort of.'

'Garbage. You wouldn't stand a chance over there on your own.'

'And you would?'

'I might. I've a shade more experience.'

'What about me?' asked Vinnie.

'Or me?' said Charlie.

'Not you, Charlie. Not this time. No offence, but you wouldn't really know what to look for. And it's no job for you, Vinnie,' said Barr.

'Male chauvinist snake,' said Vinnie.

'You mean pig, don't you?' said Charlie.

'No,' she snorted. 'I like pigs.'

'It has to be me. I should be the one,' said Steve. 'And after all —' He stopped, his face flushing a little, as if he had been about to say something of which he was ashamed.

'After all what?' asked Barr.

'Nothing.'

'You were going to pull rank on me. Right?'

'No,' Steve said awkwardly. 'Well, yes, in a kind of way. I was only going to say that someone has to make the decisions.'

'OK,' said Barr quietly. 'OK. Go ahead, boss. It's your show. Will you let us know when you're ready to dish out the orders?'

'I didn't mean it like that!' said Steve.

'Don't back down. You've made your point. Go ahead. Decide.'

'Gawd Almighty!' said Vinnie. 'Look at the pair of you! A couple of grown men buzzing at each other! Two blow-flies making the same noise! I've a mind to bang your heads together. Why don't you both go?'

'Yes,' said Steve, grasping the thought eagerly. 'Great! What about that?'

Vinnie turned to Barr, who was looking doubtful. 'Don't worry about us. I'll look after Charlie.'

'Thanks a lot,' said Charlie. 'I'm obliged.'

'Anytime,' she said.

'All right,' said Barr. 'We both go in. If we can work it. I told you, I've got an idea. If it doesn't pan out, we may have to find another way.'

'Great,' said Steve, 'great. Anything you say.'

'Don't push it too far,' said Barr drily.

A scream from outside interrupted them. It was Rose. She was standing on the paved drive just outside the front door, and Barr was the first to reach her.

She was staring up at the porch which screened the door, her eyes bulging. Someone had strung a freshly dead cockerel from an upper beam. Its throat had been cut and, as the cockerel swung gently on the rope, its blood dripped slowly to the ground. And on the flagstones before the door there was a crude but unmistakable circle of blood.

'They've started,' said Barr.

'What's it mean?' asked Vinnie.

'Voodoo,' said Barr.

'The sign of death,' said Rose in a hushed voice. 'The circle of the dead.'

'For a Christian community, they sure have some good old-fashioned pagan ideas,' said Steve.

'It happened like this – two nights before your uncle was drowned,' said Rose. 'It happened just the same way. The circle, the sacrifice, and the drumming.'

'Drumming?'

'All night. The drums. Beating all night.'

'Where there are drums there are people,' said Barr. 'And people are made of flesh and blood like you or Joe or any of us.'

He tore the chicken down and would have hurled it into the bushes, but Vinnie checked him.

'Don't do that! That's a fine chicken. Waste of good food to throw it away.' She pressed the bird's plump flanks approvingly. 'Plenty of meat there. It'll go down well with some roast potatoes and peas.'

'I couldn't cook that!' said Rose with a shudder.

'Don't worry, lovey,' said Vinnie, 'I will. We'll show them what they can do with their bloody voodoo, eh?' Holding the cockerel by the legs, she led the girl away.

'That young woman is scared,' said Steve.

'It goes deep,' said Charlie. 'My mother lived in England for thirty years and went to chapel twice on Sunday. But she still believed that the souls of the dead lived in the sea – a kind of purgatory. She believed that the music of the drums could summon the dead from the sea and then, after confessing their earthly sins to a *houngan*, they would ascend into paradise with the gods.'

'*Houngan?*' said Steve.

'A sort of priest. Half priest, half witchdoctor.' Charlie looked down at the circle of blood. 'Circles come into it a lot. So do cockerels. It goes back centuries – to Africa. Voodoo comes from *vodum*, an African word. The slaves brought these ceremonies and beliefs with them, and they've been handed down from generation to generation.'

'He's not just a pretty face,' said Steve admiringly.

'He's not even a pretty face,' said Barr.

'My father was a schoolmaster,' said Charlie shyly. 'An educated man. He made a study of voodoo. I think the fact that my mother was still touched by it led him on. He was going to write a book, but he never got round to it. Now it's too late. He's dead. And I'm a fighter. An ex-fighter. I haven't got the brains to pick it up from where he left off.'

'You underestimate yourself,' said Barr. 'You're no zombie.'

Charlie touched the crimson circle with the toe of his shoe, scuffing a line across it.

'Don't take it too light,' he said softly. 'It may seem like a load of old rubbish to us, but to some people it's powerful stuff. What happened today – all this – is a warning. They've put a sort of curse on this house and the people in it.' He shook his head and said again, 'Don't take it too light.'

Barr heard the sound just before midnight.

From the velvet darkness of the West Indian night, beyond the perimeter fence, there came the steady, strident beat of drums and an insistent flow of rhythmic sound began to invade the house. At first, it was quite beautiful, especially when the tenor drums took over with a soft sweet throbbing which floated like haunted music on the scented air: but after a while even this grated and the relentless beat began to irritate the nerves.

Voices began to mix in with the drumming; chanting voices, mocking voices, voices that screamed as if in terrible anguish. It was impossible to shut out the sound, it was impossible not to listen.

A feeling of menace, like a shadow, began to slide across the house. And curiously, although the night was warm and remained so, an odd chill touched Barr's flesh so that he was at once sweating and shivering like a man with fever.

Angry with himself for this show of weakness, he went along to Steve's room, and found him standing by the open window, listening.

'What do you make of it?' asked Barr.

'It's coming from out there, beyond the gates. But I can't see any lights, can't see anything.' He turned to Barr. 'It's odd. You can rationalise it all you like, but it does get through. Eerie.' He shivered. 'Do you feel the cold?'

'Drums can drive people half crazy,' said Barr. 'I've seen it happen.' He moved towards the door. 'Get some dark clothes on and meet me in the kitchen. We'll take a closer look at this orchestra.'

They slipped out through the back door and Barr led the way into the shrubs which lay beyond the tiny yard. The scent of jasmine and bay hung sweetly in the night air, and beneath their feet the earth seemed to quiver with life. A small dark creature emerged from beneath a silver-leafed shrub, blinked at them with bright glittering eyes, and scuttled off into the darkness.

And over all this, the drums throbbed on, settling now into a steady, monotonous, wearing beat.

Barr bent down, picked up a handful of the soft earth and smeared his face and hands. He indicated that Steve should do the same, and then he moved through the garden, round to the front of the house, keeping a pace or two ahead of Steve. He skirted the drive, holding to the protection of the trees and shrubs, until they reached the perimeter fence about a hundred yards from the house.

Beyond the fence there was a narrow dirt lane and on the other side a stretch of uneven land known as Fitzwilliam Point. Two centuries before, this had been the site of a thriving sugar plantation, owned by a British colonist called Fitzwilliam whose brutality towards his slaves had passed into island legend. During the day the neglected land, long returned to pasture, was used for grazing: but at night many of the natives were careful to avoid it for they believed that, at certain times, the shades of executed slaves came back to roam the plantation.

The ruins of the old Fitzwilliam house had been removed in 1951 to make way for Tradewinds. In the hollow, a few stones and a crumbling wall, almost covered by hibiscus, were the only reminder of the slave quarters. Sturdiest of all, the old sugar mill remained almost intact, standing like an ancient defensive tower on Fitzwilliam Point itself.

They climbed the fence and crossed the road into the darkness beyond. Barr gripped his companion's arm, and they paused, listening. The drumming was as insistent as ever, but louder now.

'It's coming from down there,' whispered Barr.

He led the way towards the sound, moving parallel to the road. To Steve, trying to keep up, the man seemed to have a sixth sense, the sixth sense of the hunter that can pick up unseen obstacles and avoid them, or hear sounds which are beyond the reach of the untrained ear.

With each pace the drumming grew louder. And again, from time to time, the voices joined in with a steady hypnotic chanting and an occasional soaring scream that prickled the flesh. The drums and the drummers could not now be more than a few yards away, but there were still no lights, no visible sign of their presence. Barr checked again, and waited for Steve to come up with him.

'There,' he said. 'In there somewhere.'

He pointed forward and Steve dimly made out the shape of trees and shrubs bunched together in a small copse. He expected to see the flicker of torchlight through the trees, but there was nothing, only the darkness reverberating with sound. Barr slid forward again, head down, body tense, until he reached the outer ring of trees and waited once more for the other man to join him.

They seemed to be on top of the drumming now, almost at the heart of it. Still no sign. Barr edged forward and carefully parted the branches of a thickly growing shrub.

'The bastards!' he murmured.

Steve peered through the dark foliage and slowly his eyes took in the shape of the object. He was aware of an extraordinary sense of anti-climax. There were no drummers, no drums, no glistening bodies dancing themselves into a frenzy, no sacrificial cockerels.

Only an old dark blue truck with two ancient cone-shaped amplifiers fixed to its roof, amplifiers which were hurling the beat of the drums into the night. Steve blinked and dabbed at his face as the salty sweat teased his eyes.

Barr waited for what seemed to be a long time before moving. He made signs to Steve to indicate that he was going to get round to the other side of the truck and then he was gone, disappearing silently into the trees. Steve ducked through the shrubs, edging nearer to the truck and waited. He could now see a narrow slit of light separating the rear doors, and a dullish glow up front, in the cab of the truck. By moving a little nearer, and to the right, he was able to distinguish the faint outline of a man sitting behind the steering wheel.

He felt something beneath his foot and, reaching down, picked up a heavy club-like branch. He weighed it in his hand, gaining comfort from the thought that now he had some kind of weapon.

He wondered where Barr was and felt a brief twinge of irritation. He presumed that he was supposed to move in, co-ordinating his actions with those of Barr, but there was no way of telling. And for an equally brief moment he wondered at the strange circumstance which had brought him, in only a few days, from the cold bustle of the London streets to this weird, dark place on a Caribbean island.

The drums were still sounding as violently as before, but now they had lost their meaning; he was only angry that for a while back there, they had taken possession of a part of his mind, even given him the illusion of cold.

Where was Barr?

A whistle gave the answer, a low whistle that could be clearly heard below the drum beat. He saw Barr emerge for a moment by the front of the truck and moved in a crouch towards him.

'All clear this side,' whispered Barr. 'One man in the cab and there must be at least one other in the back with the equipment. We'll take the one up front first.'

He eased his way towards the door. Steve saw him flex a hand and then, in two lightning-swift movements, Barr swung the door open, reached in, and pulled the astonished man to the ground. As he fell, the man rolled over and a hand went to his belt, to a knife. Steve stamped a foot on his wrist, and then Barr was on the man, twisting him round, pulling his arm up in a vicious lock at the same time as he dropped a knee into the small of his back and thrust his face hard into the soft earth.

Barr held him thus for a full twenty seconds, listening. The beat of the drums continued and there was no movement from the interior of the van. Barr signalled to Steve to give him the knife and, still holding the arm-lock, he dug the point into the wall of the man's throat. The man jerked convulsively and gave a muffled cry of pain.

'Make a sound and you're dead!' Barr hissed. Then he looked up at Steve and smiled. 'I've always wanted to say that.'

He released his hold and the man rolled over, staring up at Barr with frightened, rolling eyes. He was young and black, dressed in a shirt-jacket and jeans. A trickle of blood flowed from the side of his neck. Barr put the knife to his jugular and the man cringed back.

'How many in the truck?' asked Barr, and twitched the knife.

'One.' The answer came in a terrified gulp. And when Barr pressed a little harder, it was repeated in a faint fearful squeak. 'One.'

'Armed?'

'He got a gun. A hand gun.'

'Up. Up. On your feet.'

He jerked the young black to his feet and pushed him towards Steve. 'Hold him.'

Steve renewed the arm-lock and Barr moved round to the back of the truck. He stood listening for a moment and then signalled that the prisoner should be brought to him.

'Listen,' said Barr. 'Listen good. This is what you're going to do. You're going to open that door and call your friend out. What's his name?'

'I call him Eddie.'

'Is he the boss?'

'Yes. I'm just the driver, honest. He hired my truck.'

'OK. Now, you open that door very slow and casual and you tell your boss Eddie he'd better step down and take a look, you think maybe somebody is coming. Got that?'

'My Jesus, Jesus, I do that, he gonna kill me!'

'Take your choice. If he doesn't I will. OK?'

'OK.'

Barr turned to Steve and whispered. 'Go up front, in the cab. There's just a canvas flap between that and the interior. I'll give you a count of twenty. I'll have sonny-boy now. And we'll swop. I'll take the timber, you take the knife.'

'What for?'

'Don't argue man. Do it.'

Steve exchanged the prisoner and the club for the knife and moved forward. Barr waited, counting silently. When he was ready, he released his hold on the trembling prisoner and pushed him towards the doors. Barr moved up and waited to one side, club at the ready.

The man paused and in the little spill of light from the interior, Barr could see the sweat glistening on his nose. Then, with a swift look at Barr, he swung the doors open and the light flooded out. He blinked and said tentatively, 'Eddie.' And again. 'Eddie.'

'What is it?'

'I think you'd better come out, Eddie, I think maybe somebody is coming.'

'What are you talking about?'

The unseen man moved forward, partially blocking the stream of light, which by now was swarming with flying insects. And then, suddenly, as if taking courage from the fact that Barr no longer held the knife, the driver shouted a warning.

'Watch it, Eddie. It's a trick, a trap. There's —'

He did not finish the sentence. Barr swung the club viciously and although the man ducked and tried to shield his head with his arms, the blow struck home on the side of the neck, just below the ear. He staggered and half fell and, as he did so, Barr hit him again. The club splintered and broke under the impact but this time the man dropped and lay silent.

Steve, coming through from the cab, heard the noise of this encounter. He also saw a holstered automatic lying on a shelf beside an array of recording and amplifying equipment. A tape was turning slowly on an ancient recorder. The man called Eddie, backing off into the interior of the truck, half turned and grabbed the gun, and as he did so, he saw Steve.

Tugging the automatic from the holster he let off a wild shot which drilled a hole in the roof. Steve, plunging forward, caught his foot in a jagged tear in the canvas screen and fell headlong, dropping the knife. A second and more accurate shot cut through the canvas at the point where his head had been a moment before. The trip proved to be fortuitous in another sense, for Steve managed to convert it into what turned out to be a classic tackle: his arms circled the other man just below the waist and he brought him down with a crash that shook the truck and caused the tape to stutter.

As he fell, Eddie caught the side of his head against a large can of gasolene which was held in position by a wooden cradle and a piece of rope, and he lay still long enough for Steve to pick up the gun and scramble to his feet.

'Turn that bloody thing off!' shouted Barr.

Steve searched for the stop switch and found it at last. There was a sudden sharp silence, a silence that was almost as thunderous as the earlier drumming and then, as their ears grew accustomed to it, the vacuum was filled with the buzz and whine of thousands of insects and an occasional louder night noise from the darkness outside.

'That was a beautiful tackle. Perfect timing,' said Barr.

'It seemed the only thing to do,' Steve said modestly.

'Give me that roll of flex and the knife. You keep an eye on this one while I tie mine up.'

Steve took a roll of flex from a hook and passed this to Barr together with the knife. The man on the floor of the truck groaned and sat up. Blood was pouring from his nose and there was a developing bruise on his temple. He was young and white, dressed in an olive-green combat uniform.

'Stay there,' said Steve. 'Don't move. Here – catch this.' He took a dirty swab from the table and tossed it to his prisoner, who pressed it carefully to his nose. He winced as he did so and said in a tone of genuine anguish, 'I think it's broken. My nose. It's broken.'

'I could cry for you,' said Steve. 'Big tears.'

Barr scrambled back up into the truck. A half empty flask of rum

127

lay on the shelf next to the recorder and, rubbing the rim on his shirt, he took a long swig.

'Better,' he said, 'much better. Now, let's take a look at friend Eddie.'

He grasped the seated man's thick hair and jerked his head backwards. Eddie gave a grunt of pain but his eyes, as he glared at Barr, glowed with hatred.

'Well, well,' said Barr. He glanced at Steve with a smile. 'A good night this. I'm getting to say all the right things. This is the point in movies where the good guy says to the bad guy – Ah, so we meet again! Or is it the other way round?'

'You know him?'

'Know old Eddie? Of course I know Eddie. We're old friends, aren't we, Eddie?'

The man grunted and Barr jerked his hair a little harder. 'I'm speaking to you. Where are your manners? Answer when I speak to you.'

Eddie spat contemptuously, a stream of spittle flecked with blood landing on the floor near Steve's feet. Barr released him and handed Steve the rest of the flex: he took the gun and thrust it into his belt.

'Tie him up good. He's one of the bastards we met at J. D. Winston's office. Which explains almost everything.' He looked at Eddie and shook his head. 'Your bosses must be slipping! Did they really think they could frighten us off with this bloody rubbish?'

Steve bound the prisoner's wrists behind his back and was about to tie off when Barr stopped him. 'No, that's no good. Take a loop round his neck as well, and pull down hard. It's tougher to get out of, and it is also more painful.'

'Next time —' muttered Eddie viciously, but the words were cut off as the flex bit into his throat and Steve pulled the end tight.

The trussed man was bundled from the truck and set down beside his partner, who was bound in a similar manner. Barr checked the flex and nodded. 'All right. You can start walking back to St John's. You should make it by morning. Move!'

The black prisoner, needing no second bidding, started off at once, stumbling forward. The man called Eddie waited, glaring at Barr defiantly.

'Ah, I'm glad you stayed, Eddie,' said Barr. 'I forgot something. Hold him a moment, will you, Steve?'

Steve pinioned the young man, while Barr removed his socks, sandals, and trousers. Eddie struggled violently, kicking out in protest, but the job was done eventually and Barr stood back.

'Lovely. You'll enjoy the walk and the mosquitos will enjoy you. Now, get moving or I'll strip you right off, underpants and all!'

With a last malevolent look, Eddie turned and marched off into the darkness. He tried to maintain his defiance to the last, but after a few yards he tripped and fell. They heard him curse as he struggled to his feet.

'Now,' Barr said. 'Let's have a bonfire, shall we?'

It was the work of a few minutes to douse the truck, inside and out, with the gasolene. Barr tossed a flaming rag into the interior and, standing back, they watched the flames climb and take hold. There was an explosion as the fire reached the tank, bits of the truck were hurled into the night, and a column of red and yellow flame shot upwards.

When they got back to the house, Charlie was waiting with Joe Bradshaw and Rose.

'What happened?' he asked anxiously.

'Nothing,' said Barr. 'We just fancied a walk.'

'Where's Vinnie?' asked Steve.

'I haven't seen her since she went to bed.'

'We'd better check,' said Steve.

He went with Barr to Vinnie's room. She was fast asleep, but when Steve switched on the light she stirred and opened her eyes.

'What is it?' she murmured.

'Are you all right?' asked Steve.

'I was until you buggers woke me up!'

'Didn't you hear the drums?'

She blinked at them. 'What bloody drums?'

Steve grinned at Barr. Then he switched off the light and closed the door gently behind them.

Chapter Ten

Dr Christa Bauer had hardly slept for two nights. She had lain in her bed, half awake, her mind tormented by a flow of thoughts mixed with fearsome dreams and it was all so vivid that she could scarcely tell the difference between the illusion and the reality. She roused herself each morning in a state of complete mental and physical exhaustion.

She had gone to great pains to avoid Gunnar and, to her relief, he had made no move to talk to her or to pursue their previous brief conversation. In her heart, she knew that she could not put it off much longer: a decision had to be reached. She felt torn between her deep loyalty to the Community and, above all, to Mr Dunlop, and her increasing concern about recent developments.

It was impossible to believe that Mr Dunlop would allow the high ideals of the Community to be tarnished: yet the evidence of growing corruption was there for all to see. Indeed, to her shame, she had allowed herself to be drawn into the process, partly from fear of the consequences of refusal and partly out of loyalty.

How insidious it all was, she thought.

In her green youth she had been drawn, for a brief time, to the ideas of Marx and Lenin and it seemed to her now that there was a striking parallel between what had happened in Soviet Russia and what was happening to the Community.

In Russia, the idealism and sacrifice of millions of workers and peasants had overthrown one tyranny headed by the Tsar, only to find it replaced by another, headed by Stalin. Many thousands of good, decent Russians must have had their doubts about what was happening to their beloved revolution, but out of fear of the Party or loyalty to it, they had accepted the changes, believing that one day all would come right. But that day did not come: inch by inch the old ideals were eroded until little or nothing of them was left. And by that time, the people themselves had changed: they had either become willing allies of the régime, enjoying the material benefits of the élite, or declined into embittered passivity.

It wasn't so far away, she thought, from what was happening on Jerusalem Island. Little by little, the whole experiment was changing, turning gradually into its opposite. The island, which was to have been a symbol of liberty, equality and fraternity, was beginning to look more and more like a concentration camp. An élite, led by the Comptroller, held the power of life or death over a people whose only task was to labour. She was a Founder, part of that élite: she had gone along with the Comptroller, accepting his decrees, stifling her

130

doubts. And in that process she had felt herself, seen herself, change. She had condoned measures which, two or three years ago, would have been unthinkable, unacceptable. Soon, it would have gone too far, there would be no going back, either for her or the Community. Perhaps it was already too late to reverse the march of corruption and violence, she thought sombrely.

And then, suddenly, in the middle of the third night, the solution came to her and she wondered why she had not thought of it before. It was clear, crystal clear, that Mr Dunlop knew nothing of what was happening. He had world-wide responsibilities which often took him away from the island for lengthy periods and which, together with his spiritual responsibilities, absorbed all his time. He was possessed of remarkable energy, but even he could not supervise everything. It was obvious that he trusted the Comptroller and was content to leave the day-to-day administration of Jerusalem Island in his hands.

She would go to see him, she would get in to see him somehow. That was the solution! And then she would pour it all out, explain everything to him, make him understand what was happening. The Comptroller, no doubt, would deny everything but the evidence was all on her side. She could show Mr Dunlop the hunger and weariness of the people, show him the Beach of Pleasure, show him children who had been savagely beaten, show him what happened at the Lagoon with the so-called Terminal Experience.

This decision gave her new life and energy: she felt purged of doubt and guilt, no longer torn by conflicting loyalties. In this mood of hope, she spoke to Gunnar, saying proudly, 'Today I am going to see Mr Dunlop!'

'You have been called before him?' he asked. There was a note of alarm in his voice.

'No, no. I am going to demand an audience. It is the only way.' She lowered her voice. 'Gunnar, I know how you feel about some of the things that are happening. I – in many ways – I share your apprehension. But Mr Dunlop doesn't know, I'm certain of that. He has so many things on his mind, he leaves the running of the Community to the Comptroller. Once he knows, he will stop these excesses. Do you understand what I am saying?'

'Have you forgotten,' said Gunnar, 'have you forgotten that everything done in the Community is done on Mr Dunlop's instructions?'

'Done in his name,' she cried triumphantly. 'Done in his name but without his knowledge. Gunnar, you know him, you have read his teachings. Do you think it conceivable that such a man would lend his authority to some of the things that have been happening?'

He hesitated and, in the end, avoided the question. Instead, he said, 'The Comptroller will never allow you to see him.'

'He dare not refuse,' she said firmly. 'I am a Founder, I have the right.'

'Don't go. Please. I beg you,' he pleaded.

'Why not?'

'It is too dangerous. If you make an enemy of the Comptroller —'

'I think I may have done that already,' she replied, and added impatiently, 'I thought you would understand. I thought you would agree that something ought to be done.'

'Not this way,' he said.

'How else?'

'There are others who feel as you do.' He spoke carefully, choosing his words. 'People in various parts of the island. You are not alone.'

'That is treason!' she said in a shocked voice.

'Treason? Because they think the same thoughts as you, share the same doubts?'

'My loyalty is to Mr Dunlop! I owe everything to him – as you do.'

'He was a good man,' said Gunnar carefully. 'But even good people can change.'

'It seems to me,' she said sternly, 'that you need another term of service with the Waverers! The last one doesn't seem to have done you much good!'

And at this moment, as if on cue, a peal of organ music came flooding through the fixed amplifiers, followed by the voice of an announcer: 'Stand by, brothers and sisters, for a special message from our beloved Teacher and Leader, Mr Dunlop.'

They looked at each other, guiltily, as though caught out in an act of treachery. Nowadays, a speech or a message from Mr Dunlop was a rare occurrence. The Doctor felt herself trembling: as always the mention of his name or the sound of his voice filled her with love, a love that in its pure ecstacy was almost unbearable.

'Good morning, brothers, sisters, children,' said Mr Dunlop, 'good morning. Hello to you all. Now, listen, listen. Put aside whatever you may be doing, will you? These next few moments belong to God. I'm asking you to join with me in prayer and worship. Let us link our hands together, wherever we may be, and start this new day, God's new day, with love. That shouldn't be too difficult, should it?'

The voice, though deep and resonant, had none of the tricks of the ordinary preacher, no calculated rise and fall, no artificial smooth-ness, no hint of condescension. The tone, if anything, was casual, and even in these few opening words the speaker managed to convey the impression that he was talking not to a group but to each person as an individual.

The organ began to play once more, the sound swelling into the music of the hymn, *O Happy Band of Pilgrims*. A recorded chorus took up the words: not a choir, but a vast gathering of voices, an assembly of people singing naturally at the pitch of their voices. When this faded, Mr Dunlop spoke again.

'My brothers, my sisters, my children, I will not keep you from your daily tasks for long. For as we all know, labour is the highest tribute we can pay to God. He gave us the earth and the trees and by our labour we multiply the fruit of the trees and increase the bounty of the earth. My message to you this morning is brief, but serious. You all know that we have enemies. Satanic enemies who would destroy what we have built here. In the past, these enemies have operated from outside – and they still do. They are powerful, tenacious, evil. But do no concern yourselves with them – I have seen to it that they will never succeed. But now I have to tell you, with regret, that we have another kind of enemy, an enemy who operates from within, an insidious Satanic enemy who works like a rat in the darkness, gnawing away at the faith and the ideals which are the foundation of our Community. This morning I want to draw your attention to these agents of Satan, and ask you to join with me in exposing them and destroying them.'

There was a pause and then the voice began slowly to gather pace and to throb as though in anguish.

'Who is this enemy? How shall you recognise him? I will tell you. He is the grumbler. He is the complainer. He is the cheat who skimps his work. He is the peacock who thinks he is too good to labour in the vineyard. He is the waverer. He is the ingrate who forgets that the Community has given him new life. He is the liar, the slanderer, who whispers falsehoods and questions our achievements. All these are the servants of Satan, agents of the Devil! Be on your guard, brothers and sisters! Expose these enemies! We are under threat and the time has come for vigilance, for revolutionary vigilance. Tolerance comes naturally to the human heart, but it is a luxury we can no longer afford. Remember this – I gathered you out of many countries and brought you here into your own land. I have pledged my life to our Community and I would sooner lose that life than see our work destroyed. My arm is long, my eyes are everywhere, and I tell you, I shall be ruthless in defence of our dear Jerusalem. Let the Bible speak for us all:

Mine eyes shall be upon the faithful of the land, that they may dwell with me:
He that walketh in a perfect way, he shall minister unto me.
He that worketh deceit shall not dwell within my house:
He that speaketh falsehood shall not be established before mine eyes.
Morning by morning will I destroy all the wicked of the land;
To cut off all the workers of iniquity from the City of the Lord.'

The voice rose to a sobbing scream on the last words and then there was a short tense silence. Finally, in a tone that was subdued, humble, he said simply, 'I am sorry about that. Sorry to burden you. But it had to be said. Brothers, sisters, children, I ask you now to join with me in the Lord's Prayer. And remember this, never forget this. I embrace you, I hold each one of you in my arms. I love you.'

Gunnar and the Doctor spoke the prayer clearly, even fervently, and when it was finished she felt tears glittering in her eyes.

'Now,' she said, 'now do you see why I must go to him?' And when he did not answer, she went on, 'To explain. To make him understand that some complaints are justified, that people are restless because terrible things are being done in his name.'

He nodded. His mind was clouded, he found it difficult to think clearly. Part of him was still pulled towards Mr Dunlop: reason had been set aside and he was still held, despite himself, in the spell cast by that throbbing voice.

'Go if you must,' he said. 'And good luck – for all our sakes.'

'This,' said Sister Eleanor, in a reverential tone, 'this is the Comptroller.'

She touched Kitty's arm and the girl glided gracefully towards the desk. Her face was pale and set in a fixed look, her wide green eyes glittered strangely, as though touched by frost. When she was within a few feet of the Comptroller she stopped, inclining her head and shoulders in a respectful bow. She did not lift her eyes until he spoke.

'Excellent,' he said, 'excellent!'

'This girl is healed, Comptroller,' said Sister Eleanor fervently. 'From the top of her head to the tip of her toes, she has been renewed.'

'Thank you, Lord, thank you, Lord Jesus.' He intoned the words like a prayer.

'Satan has been driven out, the evil has gone from her flesh. In mind and body, she is ready to serve the true faith.'

'Thank you, Lord, thank you, Lord Jesus,' he said in the same chanting fashion. And then, in a more matter-of-fact tone, he continued, 'A remarkable result, in a very short time, Sister.'

'It often happens that way, Comptroller. The ones who are naturally resistant, who have strength of spirit and intelligence, are usually the first to respond.'

'Respond?'

'To the healing process. To concede that they have been wrong, to accept the teachings of our Community. Tell the Comptroller what you believe, Kitty.'

'I believe in the Community of New Jerusalem, and in Mr Dunlop our Teacher and Leader. I offer my soul and body to the Community,

134

and ask only that I may serve obediently, without question, so long as I am considered worthy.'

The girl's voice was low and humble, and she spoke quickly, mechanically, as though reciting a lesson learned by heart. When she had finished, she glanced anxiously at Sister Eleanor as though fearful that she may have got it wrong.

But Sister Eleanor beamed her approval, and patted Kitty's shoulder reassuringly.

'She has not been drugged?' asked the Comptroller.

'No, Comptroller, I assure you not. On the first day I did use Electrical Impulse Therapy for a short time, to help break down the resistance. After that, there was little or no problem. She was fairly co-operative and anxious to learn. I am sure that when Dr Bauer carries out the tests and makes the final assessment —'

'That will not be necessary!' said the Comptroller sharply. 'Dr Bauer has been assigned to other duties.'

'As you say, Comptroller. In this case, I am sure that we can dispense with the final assessment.'

He nodded, and turned to Kitty. 'Remove your robe.'

Her hesitation was only momentary and then she pulled aside her loose white robe, letting it fall between her feet and the desk, and stood before him naked. He studied her impassively, his eyes moving from the firm, lightly tanned breasts to the smooth rounded whiteness of her stomach and thighs. He moved round and surveyed her from the back in the same way. She trembled slightly as he ran a finger down from her shoulders to her buttocks but made no sound. The bracelets on his wrist jingled as he drew his hand away.

'Beautiful,' he breathed, 'beautiful.' Then, more sharply, 'Cover yourself, my child.'

As Kitty retrieved the gown and put it on again, he moved aside with Sister Eleanor. Kitty watched them with heavy eyes, her back to the desk, her left hand groping behind her.

'You are sure about this one?' the Comptroller asked, in a low voice.

'Quite sure, Comptroller,' said Sister Eleanor.

'In such a short time?'

'She was with Dr Bauer for some weeks. The process of disorientation was well advanced. It made my task that much easier. Of course, if you would like me to continue with her for perhaps another week —'

'No. No. I have a particular reason for wanting her absorbed without delay. So long as you can assure me that there is no possibility of a relapse —'

'If she is kept isolated from all outside, alien influences, there will be no danger of that.'

135

'You are prepared to take the responsibility?'

She hesitated briefly. 'Of course, Comptroller.'

'Good. Excellent.' He moved back to Kitty and said, in a louder sonorous voice, 'I see in this girl, in this our new Sister, the power of the Lord. I feel his strength working in her. He who made her beautiful has reached down in his mercy and healed her. Her soul is cleansed, and her beauty is now whole. Oh, it is at such moments, Sister Eleanor, that I feel truly humble. I give thanks to Mr Dunlop, our Teacher, for calling me to God's service.'

'Amen!' whispered Sister Eleanor. 'Amen!'

He put a hand on Kitty's shoulder and looked into her eyes, smiling. 'Oh, you are privileged, Sister, so privileged! You have joined us in a great work. By your service and your beauty you will enrich our Community, and you, in turn, will know the happiness that follows love, the joy that comes from fulfilment.'

He dropped his hand and turned to Sister Eleanor and now his fleshy face creased into a thoughtful frown. 'Kitty,' he said, weighing the name, 'Kitty. It won't do, it isn't right. Have you any ideas?'

'I hadn't thought, Comptroller.' She stammered guiltily, as though she had been reproved.

'No, no. It doesn't sit right, it doesn't sound right. Sister Kitty – no, no, no, no.' He walked a pace or two, and then his face brightened. 'Helen! That's it! Sister Helen! Helen! Beauty to match beauty! Of course. What say you to that?'

'Excellent, Comptroller, excellent,' said Sister Eleanor. 'So much more – so much more suitable. Excellent.'

'Helen.' He faced Kitty again. 'Do you like that, Sister? Do you like that name?'

'Yes, thank you,' she said quietly, without expression.

'Then it shall be yours! And it is apt, after all. Kitty, the old Kitty is dead, slain by the right hand of the Lord. And in her place we have you, our new and beloved Sister Helen!' He raised his arms and seemed almost beside himself with pleasure as he intoned:

'Helen, whose beauty summoned Greece to arms,
And drew a thousand ships to Tenedos!'

He looked at the two women for a moment, smiling, and then, as if remembering himself, lowered his arms and went to his desk. When he looked up he was frowning again like a spoiled child, and his voice was peevish: 'She doesn't smile, Sister Eleanor, she doesn't smile! And she hardly speaks!'

'That will come, Comptroller,' said the woman hastily. 'She is tired, naturally she is a little tired.'

'See that she is rested. And tomorrow morning take her to the High Place for the induction.'

'Certainly, Comptroller.'

'God go with you, Sister Helen,' he said sharply, watching the girl.

She inclined her head respectfully and backed away. As she turned and went out, she kept her left hand in the pocket of the robe, tightly clutching the dagger-shaped paper-knife she had taken from the desk.

The jeep soon left the smooth new road and headed towards the west of Jerusalem Island along a rough stony track. The driver scarcely altered speed and the jeep, which had seen better days, bounced and rattled over the rutted surface.

Dr Christa Bauer, sitting in the back, was not conscious of discomfort. Her mind was still in a state of shock, her flesh crawled with the fear of what was to come.

It had all happened so quickly. An hour before she had been standing in the Comptroller's office, demanding as was her right as a Founder, an audience with Mr Dunlop. The Comptroller had been suave and even sympathetic but he had refused her request. His words rattled like bones in her head.

'I am sorry, Doctor. You know how it is. Mr Dunlop's day is fully taken up, there is simply no time.'

'Tomorrow then?'

'Tomorrow he has to entertain an important visiting delegation. I really am sorry. Can you not tell me the problem?'

'I must see Mr Dunlop personally.'

'Do you not trust me?'

'That's not the point.'

'Then what is the point, Doctor? Mr Dunlop is an incredible man, but he is human. He carries a giant's burden on his shoulders. It is my task to save him as much as possible, to preserve him for his wider tasks. I don't want him bothered by petty complaints —'

'Petty! How can you possibly suggest —'

And then the Doctor checked, realising that she had walked into the very trap she had been determined to avoid. The Comptroller continued smoothly, as though unaware of her agitation, 'I am sure Mr Dunlop would be delighted to see you if his calendar would allow it. You must know that he has a special place in his heart for you. Why, only last night he was speaking of you, expressing his concern.'

'Concern?'

'He is concerned for us all, isn't that so? It is remarkable, quite astonishing. He seems to know each man, woman and child in the Community. And more than that, he knows what they are thinking, what is in their hearts and minds. Extraordinary.'

'Why would he speak of me, why should he be especially concerned for me?'

'He knows that you are tired, Doctor. You have been working hard,

137

perhaps too hard. As I think I said the other day when we spoke together, the trouble is that we seldom understand our own needs. We become so immersed in our work that we fail to perceive the need for renewal.'

She felt a sudden icy surge of fear. 'I assure you that I am in good health —'

'Of course, of course. But Mr Dunlop was not thinking of physical health. No, no. To put it in a nutshell, he believes that you need a change, Doctor. A spell with the Regeneration Experience.'

'No!'

'Come, Doctor. You admitted yourself that the three days you spent on the Clearance Project at Morgan's Bay helped you enormously.'

'I do not need —'

'Are you saying that you know better than Mr Dunlop?'

'No, of course not. But —'

'Then it is settled. Mr Dunlop wishes you to join the Regeneration Experience immediately. It will be for twelve weeks. A wonderful opportunity, Doctor. The vital one-to-one relationship with the earth – you will return to us enriched. I envy you, I envy you.'

She had tried to argue, even plead with the Comptroller, but to no avail. Two of the Guardians had driven her back to the hospital, where she was allowed fifteen minutes to pack a few personal things. She had seen Gunnar briefly and told him in a whisper, 'They are sending me away.'

'Away?'

'The Regeneration Experience.'

'To Hawkins Bay?'

'I don't know.'

In a hurried whisper he said, 'If you are sent there, look out for a man named Roberts. He has a number – they all have numbers. His is K31. Number K31. He will help you.'

One of the Guardians had ordered Gunnar out before anything more could be said, and five minutes later she was on her way.

Her heart contracted as the jeep reached the top of a rise and began the descent towards Hawkins Bay. A team of men and women were at work on the scrawny and desolate land, levering roots and boulders from the earth and carrying them to the edge of the plantation where others were building a wall. As the jeep passed they looked up, their faces gaunt with exhaustion. Some of them straightened up, staring curiously, and a few managed a tired wave. She noticed that a number was prominently displayed on the back of each coarse green working tunic.

Below, the Doctor could see the encampment itself, a group of long, low huts surrounded by a white picket fence. At first sight, it looked harmless enough, even pleasant: the huts were freshly painted, there were a few trees – chinaberry, lemon and mango – and around each hut and on either side of the gateway she saw clumps of flowering shrubs. In the centre of an arch which spanned the gateway there was a boldly lettered sign which read: 'LABOUR WITH YOUR HANDS AND YOUR HEART AND YOU SHALL KNOW JOY.' Mr Dunlop.

The Doctor was set down just inside the gate, where a young woman greeted her with the ritual salute. Then, smiling, she took the Doctor's face in her hands and said, 'Welcome, Sister, welcome.'

The jeep went back the way it had come and the Doctor was led to a large hut which stood apart from the others. On the door was the single word, SUPERVISOR. Here the young woman handed her over in turn to the attentions of a thin, balding, sharp-faced man who sat behind a desk in a small office.

'Welcome, Sister,' he said, with a small, cold smile. 'Welcome.' He licked a finger and began to turn the pages of a thick register. 'Name?'

'Dr Christa Bauer.'

He looked up at her and sighed, shaking his head. 'No, no. *Sister* Christa Bauer. Here, we have no professional titles, no such nonsense. We are all here to renew ourselves by labour and as such we are all equal.' He wrote her name in the book, repeating it aloud, and adding the date, then he looked up at her again. 'While you are here, you will bear a number. You will be known by that number and you will use it always.' Once again, his face lifted in that small chilling smile. 'Don't be alarmed by that, and don't read too much into it. It is simply that here, of our own free will, we agree to renounce our individuality. It is important. It levels us all, you understand. Your number will be C121. Would you please repeat that?'

'C121,' she said woodenly.

'Excellent. Now, come with me.' He stood up and rapped on a door marked PRIVATE. As he did so, the Doctor noticed that he, too, wore a number on his tunic. A voice from within, a deep male voice, replied, 'Come in.'

He opened the door and the sound of music reached their ears. Without moving further he said in a tone of deep respect, 'The new Volunteer has arrived, Supervisor.'

'Ah, send her in.'

He stood aside, motioned to the Doctor to enter, and then withdrew, closing the door behind him. She found herself in a long, pleasant room; the furnishings were new and modern, and bowls of flowers stood on the table and the desk. The windows were open and a gentle cooling breeze from the sea brushed her face. The music, which she now recognised as Brahms' Piano Concerto No 2, came from a rosewood cabinet near the desk.

Smiling, the Supervisor got up and came towards her. 'Welcome, Sister, welcome.' He took both her hands in his and shook them warmly: she was too stunned and bewildered to resist, or to answer him. He was a large cheerful man, with a mane of white hair, bright twinkling eyes, plump brick-red cheeks and a wide, generous mouth. He beamed into her eyes and said teasingly, 'You don't recognise me?'

She looked at him more closely, trying to place the face, and eventually her reluctant memory came up with part of the answer at least.

'You were in the hospital?'

'That's right!' He laughed. 'Go on.'

'About two years ago. You had a kidney stone – something like that.'

'Exactly right. It was a kidney stone. I was in great agony. You gave me morphine to relieve the pain and you told me that I would almost certainly need an operation.' He laughed again. 'But I fooled you, Doctor. During the night I passed the stone. It hurt like the devil, but it was better than an operation. Now, do you remember all that?'

'Yes. Yes, I do.'

He had been thinner then, and his hair shorter, but she recalled him now. He was an Englishman, Vincent Hemmings, who at one time had been in charge of the British Chapter of the Community. He had a great reputation as an evangelist and she had heard him spoken of as a possible successor to Mr Dunlop. At one time, if not now, he had certainly been associated with the higher councils of the Community.

'What are you doing here?' she asked.

'I am like you, I came as a Volunteer.'

'I did not volunteer!' she said sharply.

'Ah! Then you were sent because you did not recognise the need in yourself. It happens that way sometimes.'

'The need for what?'

'Renewal. The renewal that can only come when we go back to the very beginning and bend our backs in harmony with the earth. When we shake off the debris of so-called civilisation. There is joy and fulfil-ment in such labour, Sister. Oh, it will be hard for you at first, I don't disguise that fact. We have a strict régime here, we work like peasants from dawn to dusk. We live on the simplest food. There is punish-ment for those who do not fulfil their daily task. But at the end, our Volunteers go back to the Community like giants refreshed!'

'Do you labour in the fields?' she asked pointedly.

His smile was unwavering. 'I did, of course, when I first came here. And then, because I saw so clearly the benefits of the Regeneration Experience, the Comptroller asked me to stay on, in charge. So, alas, I am now a bureaucrat. On the other hand, I tell myself that somebody has to do it.'

140

Glancing at his watch, he continued more briskly, 'Well, there is still plenty of daylight left. The sooner we get you assigned to a Work Unit, the better, eh? But first give me the ring.'

She closed her left hand around the ring, the special ring that marked her as a Founder, a person specially chosen by Mr Dunlop.

'Come,' he said, 'it will be returned to you. But in this place, as you've been told, we are all equal. No names, no rings, no special status. The past is nothing, only the present and the future are important.'

He held out his hand and, with difficulty, she eased the ring from her finger, leaving behind a circle of white and puckered skin.

Thirty minutes later, clad in a working tunic with the number C121 on her back, she was sweating on the hillside with the others, staggering under the weight of the rocks she carried to the wall. And when in the mid-afternoon she could do no more and sat down to rest, her Unit Supervisor came hurrying across to her.

'Get up. Get on with it!'

'I can't,' she moaned, and held up her sore and bleeding fingers.

'Those that don't work, don't eat!' he said roughly. 'And what is more, our Unit, the whole Unit, suffers. We shall have to perform your tasks in addition to our own.' Then, in a kinder tone, he added, 'Try, Sister. For everyone's sake.'

She looked around and saw the other members of her Unit staring at her with hostile eyes. With a faint nod and a sigh, she dragged herself back to work. The Unit Supervisor watched her for a few moments and then turned away. As he did so, she saw the number on the back of his tunic, and for the first time on this shattering day she felt a tiny but positive surge of hope.

What was it Gunnar had said?

You are not alone. There are others who feel as you do. People in various parts of the island.

And later, as she was about to leave?

Look out for a man named Roberts. Number K31. He will help you.

That number, K31, was staring her in the face now.

Chapter Eleven

The British Airways midday flight from London was only a little behind schedule. Tom Barr and Steve Ugley, watching from the observation area of the Terminal Building at Coolidge Airport, saw the 747 touch down and start its slow run towards them.

'How did you get to know about this delegation?' asked Steve.

'You should read your friendly local paper,' said Barr. 'It was reported there the day we arrived. It's no secret.'

'Ten people?'

'Ten people,' said Barr patiently. 'Eight from the States and two from Britain. The two Brits should be on that plane, the Americans arrive later this afternoon. They all go over to Jerusalem Island in the morning.'

'You're sure they took this flight?'

'Yes. I rang British Airways. A Professor Beaumont and a Mr Ivor Lambert are confirmed as passengers. Travelling first class, no less.'

Steve wiped his streaming forehead. There had been a freshening breeze earlier in the morning, but this had faded and the stifling air seemed to press on his skin like a rough, unwelcome blanket. 'It's odd,' he said. 'The Community bends over backwards to keep strangers out. Why should they let in a delegation?'

'It must be a whitewash job. The delegates are probably sympathetic to start with. My hunch is that the Community is picking up the tab for their fares and expenses. They'll be trotted round a few show places, introduced to some of the faithful, and then they'll go home and tell the world that Jerusalem Island is heaven on earth – or next door to it.'

'Then the Community could be sending someone out to meet our two people.'

'Could be. But I doubt it – that would make it look a bit too obvious.'

The plane had stopped now and within minutes the passengers were stepping down into the fierce hammering heat of the Caribbean noon. In a few hours they had been whisked from one world to another and they moved uncertainly, without co-ordination, as if their minds were struggling to keep up with their bodies. Even before they reached the Terminal Building, they were stripping off coats and sweaters and mopping the sticky sweat from their faces.

'There isn't a full plane load,' said Barr, 'so it shouldn't take them too long to clear customs. Better nip out and tell Charlie to come and do his stuff. I'll be inside.'

Barr left the observation area and edged his way through the

142

waiting crowd to the Information Desk. He exchanged a smile with the pretty uniformed girl on duty and passed her a piece of paper.

'Would you mind paging these two gentlemen? I'm supposed to meet them, but I haven't a clue what they look like. Could you ask them to come here when they're through customs?'

'Of course.' She reached for the microphone and switched it on. 'Will Professor Beaumont and Mr Lambert, passengers on British Airways Flight 121 from London please report to the Information Desk in the main hall. Professor Beaumont and Mr Lambert – please report to the Information Desk.'

Barr was joined by Charlie Brown, looking distinctly hot and uncomfortable in a blue chauffeur's uniform. They had to wait twenty minutes and have the girl repeat the announcement once more, but, at last, two hot and dishevelled men came to the desk. Unlike most of the male passengers they had retained their coats and ties, at some cost to their comfort. The heavy Harris tweeds of the older man and the black jacket and striped trousers of the other were more suitable for a London winter than the heat of Antigua, but they clung to them nevertheless, as if they were a kind of badge of identity.

'Professor Beaumont?' asked Barr pleasantly.

'Yes.' The older of the two, a shortish man who looked to be in his sixties, turned to Barr with a tired smile, blinking through heavy spectacles which were slightly smeared with moisture. He was bald except for a few spiky tufts of grey hair, above which his head rose in an odd dome-shaped fashion, like the top of a hard boiled egg.

'My name is Smithson,' said Barr briskly. 'Welcome to Antigua. I've been asked to pick you up. There's transport outside.' He snapped his fingers at Charlie. 'Take the Professor's luggage, Thomas.'

'Yes, sir!' said Charlie smartly. Stepping forward he relieved the Professor of his cases.

'Wait,' said the Professor. 'I rather think I'll hang on to the brief-case.' He stretched out a hand, but to no avail.

'It will be safe with Thomas,' said Barr. 'Not to worry.' He turned to the other man. 'And you will be Mr Lambert?'

'That's right.' Lambert was tall, with stooped shoulders. Unlike his companion he had an abundance of hair, which sprouted in thick black bushy eyebrows and which fell lankly down over his neck. The collar of his jacket bore a light dusting of dandruff. He offered Barr a soft, damp hand and said, 'Jolly kind of you to meet us. And in this heat, a great relief.'

Charlie took Lambert's luggage also and disappeared through the crush of passengers and their friends at the main exit. Barr made no move to follow him immediately.

'Would you gentlemen like one for the road? The bar is open,' he said amiably. 'A West Indian rum punch, perhaps?'

'I don't think so,' said the Professor.

'Not for me, thank you,' said Lambert.

'I'd like to get to the hotel and take a nice long bath,' said the Professor. He looked towards the exit, as if he was beginning to get anxious about the fate of his luggage.

'We're booked in at a place called the Arawak Bay Hotel,' said Lambert. 'I understand that the other members of the delegation will be staying there also.'

'Oh,' said Barr, 'there's no question of a hotel. We have a house which is at your disposal.'

'We?' said the Professor.

'You are referring to the Community, I take it?' asked Lambert.

'It's a twenty-minute drive. On the beach. Better than any hotel, I promise you. You'll be able to relax there for the rest of the day and be fresh for tomorrow,' said Barr. 'Shall we go?'

He led the way outside. Charlie, standing by the station-wagon, opened the rear door and the Professor climbed in. Lambert moved to follow, but checked and turned to Barr.

'Will our colleagues be joining us? The other members of the delegation, I mean.'

'You'll see them in due course,' said Barr. As Lambert settled in beside his companion, he looked at Charlie. 'Our guests' luggage – you've got it all?'

'All safe, sir,' said Charlie.

'Aren't you coming with us? Lambert frowned up at Barr.

'I have things to do in town. In connection with the delegation, you understand. Thomas will take you to the house and Mrs Wilmot, the housekeeper, will look after you when you arrive. Don't hesitate to ask her for anything you want. I hope to see you later.'

This answer seemed to relax the two passengers and they settled back in their seats. Barr watched Charlie drive away and then walked a few paces to where Steve was waiting at the wheel of a car.

'That wasn't too difficult,' said Barr, climbing in beside him. 'Have you got all their luggage?'

'In the back,' said Steve.

'It's the Arawak Bay Hotel. That's near where we hired the boat. We'd better stop somewhere on the way and check through their papers.'

'I caught a glimpse as they came out. I must say, we don't look much like them.'

'Who'd want to? No, I'm gambling that the other members of the delegation won't know them by sight.'

'What about people in the Community?'

'I'm still gambling. Shorter odds maybe – but I'm hoping they won't know Beaumont or Lambert either.'

144

'Moody. It's dead moody,' said Steve doubtfully.

'Yes. But it's only got to work long enough for us to get on to that bloody island and get a close look at the set-up. That's all we need. Come on, let's go.'

Steve switched on the ignition and started the engine. Before engaging gear, he looked at Barr with a smile. 'Which one was the Professor?'

'The older one, with the head like a monk.'

'In that case, I'll be Mr Lambert,' said Steve.

'Thanks,' said Barr.

'Any time,' said Steve.

'I'll tell you something, sonny boy,' said Barr. 'While I was waiting for them to come off the plane, I had a terrible thought. Suppose the Professor had turned out to be a woman? We could have been in real trouble.'

'Oh, I don't know,' said Steve airily. 'You'd have looked great in drag.'

Van Norden was fantasising again. He heard little or nothing of what the Comptroller was saying because the hatred was roaring in his head like a high wind and his mind was fixed once again on the stiletto. Only that morning he had put the sliver of shining steel back in its sheath and left it in his cabin: yet somehow he could feel it in his hand now, see himself standing over the Comptroller, see the man writhing and thrashing like a harpooned fish.

It was strange: he was not a person who was given to any depth of feeling one way or the other. When he killed it was without malice; the deed was performed coldly and clinically, unclogged by emotion. And by the same token, he had never loved anyone, man or woman, or felt the need to do so. But with the Comptroller, emotions to which he had been a stranger all his life welled up inside him with such intensity and venom that it seemed as if some voodoo spirit had taken possession of his body.

Something of this must have shown in his expression or passed through the air between them like a radio signal, for Van Norden became aware that the Comptroller had stopped talking and was looking at him with cold, curious eyes.

'If I might have your attention,' he said. 'If it is not too much trouble.'

'I was listening,' stammered Van Norden.

'No,' said the Comptroller, 'you were dreaming. What about, I wonder? How to dispose of me, perhaps?'

Van Norden stood rigid, fighting to hide his astonishment and fear, but his eyes and his mouth, which slackened a little, betrayed him.

Before he could voice his denials, the Comptroller cut in, with a wave of his jingling hand and a bland smile, 'No, no. I know, you see, I know more than you think. It's been in there, within you, for a long time. Oh, don't flatter yourself that you are unique, my friend. There are many like you. I am the focus of a great deal of hatred. And I don't mind. That, in a sense, is my role.'

He dabbed delicately at his forehead with a handkerchief, and the sharp scent of cologne drifted towards Van Norden.

'You see, Mr Dunlop is the focus of love, of the Community's love. And I, in a sense, am the reverse,' the Comptroller continued. 'In their daily lives, our people quite freely attribute all that they find good to Mr Dunlop and all that is bad to me. I don't object to that, indeed I welcome it. It directs towards Mr Dunlop the support and faith he needs to continue his mission and, at the same time, it gives the people an outlet for their feelings of dissatisfaction, jealousy and hatred. Oh yes, I am a necessary element. Without me to deflect them, these primitive, brutal emotions – which are as natural to man as breathing – would turn inwards and destroy our Community. God and the Devil, we need them both, isn't that so? If I did not exist, the Community would have had to invent me'

He rose and poured some amber-coloured wine from a decanter into two goblets, and handed one to the silent, bewildered Van Norden.

'Here,' he said brusquely. 'You don't understand, I can see that. You haven't understood a word I've said. But drink anyway. And hate me if it pleases you to do so.' He raised his glass. 'To hatred, the inseparable companion of love.'

Van Norden sipped the wine and, finding his voice, said, 'What do you want me to do, Comptroller?'

'What do I want?' echoed the Comptroller, moving back behind the desk. His tone was sharp and contemptuous. 'I want you to do a great deal better than you have been doing, otherwise you may feel the weight of my displeasure.'

'I don't understand, Comptroller,' stammered Van Norden. 'I did what you said. You've got the file and the photographs in front of you. We know who these people are now, and what they want.'

'You've also succeeded in putting them on their guard! They'll know who took this file and why. And if the break-in didn't warn them, that stupid business with the truck and the voodoo tape most certainly did.'

'It has worked before, Comptroller.'

'It didn't work last night, did it?' said the Comptroller scathingly. 'These people are not children, to be frightened by noises in the night. They're tough and they're professional. Did you know that yesterday they came ashore – yes, came ashore here – and knocked out two armed Guardians? Not to mention what they've got in this file! They've checked the *Leandro* in and out of every port she has called at in the last eighteen months, and made a link with the girls. That is the sort of people they are, that's the sort of people we're dealing with!'

'Do you think they're from the Relatives Rescue Association?'

'The RRA? That conglomeration of milk-sops! No.'

'Police? Investigators of some sort?'

'We don't know, do we? There's nothing in this file to tell us. But there is enough to tell us that they already know too much.' A sudden thought occurred to the Comptroller. 'Where are they now?'

'At Tradewinds. The Ugley house. On Antigua.' Van Norden looked puzzled by the question.

'Do you know that? Are you sure of it?'

'No. But —'

'But! But! But!' The words cracked in the air like a whip. 'Do you mean to tell me that after what happened last night you didn't even think to put a watch on the house?'

'I thought I'd better report —'

'Thought! You thought! I doubt if you've ever had a thought in your life! Get back there. Now! I want a round-the-clock surveillance of the house. I want to know who comes and who goes. I want them followed wherever they go. I want their movements reported to me – direct to me – every four hours. Do you understand that?'

'Yes, Comptroller.'

'Good.' The Comptroller's voice took on a quiet, silky note that made Van Norden's flesh tingle. 'You won't let me down this time, will you?'

'No, Comptroller.'

'No, I'm sure you won't. That would be very boring. And I do so dislike being bored.'

The next morning, when Sister Eleanor came for Kitty, the girl obeyed meekly, without demur. She had no idea where she was going or what awaited her and she was now almost past caring. She felt very near to defeat.

In one of the wide corridors through which they passed she caught a reflection of herself in a long wall mirror, and it seemed to her at this moment that the double image was true, that she had, indeed, become two people.

There was Sister Helen, who glided like a mechanical doll through this strange world, responding without question to the word of command, bowing her head in deference to those in authority. And there was Kitty Higgins, who waited stubbornly in the depth of her being, refusing to give in, fighting fiercely for survival.

She remembered how, two years before, on that Mediterranean cruise with Lucy, she had come near to drowning when they had gone bathing from a beach near Athens. Caught by a current she had found herself being carried out to sea: swimming with all her strength, she fought to get back to shore, but it seemed to get no nearer. She cried out and waved, but the only response from Lucy and others on the beach was a cheerful wave in reply.

Nearing the end of her resources, she became almost overwhelmed by the feeling that further effort was useless, and with this came the thought that it would be sweet to relax, to stretch out in the warm blue water and let the sea carry her where it would. She had experienced, at this moment, a sensation of release, of utter peace and calm. And then her will had revived: striking out in a final desperate battle with the current she had, at last, felt the blessed firmness of ground beneath her feet.

Much the same feeling was with her now. Exhausted by the struggle, she longed for an end to it all, she longed for the peace that would come with total submission. Yet each time she prepared herself to give in, the old Kitty came fighting back, urging her to hold on, not to lose hope. It was this Kitty who had told her to take the paper-knife from the Comptroller's office. As a weapon it was next to useless: it was the gesture, the act of defiance itself, that mattered.

How much longer could the real Kitty Higgins survive? With each hour she seemed to diminish in strength while the person of Sister Helen grew stronger and more dominant. Instinct, a touch of native cunning, had told her to go along with her captors, to make them believe that they had won her over until the time came when she could make a bid for freedom. But it had not been easy. Even now she found herself half believing the things they had drummed into her head, half believing them when they said that her kidnapping had been a kind of 'divine deception', justified by the fact that she had been rescued from a world at war with itself and brought to a place where there was equality and brotherhood, and love and peace.

Concerned with these thoughts, she was only partly aware that they had arrived at the entrance to a large courtyard and it was this sudden touch of warm, scented air on her face that roused her. A negro albino, in a smart white high-collared tunic, stood on guard before tall golden gates beyond which Kitty caught a glimpse of trees and bright flowering shrubs and the flash of blue water. More surprising, she heard music and the sound of laughter.

The guard surveyed them with sharp blue eyes for a moment and then sprang to attention, with one clenched hand on his heart. Sister Eleanor responded in kind and, moving aside, he depressed a switch. The gates slid open with a low whisper and they passed through.

148

Kitty was almost past the point of surprise, but what she saw now made her draw breath. The courtyard itself was huge, and bordered on three sides by a wall so high that it brushed the fronds of the palm trees standing on the other side. The wall itself was scarcely visible under sweeping folds of white, red, salmon-pink and purple bougain-villaea, and below these there lay a vivid riot of ixora plants and delicate ferns.

A large pool of irregular shape occupied the centre of the court-yard, and beyond, surrounding the pool, and spreading outwards to the wall, was a wide swathe of trim emerald-green lawn. Here and there, the smooth flow of the grass was broken by lime and lemon trees, standing singly or in pairs.

From a dovecote set near the top of the wall, a small colony of white-bellied doves made occasional sallies or sat together in pairs cooing plaintively. Parson sparrows pecked for crumbs on a cane table which stood under one of the trees. Warblers, their plumage splashed with yellow and green, were singing in the hibiscus near the pool.

The setting was obviously man-made, but it had been cunningly designed to suggest otherwise. Apart from the wall, there was no formal pattern. The pool, partly shadowed by the low-hanging hibiscus tree, looked like a small natural lake or pond, set in the heart of a cool and tranquil glade.

But it was the human element in this spectacle that startled Kitty. A number of girls – perhaps ten or twelve in all – were relaxing around the pool or in the shade of the trees.

They were different in colour and race – Indian, Chinese, African, Eurasion, European. They were also very, very beautiful and they were all naked.

A tall blonde girl, her body tanned to a russet brown and shining with moisture, stood poised on a low diving board at one end of the pool. Her magnificent breasts quivered and gleamed as she raised her arms above her head and plunged gracefully into the water. She turned on her back as she surfaced and floated gently among the scattering of fallen hibiscus blossom which decorated the surface of the pool like red water-lilies.

A girl with glistening black hair sat nearby, a guitar held against her full dark body. She was playing a Cante Flamenco, plucking the strings with a certain wistful fluency; the music had a mournful, haunting quality and she held her head high, her eyes half closed, as though in a waking dream.

Two girls, their brown and white bodies in sharp contrast, lay together on a rug in the shade of a lime tree. They were turned towards each other and appeared, at first, to be asleep. And then Kitty saw a brown hand gently moulding a white breast, a white hand

149

sliding almost imperceptibly along a smooth brown thigh.

A girl with delicate oriental features sat in great concentration before an embroidery frame, her needle flashing in and out of the half-covered canvas. Two more girls were squatting near the pool, their heads bent over a game of checkers. Yet another, with a boyish figure and small high-riding breasts, was moving slowly around the wall, gathering a bouquet of flowers and fern. A group of three in the furthest corner were playing with a coloured ball, tossing it languidly, without too much exertion, from one to another.

'These will be your friends,' said Sister Eleanor, and then, seeing the look on Kitty's face, she added with a smile, 'Oh, nudity is not compulsory. It is simply that Mr Dunlop prefers it. He believes in all things beautiful –and he has said that God-given beauty should not be hidden. And, let's face it, in this climate, it is so much more sensible. Still, you have some pretty clothes, I know. You may wear them here if you wish.'

'Is this the High Place?' asked Kitty in a low voice.

'Oh, no. No, my dear. This is called the Grove. Yes, the Grove. This is where you will relax between your duties.'

'Duties?'

'We shall come to those presently. You will not find them too arduous, I assure you.' Sister Eleanor clapped her hands and the activity around the Grove stopped almost at once. 'Sisters,' she called, 'I want you to come and greet our new Sister, Sister Helen.'

The Chinese girl came first, her high-boned face shining with happiness. She cupped Kitty's face in her soft, cool hands, looked deep into her eyes, and kissed her gently on the lips.

'Welcome. You are very welcome, Sister Helen,' she said.

One by one the others came to her, and although each followed much the same ritual, the greetings seemed to possess a genuine, even spontaneous warmth.

'You see,' said Sister Eleanor, 'you see, they already love you.' She waved a hand around the Grove and sighed, 'Who could wish for anything more than this? Out there, beyond our island, a world of turmoil and confusion. And here, safe from all that, we have peace, love and beauty.'

'Peace, love and beauty,' intoned the Sisters.

Sister Eleanor smiled approvingly at the semi-circle of smiling girls and said in a brisker tone, 'You will be needed in two hours, Sisters. In the High Place. For the induction of Sister Helen. Be ready.'

She touched Kitty's arm and led the way back towards the golden gates. As she turned to follow, Kitty looked upwards at the wing of the Tabernacle which, in effect, formed the fourth wall of the Grove. At its highest point, about four floors up, she caught a winking flash, as of sunlight on glass, and, shading her eyes with a hand, she saw a

150

balcony. Shaped like a cupid's bow, its prevailing white was picked out in gold.

A man was seated on the balcony. She could not see his face because it was masked by a pair of binoculars through which he was looking down at the Grove. She could not be sure, but she felt instinctively that the glasses were trained on her.

She lowered her head quickly and hurried after Sister Eleanor.

Tom Barr and Steve Ugley arrived on Jerusalem Island with the visiting delegation in the early hours of that morning. So far, their luck had held. They had been accepted and warmly welcomed into the circle by Greg Cortez, the New Yorker who had been elected as leader and spokesman of the group. He explained that the plan was to visit as many of the Community's projects before the heat of the day made travelling too uncomfortable.

Greg was a handsome, elegant, articulate attorney in his early forties, who had earned something of a reputation in the USA by his support for liberal causes. His brief to the other members of the delegation before they set out from the hotel underlined both his general approach and his skill.

'As you know, I'm the one who put this thing together. There has been a fair amount of criticism of the Community of New Jerusalem in recent months, some, if not all of it, inspired and orchestrated by reactionary elements in the US and Europe. I thought it was about time to set the record straight, so I looked around for men and women whom I knew to be without prejudice. People who would see this fascinating and unique experiment through clear eyes and with open minds. People like you. Some of you I haven't met before except through correspondence – but that's all to the good. At least I can't be accused of packing the delegation with my friends!'

Greg paused at this point, in the manner of the practised speaker, and waited for laughter. It came as he knew it would, in a small, easy ripple and when that had passed, he went on:

'I think you all know where I stand, I've made no secret of it. Quite simply, I believe that Mr Dunlop is a unique and remarkable man and that his work should have the support of all those who are committed to the struggle for a better world. Yes, I have to tell you frankly that I am one hundred per cent behind the basic principles of the Community. Criticism – yes. There may be some minor issues on which I disagree, but I stand four-square behind the main thrust of the movement. I am going to Jerusalem Island as a friend. As an ally. If I see anything that I don't like, I shall say so – as one friend to another, in the spirit of fraternal co-operation. I ask only that you do the same.'

151

This approach appeared to sit well with the clear-sighted, open-minded members of the delegation and there was no argument. So before sun-up, they had set out from the jetty of the Arawak Bay Hotel in a hired boat, arriving at St Marks on Jerusalem Island as the first hint of dawn began to glow on the horizon.

They were given fruit juice, and a welcome from an officer of the Community who introduced himself as Brother Vincent Hemmings. 'But you must call me Vincent,' he said, with a smile that seemed to embrace them all.

With his ruddy cheeks and bright eager eyes, with his shining silver hair and air of jocular sanctity, Vincent reminded Barr of an old-time, tub-thumping preacher who had once set up his evangelical tent in a field just outside the Devon village near where he had lived as a child. Barr would have been surprised to learn how near the mark he was with this assessment.

In the course of the next two to three hours they were whisked from point to point in a small bus. They were shown trim plantations, irrigation projects, land reclamation and the restoration work which had been carried out at Nelson's old fort on Dreadnought Hill. And all the time, chirpy as a guide, Vincent bombarded them with information and statistics about the area of land under cultivation, the monthly export of soft fruits, the experiments the Community was making with cassava flour, the annual targets for production.

For the most part they kept on the move, but at the two or three places where Vincent did call a halt, the party was immediately surrounded by small groups of eager, smiling workers. Coconuts were topped to provide cooling milk refreshment, freshly picked fruit was everywhere at hand.

Vincent did not allow them to linger too long, but there was time to ask questions. Without exception, the Community workers spoke with joy of their new life. Several admitted quite freely that their lives had possessed no meaning until Mr Dunlop and the Community had raised them up. One smiling middle-aged worker told them that he had once been a millionaire businessman.

'I gave it all up to the Community when the call came,' he said cheerfully. 'I am free now and I have never known such joy.'

Greg, who sat up front with Vincent, could hardly contain his enthusiasm. He dictated his impressions into a pocket recorder, with much use of superlatives and, from time to time, he turned to his colleagues with a shake of his head and murmured some such phrase as: 'Fantastic! Isn't it incredible? All this from nothing. Fabulous!'

His excitement was echoed by the others with smiles and nods and murmurs of approval and there was much taking of notes. Vincent's smile grew broader as time passed: he was evidently well pleased by the way things were going.

Barr and Steve did their best to maintain the roles they had chosen but neither man found it easy. Greg and most of the others seemed to be sincere people, but Barr, in particular, found their uncritical acceptance of what they were shown and their willingness to embrace the general air of bonhomie sickening to the point of nausea. Not for the first time in his eventful life, he reflected that sincerity and naïvety could make a lethal combination.

At one point, he could not resist the temptation to put a question to Vincent. 'I was interested in the man who said he had once been a millionaire. Do you get many recruits like that?'

Vincent rebuked him with a gentle affability. 'We like to refer to them as converts, Professor.'

'Of course. I'm sorry,' Barr said. 'But do you convert many rich people?'

'A number, naturally. Our message is for everyone, regardless of what or who they are.'

'And they all give their fortunes to the Community?'

'If that is their wish. The act is a voluntary one, you understand.'

'What happens to the money?' asked Steve and was immediately rewarded for his bluntness by reproving looks from other members of the delegation and an elbow in the ribs from Barr. 'What I mean,' he went on hastily, 'what I mean is, I presume that the money is paid into the Community funds and used for various projecets?'

Vincent favoured him with the sort of sad but benign look that a Sunday School teacher might wear when confronted by a child who has not learned a set piece of scripture.

'We have no money on Jerusalem Island, Mr Lambert,' he said with a sigh. 'We have no need for it. Would you believe that there are young children here who have never even heard the word? It is not in our dictionary. From the beginning, Mr Dunlop established the principle by which our people live – from each according to his ability, to each according to his needs. Money, materialism, the consumer society – we have turned our backs on these evils, these absurdities.'

A vigorous murmur of approval, led by Greg, followed this little speech. Vincent had skilfully side-stepped the question, but Steve decided not to press it. He smiled sheepishly and nodded as if in agreement with his colleagues.

There was no air-conditioning on the bus and the atmosphere grew steadily more clammy and oppressive. Outside, the rosy promise of the dawn had not been maintained: the colour seemed to have been drained out of the sky and the sun blinked palely down from behind the prevailing grey. There was no breeze, no movement of air, and even the open windows brought little relief.

So far everything had happened as Barr had predicted. They had obviously been shown the best projects and allowed only to meet the most whole-hearted disciples. There had been no sign of guards, armed or otherwise. And, Steve thought ruefully, no sign of Kitty or of any place where she might be held. If she was being held . . .

The thought shook him. Suppose she had joined the Community as a genuine convert, of her own free will? He knew that she was not entirely happy in her personal life: embittered was too strong a word to use for a person like Kitty but he guessed that she had been let down by someone she loved and trusted and that the experience had made her wary, if not cynical. He knew too, for she had told him, that she had grown sick of the phoney, tinsel world of beauty contests.

In such a mood, the idea of joining a Community which not only talked of service and love and brotherhood but which had, seemingly, found a way to put such ideals into practice might, just might, have appealed to her. Her disappearance could have been faked, she might wish people to think she was dead so that there would be no pursuit and the break from her old life would be quick and clean.

He shook his hot and aching head as if to clear it of such alien thoughts. The humidity was clearly softening his brain. There was too much evidence the other way – the other girls, the *Leandro,* the armed guards and, above all, Kitty herself. She had too much character to succumb to the Pied Piper blandishments of the Community, too much spirit ever to allow herself to become one of its willing zombies.

It began to rain now, fierce driving rain that rattled on the roof like a downpouring of pebbles. He held up his face as it came through the open window and, in moments, his head and shoulders were soaked.

And then he became aware that the bus was slowing down, that Vincent had risen from his seat and was standing by the driver, urging him to drive on. The bus began to pick up speed again, but now Barr moved forward quickly. He elbowed Vincent aside, and, in almost the same movement, grabbed the wheel with his right hand and wrenched it round.

The bus slewed across the narrow road and shuddered to a skidding halt as the driver instinctively rammed on the brakes. Steve disentangled himself from a bony New York social worker who had been hurled from her seat across the aisle into his lap and went forward.

Like the sky, Vincent had lost his colour, and he was gibbering at Barr, 'You could have killed us!'

'You could have killed him!' said Barr, and pointed ahead.

Vaguely, as in a mist, Steve saw through the streaming windows a man standing in the middle of the road, about ten yards ahead. He was black and bareheaded; the rain streamed down his face and his baggy olive-green clothes hung about him in sodden folds. He held his hands up before him as if he was making some mute appeal, then he looked quickly over his shoulder, dropped his arms, and came towards the bus in a staggering run.

Barr pressed the release button and the doors slid open as the man reached the bus. He was in his middle years, with greying hair and a thin, haunted face. The nails on his hands were chipped and broken and blood bubbled up from a scratch on his wrist. He was clearly at the end of his resources for he clung to the rail, unable to haul himself up or to speak as he sucked in air with great, panting breaths. His moist brown eyes, eloquent with fear, looked from Steve to Barr to Vincent and then back to Barr.

Barr moved to help him, but even as he did so, two men appeared out of the rain and took his arms. He struggled feebly for a moment or two, and managed to free one arm which he extended towards Barr.

'Help me!' he croaked. 'Sweet Jesus – help, help me.'

One of the two men pulled him away and the other swung himself up into the doorway. He was young and white, with thin lips and even teeth, and the moisture pouring from his uniform made a small puddle on the floor.

'Sorry about that, folks,' he said with an arrogant, easy smile. 'I'm afraid our dear Brother Luke is sick. You understand, I'm sure. Lost his wife in a hurricane and rain like this kind of frets his nerves. But not to worry. He's in good loving hands and he's getting better all the time. Sorry you've been troubled. Have a good day.'

He dropped to the ground and Vincent, who seemed to have recovered his composure, closed the doors quickly.

'You see,' he said, 'not even the Community can work miracles all the time.'

The tension broken, some of the passengers smiled with relief and Vincent continued: 'Most people – the vast majority – put aside their old lives when they come here, they start anew, they are reborn. But there are a few, particularly those who are not so young, for whom this is difficult. It is partly guilt, I think. That man, for example. I know the case. Just before the hurricane struck, he sent his wife out into the yard to get some kerosene for the stove. There was a high wind, as you can imagine. A sheet of corrugated iron was blown off the roof and – well – she was decapitated.'

'God, how terrible!' murmured Greg, and reached for his notebook.

'Naturally, for he is basically a good man, Brother Luke felt responsible for the tragedy. His mind became – shall we say – unhinged. There was talk of putting him away. But Mr Dunlop heard about the case and invited him – without strings, mark you – to become a guest of the Community. And I'm happy to say that he is

155

making progress. With every day, there is an improvement.'

'Wonderful,' said Greg.

'Terrific,' said the social worker.

'I want to thank you, sir,' said Vincent, turning to Barr. 'I didn't see him on the road and I guess our driver here didn't see him either. But for your speed of thought —' He stopped, shook his head, and then smiled. 'Well, enough of that. Let's get the show back on the road, shall we? We've lost precious time. In an hour, we are due at the Tabernacle where you are to be Mr Dunlop's guests at a most fascinating ceremony.'

Outside, the rain had stopped. The heavy grey blanket was breaking up quickly and patches of brilliant blue, dotted with small white innocent clouds, were moving in. Pillars of steam began to rise from the fields on either side as the bus was urged back on to the road and they resumed their journey.

Chapter Twelve

At the Regeneration Centre, morning assembly was held at first light, rain or shine, on the small grassed area in front of the Supervisor's hut. Hymns were sung, prayers chanted, and a recorded message of exhortation from Mr Dunlop played to the gathering. Then the normal practice was for the Supervisor, Brother Vincent, to report on the previous day's work, praising some Work Units and castigating others.

Individuals were encouraged to indulge in public self-criticism and to comment – in a spirit of brotherly love – on the shortcomings of their fellow Volunteers. Any tendency, however slight, towards vanity, pride, greed, love of personal possessions, and idleness was always a popular subject of discussion. In a sense, these morning debates were their only form of entertainment – the Community's answer to the TV soap opera.

Working targets for the new day were issued next and, after a last hymn, the assembly concluded with what was known as the Touching. Each day three or four Volunteers, chosen at random, moved along the ranks from person to person: pausing before each one they would smile and gently cup his (or her) face in their hands, and say, 'I love you.' To which the Volunteer would respond, 'I love you.'

The smile was most important. Indeed, on the Regeneration Experience, the participants were expected to wear a permanent smile as a visible sign of their profound joy in being there. Anyone seen without a smile was marked down for public criticism.

Nobody was allowed to miss morning assembly. Penalties for lateness on parade or for non-attendance ranged in severity from an extra work imposition, curtailment of rations or, worst of all, an extension of the offenders' period of service with the Regeneration Experience.

Dr Christa Bauer was guilty of an offence on her first full day at the Centre. Exhausted by the unaccustomed strain of her work in the field, she had fallen into a sleep so profound that even the amplified recording of the Community Choir singing *Thanks for the Day* failed to rouse her. This hymn was always used as a kind of reveille and it was customary for the more energetic members of the Centre to add their eager early-morning voices to the chorus:

Morning has broken
Like the first morning,
Blackbird has spoken
Like the first bird.
Praise to the singing
Praise to the morning
Praise to the springing
Fresh from the word.

But Dr Bauer's ears remained deaf to the word, her sleep unbroken. Her hutmates made no other effort to rouse her; they loved her, of course, as they loved every living creature, but since they'd had to learn their lesson the hard way they felt that this newcomer should follow the same course, for her own good. She would have missed assembly altogether had not her Unit Supervisor, Roberts, otherwise known as K31, come in to check and used desperate methods to get her on her feet.

Even so, the opening hymn was almost over when she stumbled into the grey light and took her place uncertainly in the ranks. Brother Vincent had been called away on other duties that morning and his place was occupied by Sister Miriam, one of his deputies. Sister Miriam was a small bright-eyed woman in whom the faith burned with a fierce intensity and it was clear from her look that she had observed the Doctor's tardy appearance and made a mental note of it.

Gradually, as the sky grew lighter, the Doctor shook off her weariness and began to order her thoughts. She was aware, with a sense of shock, that some fundamental change had taken place within her. It was as if, during her long, deep sleep, the subconscious mind had taken a dramatic leap forward, leading her towards one inescapable and frightening conclusion. She did not understand clearly as yet, but she knew that the faith, which had once flamed in her as fiercely as it did in Sister Miriam, was dead, or at least dying.

She looked at the faces around her, and saw them with new eyes. Most of the people there were true volunteers who had asked to join the Regeneration Experience because they believed that by such service to the Community they would find a new spiritual strength. They were listening now to Mr Dunlop's recorded address, their eyes shining, their weariness forgotten, a band of Christian soldiers eager for battle.

Spiritual strength maybe, she thought, but on almost every face there were the tell-tale signs of malnutrition and exhaustion. She felt a sudden surge of pity for what she now saw as their naïve innocence, coupled with anger at those who had manipulated them.

158

Mr Dunlop! Strange to think that only a short time ago that throaty voice would have held her enthralled and trembling. Now she was only half listening, her mind feverishly playing on other things. It was in Mr Dunlop's name that she had accepted so much in the past; in his name and for his sake she had condoned one iniquity after another, to the point where she herself had become involved and tainted. And all the time she had comforted herself with the thought that so long as Mr Dunlop was there, all would be well in the end.

All that was dead now, suddenly dead, and as if the thought were caught in a clear, bright light, she understood now that she had been duped. She and hundreds, thousands, of others. Their longing for certainty, their unhappiness, their weakness, their need for hope, had made them ripe for the picking. Mesmerised by Mr Dunlop and his promise of a New Jerusalem, they had been brainwashed and exploited. They had journeyed from the dream of freedom to the extreme of servitude. They were robots, serfs labouring to serve Mr Dunlop, the Comptroller and the ruling élite. Willing serfs for the most part, that was the real tragedy of it all, walking into bondage with a smile and a hymn on their lips: and even now, as the chains tightened around them, they cherished the illusion that they were free and happy.

What would happen, she wondered, if one day Mr Dunlop's magic ceased to work, and the people of the Community came to see, as she had seen, that the dream was false, that they had been tricked? She shuddered at the thought. How terrible their wrath, how bloody their vengeance!

She was brought back from these thoughts by a sharp nudge in the ribs and realised that Sister Miriam was looking in her direction, speaking to her.

'C121. Are you listening?'

C121? Another nudge reminded her that this was her number now, her badge of identity, and she said quickly, 'Yes, Sister.'

'You were late for assembly. We would like to know why.'

'I'm sorry, Sister. I must have overslept,' she réplied, surprised by her own calmness.

'Oh, dear. Oh, dear,' Sister Miriam sighed. 'On your first morning with us, too. Not a very good start, is it?'

'No, Sister.'

'Well, what shall we do about it, eh?' Sister Miriam looked around the gathering as if seeking an opinion, but before there could be any response she went on, 'Suppose we ask C121 to clean the Amenities Block as an extra duty? Do you think that would be a reasonable penalty?'

'And no lunch!' said a woman in the front rank. She turned towards the Doctor, smiling and shaking her head, as if to indicate that she bore no malice.

'And no lunch. Clean the Amenities Block – and no lunch. Is that agreed?' There was a general murmur of approval and Sister Miriam continued, 'We have been lenient with you, C_{121}, because you are new to the Centre. Try not to let us down again, won't you? We all love you and it hurts us to see your lack of self-discipline.'

She closed with the rather surprising announcement that there would be no work in the fields that morning: Brother Vincent had left instructions that no-one should leave the compound until after the midday meal and that the Volunteers should occupy the time by cleaning out the huts and on other domestic duties.

After the final hymn and the Touching, the Doctor went to the Amenities Block to start her working penance. The block consisted of two long huts, one for either sex, each of which contained a row of open lavatories, washbasins, and four showers. She had used the women's hut the previous evening and she knew that this, at least, was in bad shape. The water supply was erratic, the plumbing decrepit, and many of the Volunteers had a casual approach, to say the least, to the subject of personal hygiene. Cleanliness and Godliness did not, in this instance, stand side by side.

Dr Bauer did not mind the punishment; indeed, she almost welcomed it. Last night's supper had been a soggy concoction of beans and half-congealed gravy and, if today's midday meal was anything like that, she would be happy to pass it by. As for the cleaning, the physical activity would give her time to think.

Later in the morning, when she was scrubbing the rough cement floor in the men's hut, a shadow fell across her face and, looking up, she saw her Unit Supervisor.

'This place is closed until I've finished!' she said crossly. 'Didn't you see the notice on the door?'

'I came in to talk to you, Doctor,' he said.

'Doctor! I thought titles were forbidden here, I thought we were all numbers!'

'I saw Gunnar last night,' he said.

'Gunnar!' She dropped the brush and sat back on her haunches. Of course, this man was Roberts, K_{31}, the one Gunnar had told her to look out for. 'Gunnar?' She went on. 'Is he here?'

'No. We met.'

'How? Isn't it forbidden to leave the Centre?'

'Many things are forbidden,' he said. 'He told me about you – he told me of your feelings. Don't be afraid to speak what is in your heart.'

She brushed a wisp of hair from her forehead with the back of her hand and stood up.

'Gunnar said – he said you could help me,' she stammered.

'I doubt it,' he replied. 'We all have to help ourselves, isn't that so?'

160

'I want to get away,' she said.

'From the island?'

'Yes. From the island.'

'Why?'

'Isn't that obvious? I want to get away and tell the world what is happening here, what is really happening.'

'If you did get away,' he said, 'they would come after you. You are a Founder, they dare not let you slip through their fingers. You are too important, you know too much. They would come after you and kill you. Or, at least, find some way to silence you.'

'I must try,' she said. 'I can't stay here now. I can't stay here.'

'You must, for the moment. You must.'

'For the moment?'

'Escape is not the answer,' he said. 'Individual escape, at any rate. Listen, a great deal has been accomplished here, not by them – not by the people who sit in the Tabernacle and hand down their commands – but by us. Us! This is our island, our movement, not theirs. Life here could be good. Why should we sit back and let them enjoy the fruits of our labour? Why should we abandon all that has been created by our sweat, our blood?'

He spoke in a low voice that trembled with controlled passion. She had never before heard anyone speak so directly and openly against the leaders of the Community and it frightened her: at the same time, beneath the fear, she felt a growing sense of elation, of liberation.

'What can we do?' she asked. 'What can we do? They have the Guardians, the power. And the people would never move against Mr Dunlop. Did you see their faces at assembly? They worship him.' And she added wryly, 'I know how they feel. It is not so long ago that I felt that way myself. Even now, the thought of doing anything against him . . .'

She left the sentence unfinished, shaking her head. He dropped a hand on her shoulder.

'I know, I know. It is hard to break the spell. When I first began to be critical of him in my mind, I felt guilty as though in some way I had betrayed the cause. But I came through it, and you will too. As for Mr Dunlop, he will not last forever.'

'What do you mean?' She felt the fear come flooding back.

'He is a sick man. It is months since he appeared in public. I think he will die soon.'

'How do you know this? I am a doctor, and I don't know it!'

'Because the Comptroller didn't want you to know. Don't you see that? Precisely because you are a doctor. You might have been able to do something about the disease – prescribe a course of treatment. The right drugs, perhaps.'

'Mr Dunlop is opposed to the use of drugs! Absolutely opposed!'

161

'Not in all cases,' he said drily. 'Didn't you use drugs on some of the people who passed through your hands? Those girls in the Special Rooms, for instance?'

'Did Gunnar tell you about them?' she asked angrily.

'Does it matter?'

'No, I suppose not.' She sighed. 'What I meant is that Mr Dunlop would never take drugs himself, not even an aspirin. He condoned their use in others, but only very reluctantly. He believes in natural medicines, natural cures. With him it is a matter of principle.'

'In this case, he might have been persuaded. When one has to choose between one's life and one's principles, it is surprising how elastic the principles can become. But never mind. The point is – Mr Dunlop will die soon. By soon, I mean six months, a year, eighteen months. His death will create a new situation. There will be confusion, chaos. The Comptroller will then take over the Community – or try to. And that will be our moment. You know that he is the most hated man on the island. We shall lead the people against him – and we shall win. Until that time comes, we must wait in patience, and build up our organisation so that we are ready.'

'Why do you do this?' she asked, looking at him directly. 'Do you want to sit in Mr Dunlop's chair?'

He flushed. 'I want only to see the Community return to its old ideals. To put an end to corruption.'

They all say that, she thought, they all say that in the beginning. Afterwards, it is a different matter. But she did not give voice to this opinion.

'I must go,' he said. 'Be careful. We must not be seen talking together too much. Will you join us?'

'I think I have already joined you,' she said. 'But give me a little time.'

'Time?' he said, with a tight little smile. 'That's the one thing we're not short of.'

As he moved to the door, she said, 'Wait. Tell me, since you seem to know so much. What is the nature of Mr Dunlop's disease?'

He paused, sliding his tongue along his upper lip. 'It's ironic, really.'

'What is it? What is he suffering from?' she asked impatiently.

'Neurosyphilis,' he said.

Vinnie Harcourt had half expected to be followed and she was not surprised when she caught sight of the green Ford Escort in the Range Rover's rear-view mirror. Just to check it out, she pulled up in one of the villages on the way to St John's and went into a small bar. When she came out with two cans of cold Heineken lager, the Ford was parked about two hundred yards away.

She ripped open one of the lagers and quenched her thirst, draining the can: as she did so, she studied the other vehicle. A white man, whose face seemed vaguely familiar, was standing by the open door on the passenger side, mopping his neck with a khaki handkerchief. He looked directly at Vinnie, and she had the impression that he was smiling. The driver, a slim West Indian youth, sat impassively behind the wheel.

When she set off again, the driver pulled in behind her, keeping the same distance between them. It was quite obvious that the two men were content, even anxious, to let her know that she was being tailed. She drove on into St John's with the Ford behind her all the way and pulled up outside the Central Post Office. The Ford slowed down, stopped, and reversed into a parking space almost opposite.

Vinnie collected and signed for a cable addressed to Barr and opened it as he had instructed. It read:

PUTTING YOUR GEAR ON BA FLIGHT 121 ARRIVING
ANTIGUA THURSDAY NOON STOP SIX PIECES STOP
CHEERS STOP NOONAN

She tore the cable into tiny pieces and threw them into a bin. When she went out into the street again, the white man was standing by the Ford in much the same attitude as before. She remembered him now. He was the tall thin man she had seen at the office of J. D. Winston shortly after her arrival on the island, the man called Simon Lavender. He was wearing the same olive-coloured uniform and he stared across at her quite openly, even arrogantly.

The arrogance irritated her. She noted how passing pedestrians were making a wary detour, avoiding the section of crumbling sidewalk where Lavender was standing. The car parked in front of the Ford had already moved off and the one behind was beginning to reverse out of its parking space. It was odd, she thought, that these people, supporters of a movement which professed itself to be Christian, should inspire such fear. Vinnie herself, when she stopped to think about it, had never thrown off the good old Methodism in which her parents had raised her, nor had she ever had the slightest inclination to do so.

It was years since she had seen the inside of a chapel but she held firmly to her belief in a straightforward, no-nonsense, old-fashioned religion. She had no time for the weird new sects which had sprung up in the last few years and she reserved a particular disgust for the people at the top – the unctuous men who used religion to satisfy their own lust for money and power.

Discussing these top people with Steve a couple of days before, she had expressed her feelings with characteristic bluntness: 'I'd shoot the bastards! I would. I'd shoot every bleeding one of them!'

The more she thought about it and the longer she looked across that dusty, rutted road at the insolent figure on the other side, the more angry she became. She longed to go across and take his scrawny neck in her hands. But she had other calls to make, other things to do for Barr, and she knew that it would be a mistake to allow herself to be provoked by Lavender.

On the other hand, it was important that she should shake him off somehow. She did not want him to learn the whereabouts of her next two calls or to put the people concerned in any danger. The Heineken was beginning to bubble up through her skin in the form of sweat and, as she wiped it away, an idea came to her, an idea which brought a smile to her broad red face.

Turning away from Lavender's steady gaze, Vinnie hauled herself up into the Range Rover and started up the engine. She waited until a heavy truck had lumbered past, engaged gear, and drove about a hundred yards to a junction, where there was just about enough room to execute a full turn. Wrenching at the wheel, she brought the Range Rover round, its wheels churning the dust. She brushed a lamp standard in the process and a car moving across the junction had to take screaming evasive action, but she was now heading back down towards the Post Office and picking up speed.

The Ford had moved off in pursuit and was in the centre of the road, in the direct path of the Range Rover. She caught a glimpse of the frightened bewildered faces of the two men, and saw the driver straining desperately at the wheel. He managed to turn the car to the left but the only result was to present Vinnie with a bigger target.

The Range Rover hit the Ford on one side, towards the rear, with shuddering force. The body panels crumpled inwards under the impact, shards of glass crashed to the road, and the car slewed round as if it was mounted on a turntable. Still travelling, it cracked a wooden verandah post in half, finishing up with its nose half way through the window of Bramley's Cut Price Liquor Store and with most of the verandah draped across its roof.

Vinnie pulled up and waited just long enough to see the two men stagger drunkenly from the wreckage. Then she drove on, putting four blocks between herself and the scene of the crash before stopping to check the Range Rover for damage. The front fender was badly twisted and the lights on one side were smashed but otherwise the vehicle was in good shape. She saw a teenage girl, wearing the uniform of the Girl Guides, standing on the sidewalk and called her over.

'How would you like to earn yourself five dollars, sweetheart?'

The girl looked at the big, perspiring woman with clear, wondering eyes and said cautiously, 'For what?'

'There's been an accident back up there, near the Central Post Office. A car ran into a liquor store. Bramley's. Will you take a note to Mr Bramley, or whoever owns the store?'

The girl hesitated. 'You'll give me five dollars for that?'

'Yes.'

'Five US dollars?'

'Yes,' said Vinnie patiently.

'Five US dollars is too much,' said the girl. 'I'll do it for two. Can't be worth more than two.'

It was a long time since Vinnie had encountered such virtue and for a second or two she was lost for words. She fished in her handbag for the money and came up with a fiver.

'This is the smallest I've got. Take it, take it,' she said, thrusting it at the girl.

'I'll get change in one of these shops,' said the girl and was about to turn away when Vinnie, who was beginning to feel that the Girl Guide code was being slightly overdone, restrained her.

'Look, sweetheart. Take the five dollars. You can split it later – take two for yourself and give three to the fund for retired Girl Guides. How about that?'

The girl considered this and then nodded gravely. 'Very well. I'll do it.'

'Good. I'm glad that's settled.'

Vinnie took pen and paper from her bag and scribbled a note. Handing it to the waiting girl, she smiled, 'Take that to Mr Bramley or whoever owns the liquor store. Tell him it's urgent. OK?'

'OK.'

'I was in the Guides myself once,' said Vinnie. 'Second troop, Camberwell Green. That's in London.' She held three fingers up at the level of the left shoulder in the Guide salute.

The girl's shining black face broke into a smile for the first time. 'You saluted with the wrong hand!' she said and showed how it should be done. Clutching the note and the money she scampered off.

Five minutes later, Mr Bramley, still in a state of near-hysteria as he surveyed the wreckage of his store, took the note from the little Girl Guide and thrust it into his pocket. He was too concerned to deal with messages, too busy trying to stop the curious crowd from laying hands on what was left of his unprotected stock.

It was only much later when he was preparing for bed, his head aching with calculations about the cost of the damage, that he found the note and unfolded it. What he read there brought him almost instant relief for, in her big bold hand, Vinnie had written:

Sorry about the damage, old cock. Send the bill for the lot to Steve Ugley at Tradewinds. He'll pay. That's a promise.

165

And she had signed the note, in what seemed like an afterthought, with the words: *A Friend.*

'This,' said Brother Vincent, his voice edged with pride, 'is the Square of Peace and Love. And there is our Tabernacle!'

The bus had stopped in the shade of the palm trees and the members of the delegation were standing beside it, looking across the wide grassed arena towards the Tabernacle and the glowing golden cross that surmounted it. For the first time that morning even Greg Cortez had difficulty in finding the words to express his enthusiasm and it was a good twenty seconds before he came up with his favourite clutch of superlatives: 'Fabulous! Great! Incredible!'

Barr had reached the point where he felt that if he heard those words once more he would ram Greg's agile tongue down his throat, but even his impatience was stilled by what lay before him. To have created such order and beauty on this remote West Indian island was an achievement by any standards.

Other members of the delegation gave voice to their enthusiasm and Vincent, delighted with the reaction, smiled with pleasure. 'You will see more of the Tabernacle in a few minutes. First, I want to show you something that you may find quite interesting.'

He led them across the avenue to what seemed to be a kind of small modern supermarket except that, like all the other buildings, it was partly shielded by a riot of flowering shrubs and small trees. They were obviously expected, because they were met at the entrance by a round pink-faced man who was introduced as Brother Brian, the manager. He was clad in the inevitable olive green uniform and, like Vincent, he was wearing a ring with the distinctive seal.

On the inside, the building did not appear, at first glance at least, to differ over much from other supermarkets of similar size, except that it was not so well-stocked as the one Barr occasionally patronised at home. There was a fair supply of fruits and vegetables and such staples as bread and cheese, but meat and canned and packaged goods with their familiar brand names seemed to be in short supply.

A dozen or so customers were moving round the shelves, selecting goods and stacking them into trolleys. Again Barr noticed that, without exception, men and women alike were wearing the special ring. It was beginning to intrigue him.

'Now, ladies and gentlemen,' said Vincent, 'have you noticed anything different about our little store?' He beamed round at them. 'Come on. There is something here that you will never see in a supermarket in London or New York.'

The New York social worker who had landed on Steve's lap on the bus put up her hand in the manner of a schoolgirl responding to a

166

teacher. She was shaking with suppressed excitement.

'I've got it! I think I've got it!'

'Good!' said Vincent. 'Mrs Sykala has the answer. Well, Mrs Sykala, don't keep us in suspense!'

Mrs Sykala pointed towards the exit, and almost screamed the words. 'There are no cash-desks! I don't see a single cash-desk! These people are going out without paying!'

'Absolutely right!' said Vincent and for a moment Barr thought he was going to embrace and kiss the woman. 'One hundred per cent correct!'

'Incredible,' said Greg. 'Fantastic!'

'But how do you do it?' asked Mrs Sykala.

'Very simple,' said Vincent. 'I told you on the bus – we have no money here. I also told you that we operate the principle of from each according to his ability, to each according to his needs.' He spread his arms wide. 'Here is the proof!'

'You mean,' said Mrs Sykala, 'you mean, they just walk in, take all they want, and walk out?'

'That is just what I mean.'

'And they don't pay?'

'Not directly. They work for the Community, and in return, the Community gives them food, shelter and so forth, according to their needs.'

'But somebody could walk in and clean out the whole store if he had the mind.'

'He could,' said Vincent, 'he could, but he wouldn't. There would be no point. Why take two loaves when you only need one?' He smiled. 'There is no greed on Jerusalem Island. We have abolished it.'

'I have never seen or heard anything like it!' said Greg. 'This beats everything. The complete answer to the materialist society! Incredible!'

The enthusiasm was reaching the top of the thermometer again and Barr, who was still trying to work out the significance of the rings, felt that it was time to intervene. He touched Vincent's ring.

'Tell me about that.'

'The ring?' Vincent looked surprised by this sudden change of subject.

'Yes,' said Barr, 'the ring. They seem to be very fashionable. I see that Brother Brian is wearing one.'

'Ah,' said Vincent. 'This is a rather special symbol. Whoever wears one of these is known as a Founder. It means that he or she occupies a special position in the Community.'

'It's an honour?' asked Steve.

'Oh, indeed, a very great honour,' murmured Brother Brian. 'These

167

rings are conferred by Mr Dunlop himself.'

'So not every member of the Community has one?'

'Oh, no. No, indeed. A small number – perhaps five per cent of the people on the island.'

'The Founders – those who have the ring – they enjoy certain privileges?' asked Barr.

'Yes,' said Vincent warily. He was becoming concerned about the direction and purpose of these questions. 'Yes. You might say that. But you must remember that Founders also have very great responsibilities.'

'Shopping in this place,' said Barr casually. 'That's one of the privileges, right? I noticed that all the customers were wearing the ring.'

'Yes, that is so,' said Vincent. He looked at his watch and said briskly, 'Heavens, time to move on.'

'What you're saying is that the privilege of collecting free food here is confined to about five per cent your members?' said Barr relentlessly.

Vincent looked at him severely. 'Professor Beaumont. It is not quite as simple as that.'

'No,' Barr said. 'I understand. It's interesting though. I believe they have a similar system in Russia. The only difference is that over there the privileged ones don't wear a ring – they carry a party card.'

'There is no basis of comparison!' said Vincent sharply. 'However, we cannot debate the subject now. Time to go to the Tabernacle.'

'I'm really looking forward to that,' said Barr. He gave Brother Vincent what he hoped was a big loving smile, just to show that there was no ill-feeling. But on this occasion, the good Brother did not return the compliment.

Neither Steve nor Barr could claim to be experts on the subject of churches, but the interior of the Great Hall of the Tabernacle was unlike any religious meeting-place that they could remember. It had been built in the style of an amphitheatre, with semi-circular tiers of seats looking down on a wide stage, and the impression of being in a theatre was heightened by the two huge Grecian-style pillars which framed the stage area like the sides of a proscenium arch.

A wooden frieze, depicting the life of Christ from Bethlehem to Calvary, ran round the walls just below the high ceiling beams: the arched windows were masked by heavy white curtains edged in blue which hung down like banners, obscuring the outer light. The interior illumination came from cleverly concealed overhead lamps which discreetly highlighted the stage and bathed the auditorium in a subdued golden glow.

The sharp resinous scent of incense drifted on the air and, in the background, they could hear the low solemn murmuring of an organ. The atmosphere, so mellow and cool after the gritty heat and glaring brightness outside, seemed to rest on the skin like silk.

The hall was full, row upon row of people sitting in silence; their dark olive uniforms seemed almost to be lost against the dim background so that, at first, Barr had the feeling that he was seeing lines of disembodied faces glowing in the amber light. But as the delegates were led down a flight of steps through the auditorium to reserved places in the front row, there was a rustle of movement as the congregation rose in unison and offered them the tribute of the Community salute.

As they settled in their seats, Mrs Sykala addressed Vincent in a hushed, respectful whisper: 'Will we see Mr Dunlop?'

'It is possible,' he replied in a low voice. 'At the moment he is fasting and meditating, so one cannot be sure. It is possible.'

'Why do you call him Mister – why not Brother?'

'It has always been that way. He is special to us, he is a great man, but he would take no other title.'

Greg was about to speak but Vincent held a finger to his lips and nodded towards the stage. The music began to surge dramatically, rising in volume, and then a light faded up slowly, illuminating a raised pulpit to one side of the stage. The organ music died away and the head and shoulders of a man appeared above the rim of the pulpit. He was dressed in a plain blue tunic, cut in the Chinese style, and he was wearing the ring of a Founder.

'The Comptroller,' whispered Vincent. 'Mr Dunlop's first lieutenant. A wonderful, wonderful person.'

Lifting his head, as though listening for some heavenly voice, the Comptroller waited for a few moments. Then he began:

'Brothers and Sisters – and friends – I have just come from an audience with our beloved guide and teacher, Mr Dunlop.'

A murmur, as of suppressed ecstasy, rose from the audience.

'He opens his loving arms to you all,' continued the Comptroller, 'he embraces you with his love. He is with you always, he lives in your hearts and minds.'

'Amen, amen!' came the hushed response.

'There is not a moment of your day when he is not with you and when you lay down to sleep his hand is on your brow. He knows your thoughts, he understands your problems, he forgives your weaknesses. He loves you.'

'Hallelujah!' A woman's voice rang out, and her cry was echoed by a hundred others.

'That is the message he asked me to bring. And he asked me, also, to embrace in his name those dear friends from beyond our island shores, who are with us today.' He extended both arms towards the delegation and the audience rose to applaud.

Now the organ music crept in again, and the lights expanded to take in the whole stage, as a line of women emerged, smiling, from the shadows at either side. Each one carried a single red rose, and each was so stunningly beautiful that a collective murmur of admiration rose from the audience.

Once again, the Grecian motif was mirrored in their dress: the white robes, threaded with gold, fell in strong but not rigid folds about their bodies, emphasising rather than obscuring their femininity. Strangely, the impression was both chaste and sensual.

'The Handmaidens of the Tabernacle!' whispered Vincent.

'Fantastic!' Beautiful!' said Greg in a whisper that seemed to cut the silence like a knife.

The Handmaidens came down the steps on either side of the stage and, still smiling, advanced on the delegates. They seemed to glide rather than walk and in the golden glow from the lamps their smiles had an extraordinary, madonna-like radiance.

The girl who came to Barr was, he guessed, about twenty years old and probably came from the Philippines. She offered him the rose and then, with a graceful motion, cupped his left cheek in her right hand. He looked up into dark, eloquent eyes and a face of such loveliness that he felt his heart quicken.

'Welcome,' she said. 'I bring you our love.'

'Thank you,' he murmured, and then, as memory prompted thought and the recollection of a photograph flashed into his mind, he added, on a sudden impulse, 'You are Mila! Mila de Jesus!'

The eyes clouded momentarily and he noted the small suppressed intake of breath, the quickening swell of her full breasts, a slight tensing of the hand on his face. She recovered almost immediately and the smile returned as she drew back.

'I am Sister Angela,' she said softly.

She joined the other girls and they filed back on to the stage, to disappear into the wings. Four of them reappeared with flaming tapers and lit two banks of candles which stood upstage. Barr leaned forward, studying the faces, trying to match them with the photographs which he had seen so many times.

He felt a pressure from Steve's arm and glanced at him. It was obvious from the animation on his friend's face that he, too, had recognised some, at least, of the so-called Handmaidens. Steve nodded, almost imperceptibly towards a Chinese girl: the taper, the flickering candles, clearly illuminated her beautiful high-boned face.

'The Hong Kong girl!' he whispered. 'Hua Yen-ping.'

'Shh! Shh!' hissed Mrs Sykala, looking towards them.

'Cool it, cool it!' Barr spoke out of the side of his mouth to Steve, giving Mrs Sykala an apologetic smile at the same time.

The organ started up again, and the lights faded, leaving only the dancing flames of the candles and a small spot over the pulpit. The music was familiar, but it took Barr a full twenty seconds before he could put a name to it: when he did so, it was with an odd, indefinable sense of apprehension.

The unseen organist was playing the Bridal Chorus from Wagner's *Lohengrin*.

The four Handmaidens had taken up position, two beside each rack of candles. Their companions entered next, holding a canopy of white flowers over a slowly-pacing girl. The new entrant was dressed as the others, except that she wore a headdress and a veil. The procession stopped and turned so that the girl and the canopy were framed by the candles. The last notes of the music lingered on the air and slowly died away.

'Brothers and Sisters,' intoned the Comptroller, 'we are gathered here together in the sight of God to welcome Sister Helen to the Community of New Jerusalem and to bind her in solemn service and duty to the Tabernacle of the People. When Mr Dunlop, our guide and teacher, led us out of the wilderness into this land, it was already fair, an island touched by the finger of God. But Mr Dunlop decreed that by our love and our labour we should build it into the perfection of beauty, so that the whole world would see and marvel and proclaim, in the words of the Bible, *Thou art of perfect beauty. Thy borders are in the midst of the seas, thy builders have perfected thy beauty.*

'It is fitting, therefore, that here, on Jerusalem Island, in the Tabernacle of the People, we should make a tribute of beauty to the Lord. It is fitting that the fairest among women should offer themselves in service to God and to our Community. It is fitting that Sister Helen should come before us today as a bride, to dedicate her beauty to our Tabernacle as one of its chosen Handmaidens.'

The Comptroller paused. A slow solemn roll on the organ punctuated the silence, and then faded. He continued, 'Sister Helen.'

The girl in the veil lifted her head in response.

'Do you come here today of your own free will?'

'I do.' The voice was low but firm.

Barr felt Steve move at his side, and he put a restraining hand on his arm.

'And do you freely offer yourself in service as a Handmaiden to the Tabernacle of the People?'

The girl hesitated. She seemed to be looking towards Steve: she could not see him but it was almost as if she could sense his presence. Then, in the same low voice she said, 'I do.'

'Do you solemnly pledge yourself to follow the wisdom and teachings of our beloved teacher, Mr Dunlop, to obey him in all things?'

'I do.'

'It is good. Handmaidens! Let the Community gathered here look upon our Sister and know that she is fair.'

Two of the Handmaidens stepped forward, and as they lifted the veil, there was a burst of applause from audience and delegates alike. Barr felt Steve quivering at his side: 'It's Kitty! It's Kitty!'

Barr tightened his grip, holding him down. 'Quiet, you damned fool, quiet!'

'It's Kitty!'

'All right. But shouting won't help anybody. Cool it, for God's sake, cool it!'

The applause had died down and Barr's last words were clearly audible. Greg looked along the row towards him with a reproachful eye.

'Professor – please!'

'Sorry,' murmured Barr. 'It's the ceremony. So moving. Mr Lambert is quite overcome. I think I'd better take him out.'

Once they were out on the low verandah which ran the length of the building, Steve turned on Barr. 'What have we come out for?'

'Because if we'd have stayed any longer, you'd have blown it!'

'We can't just leave her!'

'We can't take her with us. We'd have the whole Community at our throats if we showed our hand now. That wouldn't help Kitty, would it? Use your head, man! A bit more of the old Sherlock Holmes and a bit less of the James Bond is what we need right now. Look, we know where she is, we've got some idea of the lay-out. The trick now is to get ourselves back to Tradewinds in one piece and work out what to do.'

'But what about Kitty?'

'They don't seem to have harmed her yet – at least, not physically. They're not likely to hurt her before we make our move. Besides, it's not just a question of Kitty. There are the other girls. We can't snatch one and leave the rest.'

'They're crazy, Tom. That fat guy in the pulpit – the whole lot of them. Crazy. They're capable of anything.'

'They're not so crazy. The top boys have built a multimillion dollar business out of all this. They know what they're doing. I wonder how many numbered bank accounts they've got in Switzerland. No, they're not crazy. Cunning – yes – as cunning as a wagonload of monkeys. That's why we've got to work this thing out properly.'

'OK,' said Steve reluctantly. 'I just hope you're right.'

'I am,' said Barr. 'Didn't you know – I wrote the book?' He put a hand on Steve's shoulder. 'I'll tell you something. You didn't exaggerate. That Kitty Higgins of yours is a real crackerjack.'

'She isn't mine,' said Steve.

172

'Good,' said Barr. 'Then it's a fair fight.' He checked his smile and added in a low voice, 'Don't look now, but I think we've got company.'

'Who?'

'I'm not sure, but I think it's one of the guards we met on the beach.'

Steve turned casually. The guard had just turned the corner of the building and was standing watching them. Steve knew him instantly as the man he had fought with on the day they had slipped ashore.

'Do you think he has recognised us?'

'Yes. But he's puzzled. Can't understand what we're doing here.'

'Doesn't seem to be armed.'

'They're not going to walk around with rifles while the delegation is on the premises, are they?'

'What do we do?'

'He's as thick as two planks, but pretty soon he's going to make it add up. Then he'll blow the whistle. I don't think we'll wait. Hold on.'

Smiling as if in recognition of an old friend, Barr strolled towards the guard. The man eyed him suspiciously, holding his ground uncertainly. Barr held out his hand in greeting: 'Hello, there, hello. We really must stop meeting like this. People will start to talk.'

The guard looked at the outstretched hand and took a wary step backwards.

'Don't be like that,' said Barr reproachfully.

As he spoke, he moved in quickly. Grasping the guard's tunic at the neck he pulled him forward sharply and then slammed him back with greater force against the heavy verandah post. A cry gurgled in the man's throat as his head crashed against the solid wood and when Barr gave a repeat performance he slumped to the ground unconscious.

'You're a rough bastard!' said Steve.

'Bloody amateurs!' said Barr, brushing his hands together in a gesture of contempt. 'The oldest trick in the book, and they fall for it. Not once, but twice!'

He hoisted the man up and dropped him over the verandah rail into a clump of thickly-growing shrubs, where, for the most part, he lay hidden from view. As they turned away, the side door to the Great Hall opened and Vincent emerged with the delegation.

'Are you all right now, Mr Lambert?' he asked.

'I think so,' said Steve. 'But I'd rather like to get back to the hotel as soon as possible.' He put a hand to his forehead. 'I – I found the whole thing so – so overwhelming.'

'We're going back to the boat now,' said Vincent.

Greg Cortez took Steve's hand and pressed it firmly, nodding his head in sympathy. 'I understand,' he said. 'I completely understand. It is hard for the mind – for our sort of minds, that is – to take it all in. I feel as you do, friend. I feel humbled. Those girls – those lovely creatures – dedicating themselves to the Community. Sister Helen – oh, she has to be the most beautiful girl in the world! In America we exploit and merchandise that sort of beauty. But here it is respected and loved. Oh, yes, this visit has been shattering – in my book it has to rate as the greatest spiritual experience of my entire life. The truth is – the basic truth is – I have seen the future and it works!'

Barr had the feeling that he had heard that last phrase somewhere before, in another connection, but he made no comment. He had noticed a small movement in the shrubbery below and he wanted to get the hell out.

Chapter Thirteen

After the induction ceremony, Kitty was taken up to the auditing chamber. As a matter of routine, all the Handmaidens were given sessions of 'mental guidance' and spiritual instruction twice each week and, strictly speaking, Kitty should not have been required to attend for at least two days.

However, Sister Eleanor was concerned about the girl's slight hesitation during one of the responses and, mindful of the Comptroller's warning that she would be held responsible if anything were to go wrong, she had decided that another, immediate session would do no harm. At any time now Kitty might be called to attend Mr Dunlop and Sister Eleanor had to be sure that the new Handmaiden was properly docile.

At first, the routine was much as before. They sat knee to knee in the subdued light, with that strange metronome ticking like a heartbeat in the background, exchanging questions and answers, often going over the same thing again and again.

'What is your name?'

'Sister Helen.'

'What was your former name?'

'I have forgotten.'

'What was your former name?'

'I don't know.'

'Good. That's very good. Why are you here?'

'Because I have sinned. Because my former life was worthless.'

'How was it worthless?'

'I thought only of myself.'

'And now?'

'I have been saved. My soul has been cleansed. Through Mr Dunlop I have learned that love and service are the true purpose of life.' Kitty spoke quickly, eagerly, as though anxious to please.

'Service to whom?'

'To Mr Dunlop and the Community.'

'Who is Mr Dunlop?'

'He is God's voice on earth. To serve him is to serve all mankind.'

After an hour of this, the questioning became sharper and Sister Eleanor seemed to abandon the role of loving friend.

'Tell me your name again!'

'Sister Helen.'

'What was your former name?'

'I have forgotten.'

'Tell me your former name!'

'I can't remember.'

'You're lying, aren't you? You are lying to me!'

'No – no.'

'Stand up! Take off that dress! You are a liar, you are not fit to wear the dress of a Handmaiden! Quickly! Take it off!'

The bewildered girl stood up and, as she fumbled with the dress, Sister Eleanor ripped it from her body.

'What is your name?'

'Sister Helen! Sister Helen!'

'What was your former name?'

'I don't know!'

'You are lying! Pick up that chair! Take it over there – to the wall. Now!' Struggling with the heavy chair, Kitty went to the wall. 'Sit! No, not like that! I don't want to see your lying face. Face the wall!'

A long, long silence. Then: 'Kitty.'

The girl did not move.

In a kinder tone: 'Sister Helen.'

'Yes?'

'Turn round. You may turn round.'

Sister Eleanor moved across and cupped Kitty's face in her hands. The girl's eyes were moist, she was near to tears.

'We love you and we want only to help you. You know that, don't you?' said Sister Eleanor. Kitty nodded. 'Have you heard of the Beach of Pleasure?' Kitty shook her head. 'It is a bad place. Handmaidens who fail in their duty, Handmaidens who do not speak the truth – we send them to the Beach of Pleasure. To pleasure the Guardians. To become whores. Do you want to be a whore?'

'No. No.'

'Then will you promise to tell me the truth?'

'Yes.'

'What is your name?'

'Sister Helen.'

'What was your former name?'

'I don't know.'

'You're lying! Lying!' Sister Eleanor drew back her hand and gave the girl a stinging blow across the face. Kitty cried out, and now the tears flooded out. At once, the other woman bent over and cradled her in her arms.

'There, there, my baby. I didn't want to hurt you. But you must understand – I only want to purge you of evil, to cleanse you. It is for your own good!'

Kitty leaned against Sister Eleanor, exhausted by these swings and roundabouts of emotion. She felt lost and mindless, she could struggle no longer: her only thought was to win this woman's approval, to surrender to her will and thus find the peace her body was aching for. She slid down from the chair and, clasping Sister Eleanor's legs, rested her head against her thighs, in a gesture of total submission.

She quivered as a hand glided across her hair: through the light cotton robe she could feel an answering tremor, feel the soft warmth of flesh against her cheek.

'Look at me,' commanded Sister Eleanor softly. Kitty raised her head. 'What is your name?'

'Sister Helen.'

'What was your former name?'

'I have forgotten.'

'Do you wish to forget?'

'Yes.'

'Good. Good. Are you very tired?'

'Yes.'

'One more question. During the ceremony today, you hesitated on the second response. Why?'

Kitty thought for a moment. 'I don't know.'

'Think. Were you disturbed by anything?'

'Yes. I – I felt – I felt something – out there – among the people. It was strange – like a presence, a kind of presence.'

She frowned, trying to remember what had happened. The experience had lasted no longer than the tick of a clock but in that second she had felt the Kitty she had once been surge within her. She had been filled with an almost uncontrollable urge to cry out, as if this was her last chance. And then, something seemed to snap inside her head, as though the old Kitty had finally broken free and was drifting away. After that, a sort of tranquillity had enveloped her like a cooling shade, a peace and a feeling of quiet content that was beyond anything she had ever known. And now, all her being ached to recover that peace.

'I understand,' said Sister Eleanor. 'There were strangers there today. That is what upset you.' She leaned forward and ran a fingertip over the girl's lips. 'Would you like me to love you?' she whispered.

Kitty drew the gliding finger into her mouth and began gently to caress it with the tip of her tongue. She heard Sister Eleanor's voice. It crackled a little and seemed to be coming from a long way away.

'Go to the couch, my darling. Go and lie on the couch.'

Van Norden, on his way to Jerusalem Island to report to the Comptroller, was a troubled man. He had two matters of some moment on his mind. First, there was the little problem of the car crash and the fact that the Harcourt woman had thus been able to give her pursuers the slip. The two men who had remained on watch at Tradewinds reported that she returned 'to the house some two hours after leaving it but, apart from her visit to the Central Post Office, Van Norden had no way of knowing how she had spent that time.

Second, and more serious, there was the curious circumstance of the two white men, Ugley and Barr. Van Norden's men had held the house under surveillance since early the previous evening. There had been very little movement. Apart from Vinnie Harcourt they had seen no-one leave the place and so concluded that the men were inside. Thus, there was a certain amount of surprise, not to say bewilderment, when Ugley and Barr drove up to the house in the late afternoon. It was unlikely that they could have gone out in the car without being observed. So – how had they got away, and where had they been?

Should he tell the Comptroller all this and risk his anger, or should he simply say nothing and just ride it out?

He had still not resolved what to do when he arrived at the Comptroller's suite. On his way in, he met a man whom he vaguely knew as Brother Vincent coming out. Vincent threw him a quick glance and hurried on. Van Norden remembered him as a smooth, unruffled man, but at this moment he wore the doleful look of a frightened sheep.

Van Norden was admitted at once and the Comptroller wasted no time. 'Well?'

'It's quiet. They're all at Tradewinds.'

'How long have they been there?'

Some animal instinct prompted Van Norden towards caution. He sensed that he had been handed a loaded question and he decided that, in this instance, truth would serve him better than prevarication. He told the Comptroller about the return of Ugley and Barr.

'I've been trying to work it out,' he said. 'They couldn't have slipped away without us seeing them. So I reckon they must have left before I set up the watch. Which means they must have been out all night.'

'But you don't know where?'

'No. Of course, it can't happen again, I —'

The Comptroller interrupted. His voice had the cutting edge of a razor. 'Would it interest you to know that they were here?'

'On Jerusalem Island?' Van Norden stiffened in his chair, unable to suppress his astonishment.

'On Jerusalem Island,' repeated the Comptroller. He briefly described the events of that morning. 'Brother Vincent gave them a free tour of the island, let them look over the Tabernacle. And, more to the point, they saw the girls, the Handmaidens.'

'How did they do it?'

'They impersonated two members of the delegation. Stayed at the

178

hotel last night and came on the visit this morning.'

'You mean – you mean no-one picked them out, no-one suspected?' Van Norden's eyes were wide with disbelief.

'No-one. Not even our good Brother Vincent. No – wait. There was someone. A Guardian. He ended up with a broken head.'

'Christ!'

'That is not the expression I would use, but it does make the point.'

'Would they have recognised the girls?'

'They're not blind. And they are certainly not idiots. At the very least, they will have recognised the English girl.'

'Do you think they'll go to the police?'

'It's possible.'

Van Norden felt the panic curl in his guts like a snake. Jerusalem Island was technically under Antiguan jurisdiction: if the police did decide to investigate, if they found the girls, the consequences could be horrendous. Especially for him. It wasn't just Antigua he had to be concerned about: the law in a dozen other countries would be after his head.

The Comptroller sensed what was going through the man's mind and for a moment he played with the idea of leaving him to sweat. And then he decided that this would not be wise. The last thing he wanted just now was to have Van Norden work himself up into a state of nerves. In that condition, he could be a danger to himself and to the Community. So he said, 'Don't worry. It is unlikely that they will approach the police.'

'Why? What's to stop them?'

'In the first place, their own hands are not too clean. They must have abducted the two Englishmen in order to take their places on the delegation. In the second place, we are not without influence in Antigua or elsewhere. If they were foolish enough to go to the police, they might encounter a certain, shall we say, resistance. And in the third place, I suspect that these men are cast in a different mould. I rather fancy that they are the sort who prefer direct action.'

Van Norden nodded. It was a fair assessment. He sat back as the tension began to leave his body, and his mind turned towards a solution of the problem. He could see only one safe and sure way to solve it. And, once again, the Comptroller seemed to read his thoughts.

'Of course, I could ask you to remove them,' he said amiably. 'Remove them permanently. We have a clear commission from Mr Dunlop to protect the Community against threats of this kind. I'm sure you could arrange something.'

'It would be a pleasure,' said Van Norden. His initial feeling of panic had now turned to anger: since their arrival, Barr and the others had disrupted the even flow of his life and given him nothing but trouble. 'It would be a real pleasure,' he added savagely.

'I don't doubt that,' said the Comptroller. 'You are a lucky man, Van Norden. Not everyone finds such fulfilment and satisfaction from his work.'

Van Norden did not understand this remark but he suspected that the Comptroller was getting at him and decided not to comment.

'However,' continued the Comptroller, 'I think we should hold you in reserve, so to speak. A last resort if all else fails. In the meantime, I want you to wait in the ante-room. In due course, I shall have a letter which I want you to deliver in person.'

'A letter?' Van Norden blinked.

'That is what I said.' And as the other man frowned, he added: 'I know that rational thought is an effort for you. So don't try and think this one out. Just do as I say – it will be better for both of us.'

When Van Norden had gone, the Comptroller poured himself a glass of wine and sat twirling the glass in his hands, taking an occasional judicious sip. It was now clear to him that Van Norden would have to go. The man had never been too bright, but that, in a sense, was one of his attractions. His lack of imagination, his coldness, the absence of feeling – all these things had made him a superb and efficient tool. But in the last months there had been a change: a certain nervousness had begun to show, the edge had gone. The tell-tale signs were there, in the eyes, in the odd twitch that had developed in the man's cheek, in half a dozen other almost imperceptible mannerisms. He was like a man who, having lived on the edge of danger for years, had suddenly begun to fear that he had used up his luck.

A pity, thought the Comptroller. Van Norden had served him well and he would not be easy to replace. When this other, more immediate problem had been resolved, he would have to work out a way to dispose of the man. The Lagoon, perhaps, that would probably provide the simplest and easiest answer.

The Comptroller sighed. This was always happening. Just when things seemed to be running smoothly, some irritating problem would present itself for his attention. He had been hoping to get away from the island for a few weeks, to go to New York, and possibly even London, to take in the latest plays, hear a few concerts, browse in the great art galleries, eat in the finest restaurants.

He had been too long on the island: New York and London could give him the sort of mental refreshment and stimulation he needed. But there was no way that he could go now. It had been his intention to leave Vincent in charge, but he no longer felt able to rely on the man.

A tap at the door interrupted his thoughts. The small closed-circuit monitor on his desk, discreetly housed in a rosewood case, indicated that Sister Eleanor was waiting outside the door. He pressed a button and a light glowed outside, to indicate that she might enter.

'Ah, Sister Eleanor. Come in and take a chair. Would you like a glass of wine?'

'Thank you, Comptroller.' Sister Eleanor smoothed her skirt as she sat down and he noted, with interest, that there was a touch of relief in her manner, as if she had been expecting a colder reception. And her face, normally without much colour, bore a distinctive flush.

As he handed her the wine, he said casually, 'I thought Sister Helen did very well at the induction.'

'Yes. She is coming along nicely. Quite nicely.' A small apprehensive shadow passed across her eyes and was gone as quickly as it had come.

He lowered himself into an armchair facing her and allowed almost a full minute to pass in silence. She moved uneasily once or twice. He gave her a sympathetic smile and spoke at last:

'Are you well?'

'Yes. Yes. Quite well, thank you, Comptroller.'

'You look a little —' He paused, as if seeking the right word. 'Tired. A touch tired. Not overdoing things, I hope?'

'No. I don't think so, at any rate. Of course, it has been an exacting day. And these sessions of mental guidance can be exhausting.' She smiled. 'One is giving out all the time, giving of oneself. I sometimes think it is more tiring for us than for the subjects.' And she added hastily, 'But it is so rewarding. So rewarding in the end.'

'Of course. I know the feeling. To be able to purge someone of evil, to bend and shape someone's mind and soul until she becomes an eager, smiling servant of the Community — that requires a very special dedication.'

'Indeed,' she said, 'indeed.' She was used to the Comptroller by now, she knew that he would take his own time to reach the point. All the same, she wished fervently that he would get on with it.

'I am surprised that you should have been involved in mental guidance today, Sister,' he said. 'I would have thought the induction ceremony was enough.'

'Yes,' she said. Her voice faltered a little. 'In normal circumstances, yes. But I felt, in view of all the circumstances, that I should give Sister Helen an additional session.'

'Circumstances?'

'She has not been assessed. You said yourself that Dr Bauer would not be available to make an assessment.'

'Quite right. I did. I commend your caution. And are you satisfied?'

'Completely. There is a critical point, as you know, when the subject is poised, so to speak, between the past and the future. In Sister Helen's case, that point has been passed, I'm certain of that.

What she was is behind her. She now accepts what she is and accepts it willingly, eagerly. There is no resistance. At the moment, of course, she is passive. Her only desire is to be accepted, to please. That is a common reaction after the process of disorientation. But she has a strong mind and personality and, given her present rate of development, she will quickly proceed to the next stage and become a positive, dedicated disciple of the Community.'

'Excellent. Excellent.' The Comptroller rose and made an adjustment to the air-conditioning, then turned towards Sister Eleanor. 'At the moment, of course, you are the one she looks to. Correct?'

'Yes, in a sense, yes. That is natural. I am the one fixed point of authority in her life at the moment. It happened with the others. And it will pass.'

'I want you to persuade Sister Helen to write a letter,' said the Comptroller abruptly. 'Can you do it?'

She hesitated, the surprise showing in her eyes. 'Yes. That should present no problem. May I ask —'

'The letter is to someone – a man – with whom I suspect she had a close relationship at one time. Do you see a danger in that? Would such a reminder cause her to revert?'

'I don't think so,' she said carefully.

'Think! I don't want you to think, woman, I want to know!'

'She will write whatever I tell her, Comptroller. There will be no reversion.'

'Good. Now, suppose as a result of such a letter, she were to meet this man – meet him here – how would she react then?'

'That would depend.'

'On what?'

'On their past relationship. If they were lovers – if she was in love with him in the recent past – then I believe there could be a reaction. Such an emotional reminder of her former life might possibly break down the mental barriers we have erected. One cannot be sure. On the other hand, if you could postpone such a meeting for two or three weeks, I am certain —'

He interrupted her, his voice curt. 'That is not possible. The meeting will take place tomorrow – if it takes place at all. And I want her to be strong enough to reject this man completely – to convince him that she came here of her own free will and intends to stay here. Can that be done?'

'There are so many unknown factors,' she replied, shaking her head.

'Can it be done?' he repeated impatiently. 'Yes or no?'

'Yes. There is a risk, but if I could have one more session with her before the meeting – one or even two – then I believe I could keep her under control.'

'Good.' He went to the desk and picked up a sheet of paper. 'I have written an outline, a draft, no more. It is very much up to you. I do not know the exact nature of her relationship with this young man. You must find that out – and the letter must be written accordingly. See that she also puts in something that will convince him that it is genuine – mention of a meeting that only they would know about. I have indicated the sort of thing I mean.'

'I will see to it, Comptroller.' She took the paper and stood up. As she went towards the door, his voice checked her: 'Have you had the girl, Sister?'

The blood surged into her cheeks as she turned. 'I don't understand,' she stammered.

'Oh, come,' he said blandly. 'You don't have to be coy with me. Don't you think I know what goes on? I've watched some of the antics down in the Grove. I find them vastly entertaining. It is only to be expected, after all. You are a company of women, cut off from any meaningful relationship with the opposite sex – it is natural that you should turn to each other for – shall we say – satisfaction?'

'Some of the Handmaidens have –' she began, but he cut through her words and went on relentlessly, 'And, as you have said, Sister Helen is in that state of mind where she looks upon you as the centre of her life. She is dependent upon you – she fears your anger and longs to win your approval. These are familiar symptoms at the final stage of the auditing process, as you said yourself a moment or so ago.'

'The girl *is* eager to please,' began Sister Eleanor defensively. 'But, all the same —'

'Of course,' said the Comptroller, interrupting again. 'I am not criticising. It means you have done your work well. She longs for tenderness and she wants to please you. So, naturally, the two things come together.' He chuckled. 'Or unnaturally, depending on one's prejudices. Either way it is probably all to the good.' He gave her a smile which was not far short of being a leer. 'Carry on with the good work, Sister. The more you can do to strengthen her dependence upon you the better. It could be crucial to the meeting I mentioned.'

He put a clenched fist across his chest in a salute that was also a signal for her to go. As the door closed with a click behind her, he picked up his goblet and shook his head. Sexuality, other people's sexuality, intrigued him. He thanked God that he had been created without any such destructive urges, one way or another. It amused him to watch two or three human beings thrashing around together in a welter of passion but he had never felt the slightest desire to participate, or the smallest twinge of envy.

If anything, his reaction was one of contempt that people should lose control of themselves in this crude animal fashion, that they should allow their need for physical gratification to overcome all reason.

His thoughts went to Mr Dunlop. If there was one person in the world he admired to the point of worship it was Mr Dunlop. He had created the Community, performed miracles. Yet even this extraordinary man, for all his great gifts, had allowed his love of women to reach the level of an obsession. He had learned nothing from his youthful excesses and they had ruined him in the end, destroyed that magnificent brain. And even now, when the vigour had gone from his flesh, he lived a continuous sexual fantasy in his mind.

He thought of the old man, lying in his huge bed in the East Wing of the Tabernacle, or sitting hunched in a chair, endlessly sifting the photographs and clippings which arrived regularly from all over the world. He played little or no part in the life of the Community now, though few people knew this. He had occasional periods of lucidity, when the Comptroller could persuade him to record a message for his people, but these were growing less frequent.

He lived as a virtual prisoner in his rooms, cut off by his own choice from any outside contact, surrounded by his Handmaidens and seeing only the Comptroller, to whom he had delegated all authority over the Community.

In the beginning, the Handmaidens had been chosen from the Community itself: there had always been a ready supply of girls eager to enjoy the honour of serving Mr Dunlop. They had come and gone – and such was the force of his personality that they had largely gone without malice, proud to have been favoured even for a little while.

But later, as the disease ravaged his mind and body, a kind of monomania had developed. It sprang, the Comptroller suspected, from two things. Mr Dunlop had never succeeded in having a child and this infertility, which had always haunted him, assumed greater significance as time went by. The monomania had then been given fresh impetus by a decline in his own powers which had led finally to complete impotence.

Oddly enough, these failures seemed to increase rather than diminish his fever. Whatever else had failed, the desire seemed still to be there. It was as if the mere presence of beautiful women was in itself a sexual satisfaction; or perhaps he believed that somehow he would be touched by their beauty and made whole. It was probably a combination of both, the Comptroller thought.

And so Mr Dunlop had begun to collect the loveliest of women as other men collect paintings. Or rather, the Comptroller, using the worldwide organisation of the Community and hirelings like Van Norden, had collected them for him.

Gradually, the net was spread wider and wider. Mr Dunlop studied news reports, pored over films and photographs. Only extraordinary physical beauty would satisfy him. His collection had to be the finest in the world; he dreamed of discovering the ultimate perfection in feminine beauty.

It was a kind of madness and, at first, the Comptroller had refused to indulge it. He dared not oppose Mr Dunlop directly at that time, but he had tried, in devious ways, to frustrate the obsession. The operations it entailed were a minefield of dangers for the Community. But, in the end, he had given way, as he always did with Mr Dunlop, for he could deny him nothing. He could never forget what the man had once been, his magnetism, his strength, and – yes – his idealism. Whatever people said, in those early days, he had given thousands of people a new sense of purpose. Not least the Comptroller who had been a near-hopeless drug addict before meeting him.

Many men develop obsessions in their old age, and Mr Dunlop's was more extreme than most. But in the Comptroller's view, there was no man on earth who had a greater right to be indulged. The Community owed Mr Dunlop that at least, and so long as he was in charge he would see that the debt was paid in full.

The Comptroller lifted his goblet so that the light struck prisms of colour through the delicate glass. He also loved beauty. He could appreciate, dispassionately, the form and grace of a beautiful girl or boy: but his enthusiasm was directed elsewhere. It was his dream to build on the island, for his private pleasure – for the joy lay in personal possession – a great gallery in which he would house the greatest art treasures of the world, preserving them from the coming holocaust in which the so-called civilised nations would surely destroy themselves.

He sighed again as he studied the goblet. An inanimate object. But what could compare with the eternal beauty of such craftsmanship. Inanimate! He smiled, certain beyond any measure of doubt that there was more grace, vitality and meaning in that one object than in a hundred of Mr Dunlop's Handmaidens!

Charlie Brown, who was watching from an upper window, saw Van Norden enter the drive and move towards the house. He went downstairs, opened the front door, and waited to greet the visitor. After the coolness inside, the late afternoon heat hit him like a fist. You're not a West Indian, he told himself ruefully, you're a black cockney: you react to this climate like any pink faced European.

He eyed the man crunching towards him across the gravel. Well-built, probably in the middle-thirties, wearing a well-cut fawn linen suit and tie, moving easily. The tan suggested that he had been in this part of the world for some time. He didn't look like one of the

Community guards. A policeman, perhaps, a plain-clothes cop? Charlie thought of the two Englishmen locked away upstairs and wondered if the man had a warrant to search the house. Then he dismissed the idea: if the man was a detective and had come to look over the place, he would certainly not have come alone.

'Hi,' he said, with a friendly nod as Van Norden reached him.

'Hi,' said the visitor, smiling.

Charlie noticed that the smile did not extend beyond the muscles of the face and his long training in the boxing ring told him that behind those icy blue eyes the man was measuring him up. He noticed also that there was no sweat on the man's face: he seemed cool and composed, impervious to the heat.

'What can I do for you?' he asked.

'Is Mr Ugley in? Mr Steve Ugley?'

'Who wants to know?'

'My name is not important. Just tell Mr Ugley —'

'No,' said Charlie. 'Mr Ugley don't like no-name visitors. Come to that,' he added amiably, 'I don't much like them myself.'

For the merest fraction of a second the blue eyes darkened and then Van Norden smiled. At first, he had taken the other man to be one of the servants, but now he realised that this must be Charles Brown, one of the group around Steve Ugley. He was glad of this opportunity to meet a member of the opposition and to be able to weigh him up. One day soon, he reflected, I may have to kill you.

'If you insist,' he said. 'The name is Van Norden.'

'Van Norden.' Repeating the name didn't help Charlie, it rang no bells in his head.

'That's right. Now, would you mind telling Mr Ugley that I have a letter for him?'

'I don't think he'll want to be disturbed right now,' said Charlie, extending a hand. 'I'll see he gets it. No problem.'

'I'm sorry,' said Van Norden. 'My instructions are to deliver the letter to Mr Ugley. To put it in his hands.'

'I see.' Charlie considered this one carefully. 'Instructions? Who did they come from?'

'Mr Ugley will know when he has read the letter.'

'All right,' said Charlie, after a further moment of thought. 'I'll take you to him.'

'Thank you,' said Van Norden, with just a hint of sarcasm.

'First, Mr Van Norden,' said Charlie, 'first of all, would you like to stand facing that wall and spread your arms and legs?'

'What for?'

'We've had some funny characters hanging around lately. And I've got a very suspicious nature.'

'I'm not armed, if that's what you're worried about,' said Van Norden.

186

'I believe you. But I'd still like to check.'

Van Norden shrugged and faced the wall while the other man frisked him.

'OK,' said Charlie, 'let's go.' He pointed to the right. 'Thataway. You go first.'

Directed by Charlie, Van Norden moved around the side of the house. He allowed himself a small smile of amusement. Charlie's search had been perfunctory and amateurish in the extreme: he had completely missed the stiletto in the padded case. He could feel it now, nestling against his leg, and drew some comfort from its presence. Not that he expected to use it on this visit, but it was interesting to know that Charlie was not as bright as he appeared.

He heard a murmur of voices and a woman laughing hoarsely, and then the sounds died as they approached the terrace. The two men were in swimming trunks, with towels around their shoulders, and the woman – whom he assumed to be Mrs Harcourt – was wearing an old-fashioned but extraordinarily flamboyant bathing suit. The description he had been given was, he decided, a gross under-estimation. She was massive, with muscled arms and thighs that would have done credit to an all-in wrestler.

'Gentleman wants to see you, Steve,' said Charlie. 'Name of Van Norden.'

Steve rose to meet the visitor. Like his uncle, thought Van Norden, like his uncle. The same sort of plain craggy face, the same obstinate set to the jaw. Unlike the uncle, however, this man was young and fit, with broad shoulders and no hint of flab.

'What can I do for you?' asked Steve. He waited expectantly, warily, making no gesture of welcome.

'You are Mr Ugley, Mr Steve Ugley?'

'Yes.'

'I've brought you this.' Van Norden reached into an inner pocket and produced a white envelope. As he handed it to Steve, he added, 'I was told to wait for an answer.'

Steve glanced at the firm italic-style writing on the envelope and frowned. He gave Van Norden a quick, puzzled look and moved away a little.

While Steve was reading the letter, Van Norden studied the other man, Barr. He, too, was strong and well-built but there was some-thing more to this one. The relaxed manner was deceptive, cloaking the kind of coiled alertness that comes only from long and varied experience in dangerous places. Van Norden had seen a few profes-sionals in his time and he recognised the type. Moreover, he suspected that this man was good. Killing him would not be a simple matter.

Barr looked up at him. 'Do you reckon you'll know me if we meet again?'

187

'Sorry. Was I staring?' Van Norden smiled.

'Help yourself,' said Barr. 'There's no charge.'

Steve turned suddenly back to the group and grabbed Van Norden's arm. 'Who told you to bring this?'

'Don't do that, sonny,' said Van Norden, shaking himself free. 'I just had this suit pressed.'

'I said – who told you to bring this?' Steve took a threatening step towards Van Norden who stood his ground insolently.

'I didn't come here to answer questions. Just to bring the letter and wait for a reply. A straight yes or a straight no.'

'Kitty. How is she?'

'I told you —'

'Kitty! Kitty Higgins! How is she?'

'I don't know any Kitty,' said Van Norden. 'I'm just the messenger boy. Can I have an answer – yes or no? Would you mind? I want to get back before dark.'

Steve hesitated, tensed and angry, on the point of explosion. And then, controlling himself, he said quietly, 'Yes. The answer is yes.'

'Now, hold on,' Barr said, 'hold on! What is this?' He pulled himself up out of his chair.

'Look,' said Steve sharply, 'I can handle it! Will you let me handle it?' He turned back to Van Norden. 'Yes! I told you – yes! Now, get out, get out!'

'My pleasure,' said Van Norden lazily. He measured Barr with his eyes. 'We will meet again. I'll make a special point of it.'

'On your way!' said Charlie, giving him a little shove.

Van Norden turned quickly, a snarl growling in his throat, a muscle twitching in his cheek: he checked himself almost immediately and, with the same insolent smile, said, 'Don't push, boy. I don't like to be pushed. Let's go.'

He walked away with Charlie in tow, and in a few moments they had disappeared along the path which led through the garden.

Steve looked at Barr and said in a half embarrassed, half apologetic tone, 'I need a beer. Would you like a beer?'

'I'll have a Scotch,' said Barr quietly.

Vinnie looked at the two men and got to her feet. 'I'll get the drinks,' she said. She gave a little cackling laugh and added, 'Don't start the fight until I get back.' She slipped on a gown and padded away.

'Sorry,' said Steve.

'That letter has something to do with Kitty?' asked Barr.

'It's from Kitty,' said Steve. 'You'd better read it.'

'You sure you want me to?'

'Read it, for God's sake!' said Steve irritably. 'I'm going to take a swim.' He gave Barr the letter and vaulted over the low terrace wall

188

on to the soft snowy sand below. In a few seconds he was in the water swimming strongly, almost desperately, out to sea. Barr watched him for a few moments, then unfolded the letter.

My dear Steve – I have been told by friends that you are in Antigua, and I am taking this opportunity to contact you. If you can spare the time I should like very much to see you again, if only for a half-hour. Could you possibly come to Jerusalem Island tomorrow morning at about noon? The bearer of this letter will meet you at the office of J. D. Winston in St John's and bring you to me. Do come. It will give me a chance to explain why I left England so suddenly, without a word to my friends, or my parents.

Do you remember that evening when we went to the Duke of York's Theatre to see Glenda Jackson in *Rose*? Afterwards you drove me home in your car (your minicab!) and we had coffee and talked. I told you then that I felt as if I was living a useless life, without purpose or meaning. All that is past now, thanks to the Community. I have never been so happy or felt so fulfilled. I have truly found a new and meaningful life here on Jerusalem Island.

You will remember me as Kitty Higgins but all that is behind me now, which is why I sign myself,

Yours in Christ,
Sister Helen.

PS. Please say you will come, for old time's sake.

Ten minutes later, when Steve returned from his swim, he picked up his beer and the letter and went straight to his room, without saying a word. Vinnie gave Barr an enquiring look and he told her what had happened. When he'd finished, she asked, 'He's going, is he? He's still going?'

'Yes. Unless I can talk him out of it.'

'You won't do that. He was – he is – very fond of that girl. Fonder than he will admit.'

Barr rose and picked up his drink. 'You never put enough ice in the Scotch.' It was a statement rather than a complaint.

'The bar's over there,' she said. 'You're not paralysed. You can walk that far and help yourself.'

'Thanks,' he said, 'I'll do that. Then I'll go and talk to Steve.'

'Tom. Wait.'

'Yes?'

'I think Steve should go and see the girl.'

'Oh, yes?' he said politely.

189

'Listen,' she said, 'sit down a minute and listen.' He settled back in his seat, the impatience showing on his face. 'And take that look off your face!' she commanded. 'You look as cheerful as a dying duck in a thunderstorm!'

He managed a small smile. 'Go on.'

'This is the way I see it,' she said. 'They know we're here, and they know we've come after Kitty. They also know we can make trouble for them. They want to head off that trouble. If they can convince Steve that Kitty is there of her own free will —'

'Garbage!' said Barr savagely.

'Listen, listen! Don't let your temper get the better of your judgment!'

'She was snatched – kidnapped!'

'Maybe, maybe. But suppose she tells Steve that it didn't happen like that? Suppose she tells him she came out here willingly, to start a new life with the Community?'

'If she does that, it can only mean one thing. She's been got at. Brainwashed. That's what they call it.'

'I know. There was a case in Britain not long ago – a cult called the Loonies or something.'

'The Moonies,' said Barr patiently.

'The Moonies. I was near enough. They were accused of doing the same thing. But that's beside the point.'

'Is it?'

'They wouldn't let Steve go near Kitty if they weren't pretty sure of their ground. If they can get her to convince him that she is a genuine convert, then they figure he'll be up the creek without a paddle. He can't press charges of forceful abduction if she says it didn't happen that way. He can't go ahead and rescue Kitty if she doesn't want to be rescued.'

'It has been done.'

'Maybe. But they're hoping that Steve will be convinced enough to call off the dogs.'

'And if he isn't?'

'What have they lost? Nothing. They'll be no worse off than they are now. If you were in their shoes, wouldn't you rate it a worthwhile gamble?'

'Yes,' he said grudgingly. 'Yes. You could be right.'

'Don't overdo the enthusiasm, will you?' she said drily. 'Don't strain yourself.'

'There is another possibility,' he said softly. 'One you haven't mentioned.'

'And that is?'

'They know about Steve now. They know that he is loaded – a very, very rich young man. It could be – it just could be – that the idea is to use Kitty as a bait to get Steve over there alone. Then they go to work on him with all their techniques. Do the same job on him as they seem to have done on the girl. Eventually he sees the light – their light – and signs his money and property over to them. He wouldn't be the first rich man to do that.'

Vinnie looked at him for a long time before she spoke. 'They'd never break Steve,' she said at last, but there was a touch of doubt in her voice.

'Famous last words,' said Barr. 'I wouldn't bet on it. Vinnie – these people are running a racket, not a religion, and they're experts. Maybe, like Gordon Pullar said, maybe it started off as a worthwhile idea, but it's gone rotten. Corrupt. The Community has worldwide property worth billions of dollars. They've got thousands of kids out collecting on the streets in New York, London, San Francisco – a dozen cities. If they don't collect enough, they don't eat. Over on Jerusalem Island they've got a virtually unpaid labour force slaving away to maintain a small élite. Where the money goes, God only knows, but I'd lay odds that the Community leaders won't starve in their old age.'

'How the hell do they manage to keep their hold on people?' asked Vinnie.

'Maybe the alternative isn't so hot. I mean our world, our way,' said Barr. 'It's greedy, cheap, tawdry and there's no sign that it's going to get better. In the thirties and forties it was politics – the brave new world where there'd be no poverty, no war and all men would be equal. But the politicians screwed that one up. So now, in desperation, the youngsters turn to religion. Not the old-fashioned kind – that's part of the establishment. It has to be something different, challenging, that appeals to their idealism. No, Vinnie, we created the conditions. The people who lead the Moonies and the Community and all the other cults simply cashed in on them.'

After this, they sat in silence for a long time. A breeze had sprung up, stirring the branches of the sea-grapes, brushing their faces. The sun was low on the horizon, a glowing disc surrounded by flashes of purple and crimson: and, reaching from sun to shore like a bridge laid on the rippling water, there was a broad ribbon of gold.

'God didn't make a bad job of things,' said Vinnie.

'No,' said Barr, 'no, he didn't.' He glanced at his watch and stood up, stretching his shoulders. 'Must get moving. Lot to do. I've got to see Acky about the boat for one thing.'

'Your friends arrive tomorrow,' said Vinnie. 'You're not thinking of putting them off?'

'No. One way or another, I reckon we're going to need them.'

'You didn't get your ice.'

'Too late now.' He tipped the glass to his mouth and drained it.

'Before you go,' she said, 'I have one small suggestion.'

'Go on.'

'I'll go in with Steve tomorrow,' she said. 'As a sort of back-up. It will make it just that bit more difficult for them to swing anything. Maybe I won't be able to do much, but at least he won't be on his own. He'll have company.'

She had expected an argument but, surprisingly, he nodded agreement. 'You'd do that?'

'Of course. What do you think? Be a damn sight better than sitting here on my backside. And besides —'

He prompted her gently, 'Besides what?'

'I was going to say that meeting Steve – knowing that boy – is the best thing that ever happened to me.'

Barr patted her shoulder. 'You go in and talk to Steve, Vinnie. If you can't argue him out of going, persuade him to take you along. I'll go and see Acky before he shuts up shop.'

It was dark by the time Barr reached Sugar Bay and from the look of things Mr Daniel Ackland-Pryce had already packed up for the night. The bigger boats were lapping at their moorings, the lighter craft had been hauled up on to the beach. He was about to reverse out and go back, cursing his stupidity in leaving it so late, when he saw a flicker of light in the cabin.

He parked the car, switched off the lights, and locked the doors. It was very dark, with a low, black threatening sky pressing on the earth, holding in the stifling heat of the day. Tossing the keys in his hand, he looked back along the road. He had been tailed from Tradewinds by someone on a motorcycle, and suddenly the headlamp cut a swathe of light through the darkness towards him.

For a moment, Barr considered the possibility of circling round behind the man and dealing with him, but he dismissed the temptation. He would have to defer the pleasure until later: his business with Acky had to come first. As he turned towards the cabin, the motorcycle lights went out.

There was no answer either to his first or to his second knock, so he pushed open the door. A spill of light came through the curtains at the end of the room. He called out, 'Anybody home?'

There was no reply. He moved cautiously towards the curtains, pushing one of the canvas chairs aside.

'Anybody home?' he repeated.

Again, there was no answer. Then he became aware of the steady sound of running water. He went through the curtains into the room beyond. Most of the space was occupied by the king-size bed, which had been freshly made. A white bikini top and bottom lay on the floor and some shirts and dresses hung from a rail at one side. A bedside lamp perched on a small white table and a large coloured poster-portrait of the Beatles in their early days provided the illumination and the decoration respectively. The place was cramped and the furnishings fairly basic, but it was fresh and clean, giving Barr an altogether more favourable impression than he'd received from the brief glimpse on his earlier visit.

The sound of water stopped suddenly and Barr, feeling that he had intruded too much and too far, stepped back. But before he could get through the curtains, a door at the rear opened and a girl appeared. She was wet and, apart from a floppy shower-cap, she was naked. She was half in shadow at first, and it took Barr a moment to realise that it was Lindy, the Australian girl who worked for Acky.

She was humming as she came in and drying herself with a white towel which seemed to highlight the glossy smoothness of the tanned skin, but she stopped when she saw Barr and drew the inadequate towel over her breasts. Half frightened, half angry, she cried, 'What are you doing here?'

Barr stepped back, holding up his hands in apology. 'Sorry. Sorry. I was looking for Acky. I saw the light and – sorry.'

'Acky's not here. He's gone to town.'

'When will he be back?'

'He won't come back. Leastways, not till morning when we open up.' Her fear had gone now and she smiled. 'Ah, I get it! You think Acky lives here!'

The smile turned to a laugh. With a quick, teasing, graceful movement she removed the shower-cap and released her hair. Then, dropping the towel at her feet, she took a shirt from the rail and slipped it over her head.

'Acky wouldn't live here,' she said. 'He wouldn't be seen dead in a dump like this! He's got a fine house over by Runaway Bay. He couldn't live here.'

'This is your place then?' Barr tried to make it sound casual, but he was aware of the tremor in his voice. The fresh, piny, tantalising scent of her body drifted on the air between them.

'Only for the moment,' she answered liltingly. 'Only for the moment, till I find something better.' She moved towards him. The dampness was moulding the shirt to her body like a second skin. 'You want to see him about a boat?'

'Yes,' he said. There was a warm mist in his mind, fuddling his thoughts. With an effort, he went on, 'I want to hire the *Carib Beauty* for a couple of days.'

'No problem,' she said. 'It's done.' She stood very close and looked up at him with mocking brown eyes. She was breathing quickly and the tip of her tongue showed between the full lips. It seemed a long time before she said, 'Do you want me?' She moved closer still and suddenly, explosively, he could feel her move against him, her

193

stomach rolling and gyrating against his groin. After a few moments she stopped and smiled up at him.

'Do you like that?'

He put a hand on her right breast. She did not move. The nipple peaked and hardened under his touch.

'Are you Acky's girl?' he asked.

'No.' She shook her head.

He made to move towards her, but she stepped back a pace. With a slow, teasing motion she pulled the shirt over her head and let it drop. His blood was racing now, the beat of his heart thundered in his head.

Two smooth sun-tanned arms went round his neck and she reached up for his lips. His hands glided down her back to her firm cool buttocks. They felt like satin to his touch.

She drew away again and began to undress him. And suddenly a warning signal sounded in his head, small at first but growing more insistent, and the mist in his mind dissolved. He gripped her wrists, holding her still.

'What is it?' she whispered.

He hushed her to silence, and lifted his head as though scenting the air for danger. He knew now that someone was out there: his ears had picked up the sound of a footfall on the wooden walkway which led to the cabin. He waited to hear it again. His thoughts were on the motorcyclist who had followed him from the house.

He heard the footfall again, nearer this time, and, pushing Lindy away, he stood to one side of the curtains, watching the door ahead. There was another sound now, as the intruder rapped on the woodwork: a distinct signal, three long taps followed by another three in quick succession. Barr turned his head to the girl in a silent enquiry. The motorcyclist would not have announced his presence in this way – so who could it be?

'It's all right,' she whispered. 'A friend of Acky's. He's a bit early tonight. Didn't expect him for another hour. Wait. Won't take long.'

She slipped into a dress and went through to the door. He heard her open it, saw the outline of a man in the doorway, saw him step inside quickly and close the door. There followed the low murmur of voices. He could only make out the odd word or so, but one phrase in particular made his heart quicken with excitement. He heard, or thought he heard, the man say that he had been forced to alter his schedule because the Guardians had reinforced their night patrols.

Lindy came back, holding a finger to her lips to warn Barr to keep silent. She began to pull a bundle from under the bed: it was wrapped in sack-cloth, tied with rope, and it was obviously heavy. He went to help her, keeping out of the other man's sight-line. There was a slight half-muffled metallic clang from within the bundle as he hoisted it up.

194

She took it in both arms and staggered through to the other room. The man took the bundle, there was a further low exchange, and then he was gone.

Barr went through and lifted a corner of the curtain on one of the two small windows which flanked the door. He was in time to see the shadowy figure of the man walking down the walkway towards the sea. Carrying the heavy bundle seemingly without effort, he disappeared into the darkness.

Lindy was about to bolt the door, but Barr stopped her. 'Wait,' he said. 'I'll be back.'

She opened her mouth to protest, and he held up a warning hand. 'I'll be back,' he repeated.

Outside, there was no sound but the low whisper of the surf and, in the distance, the high bark of a complaining dog. To the south, two or three miles away, he could see the orange lights of St John's. The walkway creaked beneath his tread, and he stepped off into the sand. He moved towards the water and, as his eyes adjusted to the darkness, he picked up the outline of the man once more.

Barr dropped down behind a beached canoe. The man continued on until he reached a boat. He loaded the bundle and pushed off. Barr waited, and soon he heard the sound of muffled oars. After that, there was silence.

Barr rose and turned back. Crouching in the darkness, pausing every now and then to listen, he circled the cabin. Satisfied that no-one was there, he made his way to a point just above the road, from which he could see his car. Further up, where the motorcyclist had stopped, he saw the sudden flare of a lighter, the glow of a cigarette. The man had obviously stuck to his position and had seen nothing of the comings and goings on the shoreward side of the cabin. Satisfied, Barr went back the way he had come.

Lindy was lying on the bed with the top sheet folded back, when he returned. She had removed the dress, and she held up her arms to him invitingly. He sat down on the bed beside her and slid a hand between her thighs. She smiled and tightened her legs around his fingers.

'Who was that?' he asked.

'I told you – a friend of Acky's,' she said.

'From Jerusalem Island?'

She frowned. 'I don't know.'

'You're lying, aren't you?' he said.

'Look,' she said, 'it is Acky's business. If you want to know, talk to Acky. I only do what he tells me.'

He nodded. 'OK. I believe you. Tell me, has that man been here before?'

'Twice when I've been here.'

'At night? Always at night?'

'Yes.'

'Do you know who he is?'

'Acky calls him Gunnar.'

'Gunnar.' He nodded again. She moved restlessly and he felt the warm moistness of her flesh on his fingertips. 'Let me try to work it out,' he said calmly. 'Gunnar has been here at least three times. He comes from Jerusalem Island at night. He collects arms – rifles, guns, ammunition – and takes the stuff back. Am I right so far?'

She pushed his hand away and sat up. There was fear in her wide brown eyes. 'No! I didn't say that! I didn't say that. I don't know about any guns!'

'You don't know what was in that bundle?'

'No!'

'Couldn't you guess?'

'I don't want to guess! I told you, it is Acky's business.' She shook her head. 'Do you know – he is going to kill me for this! Kill me stone dead!'

'No,' he said, 'no. I won't let him do that. I promise.'

'Who are you?' she asked. 'Who are you really?'

'You don't have to worry about me,' he said. 'I'm on Acky's side, I think. Look upon me as a friend.'

'A friend?' Smiling again, she leaned forward and began to unbutton his shirt. 'You want to know something? I'm going to make you prove that statement.'

Barr was still trying to think it through, asking himself who Gunnar was and who he represented, whether Acky was tied in with the Community in some way, and secretly supplying them with arms for the Guardians, when the steamy mist rolled over his mind again, and he lost track.

It was at least three hours before he came back to the problem, for Lindy was delightful, accomplished and insatiable, and Barr himself was making up for lost time.

196

Chapter Fourteen

Steve?

The name kept sounding in the back of Kitty's mind like a small distant gong.

Steve?

She had put the name on the letter that Sister Eleanor has asked her to write.

And there had been another name in the letter too.

Kitty. Kitty Higgins.

And something – something – about a theatre in London, and driving home in a car.

She sat on the edge of the bed in the curtained cubicle of the long dormitory and pressed her hands to her head, as if to coax a response from her tired mind. In the next cubicle she could hear Sister Maria crooning gently to herself. Further along, two of the Handmaidens were talking together in low voices.

Steve?

There had also been something about meeting him. When? Tomorrow? The next day?

What day was it now? What time?

She could not tell, only that it was evening. She groaned with exhaustion and with the effort of thought. In the space of a few hours she had been through two long sessions of spiritual and mental guidance with Sister Eleanor and she felt drained, mindless, so tired that she was almost beyond sleep. And in between the sessions she had been told to write the letter.

To Steve.

It had been difficult, puzzling. For days, Sister Eleanor had hammered away at the same theme. Mr Dunlop's mission was to save the world; it followed, therefore, that to serve him was the greatest work one could do for humanity. But such service had to be whole-hearted. It could not be cluttered up with selfish thoughts of oneself, or of the past. The break had to be complete.

And, slowly, the exhausted girl had come to accept this, come to believe that in her past life she had been self-centred and sinful, that to break with it all – parents, friends, lovers – was a necessary sacrifice if she was to be reborn. At first, with Dr Bauer, her compliance had been a deliberate deception, designed to throw the Doctor off guard and, for a short time, the same had been true of her relationship with Sister Eleanor.

But, inch by inch, they had worn her down, breaking through the

197

defensive barriers she had erected, and unlocking her mind. Sister Eleanor had pursued her without respite, denying her sleep and food, treating her with brutal harshness one moment and with loving tenderness the next, turning her brain into a battlefield of conflicting ideas. She began to long desperately for peace, for acceptance. The point of breakthrough had come suddenly, earlier that day, when she had thrown herself on her knees before Sister Eleanor, in a silent cry for help. And later, resting briefly in the Grove, there had come upon her an inner peace so profound and beautiful that she felt uplifted, truly born again.

It had not lasted long.

Having closed the doors on her past, Sister Eleanor has asked her to reopen them, to reach back into memory so that she could compose the letter.

To Steve.

And then, after that, there had followed another gruelling session in which Sister Eleanor had schooled and rehearsed her for the coming meeting.

'When that is over,' she had said, 'when the young man has gone away, your past will be truly past. Your rejection of him will be your final triumph. You will be a true Apostle of the Community, a chosen Handmaiden of our guide and teacher, Mr Dunlop.'

Now, once again, she was confused and embattled, longing only for that peace which had brought her such radiant happiness and which now eluded her grasp. A new thought, born out of despair and desperation, came into her mind.

She slid her hand along the bed between the frame and the mattress until her fingers found the paper-knife which she had stolen from the Comptroller's desk. It had been hidden ever since and she had almost forgotten it. Her hand shook as she brought it out.

The knife was long and thin and made of stainless steel. The edges of the blade tapered away to a fine point and, opening her gown, Kitty tested the point on her body, just below the left breast. She did not press hard enough to break the skin, but she could feel its sharpness.

It was enough, she thought. It offered one certain way out. If she could not find peace soon . . .

The lights in the dormitory suddenly went up to full strength and Sister Eleanor entered, clapping her hands like a schoolmistress and calling, 'Come on, come on! Mr Dunlop is asking for his Hand-maidens! Come along, come along!'

Kitty just had time to put the knife back in its hiding-place before the curtains were pulled aside. Sister Eleanor stood there smiling.

'Come along, Sister Helen,' she said. 'Mr Dunlop has particularly asked to see his new Handmaiden!'

She came to Kitty and took her face in her hands. 'Heavens, you look ghastly! We must get you to the make-up room!' More gently, she said, 'We all love you. You do know that, don't you?'

Raising her voice, she called, 'Isn't that true, Sisters? We all love Sister Helen. Isn't that true?'

Back came the chorus: 'Yes!'

'We love you, Sister Helen,' they cried.

In the make-up room, while two of the Handmaidens worked on Kitty's hair and face, Sister Eleanor gave her final instructions.

'When he enters, you must prostrate yourself, as you have been taught. Mr Dunlop is the Lord's representative on earth, and you will therefore be humbling yourself before God. You will not look on him until he speaks. You will not rise until he gives the command. Do you understand all this?'

'Yes, Sister.'

'You must also understand that Mr Dunlop believes that beauty – in nature, in the human form – is the greatest gift of God. He believes that to honour beauty is to honour God. And what Mr Dunlop believes, we all must believe.'

'Yes, Sister.'

'You know that you were chosen because God made you beautiful.'

'Yes, Sister.'

'There is one other thing you should know,' said Sister Eleanor in a low voice. 'Mr Dunlop's health is not – well – let us say that he does not enjoy good health.'

'He is ill?' There was genuine surprise in Kitty's voice. The image in her mind had been formed by the portraits and by what she had learned of the man: it was hard to imagine that such a divinely-inspired person could suffer like ordinary mortals.

'Is it any wonder!' said Sister Eleanor reprovingly. 'He has devoted himself to his ministry for over forty years. He has spent himself for others. Were Mr Dunlop an ordinary man —' She checked herself, as if even this tentative suggestion was a sort of sacrilege, and went on, 'But he isn't, praise God! And we hope that our prayers and our love will restore him to his full vigour.'

'Amen,' said the two Handmaidens. They smiled at Kitty in the mirror, the bland, loving smiles which were almost a badge of the Community.

'Let me look at you,' said Sister Eleanor. She stood back and scrutinised the make-up and the hair. 'Perfect! Perfect!'

Kitty had to admit that the Handmaidens had done their work with great skill. The lines of exhaustion, the paleness, had gone from her face, and yet the total effect was so natural, so unspoiled, that it was difficult to see where the make-up had been applied. Her hair too seemed to have recovered its natural glossy sheen and, in its chestnut radiance, both matched and challenged the wide sea-green eyes. In the simple white dress with its edging of fine golden threads Kitty looked, as they had intended she should look, like a Greek goddess.

The room to which she was taken was rather like a smaller version of the Great Hall of the Tabernacle without the tiers of seats, except that the deep bronze pile with which it was carpeted – not unlike the colour of Kitty's hair – gave it a softer, warmer look. At the far end, stretching from wall to wall, she saw a curved panoramic window and a light glowing on the balcony beyond. She guessed, though she could not be sure, that this overlooked the Grove and that the man looking down through the binoculars had been Mr Dunlop himself.

An unseen hand must have pressed a switch for, at that moment, the drapes glided across the window, closing out the night and forming the backcloth to a kind of dais. Two wide steps led up to the dais on which there stood a single throne-like chair. The by now familiar portrait of Mr Dunlop hung in the centre of the rear wall, although this was obviously the original oil painting, and on either side of this, spreading around the room, there were other portraits. They were of nudes, painted in various poses and strikingly familiar: Kitty saw at once that they were paintings of the other Handmaidens, with different parts of the Grove as background.

The concealed lighting dimmed suddenly and she heard a movement from the far end of the room, near the dais. At once, the Handmaidens, who were standing in a semi-circle with Kitty in the centre, threw themselves down in an attitude of prostration, their eyes closed, their foreheads resting on the palms of their hands. Kitty followed them obediently.

There followed a long silence, broken only by the faint sound of movement from the dais. Kitty, her weariness forgotten, could hear her heart pumping, and she was filled suddenly with a wild hope that, in the next few minutes, all her agonising would be over, finally over. She was about to look upon the representative of God on earth, the man who had created and led the Community, the man who inspired such love and respect. Sister Eleanor, the other Handmaidens, all the thousands who followed him – it was impossible surely that they could all be wrong!

Into her mind there flashed a sudden memory of her confirmation, years before. For days afterwards she had been serenely content, free of doubt, happy in the thought that she had given herself to Jesus and that her burdens were now His. It had passed, of course: the world had caught up with her and she had gone her own wilful way. Perhaps, she thought, perhaps in His own fashion, He has brought me back, brought me to this! There was, there must be, a meaning, a purpose, to all the strange happenings that had led her here to kneel before Mr Dunlop!

She heard a low, sucking sound from the direction of the dais; someone was speaking but the words were too slurred and indistinct to be understood. Then the Comptroller said clearly, 'You may rise.'

Suddenly, in seconds, the solemn act of devotion was broken. To Kitty, it was as if someone had shattered the stained glass window of a church during a service.

To her amazement, the Handmaidens began to run towards Mr Dunlop with squeals of delight, and he was quickly surrounded by a gaggle of chattering, laughing girls. Two of them, the Filipino girl she knew as Sister Angela and Sister Gabrielle who was French, held back slightly from the others but not obtrusively so.

Kitty stood her ground, not knowing what to do. She could see the Comptroller's head above the crowd and, to one side, the big negro albino who had been on guard at the Grove, but Mr Dunlop was hidden behind a screen of girls. The Comptroller leaned down and whispered something and the chatter faded. The low slurred voice spoke again, but she was still unable to pick out the words.

The Handmaidens stood aside, flanking the chair, and looked towards Kitty, smiling happily. She had lowered her head instinctively, and stood there waiting.

'Come forward, Sister Helen,' said the Comptroller.

She moved towards the voice, slowly lifted her head, and stopped. For a moment, she thought that what she was seeing was an illusion. She had expected to see a resemblance to the portrait, a man who had the presence and magnetism of an Old Testament prophet.

What she saw was an old man, in a mask. A mask of white muslin, suspended from the ears by a wire frame, that fell like a curtain over the face, obscuring everything except the eyes and the upper part of the head.

The eyes. The striking violet eyes that she remembered from the portrait seemed to have been distilled of colour: palely glistening, they bulged outwards as if under some stern inner pressure. And even as she looked the lids closed over them two or three times in an involuntary motion.

There were no eyebrows and the head was bald except for some wisps of slate-coloured hair that clung to the sides like tufts of wire wool. In the very centre of the crinkled scalp a bluish vein throbbed restlessly, as if keeping time with the ceaseless gentle quivering of the debilitated body below.

As she stood there, helpless, staring at the grotesque figure, Sister Eleanor stepped forward and unfastened Kitty's gown from the rear. She pulled it downwards gradually, uncovering the firm sinuous breasts, the curve of the stomach, the hips, the thighs, and let it slide to the ground. Then, smiling, she stepped back.

It seemed to Kitty, in these moments, that she was staring into a distorting mirror. The full, waxen face of the Comptroller floated above like a zenith moon, the faces of the Handmaidens swam around her as though in a mist, approaching and receding, wearing their anodyne smiles like fairground masks.

The strange sucking sound hissed in her ears and she was half aware that Mr Dunlop had risen, swaying, from his chair. Supported by the Comptroller and the guard he leaned towards her, his eyes bulging, a stream of incoherent words issuing from behind the mask.

And then she fainted.

Kitty awoke about an hour later, chased from sleep by a nightmare, her nightdress and the sheet below her damp with perspiration. It took her some time to realise that she was back in her bed in the dormitory.

'Ah, you are awake!'

She turned her head and saw Sister Eleanor looking down at her with a compassionate smile. Beside her stood the Comptroller.

'Do you feel better?'

Kitty managed a small nod in response. It did not convey the truth, but she wanted these people to go, to leave her in solitude.

'Excellent. You mustn't blame yourself, you must not have any feelings of guilt. It is my fault. I pushed you too hard. In the circum-stances, in all the circumstances, you did very well.'

'Very well indeed,' said the Comptroller. 'And, believe me, Mr Dunlop quite understands. He is not angry. On the contrary, he was most impressed.'

'Perfection,' said Sister Eleanor. 'That was the word he used – perfection. I have never heard him say that of anyone before, never.'

'You must rest now, Sister Helen,' said the Comptroller. 'Sleep and restore yourself. Tomorrow is a special day. You have the meeting in the morning and in the evening you must go to Mr Dunlop. He has asked for you.'

Sister Eleanor squeezed Kitty's hand. 'Sleep now. Sleep. Sleep.'

They left her then and she closed her eyes, not to sleep, but in an effort to compose her thoughts. You must go to Mr Dunlop, the Comptroller had said. That was a return to nightmare and she forced the picture from her mind. A meeting in the morning? Of course, in the morning she was to meet Steve. She smiled, remembering him clearly now, the plain homespun face, the laughing brown eyes, the earnestness, the shy, gentle manner. The smile departed, to make way for slow tears. She was touched to the heart to think that he had pursued her to this strange place, followed her and found her. Dear Steve! Dear, dear Steve!

And suddenly, with a surge of excitement, she realised that she was

202

thinking like Kitty Higgins again! There was no Sister Helen any more: these were her own thoughts, her own memories. She was Kitty Higgins, Kitty Ann Higgins of 50, Parkhill Road, Hampstead, London, England, Europe, the Northern Hemisphere, the Earth, the Universe, Space!

She felt an extraordinary sense of exultation. It reminded her again of that time when she had almost drowned in the sea near Athens. Afterwards, she had fallen into a long sleep on the beach and, when awake again, she had seen the blue sky above her, she had felt a great surge of joy to know that she was alive, that she had not drowned.

Well, in the past few days she had come near to drowning again, in another, more terrible sense. But that was a time of shadows, it did not matter any more. That part of her life had been inhabited by Sister Helen, and she must bear the responsibility for it. It was Sister Helen who had been submissive and weak, Sister Helen who had misused her body, Sister Helen who had prostrated herself. No more!

Kitty Higgins was back, Kitty Higgins was in charge of herself again, there would be no more bloody nonsense!

She heard a rustle of curtains and, looking round, she saw that one of the Handmaidens had entered the cubicle. Kitty tensed cautiously and was about to speak when the girl put her fingers to her lips. She came nearer and Kitty recognised Sister Gabrielle, the French girl.

'Are you better?' Gabrielle whispered.

Kitty nodded and murmured, 'Thank you.'

Gabrielle sat down on the edge of the bed and looked down at Kitty. Concern showed on her face and in her eyes, a concern that owed nothing to the regulation love-look of the Community.

'You have had a bad time, I think.' She spoke English well, but with a slight lilting accent that added a kind of music to the words.

'I'll survive,' said Kitty and, with her newly recovered spirit, she felt that this was the truth.

There was a little silence and then Gabrielle said, 'It happened to me also. At the first meeting, it was the same.'

'Meeting?'

'With Mr Dunlop.'

Remembering, Kitty shuddered, and tried to put the image of that raddled old man from her mind.

'You must understand,' Gabrielle continued, 'he is sick. In the body and in the mind, also. Do not be afraid of that. He cannot harm you – only look. One gets used to it, and to him. Strange, but I have learned to pity him. I think that perhaps, one day, he had a good dream. You understand? I mean, a real dream of Jerusalem. He gave hope then to many people – despised people, rejected people. Now he is burnt out and the dream also. He lives only for this fantasy – what he calls his

203

collection of beauty. It is a madness, of course.' She sighed, not unhappily. 'I believe that he will die soon.'

'Who are you?' asked Kitty suddenly. She did not want to think of Mr Dunlop.

'Sister Gabrielle.'

'No. No. Who *are* you?'

The other girl hesitated, glancing quickly from one side of the cubicle to the other. 'I am Gabrielle Joyeux,' she whispered. 'I am from Paris. I was – no, I am, I am – an actress.' She smiled. 'I was not too bad, really. An American producer was quite interested in me.'

'Hollywood?' said Kitty, returning the smile.

'I think it was possible, yes.'

The other girl looked sad, and Kitty waited, letting her remember in silence. Then she asked, 'How did you manage – I mean – how –' She stopped, unable to find the right words but Gabrielle understood at once.

'At first, I didn't. I had not the will to resist. I tell you the truth. It is hard, very hard. They know how to empty your mind, pour it out like a glass of water, drain it until nothing is left, not even the smallest drop. And then, slowly, they fill you up again, with their ideas. It was like that for me. Except that in my case, one little drop of Gabrielle Joyeux must have been left behind inside my head. And, when they thought I was truly theirs, when there was no longer the same pressure, I began to come back to myself. In secret. The little drop they had left of Gabrielle Joyeux began to multiply, like a miracle.'

She paused and smiled. 'Do you know what I do at night? Every night, before I sleep, I go over some part of my old life in my head. Like saying a prayer, you understand. I think of my parents, my work, my boyfriend. All these things. They help me very much. I say this to you because it may help you also.' She added shyly, 'My boyfriend is an actor too. I wonder sometimes if he remembers me.'

Kitty's eyes filled with tears. She reached for Gabrielle's hand and clasped it. 'It is wonderful to talk like this, to hear you talk. Let me tell you this. My name is not Helen. I am not Sister Helen. I am Kitty Higgins, from London. I am half-Irish, half-English. Kitty.'

'Kitty,' said Gabrielle, as though trying the name for size. 'Kitty.'

'How long have you been here?' asked Kitty.

'A year. Perhaps a little bit more.'

'A year!' Kitty looked at her in dismay.

'Some have been here longer, two or three years, perhaps.'

'Do any of the others feel as you do?'

'There is one. Sister Angela, the Filipino girl. She is very nice, I think. We are friends, we help each other. The others – they have given no sign. They are happy to be Handmaidens.'

'Happy!'

204

'As a dog is happy if one gives him food and drink and comfort and a little pat on the head now and then,' said Gabrielle. 'When Sister Eleanor whistles, they run to her. If they had tails, they would wag them.' And she added wryly. 'Me, also. I run and smile and make the sign of love. I am worse than the others, that is the truth of the matter. I know – I know – and they do not. I run because I am afraid.'

'What is it that you know and they don't?' asked Kitty.

'I know what you know,' answered Gabrielle. 'I know that this – all this – is a sham. There is a wickedness here, a terrible wickedness.' She shivered. 'The things they do in the name of the gentle Jesus!'

'Have you ever tried to get away?'

'I have thought of it. I have talked of it with Mila.'

'Mila?'

'My friend, Sister Angela. Like you, they took her name away. She was called Mila. No, no, I must not talk like that. She *is* Mila. Yes, we have talked of escape. But it is not possible. The Guardians are everywhere. Even if we could get away from the Tabernacle, we would still be in the Compound – with more Guardians. No. We wait – and pray that our friends have not entirely forgotten us. We live in hope. Nothing lasts for ever, isn't that what they say?'

She smiled wanly, her face golden in the dim light, and rose to her feet. 'I must leave you now. But we will talk again.' They clasped hands once more. 'It is good to talk.'

'Thank you,' Kitty breathed, 'thank you.'

'Shall I tell you something,' whispered Gabrielle. She leaned forward, a glint of animation in her dark, lovely eyes. 'It is this. The worst thing about being a Handmaiden is that it is so *boring*! So terribly boring. Boring, boring, boring!'

An unfamiliar sound rose in Kitty's throat and she realised that it was laughter, the first real spontaneous laughter she had known for weeks. She suppressed it quickly, gurgling into her hands. When she looked up, Gabrielle had gone.

And, remembering what the French girl had said, Kitty thought of the past, of her parents, of her friend Lucy, of Steve. It was with the image of Steve in her mind, and the thought of the morrow, that she fell at last into a relatively contented sleep.

Barr opened his eyes, switched on the light, and glanced at his watch. A sense of urgency came crowding back as he saw that it was almost eleven o'clock. He slipped out of bed and began to dress.

Lindy stirred, reached out for him and, finding only empty space, opened her eyes.

'What are you doing?' she asked sleepily.

'Getting dressed. I'm going outside for a couple of minutes.'

'It's funny,' she said, mistaking his purpose. 'All the men I know seem to have half-pint bladders.'

He pulled the sheet away and smacked her bottom. 'You get dressed too, my girl. I want you to help me find Acky. Meet me outside by my car as soon as you can.'

'Do we have to? It is lovely in bed.'

'Yes. I must speak to him tonight. Do you mind coming? You're not afraid of him, are you?'

'Acky?' She smiled. 'No, I was kidding. Acky wouldn't hurt a fly.'

He went into the other room and, after a little searching, found a knife of the type carried by divers. He rolled up the right leg of his slacks and strapped the leather sheath to his calf. Then he went outside and made his way cautiously back, past the car, towards the motorcyclist. The man was still there, sitting propped up against a fence. He seemed to be half asleep. Barr circled round and came up behind him.

'Having a good sleep?' asked Barr.

The man looked up, startled eyes in a young black face, and as he stumbled up, Barr chopped him down. The young man groaned but lay still. Barr frisked him and found a .22 RG 14. It was a German hand gun, probably assembled in the United States from imported parts. Barr knew the gun by its nickname – the Saturday Night Special. It wasn't a weapon that he was over-fond of, but it was better than nothing. He tucked it into his belt.

Looking down on the unconscious youth, he felt a kind of pity. On the other hand, he thought, philosophically, if they will send a boy to do a man's job, they must expect to pay for it.

For good measure, he slashed the motorcycle tyres with the knife. He heard Lindy moving towards him and straightened up.

'What happened?' she asked in amazement, looking down at the motorcyclist.

'Poor guy had an accident. Fell off his bike,' said Barr. He took her arm. 'Come on, darling. He'll be OK when he wakes up.'

They found Acky, at the second shot, in the bar at Buccaneer Cove, next to the Anchorage Hotel. From the look of the tables, the tourists had been giving the bar a busy night, but now, except for a noisy group lingering in one corner, they had departed to their hotels and the few people left were mainly British and American expatriates who worked on the island. It was Barr's kind of place – plain and straightforward, with no phoney chrome fittings, no violent music, no poker machines, and no lisping barman offering to whip up the latest barbaric mixture of drinks.

Acky was sitting to one side with a half empty bottle of Teachers in front of him. He was flanked by a shapely young woman with honey-blond hair and the equally attractive and nubile Mandy.

206

The real surprise was that he was rolling poker dice with Gordon Pullar. Not the neat and precise Mr Pullar who had met Barr at the airport, but a different man altogether, in a brightly patterned, loose-sleeved shirt and yellow slacks.

Barr had gathered the impression that Mr Pullar was a non-drinker, but the glass in his hand, and the brightness in his eyes, quickly disposed of that assumption. He welcomed Barr with a ready smile, without any embarrassment.

'My dear old chap! Welcome, welcome! Take a pew. Come into the body of the kirk. Have a drink. First, let me introduce my wife. Tara meet Mr Barr. Mr Barr, Tara.'

This is my night for surprises, thought Barr, as Mr Pullar indicated the blonde. 'Delighted to meet you, Mrs Pullar,' he said.

'Tara, Tara!' said Mr Pullar reprovingly.

'Give the poor man a chance, Gordon,' she said. She smiled at Barr. 'I'm glad to meet you. You are a friend of Mr Ugley's, I believe?'

'That's right.' She had wide, honest grey eyes and there was a shrewdness in her handsome face that was very impressive. His respect for Mr Pullar increased on the spot.

'This is Mandy,' said Mr Pullar, with a wave of the hand. 'And Mr Ackland-Pryce — the esteemed and widely-respected Acky — whom I know you've met.'

'Yes,' said Barr. 'Hello, again.'

'Our pleasure,' said Acky. He pushed the whisky and a clean glass in Barr's direction. 'Scotch?'

'Thanks.' Barr helped himself, conscious that he was being studied.

'What brings you to this ungodly spot at this forlorn hour?' asked Mr Pullar.

'I came to see Acky,' said Barr directly. He saw Acky look quickly at Lindy, and added, 'Lindy just showed me the way, that's all. She's been very helpful.'

'Lindy is always helpful,' said Acky. 'It is one of her most endearing qualities. But if you want to see me about a boat, you should have told her. She would have fixed you up.'

'That part is organised,' said Barr. 'I found Lindy at your office on the beach. I've booked the *Carib Beauty* for two days.'

Acky shook the dice vigorously and spilled them on to the table. 'Do you want to come in?' he asked.

Barr shook his head. 'Not right now, thanks. What I would like is a couple or three minutes of your time.'

Acky looked at Mandy. 'Why don't you take Lindy away some-where, darling, and have a lovely chat? Also, a drink from the bar.' The two girls whisked off without argument. Acky eased himself in the creaking chair. 'Well, Mr Barr,' he said. 'I am at your disposal.'

'I am not sure whether —' Barr hesitated, looking towards the

207

others.

'Gordon and Tara are my dear friends,' Acky said. 'There is nothing, absolutely nothing, in my life that I hold secret from them.'

'That's a slight exaggeration, Acky, dear.' said Mrs Pullar. 'A touch overdone. I should hate to know all your secrets.'

'I'll amend the statement,' he said. 'Almost nothing.' He turned to Barr and added casually, 'What time did you go to my office?'

'Earlier this evening.'

'Around eight-thirty?'

'Before that. About an hour before.'

The eyebrows rose over the big round face. 'Good Lord, I hope you haven't been searching for me since then!' He looked towards a table some distance away where the two girls were now sitting, heads together in giggling conversation, and smiled. 'Of course not. Silly question. Lindy took you for a moonlight swim, no doubt. It is her second favourite pastime.'

'Something like that,' Barr said and, changing the subject rapidly, he went on, 'While I was at your office, you had a visitor.'

'That is not unusual,' Acky said lightly.

'This one was. He came by boat to collect a parcel. His name is Gunnar and he comes from Jerusalem Island. I think, though I can't be positive, that the parcel contained arms.' He saw Acky give another quick look towards the girls. 'Don't blame Lindy,' he said. 'I heard some of it and more or less guessed the rest.'

To Barr's surprise, it was Mrs Pullar who answered him.

'You've been very frank, Mr Barr,' she said. 'But before Acky answers you, may I put one or two questions to you?'

'I can't promise to answer,' said Barr.

'Oh, come. You must be fair. You wish to learn something about us. It is only reasonable that we should know more about you.'

'All right. Your shout. Go ahead,' said Barr.

'And you can bring your hand away from that gun, Mr Barr,' she continued. 'We're not violent people, and we're not armed.'

His hand was resting lightly on his lap near the .22 and he brought it up to the table, looking at Mrs Pullar as he did so, with a smile that conveyed amused appreciation.

'Who exactly are you and why have you come to the Caribbean, Mr Barr?' she asked. 'I include your friends in the question. We know a little about Mr Ugley, of course. But just to clear your mind, let me assure you of something. We do not believe that Mr Ugley came to Antigua simply to take over his uncle's property, nor do we believe that you and the others came with him just for the ride.'

Barr took a long swallow of Scotch while he worked on the problem. He had to make a judgment about these people and he had to make it quickly. In the end, he decided to take a chance and tell

208

them all, or nearly all.

When he had finished, Acky reached for the bottle and poured another round. Mrs Pullar refused, putting the palm of her hand over the glass. She was looking steadily at Barr.

'What happened to the two men you kidnapped at the airport?'

Barr looked at his watch. 'At this moment they should be on the BA midnight flight to London. Charlie had the job of escorting them to the airport.'

'Won't they talk?'

'I don't think so. They've been freeloading at the Community's expense for years. Free international trips, generous payments for the odd speech or article, God knows what else. In return, they've been supporting it without actually joining. I had a long talk with them after I came back from Jerusalem Island and told them that they were up to their ears in shit. Backing an organisation that went in for murder, kidnapping, extortion, slave labour and what-have-you. I said the balloon was about to go up, and if they opened their mouths about us, I'd see that their connections with the Community were exposed in every newspaper in Britain. I said I might even have them indicted as accessories. That frightened them, I think. If it didn't, Vinnie did.'

'Vinnie?' said Mrs Pullar.

'Mrs Harcourt, dear,' said her husband. 'I did mention her.'

'If you haven't met Vinnie,' said Barr, 'you haven't lived. She's a one-off. She did the James Bond bit. Told them that we were members of a special section of the British Secret Service and that we each had a licence to kill.'

'She threatened to kill them?'

'Not in so many words. What she did say was that if they talked she would personally come after them and cut their balls off.'

'Yak!' said Acky. 'Nasty, very nasty.'

'She is a most formidable lady,' said Mr Pullar.

'And you appear to be a very dangerous man, Mr Barr,' said Mrs Pullar. But she was smiling as she said it.

Barr cupped his glass in his hands and put his elbows on the table. 'Your turn, I think.'

'It began, for us, about a year ago,' said Mrs Pullar. 'Before that, we'd heard various rumours of what was going on over there, general rumours, but we didn't take much notice. Then, one afternoon, Acky picked a girl out of the sea.'

'She had almost run out of road,' said Acky, 'or ocean, if you prefer it. She'd swum about a mile and was in real trouble.'

'She had fled from Jerusalem Island, from a sort of punishment squad they call the Waverers. Acky took her back to his place and sent for us, as his friends. We fed her up, let her sleep. The poor

209

creature was half starved – she ate as if she hadn't seen food for months and slept the clock round. Over the next day or two, she poured out the whole story. It was so horrifying that we went to your friend's uncle, the late Mr Ugley and asked for his help and advice.'

'He was terrific,' said Mr Pullar, 'absolutely terrific. He persuaded us not to go to the police. He'd been through those channels, you see, in an effort to help an old friend, Jonah Winston. The police had investigated as best they could, but in the end they decided that there was not enough evidence to prove that Jonah hadn't joined the Community freely.'

'That is where the Community people are so clever, you see,' said Mrs Pullar. 'They even allowed Mr Ugley to go to the island and inter-view Jonah. And Jonah told him that he was happy, that he wanted to stay. Mr Ugley was convinced that the poor man had been brain-washed, and refused to drop the issue.'

'Jonah had property worth over half a million US dollars,' said Acky. 'He signed it all over to those bastards. And when Mr Ugley took the matter to court, the judge ruled in their favour. He had to. Legally, it was in order.'

'Your friend's uncle was a good man, a splendid person.' Mr Pullar sighed.

'Did they kill him?' asked Barr.

'We don't know,' Acky replied. 'We think so, but we can prove nothing. It was, as you remarked the other day, a most fortunate accident – for them.'

'I seem to remember also that you advised us to keep away from the Community. Live and let live, you said.'

'My dear old friend,' said Acky, 'I didn't know you then. Didn't know your mettle. You could have been a bunch of bungling amateurs. Forgive me.' He turned to Mrs Pullar. 'Carry on, Tara. You're telling it so beautifully.'

'Thank you, Acky, dear,' said Mrs Pullar.

They talked for the next hour. She told him how Steve's uncle had smuggled the girl to Miami and paid her fare from there to her home in Cairns, Australia. And she told him about a young Swede called Gunnar Arnasson, whom she described as the bravest man she had ever met.

Gunnar had joined the sect, quite genuinely, some three years before, but he had very rapidly become disenchanted. The Com-munity leadership, sensing the change in him, had sent him to the Waverers for renewed sessions of brainwashing. He was released only when they were convinced that he was back in the fold, but he had managed to fool them. He posed as a reformed character only to get away from the Waverers and was determined to escape from Jerusalem Island at the first opportunity.

210

When he returned to the day-to-day life of the Community he saw that the corruption and violence had grown worse. He told Mrs Pullar on one occasion that he could feel the active presence of evil on the island. He was an idealistic young man and he still believed in the Christian-Socialist principles which had attracted him to the Community in the first place. But now, as he looked around, all he could see was a strange inverted kind of concentration camp in which the prisoners were held partly by force, but mainly because all power of free decision had been washed out of their heads.

Gunnar then made an extraordinary decision. He told himself that it was wrong to think of saving only his own skin. It would, he considered, be an act of craven selfishness to do so. He determined, then and there, to stay and find some way to fight back.

Slowly, over many months, he built up a circle of trusted contacts; people who felt, as he did, that if the corrupt leadership could be overthrown, something of Jerusalem Island might be saved. But his underground movement was too weak, as yet, to challenge the established authority. Mr Dunlop's hold was still potent, there were armed Guardians almost everywhere.

Somehow, he heard of Mr Ugley's intervention in the Jonah Winston affair and made another incredible decision. One night he eluded the patrols and swam the two miles of sea between the island and Antigua. He found his way to Tradewinds and enlisted the willing help of Steve's uncle.

From then on, things began to move more rapidly. Acky and the Pullars were brought in and they found a friendly fisherman named Bobby Lamb who seemed to know every inch of the Jerusalem Island coast. Bobby Lamb had his secrets, and he shared at least one of them with the group.

And so a boat was provided for Gunnar and a short-wave radio and a few other useful items. Acky located a source of arms and gradually a small but useful arsenal was built up and hidden at various points on the island. After Mr Ugley's death, Acky and the others had continued, albeit in a smaller way, to finance the enterprise.

This was the astonishing story that Barr heard. If it was all true, he thought, then Gunnar Arnasson was all and more of Mrs Pullar's estimate of him. On the other hand, he did not share the young man's concern for Jerusalem Island. He would not care if the whole place was flattened by the next hurricane, or disappeared into the Caribbean. His one interest was to get Kitty and maybe the other girls off the island: that was why he had come.

'It's interesting,' he said, 'but may I ask what you are waiting for?'

'The right moment,' said Mrs Pullar.

'When will that be?'

'I told you he was a very direct person,' said Acky.

'You have to remember,' Mrs Pullar said, 'that Mr Dunlop is still looked on as a kind of Messiah. Worshipped might be a better description. But, according to Gunnar, he is dying. He will be dead in weeks, months. In our view, that will be the psychological moment to strike.'

'Tomorrow would be better,' said Barr quietly.

'Tomorrow?' Even Mrs Pullar's habitual calm appeared to have been shaken by this statement.

'We're going in tomorrow,' said Barr. 'Tomorrow night.'

'We?'

'I've arranged for a little help. I could also use some help from your friend, Bobby Lamb. And with one or two other bits and pieces. But with or without, we're going in and we're going to bring out Kitty Higgins – and maybe one or two others.'

Then Mrs Pullar surprised him once again. Without any further query, she said firmly, in the manner of one who is in command, 'Very well, Mr Barr. What can we do? What sort of help do you require?'

He told her.

And with the odd amendment here and there, nothing serious, she promised to arrange everything.

Thirty-two minutes later, he walked back to the car. He felt the weariness in his limbs and knew that sleep, four or five hours of sleep, was the next priority. As he opened the car door, Lindy came running up to him.

'Hey,' she said reproachfully. 'Did you forget about me?'

'Oh, sorry,' he said wearily. 'Jump in and I'll run you home.'

She put her arms around his neck. 'When we get back we'll have a little drink,' she said, 'and maybe you can stay on a while.'

'Lindy,' he said sincerely, 'I couldn't, I couldn't.'

'Oh, come on,' she said. 'I know you're getting on, but you never know what you can do till you try.'

It was the sort of remark that he could not allow to pass unchallenged.

Chapter Fifteen

They met on the terrace for a late breakfast – the Baker Street Runners, a long, long way from Baker Street – Barr, Steve, Vinnie and Charlie. It was a beautiful Caribbean day: a blue sky touched with tiny clouds of the purest white, a temperate breeze, and the lingering scent of jasmine drifting in the clear air. Below the terrace, almost at their feet, an azure sea lapped without urgency at the pale sand.

And in the distance, a little more than two miles away, there was a dark smudge called Jerusalem Island.

Barr was not a great early-morning eater but he ate well, if a trifle methodically. He had been taught in a tough school and he followed the old soldier's lore which prescribed that before going into action you ate what food was available, on the assumption that you could not be sure when you would see the stuff again.

Neither Steve nor Charlie appeared to be too interested in the breakfast and, on the same old soldier's principle, he did his best to encourage them. Vinnie, he observed, needed no urging: she tucked in with all the energy, and apparently the capacity, of a couple of hungry navvies. His respect for the big, cockney woman grew with each day: nothing, no problem, appeared to faze her. Her salty common sense, her strength and, above all, her indestructible spirit made her worth a platoon of commandos.

After Barr's return to Tradewinds in the early hours, they had talked over the plan of campaign for the day and now, quietly, they checked the details again. It was impossible to plan with any precision, since so much would depend on how matters developed.

The chief uncertainty lay with Steve and Vinnie and on the outcome of their interview with Kitty. Would they be able to persuade her to come back with them? In the light of her letter it was unlikely but, if they were successful, would the leaders of the Community allow her to leave? This was even more unlikely: to let her go free, with the possibility that she might lay charges of abduction and illegal imprisonment against the sect, would clearly be an unacceptable risk in their eyes.

No, it was obvious that this man they called the Comptroller was pretty well sure of his hold on Kitty, sure enough to take the same gamble that he had once taken with Jonah Winston.

There were other questions which remained unanswered. Was it all an elaborate trap, designed to get Steve over to the island so that he could, in time, be programmed as others had been and persuaded to sign his property over to the Community? That, also, seemed to be a long shot. Would they expect Barr and his friends to remain idle while this happened? Or did they have plans to dispose of Barr and the others, and so liquidate the threat?

In the end, it was Vinnie who put an end to the guessing game and summed up the position. She had spoken very little, choosing to concentrate her attention on the food, but as she helped herself to another fried egg, she said, with a touch of impatience, 'Look, will you lot stop arguing for one minute and let me get a word in edgeways? As far as I can see, you're all pissing into the wind. Listen, suppose Steve walks off Jerusalem Island with Kitty on his arm and a whole bloody band playing *Hail the Conquering Hero.* Is that the end of it? Do we all pack up and go home and leave the other poor sods over there to sweat it out for themselves? Leave the other girls? Call it a day?' She looked directly at Steve. 'Would your Kitty want that?'

'No,' he said, 'no.'

'In that case, what are you bloody lot arguing about? If we bring Kitty out, we'll still have to do something to help the others. And if we don't bring her out, or if they hold on to Steve and me, you'll still have to come to the bleeding rescue. So why don't we all stop chewing the fat and get on with it?'

'A fair assessment,' said Barr. 'Crudely put, but a fair assessment.' He took the Saturday Night Special from his belt and handed it to Steve. 'Do you want to take this with you?'

'No point,' said Charlie. 'They'll frisk him before he gets to the island. He'll never be able to hide that.'

'Give it here,' Vinnie said, holding out her hand. 'If anyone tries to run their hands over me, I'll flatten them!'

'Do you know how to use it?' Steve said doubtfully.

'Is it loaded?' she asked Barr.

'Yes.'

'Then all I've got to do is to get hold of it here, by the handle, point it in the right direction, and pull the trigger. Right?'

'Right,' said Barr, watching her uneasily.

'Like this?' she said, and turning, aimed the gun at a potted geranium standing on the next table and tried to press the trigger. Nothing happened and she expressed her disgust. 'Bloody thing doesn't work.'

'It will,' said Barr, 'if you slip the safety catch.' He indicated the catch and then added hastily. 'Not now, Vinnie. Save your bullets. And for God's sake be careful.'

'Where are you going to carry it, Vinnie?' asked Charlie.

'Don't ask silly questions,' she said, 'and then you won't get a silly answer.'

Steve, who had been looking very thoughtful, pushed himself slowly back from the table and stood up. 'I just want to say,' he began awkwardly, 'I just want to say – well – I got you all into this, I didn't realise at the beginning . . .

214

'Steve,' she interrupted gently, 'will you shut up, sit down, and finish your coffee? We all know what you're trying to say. And as far as I'm concerned the answer is a five-letter word. Balls.'

'I never backed off from a fight in my life,' Charlie said, 'and I'm not planning to start now.'

'I'll settle for Vinnie's five-letter word,' Barr said.

Vinnie weighed the gun in her huge hand and gave Steve a sly look. 'If it's any consolation, Stevie boy,' she said, 'being on this caper beats running a mob of London minicab drivers any day. Beats it right into the middle of next week.'

Charlie dropped Vinnie and Steve at the J. D. Winston office on Redcliffe Street, parked a block away, and then strolled back to keep an eye on developments. The main concern was to find out how Van Norden and his bosses would react to Vinnie's presence. Would he object to her going with Steve? They had decided to bluff as far as possible – to threaten that Steve would pull out if Vinnie was barred – but they had no way of knowing if the bluff would work. If it failed, they had agreed that Steve would go it alone.

Upstairs in the office, Van Norden's opposition to the plan was very quickly established. 'Oh, no,' he said, 'it's not on.' He pointed at Steve. 'You go. She stays.'

'Who says?' asked Steve.

'I say!' said Van Norden belligerently. 'I say! I was told to take you over. You and nobody else!'

'Don't shout,' said Steve. 'And don't get in a twist. Just pick up the telephone and have a word with the big boss. What do you call him? The Comptroller? Have a word with the Comptroller and tell him that I want Mrs Harcourt to be present at the interview —'

Van Norden cut in impatiently, 'I've already told you – it's not on!'

'Pick up the telephone and tell him that he has a choice. Both of us – or neither of us. If she doesn't go, I don't go.'

'OK, then,' said Van Norden. 'If that's how you want to play it. We'll cancel the trip.'

'I wouldn't rush it if I were you,' said Steve. 'I think your Comptroller is as anxious as I am to clear up this matter. I am worried about Miss Higgins and he wants me to see for myself that she is well and happy. Fine. But I've decided that I'd like a second opinion, a woman's view. Mrs Harcourt has never met Miss Higgins – her opinion is likely to be more objective.'

Van Norden was clearly less certain now, but he still hesitated. Steve pressed on.

'Do you want to go over to the island and tell him that I backed out because you refused to take Mrs Harcourt? Refused without even consulting him?'

'If this is a trick —' said Van Norden.

'Oh, it is,' Steve said evenly. 'Mrs Harcourt is actually a secret agent. She only wants to get on to Jerusalem Island so that she can blow it up.'

'I don't know,' said Van Norden, shaking his head, 'I don't know.' And he repeated, though not so firmly as before, 'My instructions were to take you – no-one else.'

'Oh, come on!' Vinnie took Steve's arm in mock impatience. 'Let's go home, Steve. The man's a pain in the arse. Let him take the rap from his boss, what do we care?'

'Wait!' The man called Simon Lavender, who had been listening to all this, glanced at his watch and stepped forward. He looked at Van Norden. 'You're running late. I know that the Comptroller is very anxious about this interview. Take the woman —'

'Mrs Harcourt, if you don't mind!' said Vinnie.

'Take Mrs Harcourt. I'll inform Control of the change,' he went on.

'Will you accept responsibility?' said Van Norden.

'Yes, yes!' said Lavender impatiently.

'Right. It's on your head,' said Van Norden with a shrug. But he seemed relieved that the decision had been taken out of his hands.

'Now all that's settled, could we start, do you think?' asked Steve.

'Just one thing,' said Van Norden. 'Are you carrying a gun – any sort of weapon?'

'Perish the thought!' said Steve.

'Mind if I check it out?'

'Help yourself.'

'You're not a very trusting lot, are you?' said Vinnie. 'I mean, considering that you're supposed to stand for love and peace.'

'We have enemies,' said Lavender. 'We have learned that it is necessary to be on guard all the time.'

Van Norden did a thorough search job on Steve and then turned to Vinnie.

'Don't look at me!' she said threateningly. She held her capacious handbag under his nose. 'You can check through this, but that is as far as you go.'

Two minutes later, Charlie saw them leave the office, get into a car with Van Norden and the man called Eddie, and drive off in the direction of the harbour.

They did not look at him but, by the smile on Vinnie's face, he knew that the bluff had worked. So far, so good.

It was so far so good at Coolidge Airport, too. Once again, Barr watched the British Airways morning flight from London come into land and taxi to the Terminal Building, saw the slow crocodile of

216

people descend, blinking in the sunlight, and trudge across the hot tarmac.

He was surprised but not displeased to see one familiar but unexpected face among them. Mike Noonan! Barr smiled inwardly. He might have guessed that Noonan would be unable to resist the chance of getting into the action. He saw two other faces that he recognised and was well-satisfied with them. If the remainder were of the same quality, Noonan had chosen well.

Moving away from the observation area, he took up a position which would give him a view of the passengers as they came through from Customs. He glanced around at the waiting crowd without too much concern: as far as he could tell, he had not been followed from Tradewinds and he assumed that, for the time being at least, the Community had called off its watchdogs. It was probable, he thought, that they were waiting on the outcome of Steve's meeting with Kitty before settling on the next move. All the same, he decided that he would take no chances.

So he made no move towards Noonan or the others as they came through. At Barr's suggestion Noonan had booked his party on a package holiday, to provide some measure of cover and, ignoring Barr, the big Irishman, with his red hair and matching red beard, strode directly over to the group which had gathered around the Kuoni tour hostess. He made a striking figure and it amused Barr to watch the fascinated looks that were cast in the Irishman's direction.

At last the girl marshalled her flock and led them out to a waiting bus. Most of them were holiday couples but, apart from Noonan and the two he had already recognised, Barr counted five young men who appeared to be travelling without company. Two of them looked rather too young and inexperienced and he dismissed this pair from his calculations. The others, at first glance, seemed to be good material, although he knew from bitter experience that big muscles do not always make a big man.

Barr went to the car, and drove to the Halcyon Cove Hotel at Dickinson Bay. On the way, he passed the Kuoni bus and he was waiting in the lobby of the hotel when its passengers arrived.

Ten minutes later, Barr was sitting on the balcony of Noonan's room with a glass of duty-free Scotch in his hand. Below them lay the swimming-pool, noisy with children, and ahead they could see the beach and the rippling blue ocean.

'Christ,' said Noonan enthusiastically, 'but it's great to feel the warmth of the sun on your bum. I haven't really been warm since we left Africa. Even the English summer has a kind of chill to it.'

'How are things back home, Mike?' asked Barr.

'Don't remind me, for God's sake,' Noonan said. 'Let me shove it out of my mind at least for a few days. The truth, if you must know, is

217

that things don't get better, they get worse. Would you believe that the price of a pint has gone up four times in the past year? Four times, mark you! As for whisky, I tell you, Tom, the time is fast coming when a man will have to take out a bank loan before he can afford to lay his hands on a bottle! And I'm a publican, I'm the poor bloody pig in the middle. I get screwed by the brewers and abused by the customers.'

'My heart's bleeding for you, Mike,' said Barr mockingly. Then he added, more seriously, 'You had no problems in London, I take it.'

'Nothing major,' said Noonan. 'That solicitor fellow – Mr Boyd – he was a bit shy about the money, first thing. I reckon he thought your friend had a loose screw in his head, the way he was pouring out a small fortune for air-tickets and the like. But he coughed up at the finish.'

Barr smiled, imagining the look on old Alexander Boyd's face when he opened Steve's cable and his reaction when confronted by this big buccaneering Irishman.

'What sort of deal did you make with the lads?'

'The way we agreed on the phone. A thousand pounds each man, half paid down and the other half to be received when the job's done. Plus all expenses. I could have got most of them for half that. The truth is that they're battleminded like me – bored out of their minds with the grey life back home and burning for a taste of the action.'

'I see you brought Joe Colleano and Clay Denham. Them I know. No complaints. How about the other three?'

'Well, I had to take a bit of a chance there, considering the shortage of time, but I think we're all right.' Noonan began to tick the names off on his fingers. 'There's Stuttering Bob Calder – an old Africa hand. You've surely heard of him?'

'Heard of him, yes. Never met him. He was at Stanleyville with John – John Peters – after my time.'

'He's a good man. A raving genius when it comes to explosives.'

'The other two?'

'Ex-SAS. Twins actually.' Noonan laughed. 'Frank and Jesse James. The James brothers, would you believe!'

'You're kidding! Frank and Jesse – you have to be kidding!'

'No. The name is James, sure enough. I guess their first names are something different but truth to tell, I don't remember what and I don't think they care. They told me that the kids called them Frank and Jesse at school and it sort of stuck.'

'Any experience outside the SAS?'

'I don't think so. But they had plenty there. Clay Denham brought them in and he reckons they're OK.'

Barr looked at his watch. He got up, took the Scotch from Noonan just as he was about to top up the drinks and screwed the cap on the bottle.

'That's enough of the hard stuff for now. And tell the others to lay off too. I want you all to get your heads down for a couple of hours. We meet for a briefing at 17.30. And then we go in.'

'Jesus, you don't hang around, do you!'

'You said you wanted action. That you will get, I promise.'

'What's the job? And where?'

'I'll tell you at the briefing. It's a tricksy one, Mike, like nothing we've done before. So get your chaps there on time and cold sober.'

'What about arms and equipment? All we've got is Clay's cheese-cutter!'

Barr smiled. Clay Denham's cheese-cutter was a piece of wire attached to a couple of short lengths of wood. In Clay's hands it was a murderously effective weapon: looped around the neck, with pressure applied to the back, it could pretty nearly decapitate its victim.

'I'm not sure what we'll have in the way of arms,' Barr said. 'A few bits and pieces. The rest we'll have to collect as we go along.'

Noonan sighed. 'One of them do-it-yourself jobs, is it? OK. Where's the meet?'

Barr gave him directions to Acky's place on the beach. 'Don't turn up in a bunch. One or two at a time, with five-minute intervals in between. I don't think they'll be watching, but better to take no chances.'

'God in heaven, but you're the great one for a mystery. Who are they?'

'The enemy,' said Barr. 'Who else?'

'I don't believe it!' said Noonan, waving a hand towards the beach and the sea and the children splashing in the pool. 'In a heavenly place the like of this? Where the devil would you find an enemy?'

'About two miles from where you are sitting, as the crow flies,' Barr said.

That morning, Kitty was allowed to wear one of the dresses that Dr Bauer had provided for her. She put on a light make-up and arranged her hair in something like its old loose-flowing style.

She wrapped the paper-knife in a hand-towel she had stolen from the washroom, and tied it to her right leg, just above the knee. Kitty would have been hard put to explain why she had felt it necessary to take this small and inadequate weapon with her: she was conscious only of the fact that even the small measure of optimism which had lulled her to sleep the previous evening had evaporated. The clear light of morning had dispelled hope and brought a new sense of realism. She understood now that these people would never let her go, they could not, dare not, take that risk. And, of more urgent concern, was the thought that, unwittingly, she had lured Steve into danger.

He was the immediate problem. If she could maintain her role as Sister Helen for a little longer, if she could convince him to leave without her, then at least he would be safe. What happened after that, what happened to her – that was something to think about later. There was always the knife . . .

Sister Eleanor looked at Kitty anxiously when she came to the cubicle to conduct her to the Comptroller's suite, where the interview was to take place. Cupping the girl's cheeks in her hands and looking deep into her eyes, she asked, 'Are you all right, my dear?'

Kitty stiffened as a feeling of revulsion churned in her stomach like nausea. The touch of those hands, the antiseptic smile, the shallow compassion, filled her with a disgust which was as much directed towards herself as to the other woman. She tried to keep a level tone as she replied, 'Yes, Sister.'

But some of the tension in her body must have communicated itself, for the smile faded from Sister Eleanor's face and, frowning slightly, she said, 'Are you sure?'

'Yes, yes!' said Kitty, easing herself free.

'Of course. You're nervous. That's understandable.' Sister Eleanor took hold of Kitty's shoulders and stood back at arm's length. 'Let me have a good look at you.' And, after a moment, she shook her head and said, 'You are lovely, you are incredibly lovely.'

Kitty watched, mesmerised, as the brown hand crawled down from her shoulder to rest like a spider on her breast. Sister Eleanor's eyes glittered and her voice fell to a whisper as she continued, 'Are you wearing any panties – knickers?'

'Yes.'

'As soon as all this is over, I want you to take them off. For me. I like to think of you without them. I like to watch you and imagine that there is nothing but you under your dress, nothing between you and me. And later, this afternoon, I will come for you. Would you like that?'

It took all of Kitty's self-control to stand there, to nod, to hide her repugnance. Sister Eleanor smiled and lightly squeezed the girl's breast. 'You are mine. Remember that, think of it all the time. Think of it as our secret. Our lovely secret. I will look after you and care for you, whatever happens. Send this boy away, darling. You don't need him. Send him away and we shall have a wonderful time together, you and I.'

She stepped back and her voice took on a brisker tone: 'What is your name?'

Kitty fell at once into the ritual and replied, 'Sister Helen.'

'What was your former name?'

220

'I have forgotten.'

'What was your former name?'

'I don't know. I am Sister Helen now. I have renounced my old name together with my former life.'

'Good,' said Sister Eleanor. 'Very good. Why are you here?'

'Because I have been saved. I have been born again in Christ. Through Mr Dunlop I have learned that love and service are the true purpose of life.'

'Who is Mr Dunlop?'

'He is God's voice on earth. To serve him is to serve all mankind.'

'Good. Good,' said Sister Eleanor. 'Now, tell me this also. Did you come here of your own free will?'

'Yes. God guided me to this place.'

'And do you wish to stay?'

'For ever.'

'Good. That's very good. I want you to remember one other thing. This young man will seek to remind you of your past life. He will call you by your former name, the name that you have put aside. You must be strong and vigilant. Answer him as you have been taught and all will be well. Do you understand?'

'Yes, Sister.'

'And do you understand that if you falter in any way, if you show weakness, you will be punished?'

'Yes, Sister.'

'Then let us go.'

Sister Eleanor led the way from the dormitory. They passed Gabrielle on their way out. The French girl stood aside, with the regulation love-look on her face, but the message of sympathy and understanding in her eyes was something altogether different.

The Comptroller was waiting for them in his office and Sister Eleanor noted, with interest, that some of his customary blandness had deserted him. There was more than a hint of nervousness in his eyes and in the way he spoke.

'I expected you sooner than this,' he said. 'They will be here in two or three minutes.'

'I am sorry, Comptroller,' replied Sister Eleanor. 'I didn't want to hurry Sister Helen – I felt that she should be settled in her –'

'Yes, yes,' he interrupted. He looked at Kitty, but continued to speak as if she were an inanimate object, incapable of answering for herself. 'And is she settled? Is she in the right frame of mind?'

'Of course, one must allow for a certain natural nervousness but all things considered –'

He interrupted her again, with greater impatience. 'Will you answer the question!'

'Yes, Comptroller. I am sure there will be no problem,' said Sister

Eleanor. Tentatively, she added, 'You said they. I thought there would be just the young man.'

'He is bringing a woman with him. A Mrs Harcourt.'

'Ah,' she murmured.

'Will that make a difference?' he demanded.

'No. No. I'm sure it will not.'

He glared at Sister Eleanor and then at Kitty, and seemed to be on the point of speaking again when the intercom on his desk buzzed an interruption. He contented himself with a further warning look and went to answer it.

As he pressed down the switch, a man's voice said, 'They're here, Comptroller.'

'Bring them in,' he replied.

To Kitty, the minute of waiting seemed like an hour. She felt as if her whole body had suddenly frozen, as if her limbs were immovably bound in ice and yet, within this rigidity, her mind was racing in a whirling kaleidoscope of thought so vivid and frightening that she was almost on the verge of panic.

Steve!

She tried to steady herself, to fix her mind on what she had to do. Would she have the strength not only to face him, but to outface him: to present herself coldly but politely as Sister Helen and to send him away? The thought, just the thought, made her heart sink like a stone.

A light tap on the door. The Comptroller's voice telling them to come in. A man whose face was frighteningly familiar (where had she seen him before?) pushing open the door and standing aside to allow Steve to enter.

Steve!

A woman was with him, a large woman, but Kitty hardly noticed her.

Steve!

The name was like a bell ringing in her heart. She wanted to rush across the room to greet him, embrace him, hug him, but she seemed to have lost all power of movement.

The Comptroller dismissed the other man and then advanced on Steve with a smile and an outstretched hand. 'Welcome to Jerusalem Island, Mr Ugley.'

Steve ignored the Comptroller and his greeting. He crossed the room in great strides, his face radiant with joy, and took Kitty's hands.

'Kitty! Oh, Kitty!'

He stood there beaming at her, shaking his head, simply repeating her name.

'Kitty! Kitty! Oh, Kitty.'

222

'Hello, Steve,' she said, and had to fight back the tears that flooded to her eyes. She felt Sister Eleanor's hand tighten on her arm, as though in warning.

'Are you all right?' he asked.

She nodded, wanting to say 'I am now, I am now!' but unable to put her tongue to the words. She saw that the big woman had advanced to Steve's shoulder and was smiling at her.

'Hello, Kitty,' said the woman. 'I'm with him, though you wouldn't know it.'

'Oh, sorry,' Steve said awkwardly. 'A good friend of mine. Mrs Harcourt.'

'The name is Vinnie,' said the woman. 'I've heard a lot about you, dear. From Steve, of course. Most of it good.' She looked directly at Sister Eleanor and added bluntly, 'And who are you?'

'I am Sister Eleanor.'

'What are you holding the girl's arm for? Can't she stand up on her own?'

'Of course!' Sister Eleanor gave Vinnie a startled look and took a step away.

The Comptroller moved in, his voice smooth. 'I think, Sister Eleanor, that we should leave Sister Helen to talk with her friends.' He turned to Steve. 'We have arranged an adjoining room for your meeting. I am afraid we can allow you only fifteen minutes.'

'I shall take whatever time we need,' Steve said bluntly.

He looked directly at the Comptroller, seeing at close quarters, for the first time, the hard metallic eyes, each one staring out of the pale moonlike face like the base of a bullet. Indeed, a sort of metallic aura seemed to surround the man, as if the folds of flesh surrounding him were a cover for a cold steel casing beneath. He emanated not only a sense of power and authority but a feeling of malevolence so intense that it nipped Steve's blood like frost.

The Comptroller arranged his face into a smile. 'We do not usually permit interviews. We try, quite deliberately – I make no excuse for it – to quarantine our people, to isolate them from the infections of the so-called civilised world. We are building a new kind of society here, Mr Ugley, we have no place for the diseased standards and morals which rule outside.'

'I think I can manage without the sermon,' Steve said.

'Forgive me. I thought, being a reasonable man, you might be prepared to listen to our viewpoint. However, we have become accustomed to prejudice, it does not deter us. As I said, we do not usually permit interviews. However, Mr Dunlop has agreed that an exception should be made in your case.'

'That's very big of Mr Dunlop,' Steve said drily. 'Tell him I appreciate the thought.'

'Frankly, it was my suggestion. It seemed to me that you were becoming troublesome. When I heard that you and your friend Mr Barr had come here, posing as members of the Anglo-American fact-finding delegation –'

'Is that what they were supposed to be doing?' Steve interrupted. 'Fact-finding? You could have fooled me!'

The Comptroller chose to ignore this remark and went on, 'I also have good reason to believe that you and a certain Mr Barr were responsible for an assault on two of our Guardians on one of the beaches the other day.'

'They were armed. Don't forget to mention that.'

'They were armed, Mr Ugley,' said the Comptroller with a sigh, 'they were armed because, although we are a peace-loving community, we are not pacifist. We shall defend our own at all times. But let us return to the point. You are clearly a troublesome, not to say, obstinate young man. I had a word with Sister Helen about you. And it was felt that perhaps the only way to satisfy your curiosity would be to allow you to see for yourself that she is well and happy, to hear this from her own lips.'

'Then perhaps we could get on with it?' said Steve.

'Of course. I only mentioned a limit of fifteen minutes because Sister Helen has certain duties in the Tabernacle which she must attend to when your interview has been concluded.'

Steve glanced at Kitty. 'You're rather assuming that she will want to stay here, aren't you?'

'I have the utmost confidence in Sister Helen,' said the Comptroller, with a beneficent smile.

'Stalemate,' said Steve. 'I have the same confidence in Kitty Higgins.' He turned towards Kitty. 'Kitty, love, let's cut all this garbage. This is Steve talking, your friend Steve. You can trust me, you know that. Look, I want you to come with me now. I have a place on Antigua. Come back there with me for two or three days – a week maybe. We can talk our heads off there. If at the end, you still want to come back here, I'll bring you over personally. That's a promise. Will you come?'

Long agonising moments of silence followed. And then Kitty replied, her voice trembling, 'I can't. I told you in my letter, I have found a new life and true happiness here.'

'Kitty, listen – please,' he said urgently.

'I am Sister Helen now. I have renounced my old name together with my past. I have been born again in Christ. I wished only to see you so that I could explain this. Go home, please. Tell my parents and friends that I am well and happy. Tell them that I love them, as I love all humankind, but that from henceforth there can be no contact between us.'

224

'Kitty – will you listen –' he began, his voice edged with despera-tion, but she cut in quickly, 'I am Sister Helen! The Kitty you knew no longer exists. Go! Please, go!'

Steve swung round on the Comptroller. 'What have you done to her? What have you done to her, you bastard!' He spoke from behind clenched teeth and there was a blaze in his eyes which prompted Vinnie to lay a restraining hand on his arm.

'You are a bad loser, Mr Ugley,' replied the Comptroller evenly. 'But perhaps you think our presence makes a difference? Very well. Go into the next room with Mrs Harcourt and discuss the matter with Sister Helen in private. You will not be interrupted for fifteen minutes, I assure you.'

'Come on, Steve,' urged Vinnie, 'let's do that. Come on.'

He nodded. To the Comptroller, he said, 'And if she agrees to leave with me?'

'Let us discuss that improbable development if and when it arises,' said the Comptroller. He opened a door on to a small salon and added with a smile, 'It is not – what is the word? Bugged, I think. Yes. The room is not bugged. We do not indulge in such technological tricks here.'

Steve hesitated, waiting for Kitty. She held back, trembling inwardly, fearful that, if left alone with Steve and his friend, she would not have the strength to sustain the masquerade. She could feel the Comptroller's eyes upon her, staring as though he could read her thoughts. But a few moments before she had suddenly remem-bered the face of the man who had come in with Steve and, in a strange perverse way, this recollection helped Kitty to gather herself. It was a face she had seen often in her bad dreams, the face of one of the men who had attacked and kidnapped her all those long weeks ago. His presence underlined the danger into which she had led Steve and gave new impetus to her resolve to send him safely away, at whatever cost to herself.

'Sister Helen?' said the Comptroller. He took her face in his hands and, despite herself, she shivered slightly under his touch.

'We love you, remember that. We all love you, Sister,' he said.

Kitty moved into the other room, followed by Vinnie and Steve. The Comptroller closed the door behind them and stood for a moment in thoughtful silence, his lips pursed.

'Sister Helen did well —' began Sister Eleanor.

'You failed.' He spoke in a flat tone, without emotion.

'I don't understand,' she stammered.

'You failed – with the girl. Didn't you see her, didn't you sense it? From the first moment – when he entered the room – didn't you sense that we had lost her?'

'But, Comptroller – she gave all the correct responses. Surely you heard —'

'I heard, but I saw also.' He sighed and shook his head. 'She was acting out a rôle. Now, why would she do that? Perhaps because she was afraid – afraid for the young man? Yes, that is the only possible explanation. Rather touching, don't you think?'

'With respect, Comptroller, I am sure that you are mistaken about her.'

'Really?' he replied, and there was still no anger in his voice, only a hint of resignation. 'Perhaps it is my fault. Perhaps I was in too much of a hurry.'

'I still don't understand, Comptroller,' said Sister Eleanor. 'She has passed every test —'

'Except this one. Take my word for it, Sister. She has reverted. I can prove it to you very easily.'

Without waiting for her response, he opened the door to the salon. Steve turned on him angrily. 'I thought we were to have privacy.'

'Forgive me,' said the Comptroller, 'but I have been giving some thought to the proposal you made earlier. I think, in fairness to you and to Sister Helen, it might be better if she were to go back with you for a day or so.'

'You would let her go?' Steve looked at the Comptroller in astonishment.

'My dear fellow, she is not and never has been a prisoner. She came to Jerusalem Island, and remained, of her own free will. But she is new to the Community and I would not like her to make a final decision which she might regret later. I should like her to go with you to discuss the matter in complete freedom. If then she decides to come back to us, we shall welcome her, as always, with our love. If, on the other hand, she elects to stay with you and return to her former life, so be it. We should regret such a decision, but she would go with our blessing.'

'She can come with us now?' Steve spoke as if he still could not believe it.

'Of course,' replied the Comptroller.

'Kitty!' Steve almost shouted the name. 'Kitty! Do you hear that!'

She held back, struggling to maintain her pose, sensing that it had all suddenly become too easy but, in the next moment, she was in his arms as he lifted her up and swung her round in wild exuberance. Laughing and weeping at the same time, she clung to him and cried, 'Steve, oh, Steve, Steve, Steve!'

He set her down and looked into her face. His eyes were moist and her own tears poured down her cheeks in an unrestrained flood. She laid her head on his shoulder and a great shuddering sigh of relief shook her body.

'It's all right now,' he murmured, as to a child, 'everything will be all right now.'

But when she lifted her head, she caught a sudden glimpse of the Comptroller's face. It was distorted by her tears but there was no mistaking the bitter look in the glittering eyes. She closed her own eyes momentarily and when she opened them the look had gone so completely that she wondered if it had ever been there. There was a smile on the Comptroller's face now, a tolerant understanding smile, as he said, 'I hate to break up such a touching scene but time presses. Sister Eleanor, perhaps you will go with Sister Helen – or perhaps I should say Miss Higgins? – and help her gather her things together. Come back here when you are ready.'

Kitty hung back, clinging to Steve's arm, and Vinnie said, 'I'll go with them.'

'I am afraid that is not possible,' said the Comptroller. 'There are certain parts of the Tabernacle which are barred to outsiders. In any case, it is not necessary. She will be back in ten minutes. While you are waiting we can talk and take a little refreshment.'

Steve hesitated, and then took Kitty's hands in his own. 'Don't worry,' he said. 'I don't intend to lose you again. If you're not back in ten minutes, we will come and get you. OK?'

She nodded and her lips framed the words, 'Be careful.'

He watched her move off through the Comptroller's office with Sister Eleanor, wondering whether he had done the right thing. The Comptroller's abrupt and totally unexpected change of mind had thrown him off balance and, after the emotional reunion with Kitty, he was finding it difficult to marshal his thoughts. Why had the Comptroller suddenly agreed to let her go? Was the offer genuine, or was the man playing some deeper game? In the end, Steve decided that he had little choice but to accept the offer at its face value. If he could get Kitty away, the major part of the mission would be fulfilled. The rest of the problems would be resolved later. One thing was certain. Neither the Comptroller nor the Community would be allowed to get away with what they had done. He thought of Barr and the plan they had made and tried to imagine the look on Barr's face when he walked in with Kitty.

It was with these thoughts in mind that he sat down to wait with Vinnie. His throat felt harsh and dry and he drank thankfully of the iced fruit cup that was placed before them. He found words hard to come by, and was content to let Vinnie and the Comptroller do the talking. The Comptroller spoke of the Community and of the great good it had done and Vinnie, in her usual manner, came back at him with some blunt questions, but Steve was only half listening.

It was by no means finished yet, but all the same he felt as if some part of the victory had been won and a pleasant sense of euphoria – a sort of languor – flowed through his body. He saw Vinnie yawn and smiled to himself. It would be good to relax, to sleep. He glanced lazily at his watch. The ten minutes had almost gone, Kitty should be back soon.

The Comptroller rose, excused himself and went into his office. Steve heard him pick up the telephone and ask for Brother Vincent. He smiled, remembering the flowing silver hair, the shining eager face.

'You have Dr Bauer in your unit,' said the Comptroller into the phone. 'Have her brought to me at once.'

He replaced the receiver with a crash that startled Steve, sending little shock-waves of pain through his head. As the sensation passed, he felt the desire for sleep close around him, lapping at his mind in gentle, insistent surges that could not be denied. His eyes seemed to keep closing involuntarily and it took an enormous concentrated effort of will to hold them open.

He looked across at Vinnie and saw, to his amused surprise, that she had fallen sideways in her chair and was fast asleep. Her mouth was half open and she was snoring. He began to laugh, but the urge to sleep, the tiredness, transformed it into a yawn. The word Kitty surfaced out of the mist in his mind and, with it, the word time. His arm felt leaden and heavy and he had to summon up all his strength to lift it so that he could look at his watch again. The dial swam before his eyes as though it was mocking him and he found it impossible to hold it still, or to focus. He saw the Comptroller standing over him and tried to get to his feet.

'Kitty – Kitty,' Steve muttered.

And then a wave of sleep swept over him in an embracing flood. He smiled happily, foolishly, at the face which was now so close that it seemed like a round yellow lantern glowing above him, reached out a hand to touch it, and slithered to the floor.

'I spoke to Mr Dunlop, Doctor,' said the Comptroller, 'and he has agreed that you should return to normal duties. I know you will be reluctant to leave the Regeneration Experience – we all know how beneficial it can be – but the truth is that we need you.'

'Thank you, Comptroller,' said Dr Bauer. She stood before him in her stained working uniform, still wearing the number C121 on her back, bewildered once again by the sudden shift in her fortunes.

'God, in his wisdom, has delivered into our hands a wonderful opportunity to increase the wealth and influence of the Community,' continued the Comptroller. 'And a chance for you to prove to Mr Dunlop how important you are to the Community. Something, I may add, which I never doubted.' He smiled and opened the door to the salon. 'This is what I mean.'

228

She checked in the doorway, staring in astonishment. At first she thought the two people were dead, but then she heard the deep buzzing rumble of the woman's breathing, and saw the young man stir in his sleep and rearrange the position of his head. She went in and bent over each one in turn, snapping open the eyes, listening to the heart.

'One could hardly describe them as sleeping beauties,' said the Comptroller.

'They've been drugged,' she said.

'Not too violently,' he replied. 'Enough to put them to sleep for a few hours.' He touched Steve with the toe of his shoe. 'This is the important one. I want you to prepare him in the usual way. Sister Eleanor has other urgent duties, so I want you to take him through the auditing process yourself. He will make a worthy convert, I think. Oh, yes, if we can bring this young man to a state of grace, Doctor, we shall achieve a double triumph. At one stroke, we will remove an enemy of the Community and gain the means to extend our mission a hundredfold!'

'And the woman?'

'She will go with you, of course. She is a sinner and we must do our best to save her. And the girl, Sister Helen. She has reverted and will require further training. But it is the man on whom you must concentrate. Use whatever means you deem necessary. Win him for Christ and the Community, and I promise that you will be richly rewarded.'

Her one thought now was to get away, to find time to think, perhaps to see Gunnar and talk the matter through with him. Aloud, she said, 'If I might use your telephone, Comptroller?'

'Of course,' he said, 'but may I ask why?'

'To ring the hospital and arrange for the two subjects to be transported to the Special Rooms.'

'I am sorry, Doctor,' he said. 'Obviously, I did not make things clear. You must go to the hospital, naturally, and collect whatever you may need. Then you will return here. At eleven o'clock tonight you, and our two friends, will be taken aboard the *Leandro*.'

'The *Leandro*?' She could feel and hear the shock trembling in her voice.

'Oh, yes,' he said smoothly. 'In view of the special circumstances, Mr Dunlop feels that it would be better if the subjects were removed from Jerusalem Island for the time being. So, Doctor, in addition to a new challenge we are giving you new horizons also! You will leave on the *Leandro*, at midnight, for the port of Arica. You will be met there by Brother Joshua, who will take you to our settlement near Magdalena in Bolivia.'

Chapter Sixteen

By four o'clock that afternoon, Barr realised that the worst had happened and when Acky confirmed his fears he was not surprised. Gunnar had sent a brief message by short-wave radio to say that Steve and Vinnie were prisoners and that they were to be taken aboard the *Leandro* at eleven o'clock that night. It was possible, although this could not be confirmed, that Kitty Higgins would go with them. One hour later the ship would set sail for the small South American port of Arica, and from there they were to be transported to the Community settlement in Bolivia.

Barr cursed Steve's folly in going to the island and his own stupidity in agreeing to it. At the time, it had seemed a reasonable risk, but he saw now that he had badly misjudged the situation. Originally, the plan had been for the entire group to go in under cover of night and set up a base on or near Dreadnought Hill. Then, at first light, they would be in position to move on the Compound and the Tabernacle; at the same time, Gunnar and his friends were to stage diversionary incidents in other areas of the island, with the object of pinning down as many of the Guardians as possible.

They were to be taken over to Dreadnought Hill by Bobby Lamb, the fisherman possessed of much local knowledge and not a few secrets.

One of Bobby's secrets went way back to Horatio Nelson. It seemed that the wily Admiral, when issuing orders for the construction of the defensive position at Dreadnought Hill, had arranged for a stairway and tunnel to be built, connecting one of the outbuildings to a cave in the rocks below, the general idea being that if the fortress was attacked and encircled from the land side, its defenders could continue to be supplied from the sea or, at worst, use the tunnel as an escape route. With the ending of the wars with the French and the Dutch, Dreadnought Hill was abandoned and the tunnel had fallen into disuse until Bobby Lamb, by a happy accident, discovered its location. The years had almost closed it up but, recognising its possible value in business, Bobby had laboriously cleared the silt and rock until the tunnel was negotiable once more.

It is probable that he would have kept this knowledge to himself if the Community had not taken over the island: but he had a healthy suspicion of excessive piety and this suspicion developed into dislike and hostility when his friend Jonah Winston virtually disappeared and made all his property over to the sect.

Bobby had another good friend in Steve's uncle. They were two of

230

a kind: Mr Ugley Senior had a variety of business interests, not all of which showed up in his annual accounts, and Bobby Lamb, with his knowledge of the Caribbean and his buccaneering approach to authority, made an ideal partner. And so he was drawn, as a matter of course, into the circle of opposition to the Community.

'I hate the whole kiss-me-arse lot of them,' he had told Barr. 'Stealing a man's property, that's one thing, but to go twisting his soul out of shape and blasting his brain, that's the work of the devil. Them people, they talk with two tongues. One tongue wags on about loving, but if you listen hard, you hear the other tongue and all that makes is the noise of a rat-trap!'

Timing was not the only problem that Barr faced. Unfortunately, Acky had not been able to do very much in the matter of arms and all he could offer were one Klashnikov automatic rifle, the older model but still in good shape, three handguns, one shotgun and a small supply of ammunition. However, Gunnar had organised two small caches of weapons on Jerusalem Island and the hope was that he would be able to make good the deficiencies. Otherwise, as Barr put it, they would have to feed off the Guardians.

It was Gordon Pullar who came up with the surprise of the afternoon. With an air of modesty which scarcely concealed his pride, he opened the boot of his car and showed Barr a large box with rope handles.

'Plaster gelatine,' he said. 'I thought Mr Calder might possibly find a use for it.'

Stuttering Bob Calder, a plumpish, mild-mannered man who looked as if he might be more at home with cuddly toys than with explosives, prised the lid open with his knife, took out one of the slabs of gelatine and tore off the waterproof wrapping. The stuff inside had a strong sickly smell and looked rather like khaki-coloured putty. He examined it carefully, running a finger along the slab and then studying his fingertip, as though checking for moisture. He began to mould the slab in his big hands, as a child would shape plasticine, except that the gelatine was harder and less pliant.

'OK,' he said, with scarcely the trace of a stammer, 'OK.' Normally, his stutter was painful to hear, but one of the characteristics for which he was famous among his colleagues was that when handling explosives the stutter almost completely disappeared. He had another characteristic which quite a few people had discovered to their cost. When Calder was overtaken by a fit of stuttering it was dangerous either to prompt him or to try and anticipate his words: he regarded such conduct as an act of condescension and usually reacted with a fury that contradicted his friendly appearance.

'You can use it?' asked Mr Pullar.

'N-not on its own,' said Calder. 'I need d-detonating fuse, safety f-fuse, d-detonators and tape.'

'Here, all here,' said Mr Pullar triumphantly. He pulled a tartan car-blanket aside to reveal coils of fuse packed in metal canisters, each clearly marked, and aluminium detonators in cardboard tubes. There was also a large roll of black tape and some gun-cotton primers.

Calder smiled like a child in a fairy grotto at Christmas time. He refused all help and began carefully to unload this unexpected treasure, checking each item as he did so.

'Where did you pick all that up?' asked Barr.

'Ask no questions,' said Mr Pullar, tapping his nose. 'Actually,' he added, 'I have a friend of a friend of a friend who is in the quarry business.'

Barr took Noonan and Bobby Lamb aside and told them the problem. 'We cross to the island as soon as it's dark,' he said. 'But there'll be no waiting until first light. We'll have to move in on the Tabernacle right away.'

'At night?' asked Noonan. 'We don't know the terrain, the lay-out, anything!'

'I've seen part of the Compound and I've been inside the Tabernacle,' said Barr. 'I've a fair idea of what it's like. In any case, we've got no choice.' He turned to Bobby. 'Do you know the island well enough to guide us across to the Compound in the dark?'

'Man,' said Bobby, 'I know that place like I know the back of my hand.'

'How far from Dreadnought Hill to the Compound, do you reckon?'

'About six miles, no more. The whole island is only twelve by fourteen miles.' He chuckled, and slapped his thigh. 'Well, be Jesus Christ, this is one party I been waiting for for a long time. Yes, be Jesus! A long long time!'

Barr had prepared a rough sketch-map of the Compound area, including the Tabernacle and, spreading this out, he gave what directions he could to the group, indicating where the defences appeared to be strong, and which key points had to be taken and held.

'Objective Number 1,' he said, 'is to get Steve, Vinnie and Kitty. The secondary objective, if things work out, is to get out the other girls, the ones they call the Handmaidens.'

'What if they don't want to come?' asked Noonan.

'We leave them. That's their affair. It's got to be quick and clean. In and out in three or four hours. If any one gets separated from the main party, make for Dreadnought Hill. That will be the rendezvous point. The *Carib Beauty* – and other boats, as necessary – will be there to take us off.'

'What's the strength of the opposition?' asked Clay Denham.

'We're not sure. About fifty men – they call them Guardians.

They're well armed.'

'I think, old chap, you should point out that we have nothing against the ordinary people on Jerusalem Island,' said Mr Pullar. 'They are victims, if you like, or dupes. As far as possible, they should not be harmed.'

'Right,' said Barr. 'What these people believe, that's no concern of ours. If they want to follow Mr Dunlop, or fall on their knees and worship the nearest palm tree, that's their business. We've no quarrel with them.'

'Do we get to share out these Handmaidens when it's all over?' said the twin called Jesse, with a grin. But the grin faded when he saw the glint in Barr's eyes and, with a shrug, he added feebly, 'Just a joke, just joking.'

'I'm glad,' Barr said softly. 'I like a man with a sense of humour.'

He turned back to the map and indicated the area known as the Beach of Pleasure. 'Our information is that there are always six to eight of the Guardians here on any one night. Mike, you'll take two men – Joe and Clay – and hit that first. That way we'll kill two birds with one stone – we'll eliminate a fair chunk of the opposition, and we'll pick up some arms. But it has to be done quietly – we don't want them raising the alarm. When we get to Dreadnought Hill, someone will fill you in with more detail about the lay-out.'

Ten minutes later, the last questions had been asked and answered, and the only thing left was to wait for sunset. Barr was conscious that the planning was inadequate to the point of being almost non-existent. There were so many unknown factors, so much would have to be left to improvisation: but he was up against the tyranny of the clock and there was nothing he could do about that. He showed none of this concern to the others, but Noonan, who knew him best of all, sensed his mood.

He chose a moment when he could speak to Barr alone. 'I feel good about this one, Tommy,' he said.

'I'm glad someone does,' said Barr.

'It's a funny thing, a curious thing, but I always get this itching in the region of the crutch when I'm about to be visited by a bit of luck,' said Noonan. He scratched himself vigorously to illustrate the point.

'Yes, I remember,' said Barr. 'The night in Brazzaville when we took that arms depot. You nearly drove me crazy with your scratching. I thought it was something else that was troubling you.'

'Never!' said Noonan. 'I'm a clean-living man.' He scratched again. 'Brazzaville. Ah, I remember that night. The two of us and twelve of them and we took the lot. We had them surprised.'

'We were lucky.'

'Of course. Didn't I have the itch? I knew we'd get lucky. Like tonight. We'll have this little lot surprised also.'

Barr smiled. 'Do me a favour, Mike, will you?'

'Anything, you know that,' said Noonan.

'Keep scratching,' said Barr.

Kitty was so bemused by her meeting with Steve, so thrilled at the prospect of getting away from the island, that she was in a state bordering on euphoria as, that afternoon, with Sister Eleanor at her side, she made her way back to the Handmaidens' quarters in the Tabernacle. She was conscious that Sister Eleanor was grimly silent, but this did not trouble her. The one thought that danced in her head was that soon, so very soon, she would be free again, and that this strange nightmare interlude in her life would be over. She did not wish to look beyond that: today was all that mattered, tomorrow would have to wait its turn.

The dormitory was empty when they arrived, and she remembered that at this time the Handmaidens would be relaxing in the Grove. She thought, then, of Gabrielle and Angela and chided herself silently for her selfishness.

'I would like to go and say goodbye to the others,' she said.

'What you'd like and what you'll do are two different things,' said Sister Eleanor sullenly. 'Get your bits and pieces together and I'll take you back.'

But when Kitty went to the cupboard in her cubicle and saw the white gowns she had worn as a Handmaiden hanging there, she turned away, sickened.

'There's nothing here that I want,' she said.

She was aware that Sister Eleanor had come in behind her and had closed the drapes around the cubicle. Suddenly the woman reached out and grasped her wrists.

'I didn't fail with you,' she said, the words hissing from behind her teeth. 'I had you, I nearly had you. They didn't give me time, they didn't give me enough time. In another month – less – I could have put you beyond reach of the devil, I could have saved you.'

Kitty tried to pull away, but she could not break that unyielding grip.

'It's not too late!' said Sister Eleanor fervently. 'It isn't too late! Do you really want to go back into that Satanic world – with all its rotten-ness and corruption? Oh, we're not perfect here, I admit that. We're human, we have human weaknesses. But at least we're trying to build something new. A society based on love. On brotherhood and beauty. On peace and hope! A new Jerusalem!'

There was a kind of shining exultation in the voice and in the eyes that somehow quelled Kitty's anger and turned it to pity.

'You believe all that, don't you?' she said, shaking her head in bewilderment. 'You really believe it!'

234

'I'd die if I didn't,' replied Sister Eleanor.

'But how can you speak of love when you kidnap people, when you hold them against their will? How can you explain what happens at the Lagoon?'

'The Lagoon? There must be retribution, don't you see? I told you, we are not perfect. People must be taught – and shown – that there is punishment for sinners, enemies. As for you – what happened to you – can't you see that we tried to save you? What we did was for your own good. And we came so near, so near.'

'Neither you nor anyone else has the right to dictate what is good for me,' said Kitty quietly. 'That is what's wrong with your Community. You won't allow people to think for themselves, or even to be themselves. You take them away from their families, their friends, even from their past – you separate them from everything that makes them real. Your Community isn't made up of human beings – it's made up of robots. The girls, the Handmaidens – look at them, just look at them! They're not people any more, they're walkie-talkie dolls! Dolls! For a sick old man to play with! No. No. Don't talk to me about your new Jerusalem! I'd rather take my chance in the world outside, thank you very much.'

Sister Eleanor released her hold and sighed. She seemed genuinely sad and Kitty realised that it was useless to argue. The woman's mind was shuttered, she heard only what she wished to hear, saw only what she wished to see.

'You talk of a sick old man,' said Sister Eleanor. 'That sick old man raised me up when I was down, so far down that everyone else had written me off as hopeless. He did that for hundreds, thousands, of others. He gave us hope, faith, a purpose. He is truly the representative of God on earth, I believe that with all my heart. He will die soon, he will go to our heavenly Father. And I tell you this, I would do anything – anything – to make his last days happy.'

'I don't know what he was or what he did,' said Kitty. 'All I know is that his new Jerusalem is rotten. It stinks!'

Sister Eleanor raised a hand to strike Kitty, but the girl grasped her arm before the blow could fall.

'No!' she said, and the green eyes flashed with something of her old spirit. 'All that's finished. You lay a finger on me again, and I swear to God, I'll flatten you!'

They walked in silence back to the Comptroller's suite. The signal flashed for them to enter and the Comptroller rose with a measured smile. He opened the door to the salon and said, 'Your friends are waiting. Perhaps you'd care to join them. Transportation will be here directly.'

Kitty moved inside and stopped suddenly. She saw Vinnie first, sprawled sideways in the chair with her eyes closed: and then she saw

235

Steve, lying motionless on the floor, as if he were dead.

With a cry, she ran forward. As she bent over him and saw to her relief that he was breathing, the door closed and she heard the key turn in the lock.

There were three men waiting in the darkness by the blockhouse on Dreadnought Hill when Barr's party arrived. Bobby Lamb had steered the *Carib Beauty* with a sort of nonchalant confidence safely through the reef to the cave below and led them in the same easy manner along the tunnel and up the crumbling stairs to the exit on the hill above.

Barr made the agreed signal on his flashlight, one of the three men responded, and then they came forward. They shook hands and introduced themselves. There was Gunnar Arnasson, whom Barr vaguely recognised as the man who had visited Acky's cabin; the two others were named as Roberts and Thompson.

'We'll post guards,' said Gunnar, 'then we can go into the block-house and talk.'

'How far is this place they call the Beach of Pleasure?' asked Barr.

'Not far. It's to the south of here. A mile – perhaps a little less,' replied Gunnar.

'My information is that there will be six to eight Guardians there. Is that right?'

'Yes. I would say that is correct.'

'We're going to take them first,' said Barr. 'I'm sending three men. Can you give me someone as a guide?'

'Wait,' said Roberts. 'I think we should talk this over.'

'There's no time,' said Barr brusquely. 'If we deal with that lot we can make a big dent in the odds.'

'I don't like it,' said Roberts. 'I don't like it.'

Barr decided that he didn't much like Roberts either. There was a touch of arrogance there which could prove troublesome.

'Sorry about that, Mr Roberts,' he said. 'If you won't supply a guide, we'll just have to find the place ourselves.'

'No problem,' said Thompson. 'I can take you there.' He spoke with a soft purling accent which stirred Barr's memory and brought a brief smile to his face.

'West Country?' he asked.

'Devonshire,' answered Thompson. 'Totnes.'

'You'll do,' said Barr.

'I still think you should wait until we've had a chance to discuss our overall strategy,' said Roberts.

Barr ignored him and turned to Noonan. 'Right, Mike. Get going. Twenty minutes to get there, ten minutes to do the job, twenty minutes to get back. Fifty minutes. It's now – what?' He turned the flashlight on his watch. '19.22 precisely. We'll give you until 20.30.'

'That's generous,' said Noonan.

'And remember,' Barr said, 'keep it quiet. Very quiet.'

'Perhaps you might find this useful,' said Gunnar tentatively. 'In view of the need to make no noise.' And to Barr's surprise, he produced a .22 High Standard automatic and a silencer. He screwed the silencer into place and it went home with a faint metallic click.

Barr weighed it in his hand before passing it to Noonan. Like most professionals he distrusted silencers, knowing from experience that they were largely ineffective, but he had heard that on a good .22 they really did work. In recent years, many of the hit men in the American underworld had abandoned their heavier guns in favour of the .22 with silencer, and that, from a professional if not an ethical viewpoint, was a fair enough recommendation.

'Just the job,' said Noonan. 'Right, let's head for them there hills.'

'We'll wait here until 20.30,' said Barr. 'If you're not back by then, we'll move in without you.'

'Oh, we'll be back,' said Noonan. He grinned at Barr in the darkness, a gleam of white teeth, and gave himself a last vigorous good luck scratch before moving off.

Noonan had been around a bit and was not a man who surprised easily, but even he was slightly taken aback when he peered cautiously through the window of the pavilion at the Beach of Pleasure. Four men and four girls were ranged around the dimly lit room, clapping and shouting. The object of their excitement soon became clear. A race was going on, a bizarre race in which two men were competing.

As naked as cherubs, with ropes in their mouths to serve as reins, the competitors – one young and slim, the other portly and on the edge of middle-age – were straddled by topless girl jockeys, each wearing bikini-briefs so minute as to be almost invisible. The girls carried short canes with which they belaboured the pink rumps and flanks of their mounts and when this seemed not to be enough, the spectators joined in with kicks and slaps. The older man was clearly flagging and when he sank to the ground exhausted, his rider, encouraged by the cheers of the others, beat his backside so furiously that the man pulled himself to his knees again and trundled off in pursuit of his rival.

'Holy Mother of God!' breathed Noonan. 'Is that their idea of pleasure!'

'My money's on the thin one,' said Joe Colleano.

'Best looking jockeys I ever set eyes on,' said Clay Denham.

Noonan turned to young Thompson, their guide. 'What's the rest of the lay-out like?'

'A kitchen to the left and bedrooms at the back.'

'Right,' said Noonan. 'Joe, you stay here and cover me from this window. Clay, come with me. As soon as we're inside, check the bedrooms. Don't shoot, except as a last resort. Remember what Major Barr said – quick and quiet!'

'What about me?' asked Thompson.

Noonan pointed back to the high wire fence through which they had just cut their way. 'Get back there to the ridge. Keep your head down. If you get wind of any patrols, or see anyone approaching this place, come and tell us pronto. Don't shout! Just come and tell us.'

As the young man slipped away, Noonan fitted the silencer to the .22. Apart from hunting knives, they had two other weapons. Colleano carried the Klashnikov automatic rifle and Denham had a Smith and Wesson .38 revolver. All the arms had been acquired by Acky in Miami and although they seemed to be in good order, no-one had been able to put them to the test.

Noonan glanced through the window once more. The race around the table seemed to be nearing its climax; the older man had narrowed the gap and his jockey was urging him on with shouts and a vigorous use of the cane.

'Let's go before she cuts that poor fellow's arse to ribbons,' said Noonan.

'Oh, I don't know,' said Colleano. 'From the look on his face, I'd say he was enjoying it.'

Noonan moved sideways, followed by Clay Denham. Denham lifted a foot to kick in the door but Noonan restrained him.

'Wait,' he said, 'you never know your luck.'

He tried the handle, turning it gently, very gently; the door opened with hardly a murmur and they stepped into a narrow hall. The main room lay to the right and the noise coming from there more than covered the sound of their cautious approach.

A door to their left was half open, revealing part of a small kitchen. Music was blaring from a transistor on a shelf above the sink, but no-one was listening to it. The room was empty.

Noonan nodded to Denham, signalling him to move to the rear and check the bedrooms. He gave him a few seconds to get clear and then he opened the door to the main room and waited in the doorway.

It took a full twenty seconds before anyone became aware of his presence and another twenty before there was silence.

'Good evening, ladies and gentlemen,' said Noonan.

One of the Guardians made a dive for a chair on which there lay a holstered gun. There was a faint pop as Noonan fired: the man screamed as a twelfth of an ounce of lead thudded into his shoulder, spinning him round. He crashed into the wall and slid down into a sitting position, moaning incoherently.

'I want silence,' said Noonan. 'Complete and utter silence. If any one of you, man or woman, opens your gob to make a single sound, I'll knee-cap you.' He looked down at the two naked men, who were still on their hands and knees, with the girls on their backs.

'Disgusting!' he continued. 'And you calling yourself a Christian Community! I would never have believed it if I hadn't seen it with my own two eyes. What's more, it wasn't a fair race. The old one there should have had a couple of lengths start. Get up, will you, get up! The sight of you down there with your poor bleeding bums is churning my stomach!'

Three of the other men had bunched together and begun to edge towards Noonan. There was a tinkle of glass and Colleano pointed the Klashnikov through the broken window in their direction.

'Back off!' he said. 'Back off! Face that wall – with your hands on your heads.'

Men and women alike shuffled into place along the wall and there was no more resistance. They were joined by another couple whom Clay had found in one of the bedrooms: a trickle of blood showed on the man's face and his temple was stained by a large fresh bruise. The girl, wide-eyed, whimpered with terror.

'What happened?' said Noonan.

'He started to argue,' said Clay laconically, pushing the man into position.

'We've got a problem,' murmured Noonan.

'What's that?'

'What do we do with this lot? It'll take a hell of a time to tie them up properly. And we can't just lock them up here – they'd break out in no time.'

'Why don't we just shoot the lot of them?' Clay deliberately pitched his voice so that the prisoners could hear, and one of the girls slumped to her knees, mumbling a prayer.

'Stand up, darling,' said Noonan. 'We've no quarrel with you. It's the men he was speaking of.'

Thompson came running in at that moment with the news that he had seen a truck heading in their direction along the road from the Compound.

'It must be coming here,' he said, 'there's nowhere else it could go in this area.'

'Quiet!' said Noonan.

The sound of the approaching truck could be plainly heard now. Noonan signalled to Clay and Thompson, indicating that they should take up positions to cover the main door. He took the gun from the

239

chair and tossed it to Thompson, who caught it clumsily. Then he moved across and stood behind the line of prisoners.

'I want quiet from you lot,' he said. 'I don't even want to hear you breathe. One peep – and we'll stitch the lot of you.'

Colleano had come into join him and he slapped the magazine of the Klashnikov, giving emphasis to the threat. The two men took up positions on either side of the door.

Silence – broken by two sounds: the voice of Ella Fitzgerald singing *Ten Cents a Dance* from the radio in the kitchen, and the noise of the truck pulling to a halt.

Footsteps rasping on the shingle outside. The indistinct murmur of men's voices, a short laugh from one of them. They were near the door.

Noonan held up two fingers to indicate his estimate of the number, and Joe nodded.

The men were in the hall now. The door opened and they came in, two burly figures in uniform, armed with Uzi sub-machine guns. The first man stopped short just beyond the doorway, staring in astonish-ment at the line of people against the wall. As he did so, Colleano moved in, jabbing the Klashnikov into the first man's ribs.

The second man was more quick witted. He sensed rather than saw that Noonan was waiting and, slamming the door against him, he backed off into the hall. The Uzi was in his hands as he turned to find himself facing Clay Denham. Before he could make a further move-ment Denham was upon him, thrusting the hunting knife in a deep upwards stroke into the man's guts. He grunted in surprise and fell forward as Denham withdrew the knife and stepped neatly aside. The man began to gurgle, his hands scrabbling on the tiled floor, his body writhing.

Denham crouched down, turned the man over and, grasping his hair, pulled his head back. The knife was at the man's throat, when a hand fell on Denham's wrist and he looked up into the horrified face of Thompson.

'No!' said Thompson. 'No! No!'

'Christ!' said Denham. 'What's wrong with you, boy?'

'You can't kill him, not like that!'

'I've half killed him already. It'll be kinder this way.'

'No,' said Thompson again. 'Please.'

'Jesus wept!' said Denham contemptuously. But he left the man and rose to his feet. 'OK. Have it your way. It'll take the poor bastard eight hours to die and every minute will be bloody agony. I hope that makes you happy!'

Thompson stared at the bloodstained knife, at the blood on Denham's hand and arm, and his face paled visibly. He turned and fled into the kitchen and a moment later he was retching into the

240

sink.

Noonan crowded everyone into the truck and Joe Colleano, who had assumed the uniform of one of the Guardians, took the wheel. The precaution was unnecessary. They arrived back at Dreadnought Hill twenty-five minutes ahead of schedule and without incident. The prisoners were shut into the blockhouse and two of Gunnar's supporters were set to guard them.

Barr was well pleased by the result of this first skirmish, although as usual he did not show it. In forty-five minutes, they had neutralised seven Guardians and taken in six Uzi sub-machine guns, four hand-guns, a truck, and a small supply of ammunition.

Clay Denham proved to be badly wrong in his estimate of the time it would take for the wounded Guardian to die. Mercifully, the man was already dead when they lifted him from the truck.

He was the first fatal casualty of the night.

Chapter Seventeen

It was almost four hours before Vinnie or Steve showed any sign of revival and, to Kitty, those hours were the longest she had ever known, far exceeding in terms of terror and loneliness even the worst of what she had experienced in the past few weeks.

She shook each one in turn, slapped their faces, splashed them with water from a vase of flowers, but they remained inert, peacefully sleeping while time ticked away. She had no idea of what had been planned for them, but she expected the Guardians to come at any moment: every sound from the direction of the Comptroller's office prickled her skin with fear. The paper-knife was still hidden beneath the skirt of her dress and, at one point, when she heard the low murmur of voices from the other room, she took it in hand and stood to one side of the door, prepared to plunge the blade into the first person to enter. But the talking stopped, the silence closed around her again and she was left once more with the feeling of utter helplessness. She returned yet again to the task of rousing Vinnie and Steve but their persistent slumber resisted all her efforts and she gave up in despair.

Forcing back the threatening tears, Kitty sat down and tried desperately to order her thoughts, to think of something she could do. She shivered as the air-conditioning, murmuring away at full strength, touched her flesh with a dry chill. It was getting towards late afternoon and the light, sliding through the slats of the shuttered windows, was beginning to wane.

The windows! She moved across and tried the catch on one of them. It gave easily, but the window remained firmly closed. It was framed in steel, divided into six small glass panels, and secured at the top and bottom by two flat-headed screws which had been driven through the frame into the woodwork beyond.

Kitty considered breaking the glass panels but this would still leave the frame, which looked strong enough to resist anything short of a sledge-hammer: and, in any case, there was the danger that the noise would bring someone in from the other room.

She tried the bottom screw with her knife but the point simply turned in the head without shifting the screw itself: when she pressed home more desperately the tip of the knife snapped off and she fell forwards, bruising her knuckles on the metal frame.

Angered rather than put off by this setback she tried again and found, with a first tiny thrill of hope, that the broken end of the knife was now able to get some purchase on the screw. She felt the screw move slightly as she applied pressure but it became difficult to get a firm enough grip on the handle of the knife. Tearing a strip from the skirt of her dress, she wrapped this around the sword-like handle and returned to the screw. It yielded a full half-turn this time and she stopped for a moment to draw breath, her heart thudding with excitement.

Suddenly she heard a sound at the door, and just had time to turn round with the knife held behind her back, when it opened. The man she had recognised earlier, her kidnapper, appeared in the doorway. He stood there for a moment, his cold eyes taking in the room, and she lowered her head, assuming what she hoped was an attitude of helpless resignation. He crossed to the sleepers, stirred Steve with his foot, lifted Vinnie's head and, when all this produced no response, he gave Kitty a quick, final glance and went out. The door snapped behind him, the key turned in the lock, and she turned back to the window with a murmur of relief.

The bottom screw began to move more easily now. It was hard and painful work still, with the head of the knife biting through the cloth into the soft flesh of her palm, but at last she reached a point where she could turn the screw with her fingers. In another second, it was free.

The upper screw was more difficult to reach and she dragged over a chair. Standing on this gave her the necessary height and she was relieved to feel the screw yield at once to her pressure. When that was free at last, she stepped down and sank into the chair. She was breathing heavily, perspiration was pouring down her face and a painful blister had formed on her hand: but her feeling of helplessness had all but disappeared.

She got up again and tried the window. It was stuck in the frame, and she had to put all her strength into the effort to push it open. It gave quite suddenly and she felt a rush of warm air strike her face.

There remained the outside shutters. Leaning forward, she pushed them gently, tentatively. The hinged sections gave slightly, creaking outwards, but then stopped. A thin vertical bar of light showed where the two shutters joined together. In the centre, breaking the bar in two, Kitty could clearly see part of the retaining hook. She had seen similar shutters in various parts of the Tabernacle and knew that the hooks were quite flimsy things, designed to hold the shutters in place when closed.

It would be easy enough, she thought, to burst open the shutters, but this also presented certain dangers. It was not simply the problem of noise: she knew that the grounds outside were patrolled regularly by the Guardians and broken shutters might invite their attention.

She slid the blade of the knife between the two sections just under the hook. A little upward pressure and she was able to lift the hook from its hold until it fell away and the shutters were free. Mercifully they stayed in place, but a light push was all that would be needed to open them.

Her heart was pounding in her ears like a drum-beat as she stood back. She still had no clear idea of what she would do, only the vague notion that she might use the window to escape and bring help. But escape to where? And to whom could she turn for help?

It was then that she heard a low sigh and turning, she saw that Vinnie's eyes were open. Kitty hurried across and took her hands.

'Wake up! Please, oh, please, wake up!'

The woman stared at her without recognition and the eyelids fluttered as if about to close again. Kitty shook her vigorously and managed at last to get her to sit up straight. She dipped the strip of cloth she had used on the knife into the vase of water and bathed Vinnie's face.

'Walk,' said Kitty, 'try and walk.'

With an effort she helped the big woman up and steadied her on her feet. They set off round the room, stumbling at first, but gradually Vinnie came back to life. In a few more minutes she was walking without assistance and Kitty was able to explain what had happened. Her account seemed to put the final seal on Vinnie's recovery.

'The bastards,' she said grimly, 'the rotten bastards! What do you reckon they're aiming to do now?'

'I don't know,' said Kitty.

'Whatever it is it won't be good,' said Vinnie. 'Well, the first thing to do is to get our sleeping prince on his feet. Here, give me that vase.'

She stood over Steve and let the rest of the water trickle in a steady stream on to his face. He groaned, his eyelids flickered uncertainly, and he tried to turn away. The two women hauled him up and set off round the room once more, holding the reluctant Steve between them.

'Walkies, duckie!' urged Vinnie. 'Lovely walkies.'

It took ten tiring minutes to bring him round to a state where he could understand the situation they were in, but by then the outline of a plan had formed in Kitty's mind. She began to drag the furniture across the room.

'What are you doing?' asked Vinnie.

'Give me a hand, both of you. I want to block the door – build a sort of barricade. It might hold them off for a while.'

'What then?'

'I managed to force one of the windows open. We can get out into the grounds. After that, I'm not sure. But at least we'll have a better chance than if we stay here.'

They piled the furniture up before the door, stacking one piece on another, moving as quietly as possible. The exercise further restored Vinnie and Steve and they needed no urging from Kitty. She opened the window and the shutter and peered out cautiously. The light had almost gone and she could see only a few yards each way, but it

244

seemed to be clear.

One by one they climbed through, Steve going last and closing the window and the shutters behind him. They scuttled across the path and crouched down in the shelter of a clump of shrubs. Even as they waited and watched, the West Indian night closed in upon them abruptly, so that the line of distant palm trees became a feathered blur and the darkness beyond seemed to hide the sky. The lights came on, lamp after lamp set high at regular intervals on the outer wall of the building, bathing the path and the ground along its edge in a faint salmon-coloured glow. They moved deeper into the grounds, away from the light.

'Where exactly are we?' whispered Steve.

'Outside the West Wing of the Tabernacle,' said Kitty.

'Which way to the bridge that leads into the Compound?'

'That direction, I think.' She pointed into the night. 'Yes, that's it.'

'How far?'

'I don't know. Quite a distance. We'd have to cross the big square.'

'No,' said Steve thoughtfully. 'We'll never make it across that bridge on our own. The place will be swarming with Guardians. And we can't stay here – when they find we're missing, they'll have teams of men searching the grounds.' He paused. 'Let's think this out for a minute.'

'I could do with a nice cup of tea,' said Vinnie in a conversational whisper. 'My throat feels like the inside of a rusty can.' And suddenly, stifling a louder cry, she grunted and slapped at her leg.

'Quiet!' said Steve.

'I've just been bitten!' she complained. 'Let's get out of here! This place is full of creepy-crawlies. I can't stand creepy-crawlies!'

'They won't kill you.'

'How do you know?' she asked.

'Kitty,' said Steve, 'listen. I've got it, I think. Somehow, we have to find a place to hide up until morning. Barr is coming in then –'

'Barr?' she interrupted.

'A friend of mine.' Steve explained about the rescue plan. 'They'll be heading for the island now. At first light, they're going to break into the Compound. What we have to do is hold out somewhere until they arrive.'

A dozen questions buzzed in Kitty's head but she refrained from asking them.

'Are there snakes on this island?' asked Vinnie apprehensively.

'Vinnie, for God's sake!' said Steve.

'I hate snakes,' said Vinnie. 'I really hate snakes. Nasty slithering slimy things. I bet there are a lot of snakes around here, it's just the place for them.'

'Will you shut up!' hissed Steve. To Kitty, he said, 'They'll figure that we're making for the bridge, to get out of the Compound. That's the obvious thing to do. So, we avoid the obvious. Now, where would they be least likely to look for us? Somewhere unexpected. Any thoughts?'

An idea surfaced in Kitty's mind. 'There's only one place that I can think of,' she said.

'Where?'

'The women's rooms in the East Wing. Men are forbidden to enter the area. But we'll never make it. There are people on guard all the time.'

'We can try,' said Steve. 'Are you game to try?'

'All right,' said Kitty calmly, 'if you say so. We'll have to cross behind the main part of the Tabernacle. I'm not sure of my way in the dark, but I'll have a go.'

'Great!' He squeezed her hand and added softly, 'It's a hell of a long way from Hampstead!'

'It's a hell of a long way from anywhere,' she said.

He sighed. 'I rang you that night. Wanted to take you to dinner. You'd just left. Maybe if you hadn't —' He checked this train of thought abruptly and said, 'Right. Let's get moving.'

'Wait!' said Vinnie. 'I've just remembered. I've got a present for you. Turn your head away a minute.'

'What?'

'Don't what me! Where are your manners? Look the other way!'

He turned aside. There was a rustle of clothing, a grunt from Vinnie and she said, 'OK.'

As he turned back she thrust the Saturday Night Special, the .22 RG 14, into his hand.

As he had expected, Barr had trouble with Roberts. The change to an earlier timing had thrown the man: he'd arranged for the diversionary attacks on the Guardians to take place the next morning and maintained that it would be impossible to bring these forward. He argued that Barr should wait also.

'You landed on Jerusalem Island this evening, Mr Barr. And tomorrow you will be gone. You are concerned with three people only, your two friends and the girl. I don't intend to risk all we've worked for – not for three people. My concern is with everyone on this island. I shall be here when you have left – and my task will be to maintain order and bring the Community back to its true purpose. I have been waiting a long time, I can wait a few more hours. I wish you would also, for all our sakes.'

'I am not waiting and I'm not arguing,' said Barr flatly. 'If you won't help, I guess we'll have to manage without you.'

'I will come with you,' said Gunnar.

'Your place is here!' said Roberts.

'No,' said Gunnar. 'I know the Compound, the inside of the

Tabernacle. I will be able to help as a guide, if nothing else.' And he added quietly, 'In any case, it would not be right to stand aside while these men risk their lives in our cause.'

'You are making a great mistake,' said Roberts. There was an edge in his voice which gave the words the substance of a threat. Then he added, 'However, in the circumstances, I will come too.'

'I thought perhaps you might,' said Barr.

'Someone will be needed to calm our people,' replied Roberts coldly. 'If there is bloodshed and violence, there may well be panic also.'

The capture of the truck had provided Barr with an unexpected bonus, proving once more how much of the night's work would depend on improvisation, on the use of whatever tools came to hand. A night march from Dreadnought Hill to the Compound would take them the better part of two hours: by using the truck they could be there in a few minutes. As an additional precaution, Charlie Brown and Bobby Lamb rigged themselves out in uniforms taken from the Guardians and Bobby took the wheel, while Charlie and Joe Colleano squeezed in beside him. The other men, with their arms and supplies, clambered into the back, and the canvas flaps were lowered. Bobby's instructions were to drive to a sheltered point about half a mile from the entrance to the Compound: from there, they would move in on foot.

The first three miles or so were covered without incident. They did meet one party of workers, about twenty strong, trudging wearily back from the day's work in the fields: the group simply stood to one side to allow the truck to pass, watching with haggard, uninterested faces. Otherwise they met nothing and no-one on the road. Gradually, as the minutes passed, the dark sky began to open up, with clusters of stars dancing attendance on a thin crescent moon and touching the crops in the neat fields with silver.

Just as it seemed as if they would reach the point of disembarkation without interruption, lights flashed intermittently on the road ahead and Bobby slowed instinctively. Colleano opened the canvas flap and called through to Barr, 'Major. Someone on the road. Signalling. Do we go through them, or what?'

'No,' said Barr. 'Stop. Don't do anything to arouse suspicion.'

The signalling grew more insistent and eventually they made out the figures of two men standing in the road. Bobby pulled to a halt and the men came round to his side of the truck. They were Guardians, and armed, but they seemed to be more relieved than suspicious.

'Where the hell have you been?' asked the first Guardian.

'What do you mean?' asked Charlie.

'Control sent out a signal. You didn't call in. We were on our way to the Beach to check.'

'Wait a minute!' said the second Guardian, suddenly suspicious. He turned his flashlight on Bobby and the others. 'I don't remember seeing any of you in —'

The rest of the sentence gurgled in his throat as the butt of Barr's gun caught him on the side of the head just above the ear. His companion went down at the same moment, under the impact of a similar blow from Noonan.

Barr holstered his gun and called the James brothers down from the truck. 'Truss them up, gag them, and put them somewhere out of sight in that field. Make a good job of it. I don't want them to get loose. And take their guns.'

While this was being done, Barr talked with Gunnar. 'The man said something about Control. Do you know where and what that is?'

'The Guardians have check points in various parts of the island. They're supposed to call in from these points at regular intervals. The central Control is just outside the Compound in a converted sugar mill, next to the generating station. It's only a few hundred yards from the bridge.'

'Generating station? Tell me about that.'

'The island used to draw all its power from Antigua. But as the Community grew, the demand began to put a strain on the supply. So now at least half the electricity used comes from our own generators.'

In five minutes they were on their way again and, in another five, Bobby pulled off the road and parked the truck in the dark centre of a group of flourishing bay rum trees. They were almost at the peak of a hill: Bobby went forward with Barr and Gunnar until they reached the top and there, below them, lay the Compound. The arena was clearly marked, surrounded as it was by chains of amber light. Other lights gleamed in various parts of the Tabernacle and in the residential area to the left of the square, but what caught the eye was the great golden cross. Illuminated by discreetly placed floodlights it seemed to hang in the sky as though having no foundation, as if it were part of the heavens along with the moon and the stars.

And, borne faintly on the tradewind, they could hear music and singing coming from the amplifiers in the Compound. It was the Tabernacle choir singing *Onward Christian Soldiers.*

Steve and his two companions could hear the hymn too, as they slipped through the grounds, round the back of the Tabernacle towards the East Wing. To them, however, the sound came over loud and clear, bursting forth as it did from the amplifiers which were located at key points throughout the Compound and, indeed, the entire island. It added a new and grotesque dimension to their situation, but at least the singing gave some cover to the sound of their own movements.

A brief, eerie silence followed the hymn and then the voice of the

Comptroller followed:

'My dear Brothers and Sisters, once again we have come to the end of another day of labour and service. To all of you, I bring a message of love from our beloved teacher, Mr Dunlop. He embraces and thanks each one of you. Brothers and Sisters, it is through the power of his great love that our Community has triumphed. Let us give thanks on our knees to God, and to Mr Dunlop, his representative on earth, who is our leader, our thinker, our brain, our heart. Let us all pledge ourselves anew to his service. May his grace and love be with us all this night and for evermore.'

They had reached the wall and the line of palms skirting the Grove by the time the Comptroller finished speaking. Ahead of them lay the dimly lit entrance to the East Wing, its arched wooden door closed. In full view, in the doorway, was one of the Guardians, leaning casually against the door, and taking surreptitious puffs from a cigarette.

The shrill blast of whistles cut through the silence, followed by the sound of voices and running feet. The Guardian straightened up quickly and flicked his cigarette into the shrubbery.

'Get down!' hissed Steve, 'get down!'

As they crouched in the shadows, two Guardians ran past them to the entrance. The first one gesticulated towards the grounds but Steve could only pick up a fragment of what was being said. It was enough to tell him that their escape had been discovered and that the pursuit was on.

The two Guardians hurried off the way they had come, and the man on duty at the entrance stepped forward a pace or two, taking a flashlight from his belt and beaming it into the darkness. For one long moment he looked directly towards them and it seemed as if they must be found, but eventually, after a final look round, he moved back into the doorway.

Steve gripped the gun. He had the advantage of surprise, it would not be too difficult to pick the man off. But the shot would bring the other guards down upon them and there was still the door. If that was locked, or bolted from the inside, they were in real trouble. Nothing that he had read in his library of books on crime provided an answer to this kind of problem, he thought wryly. This was Barr's line of country, he would have known what to do: but there was no Barr, somehow he had to work it out for himself.

He was doing just that, contemplating the idea of tricking the Guardian so that he could knock him out by a surprise attack from behind, when Barr did intervene, indirectly perhaps, but in rather dramatic fashion.

Suddenly, a tremendous explosion shivered the air and, in the distance, from the direction of the bridge, a pillar of flame flared into the sky. The tail-end of the blast fanned their faces and rattled the shutters on the windows of the Tabernacle.

The startled Guardian left the doorway and stood on the pathway staring in the direction of the explosion. The sudden flare had gone and a column of yellow-tinted smoke smudged the clear night sky, feathering out under the gentle surge of the breeze.

The Guardian seemed to stand there bemused, only a yard or so in front of where they were hiding. Vinnie was the first to react. Steve was aware of a sudden swift movement at his side and he saw Vinnie get to her feet. In her hands was one of the big whitewashed rocks which lined the edge of the path. She moved forward, lifting the rock high, and brought it down with crushing force on the Guardian's head.

The man gave a long sigh as the breath squeezed free of his lungs, and fell at her feet. Vinnie dragged the unconscious man into the darkness, brushed her hands together, picked up the gun and the flashlight, and moved over to the door. She tried the latch, and the door opened with a little whine. Holding it open a few inches, she turned to the others.

'Well, don't stand there like two cups of cold tea! Are you coming or not?'

As she spoke, all the lights went out, and they heard the sharp crack of gunfire.

Stuttering Bob Calder had excelled himself. He had been asked by Barr to blow the Control Centre and, more than that, to go for overkill. He had done just that.

'Those old sugar mills are built like fortresses,' said Barr. 'So don't stint yourself. I want an explosion and a half. Something big enough to divert their attention so that we can get across that bridge.'

Before leaving Antigua, Calder had made up twelve plaster gelatine charges in two groups of six, and two fuse assemblies. He had nursed these carefully on the way over, cursing, with an extra-ordinary fluency and range of language, anyone who even made a motion towards lighting a cigarette.

He had been given no time to reconnoitre, to calculate. Operating with a combination of instinct and experience, he had sized up the mill and decided that one of the two groups of explosives ought to give Barr what he wanted. He disliked having to work in a hurry but he had been given no choice.

Apart from a long breathless two minutes when he, together with the James brothers who were cradling the box of explosives between them, had to throw themselves flat in the darkness while two Guardians sauntered past, they had reached the mill without trouble. Arming the fuse ends, taping the detonators into position in the slabs of gelignite, setting the charges in the entrance and in recesses in the brickwork, had taken an agonisingly long time, but it had finally been done more or less to Calder's satisfaction. He had then paid out the seventy feet or so of fuse assembly and told the brothers to move on to their next target, which was to take over the generating station, some eight hundred yards distant.

Calder had then lit a cigarette, applied the glowing end to the length of safety-fuse, and waited until the fuse split alight. Then, in a stumbling run, he had headed back through the night towards the point where Barr was waiting with the others.

Barr had arranged for the truck to be brought up, and Calder swung aboard as the mill went up with a crunching roar, and the earth and the air trembled around them. Three men came running out of the guardhouse and, as they did so, Noonan and Colleano opened fire from the shadows. The Guardians went down like toy targets in a fun fair and Noonan, rushing forward, raised the barrier. The truck checked long enough to pick up Noonan and Colleano, and then gathered speed.

As it charged across the bridge, a terrified maintenance engineer in the generating station, with the muzzle of Jesse James's gun cold against his neck, pulled the main switch, plunging the Compound into darkness.

Frank and Jesse then trussed up the engineer and waited, as instructed by Barr, for ten minutes. At the end of that time they switched the lights back on, and went back down to the bridge. Charlie Brown was waiting for them and the three men took up positions behind the rampart of earth and cacti on the further side, from where they could cover both approaches. Their task was to hold the line of retreat open.

Louis, the blue-eyed albino negro, principal officer of Mr Dunlop's personal bodyguard, was not a hired hand like most of the Guardians: he and the four men under his command were ardent members of the Community and their devotion to Mr Dunlop was absolute. Moreover, Louis was not a man to panic easily and his first thought, when he heard the explosion and the gunfire that succeeded it, was for the safety of his charge. By the time the lights went on again he had discovered one of his men lying unconscious in the grounds near the door of the East Wing, drawn the obvious conclusions, and placed two of the remaining three men on full alert outside Mr Dunlop's quarters. With the third man, he began a systematic search of the rest of the wing.

The lower floor appeared to be clear and they went back up the wide stairway to the landing. To the right, towards the front of the building, his two guards stood on duty outside the heavy oak door which led to Mr Dunlop's apartments. To the left lay the dormitory and other rooms occupied by the Handmaidens. It was territory that no man except Mr Dunlop, not even Louis, was allowed to enter.

The sound of gunfire from the West Wing increased his apprehension. He went into the small duty room which served as his office and tried to contact the Comptroller on the internal telephone, but the line seemed to be dead. He switched on the Public Address receiver, hoping that he might hear some announcement which would explain what was happening. The system operated from the Radio Room in the Comptroller's suite and was linked to every home, building and working area on the island: it was over this network that Mr Dunlop, the Comptroller and others broadcast each day to members of the Community. Access to outside radio transmissions was forbidden.

A low whine and the crackle of static came from the receiver at first, and again, in the background, he heard the sound of firing. Then a voice, a strange voice, took over:

'Attention! Attention! Attention, please. This is Brother Roberts speaking, Brother Joseph Roberts. Many of you will know me. I ask all members of the Community to stay calm. Remain in your homes or settlements. I assure you that there is no need for fear or panic. No harm will come to you if this order is obeyed. The Community is not under threat – I repeat, the Community is not threatened. I speak as Chairman of the Council of Seven. The action we have taken tonight has one purpose, and one purpose only – to bring our Community back to the principles on which it was founded by our spiritual head and teacher, Mr Dunlop. Our aim is to root out graft, privilege, violence and the exploitation of our workers – all the evils which have stained the good name of our Community. I order all Guardians to lay down their arms and surrender themselves to the authority of the Council. The Comptroller has been taken into custody and, in due course, he will be brought to public trial for his crimes against the Community. A further announcement will be made in one hour. Until then – remain calm, stay in your homes. God bless you all.'

The strains of *O Happy Band of Pilgrims* started up and Louis switched off the receiver. He waited, trying to absorb the meaning of this strange message. The one thing of which he was certain was that he would not surrender himself or his arms to anyone: he had taken a pledge to defend Mr Dunlop and the Handmaidens with his life and he had every intention of fulfilling that obligation.

A door opened nearby and he heard the low sound of whispering voices. Ignoring instructions, he crossed the invisible line, the frontier of the Handmaidens' quarters, and turned the corner into their private corridor.

Two of the Handmaidens had emerged from the dormitory. They lowered their heads as they saw him but he recognised them as Sisters Gabrielle and Helen. Sister Helen? Earlier that day, he had seen Sister Eleanor take the girl away, and she had told him that Sister Helen would be leaving the island. The information had registered with Louis because of its unusual nature: since he had taken over his present responsibilities only one other girl had left the ranks of the Handmaidens, and even she had not been allowed to leave the island. That particular girl, convicted of lack of respect for Mr Dunlop, had been sent to the Beach of Pleasure.

'Stop!' he ordered.

The two Handmaidens checked and waited for him to come up to them.

'Where are you going?' he asked.

'Down to the Tabernacle, to the Great Hall,' said Sister Helen. Her face was flushed and he noticed the rather agitated rise and fall of her breasts beneath the white robe.

'What for?'

'There are flowers to arrange for the late night service.'

'Where is Sister Eleanor?'

'She is not here.'

'She is always here at this time!'

'Not tonight.'

Louis did not hear Steve come up behind him, was not aware of his presence until the gun jammed into his spine.

'Don't make a move. Don't do anything stupid,' said Steve. 'I'm taking the girls out of here – all of them. Bring them, Kitty.'

Louis stood there, the gun hard against his back, as Kitty led the other Handmaidens out of the dormitory. They glided along, demure in their white dresses, with frightened, excited looks on their faces – more animated than he had ever seen them before.

'Right!' said Steve, prodding him. 'Move!'

They took up position at the head of the strange procession and moved forward. A few slow paces and they turned the corner into the main corridor. Facing them at the far end were the door to Mr Dunlop's quarters and the two guards.

Steve checked and ordered the girls to keep back. Then, with a sharper prod into his prisoner's back, he said, 'Tell them to drop their guns!' And remembering how he had seen it done in Westerns and detective thrillers, he added, 'Slow and careful. Otherwise, you're a dead man! There are two Handmaidens in with Mr Dunlop. Tell one of your men to go in and bring them out!' He felt rather pleased with the sound of all that, but his pleasure did not last long.

'Shoot!' shouted Louis suddenly. 'Never mind me! Shoot! Get him! Get him!'

This unexpected development momentarily stunned Steve. It was not the sort of thing that happened in television series, and the situation was made worse by the fact that Louis broke away at that moment and started to run towards the other guards. His back presented a perfect target for Steve while, at the same time, the guards hesitated for fear of hitting the running man.

He fumbled with the gun, wishing that he had held on to the

handgun instead of giving it to Kitty. He was holding the Uzi taken from the Guardian downstairs and he was not familiar with the mechanism. As he raised it a shot roared in his ears and a flash of scorching air brushed his face. He saw Louis spin round and slam against the wall, he had a momentary glimpse of Kitty holding the Saturday Night Special out at arm's length, a look of amazement on her face, and then both he and Kitty went down as Vinnie tackled them from behind.

Half crawling, half dragged by Vinnie and Gabrelle, they retreated round the corner as a spray of bullets roared over their heads and thudded into the wall beyond.

As they lay there for a moment, drawing breath, Kitty said, in a voice that trembled with disbelief, 'I hit him! I hit him!'

'You damn near hit me!' said Steve.

'Well, I had my eyes shut,' she said, as if this were a justification.

They scrambled to their feet. Most of the Handmaidens had fled screaming and crying into the dormitory.

'What do we do now?' asked Vinnie.

'I don't know,' said Steve honestly. 'I suppose the only thing is to hold out here until Barr arrives.'

'He's taking his bloody time!' said Vinnie. They had heard some distant gunfire from the direction of the bridge, but none from the West Wing for a good fifteen minutes.

And then there took place the most extraordinary event of that extraordinary night. A scream echoed down the corridor and it took Steve a moment to realise that it had not come from the dormitory but from the other end of the building.

He took a cautious look around the corner. The door to Mr Dunlop's apartments was open. There was no sign of Louis or the other two guards, but a distressed girl in the white dress of a Handmaiden came running towards them.

She gave Steve a startled look and threw herself into Gabrielle's arms.

'You are safe now,' crooned Gabrielle. 'Help has come. You are safe.'

The girl pulled back a little, a puzzled look on her face, the tears staining her cheeks.

'You don't understand. He is dead.'

'Dead? Who?'

'Mr Dunlop. He was asleep. We heard him cry out. When we went to him – when we went to him, he was dead. He died in his sleep.'

Louis came out of the door at the far end, walking unsteadily, a crimson stain colouring his left shoulder. He was weeping silently, tears glistening like pearls on his cheeks. Behind him came the two guards bearing the body of Mr Dunlop on an improvised stretcher.

254

The mask, the face that lay beneath the mask, was hidden under a white sheet. A Handmaiden brought up the rear, her head lowered, her lips moving as though in prayer.

Steve moved forward with Kitty and Vinnie, but Louis ignored them. The little cortège moved off down the stairs, their footsteps slowly echoing away into silence.

Barr arrived five minutes later, with Noonan, Calder and Gunnar. It was as much as Steve could do not to embrace him, but he wisely left that to Vinnie, who enveloped the protesting man in a bear-hug of prodigious power.

'Hey,' cried Barr, 'easy, easy! Don't break my bloody back!' And when she released him he said, 'You OK? You all OK?'

'More or less,' said Steve. 'How about you?'

'We lost Colleano, Joe Colleano,' said Barr. 'And Clay got it in the leg.' He spoke without emotion, but Steve could sense the pain behind the words. In Joe, Barr had lost an old comrade and a close friend.

'I'm sorry,' he said, 'I really am.'

'Nobody lives for ever,' said Barr flatly. 'Not even Mr Dunlop.' And, as if this reminded him of the need for action, he added, 'We've got to move. When the word gets round that the representative of God on earth has checked his ticket, there'll be hell to pay down there. This place will be more like a madhouse than ever.'

'I would like —' said Gunnar diffidently, 'I would be grateful if you would allow Dr Bauer to go with you.'

'Dr Bauer?' Kitty's voice held a mixture of amazement and shock.

'She is not – how can I express it?' said Gunnar. 'Let me say, that she gave me the information that saved your lives, I think.'

'OK,' said Barr briskly, 'OK. But what about you? Are you coming with us?'

'I think I should stay,' said the young Swede hesitantly.

'What for?' asked Barr savagely. 'What for? You heard Roberts speak his piece. He's going to take over now, and it'll be just the same. Different drivers, but the same old car.'

Kitty touched Gunnar's arm gently. 'Come with us,' she said. 'Come with us, for a while at least. To sort yourself out. If you want to come back later —' She left the rest unsaid.

He nodded. 'Yes. Perhaps it was wrong to think that we could build Jerusalem in isolation away from the world.' He sighed. 'In the beginning, it was a good dream. But when you think about it, Jerusalem isn't made of islands, or Tabernacles or even fields. It is a thing of the heart, isn't that so? It must be built in the heart.'

'You're young,' said Barr, with a trace of bitterness. 'If you want to believe that, if you want to keep trying, that's your funeral.'

All the Handmaidens except one decided to go with the party, and by the time Barr had packed them and his men on to the truck, his prediction was coming true to an extent that exceeded his worst fears.

Word of Mr Dunlop's death had spread like a bush-fire and, from all corners of the Compound, men, women and children, carrying flaming torches, were hurrying towards the Tabernacle. The torches added an eerie glow to the night air and there was something else on the air too, a strange merging of voices into a low, collective, threatening growl. Barr had heard that noise before, in many places: it was the authentic roar of the mob.

As they moved forward, one section of the crowd tried to block the road ahead of the truck, but Noonan fired a volley of shots over their heads and they scattered in panic.

Looking back before they left the arena, Barr saw that Mr Dunlop's body had been placed on a bier on the steps of the Tabernacle. Men with torches surrounded the bier on three sides, facing the keening crowd. Roberts was trying to address them, but his words were lost in a great renewed roar as the Comptroller was half led, half dragged forward. For a brief moment Barr saw the great moonlike face quite distinctly: then the mob surged forward like wolves and dragged the man down . . .

One final incident occurred, shortly before they crossed the bridge. A man came chasing after the truck, running desperately, one arm outstretched as if in appeal. Behind him, thundering at his heels, was the pursuing crowd.

The man, powered by desperation, came within a few feet of the truck. The arm went up again, straining to catch the tailboard, and Kitty saw his face as clearly as Barr had seen that of the Comptroller, as clearly as she had seen it all those weeks ago in England, on the night when it had all begun.

Van Norden.

He was almost up to the truck now, his fingers brushing the canvas and, instinctively, she put out a hand to help him. His hand touched hers, clasped it for a moment, and then he slipped and the mob was upon him.

Kitty shivered and closed her eyes. She hardly noticed the truck stop to pick up the three men at the bridge and was hardly aware of the bumping, crowded journey back to Dreadnought Hill.

She sat in silence too on the deck of the *Carib Beauty,* until Steve came and put a coat around her shoulders.

'All right?' he asked.

'Yes.' She nodded. 'Yes.'

'It's all over now,' he said.

Yes, she thought, it is all over.